EMILY RENK HAWTHORNE

Copyright © 2024 by Emily Renk Hawthorne
OF MOUNTAINS AND SEAS

Published by Hawk Ridge Press
www.HawkRidgePress.com
contact@hawkridgepress.com

www.EmilyRenkHawthorne.com
hello@EmilyRenkHawthorne.com
TikTok: @erenkhawthorne
Instagram: @emilyrenkhawthorne
Facebook emilyrenkhawthorne

Cover illustration and internal formatting by Damonza – Damonza.com
Developmental Edit by Wishing Shelf – www.thewsa.co.uk
Line Edit and proofread by Paige Lawson
Special edition art by Sweeneypen
Yuras Map by Melissa Nash

ISBN (paperback) 979-8-9905979-0-7
ISBN (hardcover) 979-8-9905979-1-4
ISBN (ebook) 979-8-9905979-2-1
ISBN (audiobook) 979-8-9905979-3-8

A Note to the Reader

This is a story of magic, mystery, mythology, and adventure. While I aimed to create a mostly "clean" story, there are topics that some readers may wish to avoid.

This book includes references to alcohol consumption, grooming relationship behavior, emotional abuse from a parent, physical violence, and violence using fantasy magic. If you feel any of the above would be detrimental to your reading experience, please kindly bypass this book.

If you choose to continue, I look forward to hearing what you think! I encourage you to leave me a review as all feedback will help me grow as an author. Thank you!

For Zoe—
As strong and magical as any mythical creature

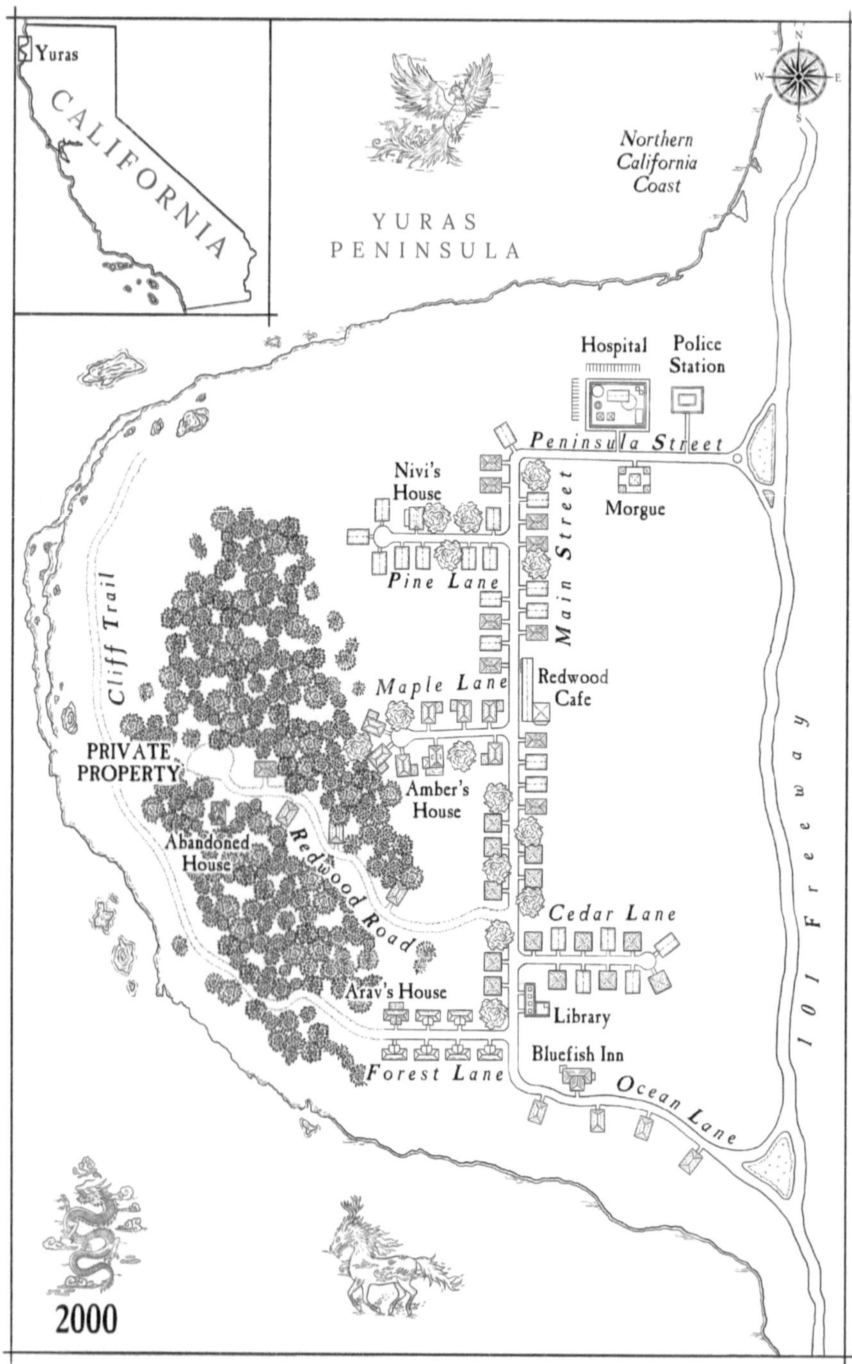

Yuras
CALIFORNIA
YURAS PENINSULA
Northern California Coast
Hospital
Police Station
Peninsula Street
Morgue
Nivi's House
Main Street
Pine Lane
Cliff Trail
Maple Lane
Redwood Cafe
PRIVATE PROPERTY
Abandoned House
Redwood Road
Amber's House
Cedar Lane
Arav's House
Library
Bluefish Inn
Forest Lane
Ocean Lane
101 Freeway
2000

"On the mountain, there are many monsters, the waters are full of peculiar fish… there are many strange snakes… an area off-limits to man."

-*The Classic of Mountains and Seas,*
4th Century BCE

PROLOGUE

Winter 1935

THE FIRST GLIMMERS of consciousness seeped in, and with a start, Randall Sun realized he couldn't see. At first, he thought it was a moonless night and he was at home in bed. But the feel of his hot breath against a cloth, the binds around his wrists and ankles, and the whirring of the car beneath him proved otherwise. He pulled against the restraints. They must be magic. Like all magic things, he could feel their power, whether it was the warm glow of another Shifter or the hum of the restraints that tingled against his skin at that moment. He doubted either of his powers would affect magical restraints, but he would try.

The car rumbled to a stop. Voices murmured to each other from the front seat. Doors opened, and the crunch of footsteps came to his door.

A vague, recent memory surfaced in Randall's mind. He had been leaving the casino when a woman and a man approached him, but that was all he could remember. Based on the situation he was currently in, one of them must have the power of magical binding, and the other must have some sort of sleep-inducing power. Randall sighed. Alcoholic fumes accumulated beneath the cloth and burned his nostrils and eyes. Maybe that second part was his own doing.

The door next to Randall opened. Hands yanked him out onto the ground and dragged him a few feet before forcing him onto his knees. A sharp pain shot through his left leg, and something clattered next to him; most likely his cane. At least they hadn't thrown it away. One of the people removed the cloth sack from his head, and he was momentarily blinded by the car headlights. He squinted and turned his head. Past the glare of the headlights, outlines of trees towered around them. Aromas of pine and dirt blended with the alcohol on his breath and the gasoline from the car. The man and woman approached from each side, becoming looming silhouettes in front of the car. Randall took his chance and transformed.

His bones and joints cracked as they lengthened and spread, a sensation that was second nature for him. Thick, coarse fur sprouted from his skin, absorbing his clothing. His nails elongated into long, yellow claws, murderous yet useless against the magical restraints. He glared at the two silhouettes that looked half their size before his growing body while snapping at the binds and bellowing to no avail.

The woman laughed. In an instant, her body elongated from her neck down, her arms and legs fusing into a serpentine body. A monstrous human-headed snake stood before him, scales glistening in the headlights. The tip of her tail lashed out, smacking Randall across the face.

"Even a grizzly won't be able to break those."

Randall huffed from the blow. He knew that voice and that Shifter form. Susan Bai. But who was the man with her? He almost laughed when he realized. How cute, Mrs. and Mr. Bai, a wife and husband gangster duo. What was his name again? It didn't matter. Susan was the one in charge. The humor faded. They wouldn't get away with this.

He shrunk back to his human form. His bones realigned and his fur resorbed into his skin as his clothes reformed. He looked down at his hands. White cords twisted around his wrists, shimmering like snakes coiling around and around. He couldn't break through the binds with sheer strength, but maybe he could burn through them or at least hurtle a fireball at his captors. A tingling sensation arose from his inner core and intensified as it moved toward his hands. In less than a second, sparks leaped from his palms, burst into flames, and coalesced into a bright, burning ball. The restraints remained intact, so he prepared to shoot the fireball at one of the silhouetted figures. At that moment, a ball of water struck the fire. Steam sizzled into the air until both elements were nullified.

This time, Mr. Bai laughed. "Did you think we didn't do our homework on you, Randall?"

That was right. Susan could summon and manipulate water. So that must mean Mr. Bai had the power of magical binding, and the somnolence had been his own fault, after all. Randall swore under his breath and made a half-hearted promise not to drink as much. He thought about forming another fireball but knew that even in a best-case scenario, that would only lead to a standoff of fire against water, and he was outnumbered here. But he had a secret weapon that most other Shifters did not, another secondary power. Thrusting his hands down onto the ground, he simultaneously melted the ground in front of him and built it back up. He intended to build a wall and then tunnel himself to safety, but suddenly his arms were jerked up from the ground. Another white rope had formed from between his wrists to a branch overhead. It pulled his arms up and away from the ground. His stonemasonry was useless if he couldn't touch the ground.

"As I said, we did our homework on you."

Randall cleared his throat. "What do you want?"

"The same thing as you," Susan said. "Purity of our kind. To remove the weaknesses of the Statics from the Shifters."

"No one wants that more than me," Randall said.

"Yet you have done little to change the situation," Mr. Bai said. "Even in your position of power and influence, your promises remain empty."

Susan transformed into human form, her black coat and trousers reforming where scales had been. She turned to her husband. "We should've expected he'd grow a soft spot for the Statics. You know what his son is, right?"

Randall spat into the dirt. "That is precisely why I'm such an ardent supporter of the cause. My son is an abomination."

The Bai's approached each other and spoke in whispers before turning back to Randall.

"You have one week," Susan said, "to change your wife's mind."

Randall scoffed under his breath. He had tried everything so far to persuade his wife, who at the young age of sixty, had achieved a higher political position than he ever could in his 362 years. And with her popularity, she would most likely be re-elected again and again. Yet, that didn't bother him. She was beautiful and strong, the strongest Shifter he knew, and he respected that. What bothered him was that she coddled the *boy*, even going so far as to be pro-integration because of him. And the longer she held that view and stayed in power, the more likely it would come to fruition. Integrating Shifters and Statics would be a death sentence to Shifter kind. His son was living proof of that. Somewhere in past generations Static blood had gotten in and wiped out his ability to develop powers.

"Otherwise," Mr. Bai said, "we'll have to resort to more drastic measures. Shifters dead at the hands of Statics is sure to increase anti-integration sentiment."

Before Randall could respond, they got into the car and sped off. As the car left, the restraints disintegrated from Randall's wrists and ankles. He sat alone in the dust for several minutes, rubbing his wrists. No one treated him that way, like an animal to be tied and thrown in the dirt. He would not be cowed by threats like some weakling. He would not only show them he could get anti-integration implemented in the Council, but he would also make them pay for what they did to him tonight.

He massaged his temples, willing a foggy memory to form. Many years ago, he participated in the creation of a special and powerful stone that had since become illegal. Despite his usual inebriation, he had swiped a few, unbeknownst to others. He needed them now for protection, in case he couldn't change his wife's mind. Otherwise… he shuddered to think of it. But, if necessary, he knew what he'd have to do.

CHAPTER ONE

Davis

Fall 1932

THE PILLOW ABSORBED his tears and quieted his sniffles. His mother's voice called from the bedroom door. "Davis?"

Davis Sun buried his face into the pillow and kept really still. He didn't want her to see him crying, but footsteps approached his bed, and a weight sank onto the bed next to him. A gentle touch rubbed his back, releasing a sob from his throat.

"Father hates me," Davis said into his pillow.

His mother took a deep breath. "He just doesn't understand you. These things have happened before, and that doesn't mean you're not a wonderful, darling boy."

Davis turned his face to his mother. "Is there any way my powers could come out later?"

His mother crouched next to his bed, a ray of sun across her face. In the golden light of the autumn afternoon, his mother's pale complexion glowed. For a brief moment, Davis's hope soared. Was this the Shifter glow he had always heard about? Were his powers suddenly manifesting? Then his mother stood up, and with her face in shadow, the glow disappeared.

"You never know." But Davis could tell she didn't believe it. His mother motioned for him to sit up. "Let me tell you a story. Before you were born, Shifters found they could imbue certain stones with powers. The process is very complex, and only certain people were allowed to know how to do it. The effects are strongest when stones are imbued while still in the ground. Whole mines were created full of magical stones. As you can imagine, this caused a great deal of excitement."

"What kind of powers did they have?"

Davis found himself drawn into his mother's story. She was a natural public speaker and looked especially distinguished with her pinned curls, red lips, and floor-length, satin evening gown. There was no doubt another political event that evening.

"Oh, all sorts of things. Some could heal a minor cut. Others changed color at random; entertainment for children. Some thought a stone could be more convenient or powerful than tinctures, leading to a lot of experimentation to replace love and forgetfulness tinctures with stones. And one is being refined as we speak; a camouflage stone that will keep Shifters disguised from Statics. Anti-integration enthusiasts are particularly excited about that one."

A stone that would keep Shifters from Statics? Davis knew that he wouldn't be accepted in Shifter society. His father had made that clear. But he hadn't expected to be physically separated as well. Would he wander the streets and never again see another Shifter?

His mother seemed to read his thoughts. "Don't worry. You know I'm for integration. As chairperson of the Shifter Council, I will never allow anything to separate us."

She put an arm around Davis's shoulder, and he tried to smile. He hoped what she said was true.

She continued. "What I wanted to tell you about is one stone in particular. This is very important. You have to promise not to breathe a word about it to anyone else."

Davis shook his head enthusiastically. "I won't."

"It's called a transfer stone. It supposedly can transfer magic from one Shifter to another Shifter, or even to a Static." Davis's eyes widened. Was she saying what he thought she was? She put up a hand as if telling him to slow down his thoughts. "This is not something to take lightly. The Council considered this stone to be too dangerous and banned it from use, and for good reason. To take magic from a Shifter is like taking a limb. So, the location of the mine was hidden, and most Shifters these days have never heard of them. All stone imbuements are now very regulated."

"But you're the chairperson! Couldn't you find out where the location is? Why tell me about this if there is nothing to be done?" The desperation in his voice was obvious, and Davis hated that he sounded so weak. But this stone could change everything for him. He was sure there had to be someone out there who didn't need their powers as much as he needed them.

"This was before my time. The current members of the Council no longer know. I only know about it because my father used to tell me about it as a child. I thought they were just stories, until one night, your father came home from the casino babbling about special stones. I couldn't get any more information from him, and by the morning, he seemed to have forgotten. But it got me thinking again about the stories my father used to tell me. And now I'm telling you because I want you to hold onto hope that you won't be left behind. If something like that stone could be developed in the past, other possibilities may come out that could help you in the future."

CHAPTER TWO

Ling
Summer 1985

On the second Monday of June, Ling Guang readied herself to meet her daughter for lunch as she did every month. An outlier of the local Shifter community, Ling enjoyed living in the more populated area of Yuras, where she could people-watch and feel more engaged with the community, even if the surrounding Statics had no idea she was there.

Today was great for people watching as Main Street was bustling with families and children enjoying their summer break. There were some tourists as well, taking photos in front of the quaint brick sidewalks lined with maple trees. A decent crowd by any standards.

Ling turned onto Redwood Road, an unpaved two-lane road that led into the forest where most of the local Shifters in Yuras lived. The canopy instantly cooled the warm summer day as she entered the forest. Along the length of the road, camouflage stones affixed to wood posts guarded against Static passersby. Their mottled green surfaces looked almost like a quarter-sized patch of moss. If a Static happened upon the road or walked by one of the houses, she would continue on by as if she had seen nothing but an extension of the forest.

Ling's daughter's house was at the end of the road. A large, lone redwood stood in front of the house on the right. She walked past it, up the porch steps, and knocked on the door. A moment later, her daughter's husband answered.

He looked surprised. "Did you two miss each other?" Ling wrinkled her brow and he continued. "She said she told you she would head out early today and meet you on the road to town."

Her daughter hadn't said anything to her about that. No sense in making a big deal until she found out more information.

"I must've forgotten. I'll head back and find her. She's probably at the restaurant already."

Ling kept her voice nonchalant but felt a little strange about the whole situation. She said goodbye and walked back to town. They usually went to the Redwood Cafe in the middle of Main Street, the only Shifter restaurant in town, so she headed there now. As she walked, she suddenly sensed a Shifter's glow down Maple Lane, a quaint neighborhood street. Turning, she saw her daughter emerge from the house nearest her. Her daughter rushed to the street, seemingly not seeing Ling until the last moment. Startled, her daughter ran her hands over her disheveled hair.

"Ma Ma. I was just coming to meet you."

Ling looked at her daughter and back at the house. She didn't sense any other Shifters in the vicinity. "Why were you in that Static's house?"

Her daughter's face flushed. "What? I was just taking a walk until it was time to meet you."

A sickening feeling grew in Ling's stomach. She glanced at the house again and saw a man peeking out the window from inside. Dark brown skin. Curly hair. Just like her daughter's husband. "Not again."

The red in her daughter's cheeks grew darker. "You're mistaken. I was only taking a walk."

"I covered for you once. I won't do it again. Please, don't ask me to. And put your camouflage pendant back on before one of our fellow Shifters sees you without it."

Her daughter gasped and touched her neck, then quickly found her pendant in her bag and put it on. The green, teardrop-shaped stone had a matte look against her daughter's glowing skin.

Her daughter gritted her teeth. "I'm not going to ask you to cover for me because there's nothing to hide."

Ling felt both numb and enraged at the same time. "I don't understand it. You have a loving husband at home, yet you insist on finding these look-alike *Statics*."

"You don't know what he's like at home."

"Then tell me. Help me understand. This sneaking around is not good for you or your family. Could you imagine what would happen to our community if Jackson were involved in a scandal like this?"

"Exactly, only our reputation matters to you."

"I care whether you end up in jail as well for breaking the law."

"Can't you see the bigger picture? My husband's ideas are too rigid and outdated. It's time for a change. Shifters and Statics should be allowed to mingle."

"And you're paving the way with infidelity?"

"It's not like you're in a traditional relationship either. What would Ba Ba have thought if he were still alive?"

Ling winced. "That's not fair. You know it's not the same thing." She had never dallied with *Statics*.

"You know what, *Mother*, I'm not hungry anymore. Maybe I'll see you next month." With that, she walked away.

Ling watched her go, her heart racing. What was she going to do? The last time the boyfriend had ended it with her daughter. Yet that didn't stop her daughter from finding someone new. If it *was* like last time, the man would be from the city. Maybe she could use an oblivion tincture and send him back to the city. She'd have to see if there was a way to convince Meng to get some from the Council for her.

Heading home, Ling pondered the stories she could tell Meng. Maybe there was a Static that had seen her Shifter form that needed his memory erased, but then Meng would insist on applying the tincture herself. That *was* her job in the Council, afterall. She rubbed her face and took a moment to compose herself outside her home. The dragon-headed qilin statues on either side of the front door peered up at her, majestic and calm. She patted one of their stone heads.

"Give me luck," she murmured before going inside.

Inside, Meng was in the kitchen sauteing food for her lunch. She looked up as Ling walked into the room.

"Hi, Darling, back home already?"

Ling nodded and tried to smile naturally as she sat at the dining table. She focused on the charming cadence of Meng's British accent to distract herself. Meng turned off the stove and the overhead fan. She brought a bowl of her food to the table and sat across from Ling to eat.

"Everything OK?" Meng said between bites of chicken and vegetables.

Ling hated keeping things from Meng, but she didn't want Meng involved in this situation either. "It's just that this man might have seen my Shifter form."

Meng put down her chopsticks. "What? When?"

"A month ago."

"Why didn't you tell me sooner? And why are you taking chances shifting around here? You know your camouflage stone isn't reliable in Shifter form. That's why we have safe spaces to transform."

"I know. I know. Sometimes, it's so hard to wait until our next trip to the city. You know how it is. Anyway, the man was a drunk tourist. I thought he'd go home and forget about it as a drunken hallucination. But he's back. And he moved into a house on Maple Lane. I saw him just now, that's why I'm home early. I think he's trying to join the monster hunters out here. Maybe you can use a little oblivion tincture to tell him to go back to San Francisco?"

Meng put up a hand and closed her eyes. She took a deep breath. "I'll take care of it. But please, my darling, let's be safer in the future? I have enough on my plate, having to fend Iris off at work."

Ling reached across the table and took Meng's hands. "Yes, of course. Thank you."

She kissed Meng's hands. Meng waved her off and resumed eating. Ling smiled and let out an inward sigh of relief. Meng didn't have to know the truth. She was doing a good thing for their community and for her daughter. After it was done, she would call her daughter, apologize for her behavior from today, and suggest they get together for lunch next week. Maybe she could suggest they start getting together more than once a month. That's what her daughter needed to keep her out of trouble: more family involvement.

CHAPTER THREE

Davis

Winter 1935

DAVIS RELUCTANTLY LET his little sister, Anna, tag along to explore one of the storage rooms beneath the house, the creepy one under the archway where the path from the house led to the stables. Several nights before, he had seen his father stumble home in the middle of the night, and he followed him to this storage room. He had listened outside while his father sifted through boxes, muttering about how he must have placed *them* somewhere in there. Curiosity gnawed at Davis ever since, but he had to wait for the right moment to return when he wouldn't be observed. Fortunately, his parents had gone into town today and wouldn't return until evening. Except for his seven-year-old sister, none of the household staff seemed to notice his whereabouts. Possibly because he was almost eighteen, they figured he could look after himself. More likely because he didn't belong.

"Stand back," Davis said while he picked the lock of the solid wood door.

The door shuddered as if something were trying to escape.

With a few skilled movements, the lock clicked, and the door gave way with a groan.

The room was dark and had a funny smell. Light streaked onto the floor from between drawn window curtains. White sheets covered boxes and unused furniture. Every move they made caused dust to sparkle and dance in the air. Anna ran forward and grabbed Davis's hand. He stiffened at her touch and shook her off a little too forcefully. Feeling instantly bad at his behavior, he looked at her and patted his side.

"You can stay beside me, but I need my hands to search."

He hated how he treated her, but he mollified himself with the knowledge that a little adversity would toughen her up for the real world if she ever encountered it. She was the favorite, afterall. Coddled and protected in a way he never was.

He walked around, looking under sheets and rummaging through old boxes while Anna huddled behind him. Some boxes were already partially emptied from his father's previous visit. Papers, clothing, a lampshade, and a broken picture frame lay strewn across the floor. He pushed the items to the side with his foot, unable to determine what his father had been looking for. After investigating the room for several minutes and peering in half a dozen boxes, he lifted a sheet off a wooden chest. Dust scattered and ballooned into the air, causing Anna to sneeze.

"Shh," Davis said. "We need to be quiet. We're not supposed to be in here."

Anna rubbed her nose with the back of her frilly sleeve. The chest sat before them, old and worn, big enough for either of them to curl up inside. It no longer had a latch, only holes where it used to be. Davis leaned over and lifted the lid.

"What's in there?" Anna whispered.

Davis rummaged through old papers and clothes. "Nothing interesting." Then he paused. "Wait a second. What's this?"

He pulled out a navy coat covered in gold trim and buttons. It looked very official. He put it on over his gray wool coat and buttoned up the front.

"Aye, aye, captain," he said, standing up tall and saluting her.

Anna stifled a giggle. Davis grinned back at her, putting his hands into the coat's pockets. Something clicked against his right hand. He grabbed the objects and pulled them out. In his fist were three shiny, gray stones.

"What's that?" Anna said. "Can I see?"

"I don't know." Davis handed over one of the stones. "They look like marbles but flatter."

Anna rolled the round stone between her hands and then jumped up and down with an excited voice. "It's moving inside!"

Davis shot her a disapproving look, and she snapped her mouth shut.

"Give it here." He took back the stone and then held each one up to the light. The insides swirled like puffs of smoke. His voice filled with curiosity. "So they are. All of them." A memory popped up about special stones. Something his mother had told him a few years ago.

"What does it mean? Should we ask Daddy?"

"No." His tone was harsh and abrupt. Anna shrunk back.

He put the stones in his pants pocket and took off the blue coat, folding and replacing it and the other items in the chest. Then he put the sheet back over it like he'd found it and took Anna by the shoulders, grasping her hard.

"Promise me you won't tell anyone we were in here or what we found."

"Ow. You're hurting me."

He shook her. "Promise!"

Anna's lower lip trembled. "I promise."

Davis let go and softened his voice. "Well, OK then."

He patted her gently without meeting her eye. She winced at his approaching hand, and he felt a sharp pain in his heart, but he knew she could handle it. He had tolerated far worse from their father over the last few years. Things that Anna would never know.

Drops of rain began to patter against the storage room roof. Their cadence quickened until they were indistinguishable, vibrating the roof like cymbals. Davis led Anna out of the room and locked the door.

"We better get back to the house before this storm gets worse."

He opened his coat and wrapped Anna in it as they returned to the house. This time she didn't wince away.

When they got back to the house, Davis and Anna went upstairs to their rooms to change into dry clothes. From outside, there was the sound of horses galloping up to the house. Davis looked out his bedroom window and saw some of his father's men riding up. They dismounted by the servant's entrance. One of them carried a wooden box under his arm.

Anna must have heard the commotion, too, because she came running into his room.

"Davy?" She joined him by the window and shook his shirt sleeve.

Davis wrinkled his nose at the nickname. She wasn't a baby anymore. Why couldn't she call him Davis like everyone else?

"Why are Father's servants riding horses outside?"Anna continued. "Isn't today their day off?"

"I don't know."

Davis left Anna by the window and walked into the hall. He headed down the stairs with the plan to peek into the servants' quarters.

Anna ran after him. "I want to come too."

Davis stopped on the staircase and turned to her. "No. Go back to your room and shut the door."

"But Davy…"

"Go. It's dangerous."

"They're just servants."

Davis knew better. They were more than simple servants. They were his father's henchmen. He pointed up the stairs and didn't move until Anna turned around with a pout on her face. She dragged her feet back up the stairs. Once Davis heard her bedroom door shut, he continued down the stairs and into a side hall toward the servants' quarters.

Narrow, shadowy hallways replaced the grand open rooms of the house. Small bedrooms lined the halls, which stretched to the kitchen. Just beyond was the servant's entrance, where another servant was conferring with the two that had just arrived. Davis snuck through the kitchen and leaned against a wall where he could listen but not be seen.

"She's sorry now about binding and abducting the master," one of the men said.

"Let's see the evidence."

There was a shuffling sound. Davis peeked around the corner and saw the man with the box pass it over to the third man. The third man opened the hinged, wooden top and tipped the box toward himself to look inside. Something dripped onto the stone floor. At first Davis thought it was just rainwater dripping off the box. But it was thicker, more viscous. And dark in color. Inside the box, something pale and gnarled rolled over with a thud. A severed hand.

Davis inhaled sharply and pulled back behind the wall. He hurried back through the kitchen and hall and didn't stop until he had gone upstairs into his bedroom. Shutting the door, he sank onto the floor, trembling all over. A cold sweat covered his body, and his head felt light and heavy at the same time. No matter how hard he squeezed his eyes shut, he couldn't get the image out of his mind. He knew that his father was involved in an unsavory business, but until now, he had been able to fool himself into thinking it wasn't that bad.

He rubbed his hands over his eyes and then started slapping his face. *Snap out of it.* He was being a weak, little boy. His father was right to look down on him. How would he ever hold a place in this family if he couldn't take a little blood? He should've been the one getting revenge for his father, not those servants. His trembling stopped. That was it. He would figure out how to eliminate his father's enemies. Not by killing them. That thought almost made him start trembling again. Something else. These were political enemies. If only there was a way for Davis to get into Shifter politics. But there wasn't. He was weak. Powerless. An abomination.

Absent-mindedly, Davis put his hands in his pockets and brought out the stones he had discovered earlier. He rolled them between his palms, watching the swirling smoke inside them. His mother had once told him about some special stones. Stones that could make him like the rest of his family. He had always assumed that was a story she made up to make him feel better, but now, as he sat there, he wondered if these were the stones she told him about. When his parents returned home, he would show them to his mother as soon as he could get her alone.

CHAPTER FOUR

Iris

Summer 1955

IRIS SAT UP and tapped the ringing, metal clock on her nightstand, bringing the crisp tones to a halt. A minute later, her mother walked into the room and handed her a pill and a glass of water. In one smooth, well-rehearsed movement, Iris gulped down the pill. She picked up the clock and turned the dial, setting the alarm to four hours later, then emptied her glass into the glossy, canoe-shaped leaves of an aspidistra plant beside her nightstand. She put on her black, browline glasses and brought the world into view. Her mother, who had been watching the whole time, nodded in approval and withdrew to the living room.

Iris lay in bed for about twenty minutes until the pill took effect. A serenity diffused through her body, extending out to her limbs. She felt as light as air, and her mind was at ease. At this point, it was safe to get out of bed. She walked to the living room where the smell of freshly baked breads and pastries wafted from the Chinese bakery below, a welcome and cozy aroma in their dimly lit apartment. On the dining room table were a couple of pineapple buns, named for their criss-crossed pattern. Iris lit up.

"Are they both for me?"

"One was for Ba Ba, but he had to go to work early. He won't miss it," her mother said. She patted her stomach in emphasis.

Iris smiled and stuffed the side of one bun into her mouth, feeling the crunch of the top crust and the soft, slightly sweet bread. It was still warm.

Her mother pulled on a jacket and tucked the cuff of her left sleeve over the stump of her wrist.

"Ma Ma," Iris said as her mother was opening the door to leave for work.

"Hmm?"

Iris fidgeted. "Is it OK if I have lunch at school today?"

Her mother sighed, closed the door, and returned to the dining table. "We talked about this."

"But—"

"I will not have you being judged for needing to take medication."

"I could just take one pill with me and hide it so no one sees."

"Too risky. And you could easily lose it."

"Couldn't I just try it today? It's the last day of school."

"Then you can come home for lunch one more day."

Iris pouted, picking at pieces of her pineapple bun. "Is it because of your hand?" she blurted out, then instantly regretted it as she saw her mother's mouth press into a thin line.

"Why do you say that?" her mother said after a pause.

Iris stared at the table, pushing crumbs around. "Because

you're already ashamed of your hand, you don't want to be ashamed of me, too."

Her mother's expression relaxed. She sat down at the table across from Iris. "Iris, I'm not ashamed of you. I'll never be ashamed of you. I'm trying to protect you."

"How? I'm sixteen years old, and you don't trust me to take my own medicine."

Her mother seemed to think for a while before choosing her words. "People can be— cruel when they know you are different." Her eyes took on a far-off look, and she fingered the cuff of the sleeve that hung over her missing hand.

Iris watched her mother's movements. "You never talk about your hand. Maybe if you told me what happened I would understand."

"It was a long time ago. Before you were born. An accident at work. I just– I don't want anyone to think you're incapable of anything."

"Even though you don't think I can manage my own medicine? You won't even let me touch the bottle."

Her mother stood up. "You're coming home for lunch today. End of story."

"Well, then, can I at least go see the new Anna Sun movie with my friends tonight?"

"You need to set your priorities straight. School first. Movies are not important."

"But it's Anna Sun! She's Chinese, too. The first Chinese American movie star."

"Hmph. Movie star. Not a good career. Focus on school so you can have a good career."

Iris continued to pout and stare at the table. "Yes, Ma Ma."

Her mother walked around the table and patted Iris on the head. "Guai. Good child." She pleated Iris's long hair into two braids, using her right hand to cross the strands and her left wrist to hold them in place against Iris's head. She worked so quickly, no one would have ever suspected she lacked an appendage. She pulled back and scrutinized Iris, pursing her lips and clicking her tongue behind her teeth in disapproval. "Ai-yo! You are getting so dark. Why do you want to look like a lowly field worker? Put on long sleeves. Wear a hat."

Iris rolled her eyes, turning her head away so her mother wouldn't see. She stuffed her mouth with another bite of the bun. She accepted the mustard yellow cardigan and conical bamboo hat her mother handed her, bowing her head dutifully and suppressing a wry smile at the contradiction. *She doesn't want me to look like a field worker, but she wants me to dress like one,* she thought while holding the hat traditionally used by rice pickers in China. Despite the repeated pleas of her parents that she achieve the Chinese ideal of a pale complexion, Iris was a sun-loving bronze.

As her mother left, she took a hard look at the clock and gave Iris a little nod as she closed the door behind her. Iris understood what that meant. She would need to be back before her alarm went off. She double-checked her wristwatch against the clock to ensure they matched.

Ten minutes later, Iris exited their second-floor apartment without the bamboo hat, tugging the door closed so she could fasten the double locks. Los Angeles Chinatown was bustling with activity. Storefronts lined the buildings, the color of paint differentiating one shop from the next. White, pale yellow, green, and pink. All had awnings in the style of pagodas, sloped and emerald green, supported by red joists and rafters. Strings of red paper lanterns stretched from building to building across the street. Women in calf-length skirts were perusing the bakery below her apartment and the sidewalk fruit and vegetable stands next door.

The sun was bright, and Iris almost wished she had brought the bamboo hat. Despite the heat, she pulled the mustard cardigan over her brown arms, moving her backpack and braids out of the way. The cardigan was short and surprisingly fitted to her skinny frame, no doubt a donation from the local Christian missionaries. The base of the cardigan ended at the top of her high-waisted, blue capris. The cropped pants had begun their life as full-length pants and had been altered many times through the years by her mother, who worked as a seamstress inside the laundromat that they owned.

As Iris crossed the street a few blocks from her home and halfway to the school, she noticed a crowd of her classmates gathered along the road. They were huddled against a metal barricade that blocked the sidewalk. An excited energy was in the air as students whispered among themselves.

"What's going on?" Iris said, tapping a student named Brian and trying to see over his head.

"They're filming a movie," Brian said. "That's Anna Sun!"

Iris sucked in a breath. "Really?"

"She's one of the first Chinese American movie stars," her friend Stephanie Chu said to her left. Her cheeks were as flushed as Iris's felt.

"I know," Iris retorted. She knew everything about Anna Sun. And she couldn't believe it. A chance to see and maybe even meet Anna Sun.

"I heard she grew up around here and maybe even went to our school, too," Brian said.

Stephanie laughed. "If you count growing up in a mansion as around here."

Iris stood on her tiptoes and squinted down the sidewalk. Chinatown was a popular place for filming, but this was the first time she was this close to the action. A cluster of men stood behind a large movie camera with spinning film reels on top. It was propped on a tripod, and the whole contraption was being pulled on a small track in front of a woman as she walked down the sidewalk. A black, satiny dress that tapered from her shoulder pads to her small waist twirled about her porcelain legs. With each step, her shoulder-length curls caught the breeze, lifting and falling with grace and allure. She looked out over the camera. Her wide-set eyes seemed to pause on Iris, and she displayed a smile that exuded sweetness, innocence, and hope.

Iris drew in a breath, a thrill rising in her chest. "It is her."

Several heads nodded around her. They all watched as Anna Sun walked back and forth, gesturing and saying things they weren't close enough to hear, until someone noticed that they only had five minutes until school started. One by one, her classmates took off in a jog. Iris reluctantly ripped her eyes away and joined them. They laughed and chatted while they scurried toward the school, knowing that as soon as they entered the grounds, they would have to be silent, obedient, well-behaved children.

Class after class, Iris stared at the chalkboard while the teacher spoke, her mind elsewhere, thinking of movie stars. Seeing Anna Sun had awakened something within her. She longed to see more, to be close again. If Anna Sun could rise to a position of prominence in society, maybe she could as well. She was no longer upset that she would have to go home for lunch. It would be another chance to stop by the movie set. The minutes dragged on until the bell rang for lunch. Iris jumped up from her desk and bid her friends a quick farewell.

"Are you ever going to have lunch with us?" Stephanie asked.

Iris turned and shrugged as she walked out the door. "You know how my parents are. I have to go help them at the laundromat."

Her friends just waved her off without asking any other

questions. It wasn't a lie. Iris often did help with her parents' business. It just wasn't the full truth. Iris would stop at home, take her medication, then stop by her parents' laundromat, which was only a couple blocks away, before heading back to school. She checked her watch while walking and saw she had a few extra minutes to stop at the movie set. Before long, she was back at the metal barricade, but Anna Sun was nowhere in sight. Her heart sank.

"Excuse me," Iris said to a man sitting next to the camera equipment. "Are you done filming?"

The man looked up from eating a sandwich. "Not yet. Just taking a break for lunch."

"How long will you be here?"

"We'll probably wrap up late this afternoon."

"OK. Thank you."

Her hope rose again. Maybe she could see Anna Sun after school.

As she unlocked the door to her apartment, the alarm in her bedroom went off. Right on time. Her mother was already home, waiting for her with lunch at the dining table. She looked at the clock and gave Iris a look like "That was a little too close." Iris took the pill her mother handed her, then set the alarm and came back to the dining table where she proceeded to shovel the steamed rice, sauteed chicken and vegetables into her mouth. If she hurried back, maybe the filming would have started up again.

"Chew your food," her mother said. "You're going to give yourself an upset stomach."

Iris didn't slow down but made a show of chewing the large amounts of food in her mouth. Her mother shook her head as she cleared away the empty dishes.

"Do you need me to come help fold clothes today?" Iris said.

"Not today," her mother said.

"OK," Iris said with a tad too much enthusiasm. She jumped up and grabbed her backpack. "Then I'm going to head back to school now."

"Make sure to be home on time to take your medicine," her mother called after her.

Iris turned and gave a thumbs-up as she closed the front door. She bubbled with excitement. After school, she'd have a couple of hours to spare to watch the filming.

The film crew was still at lunch when Iris passed by, so she returned to school before lunch was over. Her friends cheered as she joined them in their circle.

"I guess having a partial lunch with you on the last day of school is better than nothing," Stephanie said.

Iris laughed. "My parents didn't need much help today."

"At least we get to hang out a little before we leave for camp. Wish you were coming."

"Maybe next year," Iris said, knowing that wouldn't happen. She would have no friends around for the first two full weeks of summer, just like every summer. *I'm sure my parents will keep me busy, though,* she thought ruefully.

The rest of her classes dragged as the morning ones had. When the bell rang for the final class of the year, Iris and her fellow classmates sat without moving until the teacher dismissed them. They walked out of the classroom in a single file, each thanking the teacher with a slight bow of the head. Once out in the school's courtyard, the students broke into joyous laughs and chatter. Iris hugged her friends goodbye and made plans to see them when they returned from camp. Although she was sad to see them go, those feelings were overshadowed by her desire to get back to the movie set.

She left the school grounds and quickened her pace toward

the barricaded sidewalk where some classmates were already gathering. Dodging and squeezing through the crowd, she got to the front where she had a great view of the action. Except, there wasn't any action. Iris looked around the set, straining to see through her glasses. A couple men were standing near the movie camera, talking over some papers they held in their hands. No one else was around the set. Iris waited and checked her watch from time to time. They couldn't still be at lunch, could they? Maybe movie stars got extended lunches.

Little by little, the crowd began to thin around her. Iris stayed a little longer, chewing on her lower lip and hoping something would happen before she had to leave. She checked her watch again. The time ticked down. She would have to leave soon to take her medication, but she didn't want to leave without finding out if they would be back.

"Excuse me," Iris called to the men next to the camera. One of them looked up with an impatient look.

"Yeah?" he said.

"Will you be filming more today?"

"We're postponed until Monday."

"Oh."

"Sorry, hon, that's just how show business goes."

Iris was preparing to dwell on her bad luck when the time on her watch caught her eye. There were only a couple of minutes until she had to take her medicine. Her misfortunes left her mind, and she took off in a jog. She had to be home before the alarm went off.

CHAPTER FIVE

Ling
Summer 1985

T HE ENTRANCE TO Redwood Cafe was through the fire-hollowed interior of a living redwood. Wood panels incorporated the redwood into the cafe building so the tree looked like it had grown into the wall. Like all Shifter establishments, the cafe was guarded by camouflage stones, and Statics walked to and fro, unaware of its existence. Some Shifters sat at the windows that looked out onto Main Street, but Ling preferred the outdoor patio in back.

The aroma of coffee and pastries filled the air. Ling ordered an espresso and a croissant and headed to the patio. Her daughter was already there, sitting at a table in the corner, sipping a coffee. Her face was a stoic mask, but a close examination of the corners of her mouth betrayed a slight downward tilt, and there was a glistening in her eyes. Did she suspect what Ling had done? Probably not, or else she wouldn't have agreed to come today. Ling took a deep breath and headed to the table.

The patio air was cool and moist. A trickle of sunlight speckled the moss-lined stone walls, and hanging ferns rustled delicately. It was quiet and peaceful. Just what Ling needed right now.

Ling smiled as she sat down, but her voice came out more business-like than she intended. "Hello. So glad we could get together again so soon, especially after... well, you know." She waved her hand and quickly sipped her espresso to hide her nervousness.

Unexpectedly, her daughter burst into tears. Ling didn't know what to do. She glanced around to see if any other patrons were watching them, but they were the only ones on the patio. Handing over some napkins, she waited patiently while her daughter composed herself.

"He's gone." She sniffed and wiped her eyes with a napkin.

Ling patted her hand from across the table. "This is a blessing. I know it doesn't seem like it now, but this allows you to focus on and repair your marriage."

Her daughter didn't seem to be listening. "He was so happy when I told him. But it must have been all pretend."

A heavy lump dropped into Ling's stomach. "Told him what?"

Her daughter seemed to notice her for the first time. "Hm?"

"You said 'he was so happy' when you told him. Told him what?"

Her daughter's lip trembled. "Ma Ma... I'm pregnant."

Ling's mind began to whirl. "OK. That's OK. You and Jackson had been trying for a long time. He'll be so happy–"

"It's not Jackson's. He's infertile, but he doesn't know. We got tested awhile back, and I couldn't bring myself to show him the results, knowing how he'd react. So I lied."

"A *Static* child?" This would ruin everything. Her son-in-law's political career. Her daughter's reputation.

Her daughter became very serious. "No one will know."

"How can you say that? What do you think will happen when her powers don't develop?"

"I'll figure it out."

Ling's voice took on an edge, but she tried to keep it hushed to avoid attracting attention. "You'll figure it out?"

"Maybe for once in your life you could be more supportive of me."

Ling sat back in her chair and huffed. How could she even respond to this irrational talk? "Supportive of your affairs? Or supportive of you breaking the law?"

Her daughter leaned forward. "Supportive of the fact that my marriage is broken. Supportive of me as my own person. If you didn't care so much about our social standing and reputation, I could've left Jackson long ago and none of this would've ever happened."

"I just can't reason with you."

Her daughter stood up. "Don't worry, I'll make it easy for you. Stay away from me and my child." She turned and left the cafe.

Ling sat at the table, heart thudding. The secret was safe for now. Ling wouldn't dare say anything. She couldn't bear the shame of it. But the secret would come out eventually. There was no way around it.

CHAPTER SIX

Nivi

Summer 2000

IVI PLACED TWO oranges on the table in front of the picture of her parents. Her grandmother, Ling Guang, lit a candle and set it down next to the oranges.

"Ten years," Ling said with a somber look and a shake of her head. This anniversary seemed to affect her more than usual as a glistening at the corner of her eye broke her usual stoic expression.

Nivi tensed at this slight display of emotion. She didn't want to speak about her parents, and even this once-a-year ritual made her uncomfortable. To avoid making eye contact with her grandmother, she kept her attention on the photograph. The two figures in the photo were covered in shadow, their facial features obscured. These people were strangers to her. She barely remembered the day of their deaths. That wasn't her fault, though. She was only four years old at the time. All she knew of them was what she could make out in this photograph, and she preferred to keep it that way. There was no point talking about people she would never see again.

In the photo, the woman and man were the same height. Nivi couldn't tell if that was because they were both tall, short, or average height, although she assumed they must be close to her five-foot-five height. The man had broad shoulders, dark brown skin, and corkscrew curls. The woman was slim and more pale than the man. She had a prominent gray streak of hair that contrasted with the rest of her long, black hair. For a moment, Nivi imagined a little girl between the two shadowy figures with wavy hair and brown skin. A perfect blend of her African American and Chinese parents. She caught herself and averted her eyes from the photo.

She stared at the wall behind the photo instead. The boring beige wall was like all the other walls in the house. Even the house exterior was a shade of beige. It was as if her grandmother had deliberately gone above and beyond to have the most nondescript home in Yuras. The only interesting thing about their home was the qilin statues in the entryway. With the head of a Chinese dragon and the body of a horse, except covered in scales, it was associated with wisdom, serenity, and longevity, or so her grandmother said. Why her grandmother insisted on keeping them inside the house, Nivi didn't know. She thought it looked like an outdoor fixture and would look more appropriate guarding the front door.

Ling continued to speak in a low tone. Nivi wasn't sure if she was talking to herself, but she wished she would stop and stand in quiet reverence like usual.

"Ten years… Who would've ever thought? It shouldn't have been like this." Ling lowered her head. "That awful fire…"

At the mention of a fire, Nivi turned to look at her grandmother. What was she talking about? Her parents had died in a car accident. Ling was staring into space as if she were someplace else.

When Ling's gaze met that of Nivi's, Ling jumped a little. Her eyes snapped back into focus, and she looked away quickly without a word.

Nivi was glad her grandmother's ramblings had stopped, but something inside her felt ill at ease. What did her grandmother mean by "that awful fire?" It must be nothing. Her grandmother wasn't thinking clearly. Or maybe she had been thinking of other tragedies in her life. But the thought of a fire gnawed at Nivi, as if something ignited within her memory. Even though she tried to clear her mind, the feeling remained and grew like an itch that demanded to be scratched. Finally, she felt compelled to say something.

"What fire?"

Ling cleared her throat. "Hm?"

"You said 'that awful fire.'"

"I must've misspoke." Ling lowered her voice as if speaking to herself. "This aging thing…"

Her grandmother was confused, as Nivi had expected. Nivi shouldn't have said anything. She put the fire from her mind and left the altar in the living room.

"I'm going to go practice violin," Nivi said as she walked down the hall toward her room.

"OK, May," Ling said behind her.

May? Nivi paused in the hallway, her heartbeat quickening. She didn't know why she'd be affected by an unknown name. It was probably because she was worried her grandmother really was losing it. She glanced back at her grandmother.

"You OK?"

Ling rubbed the bridge of her nose. "I'm fine."

Her grandmother's face had resumed the stoic expression that Nivi was familiar with. That made her feel better.

Nivi went into her bedroom toward the violin stand next to her bed. When she reached forward with her right hand to pick up the violin, her hand shook. She grabbed her right hand with her left to stop the shaking, but now her left hand shook as well. A feeling of dread began to tighten her chest.

She stepped back from the violin and sat on the ground with her back to her bed. Sucking in rapid breaths, she gripped the carpet with both hands and stared at her toes in the beige fibers. To distract herself, she counted her toes over and over. One, two, three, four, five, six, seven, eight, nine, ten. After her tenth round of counting, her breathing slowed, and the tightness in her chest released. She continued to sit on the floor for several minutes, catching her breath and trying to figure out what had happened.

The whole exchange with her grandmother must've left her unsettled enough to cause a panic attack. She'd never had one before but remembered learning about them in health class. The mention of a fire stirred something within Nivi. And the name May. Her heart thudded as if she had just received the news of her parents' death for the first time. Maybe the car her parents were in burst into flames after it collided with the tree. That could be the fire her grandmother was talking about. But she had never mentioned a fire before. And maybe her grandmother meant Mei, as in the Mandarin word for little sister. But why would her grandmother call her that? Her grandmother had said she was fine, but what if her mind was starting to go?

Nivi stood and stared at her violin. She still needed to practice, but each time she started to reach for it, her hands would shake again. Afraid to have another panic attack, she gave up on practice for the day and took out her books for one last study session.

She sat at the desk in the corner of her room and paged through the books, unable to concentrate. After several minutes, she gave up on studying and put her head on the desk. She wasn't worried about her exams. She had been prepared for weeks. As usual, she would get straight A's and get into the elite music camp that summer.

She lifted her head and glanced around her room at the beige walls and carpet. Everything tidy and in its place. Everything so ordinary. Nothing unexpected. She should be grateful. She had food, a home, a good education, and a talent for violin, but sometimes she felt there should be something more. Or something less. Violin took up all her free time. She barely had any friends because of it. Seemed fitting. Barely any friends and barely any family.

A novel question formed in her mind. What if she quit violin? The thought somehow lightened her anxiety. She let out a small laugh. Could she really quit? And more importantly, how would her grandmother or her best friend Amber react? She let the idea percolate. What would she even do with the extra time? Did she actually want more friends? No. Of course not. Just thinking about being surrounded by people increased her anxiety again. She should forget that she ever thought about quitting.

That night Nivi couldn't fall asleep. She tossed and turned, thinking about violins, fires, and her grandmother losing her wits. She had always tried not to think about her parents' death that much, refusing to let it make her into a victim, but now she couldn't get it out of her mind. If she had more time, maybe she would be able to make a friend she could talk to about things like this. One who understood what she had been through.

She needed to stop this line of thinking. It was silly and weak. She was strong. She didn't need anyone else in her life.

As if mirroring her agitation, the tree outside her window waved its branches wildly in the wind. Nivi was used to the branches knocking against the side of the house so at first didn't think twice when there was a tapping at her bedroom window, not until a voice spoke.

"Nivi, are you awake?"

Stirring from her bed, Nivi looked up to see a face pressed against the window, a mouth suctioned to the glass, and cheeks inflated like a puffer fish. She almost screamed before she recognized Amber Su's dark, mischievous eyes.

"What are you doing?" Nivi whispered. Her heart rate slowed as she evaluated the scene. "That's gross. The glass is dirty." She made a face.

Amber pulled away from the window with a big smile and motioned to Nivi. "Come on! I've found something. You have to see it!"

Nivi shushed her while stumbling out of bed, almost knocking over her violin and music stand in the process.

"It's not really a good time. It's the last day of finals tomorrow. And we have our violin auditions right after."

"Which I'm *sure* you're already prepared for. Come on, it'll be quick. I promise."

Nivi rubbed her arm and looked off to the side. "I don't know."

"Are you afraid of the *Monster People?*" Amber stuck her arms out in front of her and formed her hands into claws, wobbling back and forth while moaning.

Nivi stiffened, unable to keep herself from glancing at the shadows behind Amber. When she saw Amber smirking, Nivi gave a weak smile as if she was too old for such nonsense. "We both know that's just a silly legend the people of Yuras made up to put our little town on the map."

Amber crossed her arms. "Keep telling yourself that."

"It's true. Why else would anyone care about one of the smallest towns in California? Sure, it was a gold rush town, but there didn't even end up being any gold here."

"Ugh. You're always so literal. Can't you just relax and have fun?"

Why *couldn't* she just relax and have fun? How was it so easy for Amber? Didn't she care about school or her violin auditions?

"I don't have time for fun unless I did something crazy… like quit violin." Nivi said the last part quickly like she was ripping off a bandaid. She braced herself for Amber's response.

Amber let out a sound halfway between a choke and a laugh. "Yeah, right. You've always loved violin."

Nivi couldn't meet Amber's eyes. But now that she had said the thought out loud, it was like the flood gate had opened, and she needed to pursue the idea more. "I think… I might have confused being good at violin and liking it."

Amber waved a hand. "You're just stressed and jumping to conclusions. All the better to come out and take your mind off things for now."

Amber's easy dismissal stunned Nivi. Amber was probably right. Nivi didn't know what she was saying. She glanced at her violin and offered a smile as if she were asking for its forgiveness after a disagreement. Her palms began to sweat. A sense of unease returned, accompanied by a strange sensation in her hands. She tried to dissipate the sensation by opening and closing her hands. The feeling only intensified. Heat spread out across her palms into her fingertips and pulsed like she had grown a heart in each fist. The heat became almost unbearable, as if she were actually holding them over a fire. She ripped her eyes away from her violin and rubbed her palms on her nightshirt.

Somehow Nivi was able to keep her voice steady. "I can't. Sorry."

"Come on. I've been waiting all day for the perfect time to show you, and you're going to miss it!"

"It can wait until after tomorrow."

Amber huffed and turned her back to the window. "Look, we both know you're already perfect in both school and violin. If you don't start letting loose a little, I really will be your only friend at music camp."

The internal knot of insecurity twisted in Nivi's stomach. She repeated to herself that she was strong and didn't need anyone else. People were overrated. They could just leave at any moment, so what was the point? Anyway, she already had Amber, her grandmother Ling, and her perfectly planned future to look forward to. None of those other kids mattered. Even if she decided to stop playing the violin, she had her immaculate grades to fall back on. She could go to any college she wanted to.

She began to walk back toward her bed. The warm sheets were calling to her. But more thoughts tugged at her resolution. Amber's grades were not the most competitive. She did have to rely more on violin and the music camp auditions tomorrow for her future, yet she was still relaxed and ready to have fun. And she *was* friends with most of the other kids at school. Was she going to tell them how much of a spoilsport Nivi was? Maybe she had been telling them all along. Maybe Amber was finally getting sick of her.

Nivi paused and turned back toward Amber with a sigh. "Alright."

Amber's mouth fell open, then curved into a smile as she jumped up and down. "Really?"

"Just this once. And we better not be gone too long."

"Of course not. It's just down the Cliff Trail."

Nivi crept to the hall to make sure her grandmother Ling was still asleep, then came back to the window where Amber was waiting, pacing back and forth. She pulled on a gray hooded sweatshirt and baggy jeans, then slid her bedroom window up as quietly as possible. The wind gushed in, whipping her bangs off her forehead. Amber half-pulled Nivi out of the window while she let out a squeal. Right away, Nivi noticed how her outfit contrasted with Amber's sleek black leggings, fitted white down jacket, and matching white beanie with two pom poms on top. She looked like a snow bunny even though it was almost summer, although the wind was cold tonight.

"Way to be inconspicuous," Nivi said.

"Oh, relax. No one's going to be awake at this time."

That was probably true, but Nivi still felt uncomfortable. It was a high risk that watchful neighbors would recognize them while sneaking around in their small town at night.

"This better be good."

"It's better than good." Amber's eyes sparkled as she grabbed Nivi's hand and pulled her down the street.

They made their way through the short stretch of down-town Yuras. Rows of floor-to-ceiling arched windows looked out from brick storefronts, their displays swallowed up in the night. At this time of year, the bars closed before midnight and the streetlamps were off. Not until school got out and the summer tourism started would businesses extend their hours and leave the lights on overnight. Even the moon was a tiny sliver in the sky, barely enough to cast a shadow. They were in a black-and-white movie. Everything was devoid of color and life.

Amber led the way with a small flashlight. She turned down Forest Lane, a side street where a classmate of theirs,

Arav Markson, lived. The wood cabin was the last house on the dead-end street. Amber paused and stared at his bedroom window. Nivi sighed.

"What?" Amber said.

"Nothing." Nivi looked away.

"Why don't you like him?"

"I don't not like him."

"Oh yes, you do. It's so obvious."

Nivi rolled her eyes. "He's just such a jock."

Amber's voice took on a tone of annoyance. "Maybe if you gave him a chance, you'd see there's more to him. And then we could all hang out together, and it wouldn't be so awkward. You have more in common than you realize. His mother died when he was young, too."

Nivi stiffened and didn't respond. Was she supposed to be friends with every kid who also had dead parents?

Amber continued. "You know, it could've been a lot worse for you. Arav's dad *saw* his mom die. He has to carry that around. It affects their whole family." She paused. "Forget it. I shouldn't have said all that."

Nivi kept her eyes on the ground and hoped that her burning cheeks wouldn't lead to tears. If Amber were a better friend, she would know Nivi's parents' deaths affected her whole family, too. She shouldn't have to point that out. They stood in silence for a few moments. For some reason, Nivi had the urge to apologize. Amber probably just said what she said because Nivi had insulted Arav. Instead, she blamed it on her grandmother.

"It's just that… I'm worried about my grandmother."

Amber still seemed annoyed, and she responded with a curt tone. "Why?"

"She said some weird things today about my parents. That

they died in a fire." Why was she telling Amber all this? She didn't want to be talking about her parents.

"Didn't they die in a car crash?"

"Yeah. That's why I'm worried my grandmother's getting confused. I heard her mumbling to herself about her memory and aging."

"That sucks."

Now, Nivi really wished she hadn't said anything. What had she expected? There was no point opening up about these things.

"My parents like keeping track of the news," Amber said. "I could ask them if they heard of a deadly fire around ten years ago."

"Really? Thanks." That was unexpected. And kind of nice.

Amber's unsolicited offer gave Nivi a sudden new hope. Maybe she would find out more information about her parents. But why should she feel excited about that? It wasn't like new information would bring her parents back. Just as quickly, her mood soured again.

They waited outside Arav's house for a few more minutes. When it was clear there was no movement inside, Amber continued down the road. Nivi envied the home, with its lights off and its sleeping occupants inside, wishing she could be at home doing the same. But here she was, tagging along with Amber as usual. At least this time, it wasn't to a birthday party she hadn't been invited to.

A footpath continued past the dead-end street into a forest and split into various hiking paths beyond. Fir, cedar, and pine took over from the maples that lined the neighborhoods and downtown. Amber trudged ahead, her flashlight and bright white jacket a beacon bobbing over the pine needles and dirt. Nivi glanced behind. The darkness had already consumed Arav's house and his neighbors. In the forest, the trees created a barrier against the wind, creating a sudden hush and sense of isolation. A twig snapped behind Nivi, and she ran forward and almost collided with Amber. It was probably just a squirrel, but she stayed close to Amber either way. Encapsulated in their own bubble of light, she felt like a deep-sea explorer. Only the sounds of their crunching footsteps and an occasional scattering of pine needles and twigs from above reminded her they were on solid land.

They exited the trees and headed along a trail on the cliffs along the south side of the Yuras peninsula. The ocean waves crashed thunderously below, and the wind threatened to blow them over. Amber walked off the trail, past a sign that read *Private Property No Trespassing*, and toward the cliff edge. She stopped by a large boulder at the edge of the cliff.

"Watch this," she said and jumped over the side of the cliff before Nivi had a chance to protest the fact that they were trespassing.

Nivi gasped and clambered to the cliff's edge, her heart racing. There, Amber stood triumphantly on a three-foot wide ledge. It had not been visible from the trail. A mix of terror and rage boiled behind Nivi's slack jaw.

"You could have warned me."

"Well, are you coming?" Amber said with a flip of her hair.

Nivi pressed her lips together. At least Amber's annoyance seemed to be gone. She climbed down. Her thin fingers, calloused from years of violin practice, easily gripped the stone wall. As she walked, Nivi hugged the wall, trying to ignore the feeling of gravity pulling her over the edge. She followed Amber as she descended the downward-sloping ledge, leaving the top of the cliff several stories above them. Focused on maintaining her footing, Nivi didn't wonder why there was a hidden, well-worn path on the side of the cliff until they neared sea level.

The low tide lapped at the damp stones they walked upon.

A tunnel extended into the jagged cliff face at the base of the path. It was large enough for them to walk side by side without stooping over.

"Is this safe?"

"Of course." Amber strode in without stopping or looking back.

Determined to demonstrate her ability to stay relaxed and carefree, Nivi headed into the tunnel. A gust of cold, moist air carried the smell of wet, ancient stones. Seaweed and must seasoned her lips. Despite her efforts, dread prickled under her skin like thousands of needles trying to break free. She focused her attention on her footsteps. One foot in front of the other.

Striations of concentric circles repeated over and over in the hard stone. The ocean sounds faded behind. After a while, Nivi estimated they were about a quarter mile into the cave. The further they went, the more nervous she got. They passed a couple of smaller tunnel offshoots to their left, and Nivi was relieved Amber didn't take them down either of those.

Finally, Amber stopped, grabbed Nivi's hand, and stepped into an opening to the right. They entered a massive room, expanding from the tunnel a foot above their heads to a dome that felt like the night sky. The walls sparkled with gemstones scintillating from the flashlight. Stars in an underground planetarium. Nivi's jaw dropped.

"It's beautiful," she breathed. Tension faded from her mind and body.

"Isn't it?" Amber said.

"How did you find it?"

"Arav and I were hiking, and we stopped to rest by that big boulder on the cliff and saw this path down. I wanted to bring you back but had to wait until it was low tide."

"We should probably get going soon. It's private property."

"Don't worry. Arav and I hike this area all the time and never see anyone. And there's no way an active mine is operating when half the time it's underwater. It has to be abandoned."

Nivi had to admit that Amber had a point about the mine. She felt a sense of awe at the antiquity of the place. A time when the tide must have been lower.

"Interesting." Nivi turned around and tapped her foot in an arc. "It's not that wet here. I'd expect more water on the ground after the tide went out."

Amber shrugged. "Maybe it absorbed into the ground."

Nivi approached an encrusted wall to the left of the entrance and examined its contents. Translucent gray gemstones, the size of large marbles, were embedded within. They were a paler gray than the surrounding dark stone of the cave wall, like dew drops on its surface.

"I wonder what kind of stone this is." She ran her fingers along their surface. "Strange. All these stones are perfectly smooth, like river rocks. I guess the ocean must have polished them over time, but wouldn't it have worn down the walls over time, too?"

"Don't ask me. You're the smart one." Amber bent over. "Look, I found a loose one." She picked it up from the cavern entrance and held it out to Nivi.

Nivi pushed up her sleeves and took the stone in her hand. The cool surface was as smooth as glass, and it was lighter than she imagined. She took Amber's flashlight to shine a light on it. Beneath the glassy surface, the gray swirled like a wisp of fog caught in the wind. Was it actually moving? She stared at it, enraptured.

In the still and thick air, Nivi's hair moved slightly on her shoulder. A breeze arose from the tunnel followed by a chorus of whispering.

"Haven't you messed with me enough tonight?" Nivi said. Why was Amber obsessed with scaring her?

"What?" Amber said from across the cave.

Confused, Nivi looked up from the stone to locate Amber, then sensed a presence at her back. Cold appendages touched her exposed arm from behind. She jumped and let out a yelp. Heat jolted through her chest. An explosion of energy coursed through her body. The frigid hand released her wrist, and the whispering retreated down the tunnel. Nivi dropped the stone and flashlight. Everything went out of focus, and she stumbled backward against a wall.

Amber ran up. "What happened?" She tried to help steady Nivi but instantly let go. "Ow! You're hot!"

Nivi looked at Amber through her blurred vision. "I– don't know." Her brain felt foggy.

Amber put the back of her hand to Nivi's forehead. "You're burning up. Let's get you home."

"I'm ok." Nivi regained her balance and felt the heat pass. She didn't want to leave the beautiful cave just yet, and she didn't want Amber to think she was wussing out.

"You're not blaming me for missing finals tomorrow. Plus, the tide will be coming in soon." Amber slipped her arm through Nivi's and led her out of the cave.

They walked back through the tunnel. All the while, the air seemed to pull at the back of Nivi's hair. She looked behind her, but all she could see was darkness. Here and there a sound would cause her to look back again, but she never saw anything.

They continued up the ramp and onto the cliffs where they rejoined the path. Through the distant crash of ocean waves, there was an occasional crunch, as if someone were ascending the rocky slope behind them.

CHAPTER SEVEN

Davis
Winter 1935

A SCREAM PIERCED THROUGH the thunderous storm, penetrating Davis's subconscious and sending him into a rigid panic. He lay frozen in bed, heart racing, skin prickling with sweat. At seventeen years old, he hadn't had a night terror in years, yet the familiar constriction of his throat squelched his breath, and his numb limbs failed to move. A flash of lightning illuminated the ceiling. Long shadows shot out from hidden corners and clawed for purchase before retreating into darkness. The accompanying thunder rattled the windows in time with Davis's trembling heart.

The stress of the day must've gotten to him. Seeing that severed hand was playing tricks on his mind.

Then, again, a scream.

Davis struggled against his imprisoned body. He could feel the sweat trickling down his brow. All of a sudden, the air returned to his lungs. He sucked in breath after breath until the chill air smothered his feverish nerves and released his limbs. Heart thumping, he scooted to the bed's edge and pushed himself up onto shaky legs. Another scream. This time he recognized the voice. It was his mother.

Davis stumbled to the chest of drawers on the opposite side of the room and pulled open the top drawer. Under a pile of socks, his hands found the smooth stones he had hidden there. He brought them out just as another bolt of lightning illuminated his room. If his mother was in trouble, the power in the stones had to be able to help in some way.

He slipped them into his pajama pants pocket. Then he went to the door and cracked it open. Cold air rushed into his room. He shivered and put on a robe over his pajamas, then returned to the door and peered down the hall. There was a flurry of activity downstairs and at the end of the hallway in front of his parents' room. Nurses in white aprons and caps hurried in and out of his parents' bedroom carrying red-stained linens which they handed to the household servants waiting in the hall. The servants rushed downstairs and returned with fresh linens. This was repeated several times while the screams continued. Davis remembered seeing a scene similar to this one ten years prior when his sister was born, but his mother wasn't expecting a child now.

The screams stopped. Davis tiptoed into the hall and approached the room. Cold marble floors bit into his bare feet. He passed his sister's room with the door cracked open. His sister snored softly inside. She could sleep through anything.

Nurses emerged from his parents' bedroom followed by a man in white scrubs whom Davis recognized as the family doctor. The doctor wiped his brow and said something to the nurses, who nodded and went down the staircase. Davis crept closer and craned his head to hear what was being said. The emergence of a man in a suit beside the doctor caused Davis to jump into an empty bedroom just past his sister's room. Davis's father looked as stern as ever. Side-swept, black hair lay tousled across his furrowed forehead, and his usual frown contradicted the curled-up ends of his thick mustache. Blood smeared the side of his face and covered his hands, and he leaned heavily on the metal-tipped cane he always carried.

Davis leaned against the wall next to the door, attempting to hear and not be seen. The doctor spoke, his voice sounding resigned and weary.

"I'm sorry, Randall. There's nothing more I can do. We need a healer."

"*You're* a healer," his father's voice boomed.

"Not that kind. I can heal surface injuries like yours. Her wounds are too deep. Her organs are failing. How did this happen?"

Davis's father was silent for a moment. "Did she say anything? Did she see who attacked her?"

"Nothing coherent."

Davis's father let out a breath. "We were returning from dinner in the city when they attacked. I don't know who they were for certain. They might have been savage Statics trying to take down another Shifter they discovered in their community. My guess is they were hirelings of the Dawan family." His voice grew louder. "I bet this was a political attack. With my wife out of the way, Jackson Dawan would ascend to Chairperson of the Shifter Council. I'm sure they hoped to kill me too, knowing that my son – being what he is – would have no way to retaliate."

"It seems too brazen. Are you sure? These wounds are not magical."

"That's so it can be spun that some Statics attacked her.

That way, Jackson can push his agenda of anti-integration. You know Chairperson Sun, my wife, was for– is for– integration, on account of our son and all."

"Integration or not, where will we be if we can't find peace within our own?"

"That is neither here nor there. Now tell me what you can do to help my wife."

After a pause, the doctor continued. "I know of another healer, but she's down in Long Beach. There may not be enough time."

"We have to try."

"I'll see if I can contact her and have her head this way."

Footsteps and the click of a cane descended the stairs. Davis peeked out from the office. Not seeing anyone, he stepped out into the hallway. To his right, an intricate, wrought-iron banister obscured the view of the entryway below, however, the lack of voices assured Davis his father wasn't near. He made his way toward his parents' room. Cracks of thunder quickened his pace.

Davis hesitated just outside the door of his parents' room. In contrast with the crisp, fresh air in the hall, the air inside the room was thick and humid. Particles shone in the air around the dim bedside table lamp. The sour smell of blood hung in the air, and his mother lay motionless on the far side of the bed, her face turned away. His stomach churned, and he rested against the doorframe to regain his balance before stepping into the room.

"Mother?" he whispered.

He crept closer and closer until he was next to the bed. A pale hand stuck out from under the covers, deflated and limp.

Suddenly, his mother let out a gurgling choke and flopped over so that her face was visible. Her usual perfectly coiffed hair hung loose around her shoulders in clumped, black strands. Gray skin shrouded the beauty of her face. Half-open crusted lids revealed bloodshot eyes. Lightning shot horrendous shadows across her face. Davis held in a yelp and stumbled backward. He regained his composure and quickly stepped to his mother's side.

"Mother, can you hear me?" He took her cold hands in his own. "Who did this to you? Was it the Dawan family?"

His mother's eyes rolled side-to-side, unfocused. Blood soaked up through bandages around her abdomen.

"If it was, I promise to avenge you." He reached into his pocket and brought out a stone. "I think I have something that can help you."

His mother took in a strained breath. "Davis?"

Davis straightened up and squeezed his mother's hand. "It's me. Remember those stories you used to tell me? The ones about the stones with special powers? I– think I found some. Maybe one of these stones can help you get better."

He held the stone out to his mother. Her eyes focused and refocused, then opened wider.

"That is a special stone indeed," she said with a labored breath.

She took the stone with a shaky hand, and it lit up with a brilliant white flash. Davis gasped and squinted from the brightness.

"Lay a finger on the stone." She held it out in her palm.

Davis did as he was told. His mother seemed to get a sudden surge of energy.

It's working, he thought. *She's getting better.*

"This is a gift I wish I could've given you long ago." Her voice was sounding stronger. "Then maybe your father would have been a little less hard on you."

The light from the stone pulsed. There was a disturbance in the air where their hands touched. Translucent threads appeared, wavering like a clear smoke. They flowed from his mother's hand, through the stone, and into Davis.

"What's happening?" Davis said as the shimmering webs absorbed into his finger.

His hand began to glow, a soft white light. The glow spread, pumping up the veins in his arms until his whole body pulsed with light. His mother, on the other hand, grew dimmer.

Then, the light was gone. His mother collapsed back against the pillows. Her hand dropped, and the stone fell to the ground. It was black and no longer shined or swirled from within.

Davis hunched forward, catching his breath. He pulled himself forward and touched his mother's face.

"Mother?"

She didn't respond.

"Mother!" He let out a sob.

A voice thundered from the doorway.

"What have you done?"

Davis flinched but didn't move from his mother's side. Step, step, cane. Step, step, cane. The telltale two-and-a-half footsteps of his father entered the room. Unexplainably, Davis felt his father's presence behind him in a way he never had before. There was a warmth and a glow in his mind's eye. But no affection accompanied those sensations.

His father leaned over and picked up the darkened stone. After examining it for a moment, he let it fall to the ground again. He lifted his cane and brought the metal-rimmed base down hard, shattering the stone into pieces. When he spoke again, his voice was shaking.

"Where did you get a transfer stone?"

Davis bit his lip. He stayed silent.

A strange expression crossed his father's face. He approached Davis, took him by the shoulders, and addressed him with a steady and serious voice.

"Listen to me, Son." Davis's stomach jumped. He couldn't remember the last time his father addressed him as *son*. "You need to leave. Now."

Tears pooled in Davis's eyes. "I don't understand."

His father's voice was almost gentle. "You must go before anyone sees what you've done. What would the Shifter Council do if they knew what *you* did? These stones are illegal. They have been banned for decades."

Davis trembled and shook his head. "No. Please. I didn't know."

"A Static killing a Shifter. And with such a dangerous and illegal stone. That deserves the worst punishment. Now, there will never be any chance of integration."

Davis's legs wobbled, yet he refused to leave his mother's side. His father lifted his cane and thrust it forward, knocking Davis back and onto the floor.

His father's eyes grew wild. "Hurry! Before it's too late."

Davis got up, panting, and ran from the room.

CHAPTER EIGHT

Nivi

Summer 2000

NIVI EXITED THE room where she had just completed the last final of her freshman year. She smiled faintly to herself, confident in her performance. Despite the transient fever she had developed the previous night, she woke up this morning feeling amazing. Her memory of the night was still a blur. There was the Cliff Trail, the tunnel, and the beautiful cave full of sparkling stones. Then the fever had come on so quickly. It must have been a reaction to the musty air trapped for who knows how long.

A massive exodus of students pushed past Nivi, excited to be done with finals, bumping into her and knocking the books out of her hands. The smile faded from her lips. She bent over to gather her scattered belongings. At least during the summer, she wouldn't have to be around so many people, especially if she didn't go to music camp.

"Hey, Nivi!" Amber waved from the end of the hall and

walked over. "Do you always have to be the last student at school?" She helped pick up a book. "We're done! Let's go party!"

"Party?" Nivi made a face. "I think I'm good after last night."

Amber formed a mock pout, then broke out in a singsong tone. "We're done! We're young! It's time to have some fun!"

She stretched both arms into the air and threw her head back as she exited the Coastal High building. A strip of her tiny waist showed between her red top and low-rise jeans as she took a deep breath. At that moment, an athletic boy swept her up, spinning her around while Nivi stood by awkwardly. Amber laughed and playfully pushed him away.

"Oh my god, Arav. You're so silly."

"Are you ready to go?" he said.

"Hold on one sec." Amber turned to Nivi. "Ready to go to the music meetup?"

"Uh, no thanks."

Amber turned to Arav. "Don't worry, we'll be there. You go ahead. She's just grumpy because she's tired."

Nivi forced a smile. Her smile faded as Arav left in a friend's car. "Why did you say that to him?"

"It's true, isn't it? You're always grumpy when you're tired."

And whose fault did she think that was? "I already told you last night I don't think I want to do this violin thing anymore."

"Yikes. You really are grumpy. And you're jumping to conclusions based on one night of poor sleep. Just come. Tonight you can rest, and you'll be back to normal."

Nivi tried to make her voice sound as calm as possible. "No. I've been thinking about this for a while now." It wasn't a full lie. She knew that somewhere deep down in her subconscious, she probably had been thinking about this. Still, she couldn't stop herself from fidgeting.

Amber looked her up and down. "Right… Then why even bring your violin today?"

Nivi shrugged, hoping she appeared nonchalant. "I already committed to the audition." She looked around. Where *was* her violin? "I'll be right back." Trying not to panic, she ran back toward the school, leaving Amber alone by the parking lot.

Amber let out a loud sigh behind her.

The darkened classrooms streaked by as Nivi jogged through the empty hall. How could she have been so careless? She hadn't told her grandmother yet about wanting to quit playing the violin, and even if she had, her grandmother would kill her for losing such an expensive item. This was all Amber's fault. If Amber hadn't pressured her into going out late last night, she would've been more clear-headed.

She entered the classroom and breathed a sigh of relief. The violin case was still under her seat where she had left it. She grabbed the case and headed back into the hall, swinging the violin by her side and smiling down at it.

The door slammed ahead. Nivi looked up and skidded to a stop. At the end of the hall, a tall, thin figure had entered the hallway and stood there, unmoving. The bright sun behind him outlined his figure, casting his pale face in shadow. Nivi looked around, very aware that she was all by herself.

"Hello?" she called out.

The person walked toward her, mumbling, whispering. His vocal raspings gave Nivi goosebumps. They were so familiar; so chilling. She had heard the same sounds before. She was sure of it. Little by little, the memory came back. Last night. In the tunnel. Someone had grabbed her arm. She didn't have time to process the memory any further because the man was getting closer. As he approached, she could see he was young and had deep, sunken eyes. Those eyes fixated on her, unblinking. Suddenly, he ran at her. Nivi screamed.

Nivi woke up on the linoleum floor of the hallway. Sweat dripped down her face, and she struggled to breathe. Then she saw why. A wall of fire engulfed the hall. Coughing, she pushed herself off the floor and hunched over to avoid the smoke. Terror propelled her toward the doors, and for a moment, she forgot about her attacker. When she remembered, she ran even faster, not looking back. She burst out of the double doors and almost collided with Amber.

She collapsed, gasping and choking. The air was heavy and thick; oxygen a precious commodity she sipped at, unable to quench her lungs. Amber grabbed Nivi and helped her to her feet. Nivi tried to motion toward the building to warn Amber of the strange man, but she was too weak and her voice too hoarse.

They walked to the parking lot as Nivi continued to cough. Her hands were red and smudged with ash. She swallowed hard and lifted her head, her eyes bleary. She tried to say something but started to cough again before going limp.

Amber shook Nivi and called out her name. She brushed Nivi's hair away from her shoulder and gasped. "What happened? Who did this to you?"

CHAPTER NINE

Iris

Summer 1955

Alarm clock ringing. Pill, water, gulp. Wait for the euphoric calm to take effect. Repeat every four hours while awake.

"It's coming soon. The cure," Iris's mother said.

Her mother had said that before, but now she said it several times a week. Iris usually nodded and said no more, but as the frequency of her mother's statements increased, Iris started to develop questions.

"How do you know?" Iris asked.

"From our community meetings," her mother said.

"What are these meetings anyway? Who goes to them?"

Her mother looked taken aback. "For members of our community, of course. To inform them of updates and situations that would affect everyone."

"Why would your meeting be talking about a cure for my condition?"

"The condition doesn't affect only you. It affects people all over our community."

"It does?"

"Of course."

"Maybe if you let me out more, I'd have found that out," Iris mumbled. She wondered if the parents of the other children with her condition were as militant.

Her mother exchanged a glance with her father, and Iris knew by the look on their faces not to push any further.

Later that evening, as Iris was getting ready for bed, she overheard a hushed conversation between her parents. She crept toward the living room, hiding in the hallway as she listened.

"We should tell her," her father said.

"No," her mother said. "Once we have the cure, we won't need to. It's the only way to keep her safe."

"Are you sure her medicine is still strong enough?"

"Any stronger, and she won't be able to get up."

There was a sound as if her father was shifting on the couch. "Maybe you should at least give her a little more freedom. You don't want her to resent you forever."

Her mother was silent for a moment. She sighed. "Forever is a long time."

The couch creaked and footsteps approached the hall. Iris tiptoed back to her room. She didn't know what to think about what she had heard. Was she dying? If she were, her parents didn't sound very sad about it. So why wouldn't her medicine be strong enough? She hadn't had a seizure in years. She couldn't make sense of it, so she got into bed and tried not to think too much about it. A little bit of excitement replaced her confusion. If anything, it sounded as if her mother were considering being a little more lenient.

A few days passed after the last day of school. All Iris could think about was the upcoming Monday when Anna Sun would continue filming. She tried to focus on her work and studies, cleaning the apartment, reading ahead for the school year, doing practice problems and tests that would prepare her to achieve more than her parents had. When that didn't work to pass the time, she voluntarily helped out more at her parents' business, sweeping, mopping, counting money, and helping to fold customers' clothes.

"Look at our daughter," her mother said to her father. "Such a diligent worker. She'll be running the family business in no time."

Iris smiled and continued to work. Other than boredom and passing the time, she had another ulterior motive for her increased helpfulness. She hoped that by Monday's arrival, she would be granted a full day of freedom to go watch the filming as she pleased. However, she knew better than to ask her parents to go out too often. Not with her pill schedule. Running errands in town was fine, though; she was often given an errand list at the beginning of the week. So she waited.

When Monday morning finally arrived, Iris emerged from her room and saw what she had hoped for. A pad of paper on the dining room table and some money next to it. The cardigan and bamboo hat were placed conspicuously next to them. Leaping over to the pad of paper, she read over the top page, adjusting her thick glasses on her nose. It was a grocery list. She squeezed the paper in her hands with excitement.

I'll go watch the filming first, she thought, *then get the groceries and be back before my alarm goes off.* She would have plenty of time after that to complete her chores before her parents returned home. They wouldn't know the difference.

Her mother joined her in the living room. She approached Iris with something in her hands, then ceremoniously handed her the bottle of pills.

"What's this for?" Iris said.

"I've been thinking about what you said. I'm sorry for being so controlling. You are my only child, so I worry about you. But you are old enough to manage your own medication now."

"Really? Thank you, Ma Ma." Iris threw her arms around her mother.

Her mother patted her back. "Could you come home the first few times to take your medication? It would make me feel better."

"Sure. I'll leave the bottle in my desk drawer and come home at lunch. Will you be here?"

"Not today. I trust you." She smiled, almost sadly, and left for work.

Iris couldn't believe her luck. Maybe she had been too quick to judge her mother. Then again, maybe this was a test. Just in case, Iris compared the time on her watch to that on the clock. Three hours before the alarm would ring. If her mother happened to come back to check on her, she wanted to be on time and prepared. She set out a glass of water and a pill on her nightstand. The bottle she placed in the nightstand drawer.

But what if her mother really wasn't coming home? Then Iris could stay longer to watch the filming. She thought about taking one pill or the whole bottle with her. There were sure to be fellow students in the filming area again. It would be difficult to take a pill without being seen. Would she be OK if people did treat her differently once they knew about her condition? And there was always the possibility that she could lose her medication. Better to just come home this time since it was only a few blocks away. Plus, she told her mother she would. She didn't want to start this new trust with a lie. She stuffed the list and money into her capri pocket, left the hat and cardigan where they lay on the table, and headed out.

When Iris arrived at the film set, her face was dewy from

the summer heat. A dozen people were on the sidewalk, a good sign that production was up and running. Suppressing an urge to skip, she walked in a more dignified manner up to the barricade, keeping a calm expression plastered on her face. The film crew bustled in front of her, and she couldn't see anything except people walking back and forth with various items. It looked like they were still setting up. Iris removed and wiped her glasses, which were fogging up from the warmth of her face.

Just then, a murmur arose around her. Her vision was a blur without her glasses on, but she suddenly had an awareness of the same awe she had had when she first saw Anna Sun. She was taken aback because she hadn't even seen Anna yet. She just *felt* her presence. Deep in her chest. A flickering spark, creating heat and drawing her toward its warmth. Last week, Iris had attributed it to the excitement of seeing a movie star up close for the first time. She was still excited, but this was something else. A familiarity or connection. Like recognizing someone in a room full of strangers and the sense of relief and comfort that came with that.

She shook her head as if doing so would organize her thoughts, and put her glasses back on. Sure enough, as the scene in front of her came into focus, there was Anna Sun. She stood before the camera, looking glamorous in the same black dress, continuing to film where they left off. And just like last time, she seemed to glance directly at Iris before looking back at the camera. It was as if she were aware of the same sensation that Iris felt.

How could that be? Iris thought before admonishing herself. *You're being silly. You don't have any special connection with a movie star.*

The sensation remained. The more she watched, the more the feeling and her sight seemed to merge. Anna started to look as if she were actually glowing. Although it was very faint, the light called to Iris like a beacon in an unfamiliar sea. No matter how much she told herself she was being crazy, she couldn't unsee this inner light. Those sensations and thoughts engrossed her.

It wasn't until the sun had crossed overhead and began to cast shadows from the buildings and trees on the other side of the street that she realized it was getting close to noon. She raised her wrist and looked at the watch. 11:30. She had plenty of time.

She watched a little longer and checked her watch again. Something was off. It was still 11:30. She looked closer at her watch and saw the second hand wasn't moving. She held it up to her ear. There was no ticking. How long ago did it stop? She couldn't be sure.

"Excuse me, do you have the time?" Iris said to a woman next to her. The woman shook her head and returned her gaze toward the filming.

She asked a few other people who also shook their heads and turned away. They were all distracted by the movie spectacle. She didn't blame them, but she was beginning to worry. She had no choice but to go home and give up her spot at the front of the crowd.

As Iris left the group of onlookers and moved farther away, the strange sensation she had been feeling faded. She didn't really pay attention to the change, though, because she was too worried about the time and her medication. In the past, missing a dose had led to seizures and fainting. That was part of the reason her mother was so strict.

Please don't let it be too late, Iris thought as she ran through Chinatown toward her apartment. Maybe her mother had been right not to trust her. She was going to mess up the first chance of freedom she had been given.

The apartment was just ahead. Iris was breathing hard, and her mouth began to taste of metal. Pulling the keys from her pocket, she ran up the stairs to her home. As she approached, she could hear the alarm ringing clear and crisp through the apartment walls. She fumbled with the keys against the locks. They refused to go in.

Steadying her trembling hands, she slipped the keys into the first lock. It clicked open. She aligned the correct key to the second lock, but it slipped from her grasp and fell to the ground. She grabbed them with clammy hands and separated the keys from one another, shoving it into the second lock. With several bumps of her hip, the door gave way. She ran into the living room, glancing at the clock as she turned toward her bedroom. Seven minutes past the alarm. *It should be OK,* she thought. *It's not too late.*

She could see the gold alarm clock rattling away on her nightstand, the glass of water vibrating in response as if they were engaged in a frantic dance. The little blue pill nearby, waiting to be taken. She reached her arm forward. Lightheadedness. Balance tipping. A tightness in her chest and up her neck. She clutched at her throat, feeling it burn, and stumbled to her knees. Her mouth dried out, and she coughed as fumes emerged from the base of her tongue. There was a residue in her mouth that tasted of charcoal.

Iris pulled herself along the floor, clawing toward the glass of water and the pill. Her heart thumped so hard her ears rang. She wheezed through her burning throat. Her vision blurred in and out, and she swore the skin on the back of her hands looked shiny and white. This was not like the other times she had missed her medication. In the past, she had passed out, and later her parents told her about the seizure. Maybe she *was* dying. This was all her fault. If she hadn't pressured her mother to give her more control of her medication, this wouldn't have happened.

Iris continued crawling along the carpet. She was almost there, just a few more movements and she could reach the glass. Her vision went fuzzy. She put her hand to her face to see if she had lost her glasses. They were still there. The world spun, the floor approached her face, and then all was dark.

CHAPTER TEN

Davis
Winter 1935

AVIS HUDDLED UNDER the archway next to the storage
room. Gusts of wind blew rain at all angles, so the
archway did little to keep him dry. He shivered and
pulled his damp robe around himself, unable to distinguish
the rain on his face from tears. The shock of the evening was
still percolating beneath his subconscious; his mother dead; his
father kicking him out. Was his mother's death his fault? No,
it was Vice Chairperson Jackson Dawan. That much he knew.
Confusion and angst tumbled within him, and he felt as tossed
and torn about as the trees in the gale.

A flash of lightning streaked the sky, and the accompanying thunder seemed to shake the whole world. Water flowed
beneath the archway, widening with each passing minute.
Davis's bare feet were almost numb. Again, a flash of lightning.
This time, as the thunder roared, he wailed like an animal shot
in the gut. He kicked at the water and banged on the walls, all
the while yelling and sobbing. He was alone in the world.

Heat radiated out from his chest to his extremities. The rain stopped blowing into his face, and his feet even felt dry. As the release of emotions faded to a stupified daze, Davis realized that the rain was still blowing around him. It just wasn't touching him. He looked down, and the same was true for his feet. The water flowed by, but in an arc like there was an invisible boundary. When he nudged a foot out toward the water, it retreated back by the same amount. The heat in his chest intensified. He lifted his hands before him and waved them slowly side to side. Ribbons of water formed, looping and twirling with his movements. Davis gasped and laughed at the same time.

As quickly as his elation had come, it just as quickly dissipated, and his grief returned. His mother had given a piece of herself to him. His father was right. He had taken his mother's power, and that shock had killed her. For a moment, he let his power lapse, and the rain resumed battering his body.

The ribbons of water returned around his feet. They curved back and forth like snakes. Snakes. His mother's Shifter form had been a terrifying, nine-headed snake. Soon, another thought entered his mind. If he had his mother's water power, could he also transform into her Shifter form?

Only a couple times did Davis remember seeing his mother's Shifter form. With anti-integration sentiment growing, more and more Shifters refrained from transforming in the general public. It was also potentially dangerous in areas with so-called monster-hunting mobs. But as Davis understood it, it became torturous to go a long time in just human form, so the Shifter Council had started buying land, stationing guards, and erecting walls where Shifters could gather in all their forms. The camouflage stone his mother once told him about would probably be handy there.

Davis held a hand in front of him. How did this shifting business work? He closed his eyes and imagined the last time he saw his mother in her Shifter form. A long and large serpentine body that branched into nine heads. Venomous fangs that easily took down a deer with a single bite. Green scales across the head and down the back. White scales on the belly. He opened his eyes. His hand was still a human hand. He tried again, visualizing and clenching his teeth, stretching his arms out, willing himself to change.

Nothing happened. He kicked at a puddle of water, inadvertently striking his toe on a stone. Pain shot through that sensitive appendage. He yelled and hopped on one foot, then slipped and fell back into the mud. It was hopeless. He was no Shifter. He didn't even know if he wanted to be a Shifter. He just wanted his mother to be alive and things to go back to the way they were, even if that meant his father would never accept him. At least he would've still had a home and his mother. This was all Jackson Dawan's fault. If he ever became powerful enough, he would make sure Jackson Dawan knew what kind of misery he caused and then make him pay.

Anger and the thought of vengeance again elicited a shooting heat through his body. This time, instead of affecting the water around him, his body began to ache. His joints cracked and his muscles strained. His skin tightened over his body. He felt as if he were being pulled apart. The pressure built and built in his back and limbs until it suddenly released. The feeling was euphoric. His legs fused together, and his arms melded into his torso. Green scales formed over his body as he lengthened, his head moving higher and higher from the ground. Another release of pressure, and Davis could suddenly see behind him as well as in front and to the side at the same time. It took him a moment to realize he now had multiple heads, although his consciousness seemed to be single and intact. One of his heads looked up as his body continued to grow, not fast enough to prevent his head from colliding with the underside of the archway.

The shock of the collision knocked Davis out of his transformation, and he shrunk back into his one-headed human form. He rubbed his head and gasped, reeling from the impact and exhilaration of the transformation. So he *was* a Shifter, afterall. It seemed that strong emotions helped to bring out his powers the first time, but now that he'd done it once, he felt that he could do it again, even if relaxed. This would change things. His father would have to accept him back into the house and family now.

The rain stopped falling, and the night sky began to lighten. A crisp breeze blew through the archway, and Davis shivered. With the help of his newfound powers, he was able to expel all water from his clothing and body. That helped with the chill. In the gray morning light, he made his way back to the house with a renewed hope for his future.

In the living room, his father sat by a window with a view of the rose garden. Every so often he picked up a mug and took a sip. Davis walked through the garden, bracing for the moment his father would see him, but his father kept sipping from his mug without looking outside. With a deep breath, Davis opened the garden door and went inside. As he approached his father, he noticed something unusual. He seemed to be glowing from his chest and radiating out toward his extremities. Davis paused and blinked. The glow remained whether his eyes were open or not.

His father locked eyes with him and put down his mug. His face was expressionless. "I thought I told you to leave."

"Father," Davis said, trying to keep his voice from shaking. "I'm a Shifter now."

His father's face didn't change. "And who do you think you got those abilities from?"

Davis gulped. It hurt so badly to know he had his mother's powers, but he still hoped his father would allow him back in the house. Before he could say anything, his father spoke again.

"And they won't last."

Davis's mouth remained half open, unable to form words.

His father continued. "You're wondering how long you have. Who knows. Months? Years? Depends on how much and how often you use them."

Davis finally found his voice. "Then let me be of use to you. Help take down your enemies. Like that woman who lost her hand."

His father seemed momentarily surprised by Davis's mention of the woman. He immediately composed himself. "I can take care of my own affairs."

"But people know who you are. They don't know who I am. I can help keep them out of your political affairs without you being suspected of involvement."

His father seemed to consider this. "It's too risky. You're a wanted felon now."

"But I didn't kill Mother. Chairperson Dawan did."

"Perhaps, but you struck the final blow."

Davis pleaded with his father one last time. He had nothing to lose. "I can stay in the shadows. Even if you let me back in the house, I can stay out of the way. No one would know I was here or that I even existed."

His father stared at him while taking a sip from his mug. He put his mug to the side and continued to stare at him. After a moment, he spoke. "Prove to me you can take down one of my enemies, and there may be a future for you in this home."

Davis nodded and quickly left before his father could change his mind. He would figure out how to make his father proud. His father would accept him yet.

He walked through the garden and into the line of trees that surrounded his family's property, down a winding dirt road over the hill, and toward the city. He had heard the servants talk about the local Shifter resource center. He just had to find it.

The dirt road merged onto a larger paved road, and soon there were buildings and lamps and cable cars packing the streets. People in suits, dresses, and coats walked around him, staring at his bare feet. Some kept their distance and gave him looks of disgust. He must've been quite a sight in his muddy pajamas and robe. Every so often, he tried to ask someone where the local Shifter resource center was. Person after person ignored him. Then he saw a man sitting on the corner with a can begging for change. Surely, this person would speak to him and potentially know where someone down on his luck could find some help. He approached the man, and sure enough, the man pointed him to a center a couple blocks away.

As Davis walked down the street, he noticed more men, women, and children sitting on the sidewalk in various degrees of destitution. Were they all Shifters? He had heard his father talk about how Shifter wealth was declining due to the Statics. Either way, it seemed he was headed in the right direction.

A row of nondescript, boxy buildings lined the street. Davis paused to read the signs in front of each entryway.

LA Rescue Mission.

CaliCares Homeless Resource Center

The Housing and Resource Center

These all sounded promising. But how was Davis supposed to know which one was for Shifters? He paced in front of the buildings. The first two buildings had long lines of people waiting to enter. It would take forever to get through those lines today, and most likely, he would end up sleeping on the street like the rest of the people here. The third building, The Housing and Resource Center, had no line. That was strange, but for expediency's sake, he walked in.

A middle-aged lady with red hair in a bun sat at the front desk. She had a glow to her, just like his father did. In his childhood, he had heard talk of a Shifter aura. The glow must be it. He glanced down at himself, hoping he also glowed even though he couldn't see anything. Would they know he was a fake Shifter and kick him out?

The front desk lady smiled at him as he approached. "Hi, hun. Aren't you a handsome one? What's your name?"

"Uh, Davis."

"Hi, Davis. I'm Frances. How can I help you?"

So far, so good. She seemed to think he belonged here. "I– I need somewhere to stay."

"Where are your parents?"

"My mother's dead."

"And your father?"

Davis looked down and shook his head.

Frances gave him a sympathetic smile. "Come in, child. You can pick up a package of clean clothing and toiletries at the counter. Just give the lady your size." She pointed to a woman folding a stack of shirts with the shelter's name printed on them. "Once you have a chance to use the locker room to shower and change, we will assign you a bed. Tomorrow, we will help you get a job if we can. I'm glad you made it to us in time. If the anti-integration bill passes, we may have to close our operations."

Davis began to walk toward the counter, then turned back. "Where is everyone else?"

Frances furrowed her brow. "Everyone else?"

"There's no line for this building like the other ones."

"Oh, we're actually almost at capacity, what with the

Depression and all. But to answer your question, the Shifter population is less than 1% of the general population, so that's why you don't see a big line here."

"What do you do if a Static comes in?"

"They don't. That is, they don't anymore. They don't even know we're here now. We have something relatively new on the sign. A stone that camouflages the building to Statics. We've been trying it out for a year, and it's really made my job easier. I don't have to turn people away and have them get all angry at me. Although, I'm still uneasy about this anti-integration business. I really hope we don't have to close."

"Why would you have to close? Wouldn't anti-integration benefit us?" Davis repeated words he had heard his father say. "Keep Statics from taking Shifter jobs and the like?"

The woman's smile faded, but she continued in a gentle voice. "That's, unfortunately, a very common misconception, and it's not true at all. The Statics in our community work closely with the Shifters, especially for the benefit of this outreach center. Without their support, we wouldn't have enough funds to run on our own. Supporting each other benefits everyone in our community in the long run. Lifting people out of poverty leads to happier, more involved, and more productive members of society, which in turn increases spending, grows our economy, and supports local businesses." She sighed. "Anyway, as you can tell, I'm very passionate about what we do here. I just hope I can continue doing it for a long time."

Davis nodded and picked up a set of clothes and toiletries, lost in thought. If it wasn't true that Statics had caused Shifters' poverty, then why was his father so anti-integration? And if it was true, it hadn't affected his family at all. As he undressed in the locker room, the sad reality sunk in. It was because of him that his father was anti-integration. He always knew he was a disgrace to his father, but now he realized it was because it showed that his Shifter family line wasn't pure. Static blood had gotten in somewhere, and it had shown up in him. He was a blemish his father couldn't hide. A sign to the world of their bloodline's impurity, and thus, weakness. But he had power now. He could fit in. He just proved it by checking into a center for Shifters in need. He could get a job and work his way up. Prove to his father that he did belong and that he could make a difference in the Shifter community. If only his powers would last long enough.

He put his dirty pajamas and robe into a bag to be laundered and heard something clatter. Two swirling gray stones bounced on the tiled floor. In all the commotion since last night, he had forgotten about the two additional stones he had. His mood lifted. He had what he needed to continue to fit in. If he ever lost his powers, he could get new ones. He didn't trouble himself about how that would work. For now, it was enough to know he had options.

CHAPTER ELEVEN

Amber

Summer 2000

Amber Su's face burned from frustration and embarrassment. The two police officers across from her, one who was Arav's older brother, Kabir, expressed looks of seriousness and concern, but she could tell they didn't believe her. To make matters worse, she could tell her parents also didn't believe her. They shifted in their brown, padded seats while waiting for her to finish her interview.

Kabir reviewed his notebook. "Let me see if I got everything. Nivi went back into the school to look for her violin. You waited in the parking lot. Then, you noticed smoke coming from the building, so you went back to the school to look for Nivi. You looked in a window and saw Nivi spreading fire with her hands. Then, Nivi ran out of the school, and you noticed hand marks on her neck?"

"Yeah, that's right," Amber mumbled.

"Is it possible that what you saw was Nivi catching on fire and trying to put it out?"

Amber closed her eyes. She saw a determined look on Nivi's face as fire burst forth from her hands. Nivi didn't seem like she was frantically trying to put out a fire. She seemed like she was just getting started. It didn't make any sense. "Maybe?"

Officer Clayton, a tall woman with short brown hair, stood up. "That's all for now,"

"We'll be in touch," Kabir said. "And please let us know if you think of anything else."

"Yeah, thanks," Amber mumbled.

She darted from the room with her parents in tow, who nodded and thanked the officers one too many times.

"Thank you, Officer Clayton. Thank you, Officer Markson."

After they were in the car, Amber's mother looked up at Amber in the rearview mirror and broached the subject with her timid, soft voice.

"Amber, Sweetie. It's normal to see strange things during a moment of crisis." She turned to Amber's father. "Isn't that right, honey?"

"Very normal. Completely normal," he said professionally.

"Oh my god, you guys!" Amber said. "I don't need you to shrink me right now. I know what I saw."

Mr. and Mrs. Su exchanged a glance and then looked at the road ahead.

"Of course, dear," Mrs. Su said. She started the car and drove from the police station. "I was just wondering, to make such an accusation… Are you mad at Nivi?"

"No," Amber said with some force but then backtracked. "Well, not really."

Her father turned around in his seat to look at her. "I don't doubt what you think you saw, but heightened emotions can distort our perception. Especially in the heat of the moment. No pun intended." He chuckled to himself.

"Oh my god, Dad! Someone died today!"

Mr. Su's face became serious. "Yes. That's very sad. I'm sorry I made light of the situation."

Amber sighed audibly and crossed her arms.

Mr. Su turned back to look out the windshield. "We can talk about it later when you've rested."

Amber stared out the window at the scenery streaking by. No one was going to believe her. Could what her father said be true? Was she so upset that Nivi didn't want to go to music camp that she would hallucinate Nivi starting a fire? On the one hand, it did conveniently get Nivi out of having to play violin for a long time with her injuries. On the other hand, Nivi was way too much of a goody-two-shoes to even think of doing something like this.

She thought back to the moment she looked in the window at Coastal High. There was Nivi with a look of concentration, looking down at her hands. A flame flickered from within her hands. Maybe it was in self-defense. That man had attacked her, after all. But why would Nivi light a fire rather than run? And the look on her face had been strange as if she had been in a trance.

They paused at a stop sign in front of the hospital. Even though the neat hedges and modern facade created a welcoming feel, it had the opposite effect on Amber. She should go see Nivi, especially before jumping to conclusions. She would. Later.

Her mother seemed to sense her thoughts. "I spoke to Grandma Ling. Nivi's awake, dear. She is going to be discharged soon."

Amber didn't respond and continued staring out the window. Why was her mother still waiting at the stop sign? Was she expecting Amber to go see Nivi right now? Amber was about to say something to urge her mother to go when a woman exited the building and walked straight toward the sidewalk where they were idling. She was a striking figure, in her 30s or 40s, slim and tall, although Amber couldn't tell if that was due to her super high heels. Her jet black hair and black skirt suit contrasted sharply with her pale skin, and the way she carried herself definitely didn't seem to be like anyone from Yuras.

Finally, her mother continued driving. As their car pulled away, the woman looked right at Amber as if she knew her. *Those eyes*, Amber thought. A glacial blue that penetrated her soul. She felt a shiver down her spine and averted her gaze. This day couldn't get any weirder.

Back at home, Amber went straight to her room despite gentle protests from her parents that she should eat something. She shut the door and flopped on her bed. Not long after, the home phone rang. Amber turned over and pulled the pillow over her head. Through the pillow, she could hear her mother answer the phone down the hall. Footsteps approached her room, followed by a soft knock at the door.

"Amber, dear," her mother's voice said. "It's Arav."

A small smile came to Amber's lips. She picked up the phone in her room and waited for her mother to hang up before she spoke. She tried to sound casual, but her voice quivered from the stress of the day.

"Hey."

"Hey Babe, are you OK? What happened?" Arav's smooth, deep voice was full of concern. "I've tried calling you a million times."

"I was at the, uh, police station."

"What? Why?"

"I saw– something." Amber's throat choked up.

"What did you see?"

"You wouldn't believe me."

"Did you tell Kabir?"

"Yeah."

"Well, I'm not him. Try me."

Amber took a deep breath but couldn't bring herself to tell him, even though something about his tone felt like he'd be open to believing her. But he wouldn't. He couldn't. What she saw couldn't be real, and any sane person wouldn't believe her. She couldn't do that to Nivi. An accusation like that would spread through the school and ruin Nivi's life.

Her lack of an answer extended into an awkward silence. She could hear Arav's gentle breathing and voices in the background. One of them was calling him to dinner.

"I have to go," Arav said. And then, after a pause, "Maybe you can come over later? Maybe we can get Kabir to tell us more about what happened. Off the record."

CHAPTER TWELVE

Iris

Summer 1955

IRIS WOKE UP on her bedroom floor. The speckled brown carpet clung to her cheek as she pushed herself to her feet. Strangely, she felt great. Her vision was clear. There was no lightheadedness or weakness. Only her throat was a little parched. She stretched her arms above her head as if she had just had the best nap of her life instead of another terrifying episode.

The alarm clock was still ringing. Iris silenced it and looked at the nightstand. The glass of water was there, but not the pill. She must have taken it just before she lost consciousness. That must be why she felt so good now. She checked the clock. Ten past noon. There was still plenty of time before her parents would be home. She could finish the groceries and her chores before they arrived. Maybe she would even have time to go back and watch more of the filming.

She gathered her things and prepared to leave the house. Out of habit, she moved her hand to the bridge of her nose to push up her glasses. Her finger encountered only skin. She stopped what she was doing and put both hands to her face. The glasses weren't there, yet she could see perfectly fine.

Confused, she stood but didn't move from that position for a few minutes. She racked her brain for an answer. Unable to think of one, she focused on where her glasses could be. A strange pressure began to tickle the back of her head like an invisible string was tugging at her. Not fully aware of what she was doing, she followed the pull toward her bedroom. In her bedroom, the pressure reoriented to the floor. Iris got on her hands and knees. There were her glasses under the bed. They must have fallen when she passed out. Relieved, she put them on her face, brushing off the pressure sensation that had led her there as a subconscious memory working its way to the surface. The world became a blur through the thick lenses. She took them off, then tried them on several more times before setting them down on her nightstand. Could they have become distorted when they fell off her face? But that wouldn't explain how well she could see without them.

Iris got on all fours again to check under the bed where the glasses had been. She wasn't sure what she was looking for, something, anything to help make sense of things. As she groped under the bed, her fingers encountered a small, round object stuck in the carpet. Plucking it from the carpet, she held it up before her eyes but already knew what it was without seeing it. Panic welled up inside her. On the palm of her hand sat the pill. She began to tremble, causing the pill to rattle around on her palm.

Her reflexes took hold. She grabbed the water at the side of her bed, preparing to toss the medication into her throat. As she lifted her chin, a movement from the corner of her eye brought her attention to the bedroom window. A pigeon had landed at the far end of a string of paper lanterns that stretched across the street, causing the lanterns to bob like jellyfish suspended in the air. The bird flapped its wings a few times while the string settled. Iris rarely paid much attention to the fuzzy blobs that roosted outside her window, but now the detail was so amplified it took her breath away. The pigeon's body was the color of the sky before it rained. Bands of dark gray lined the tips of its wings as if they had been dipped in ink. A wave of iridescent greens and purples expanded across its chest with each cooing. From the side of its cocked head, a bright orange eye darted side to side, surveying its surroundings.

She lowered her hand from her mouth and let it fall to her side, the small pill leaden in her palm. What was going on? How could her vision be so perfect? Was bad vision a side effect of her medication? This didn't make sense. Iris looked back and forth from her glasses to the pill. Should she take her medicine? She didn't want to lose her perfect vision. Plus, she felt great right now. Maybe if she kept her energy levels low enough, she could prevent another episode without having to take the pill. She wasn't sure if that's how it worked, but it seemed plausible. One more day like this couldn't hurt. She wished she could talk to someone about it to help reason things through, but what would she even say? Her parents were sure to freak out if she told them and force her to take her medication immediately. Would her friends believe her? To begin with, they weren't aware she had a condition or took medication. Even if she wanted to tell them, they were all at camp right now.

With great care, Iris set the pill back down on the nightstand. In a daze, she walked over to the bathroom she shared with her parents and splashed water on her face. She closed her eyes, letting the water drip down her chin. Was this a dream? She opened her eyes and looked at herself in the mirror. It was the first time she was seeing herself so clearly. Even with her glasses on, the edges of everything were usually a little fuzzy. Her eyes appeared smaller. Not in a bad way. Rather, she looked well-balanced. She inspected herself more. Soft skin, heart-shaped face, rich brown eyes, full lips. She might even be a little pretty.

Firm resolution took hold. Iris strode back into her room, took the pill from the nightstand, and shoved it deep into the dirt of the aspidistra plant. She walked back to the living room and paced in front of the door. Her pocket crinkled with the money and grocery list. Eventually, she cracked the front door open and peered through the slit. Her vision was just as clear from this vantage point. People moved to and fro on the walkways below, and she could see each of their faces in detail. She blinked several times, still not believing she could see so well and opened the door all the way to let the afternoon sun encompass her.

Taking a deep breath, Iris took a step out of the apartment, then another. She leaned over the railing, watching the women walk back and forth, admiring their flipped and curled hair, bright-colored cardigans and matching knee length skirts.

I can do this, Iris thought.

She closed and locked the door. At the staircase, she slowed her breathing and descended one step at a time. Apprehension and excitement threatened to throw off her steady pace. She was seeing the world through a new lens. Everything was so crisp and vibrant.

As Iris entered the mass of shoppers, the people around her seemed to smile and nod in approval. She began to stand straighter and to hold her head up taller. The apprehension faded, and the excitement grew. Everything was going to be alright.

The crowd swept her up like a stick in a stream. She flowed with the current, getting caught at a storefront here, disentangling herself from a jumble of arms there. From the right, the flower stands beckoned to her. She waded over and paused to admire the array of shapes and colors. The flowers seemed brighter as she browsed, their bonneted visages vying for attention. Sweet perfume floated in the air. She could almost hear their pleas to be chosen. The squeals of victory from the lucky ones that were bundled together and taken home, ready to star in their own centerpiece. She quelled the urge to buy a bouquet. There wasn't enough money for that. Instead, a final inhalation would have to do.

Moving on to the vegetable stands, Iris picked up a basket and pulled out the grocery list. An array of options lay before her, verdant and squeaky clean. She inspected each, turning them over with gentle fingers. Green onions, cabbage, eggplant, mushrooms, sprouts, string beans, carrots, bamboo shoots, garlic, and ginger filled her basket. Lastly, eggs and chicken. She paid and carried the brown paper bags back to the apartment. Once inside, she let out a simultaneous squeal and sigh of relief.

I did it, she thought while putting away the food. *Now what?* Should she continue to not take her medicine? She could take it right now and continue life with her rigid schedule. Her parents would never know the difference. The thought of returning to business as usual depressed her, so she put it from her mind for the time being.

Until this point, Iris had been so distracted by the events surrounding her medication and eyesight that she had forgotten about returning to watch the movie filming. She considered going back out but was too afraid of the possibility of having an episode to venture out again, and she still wasn't sure if she was ready to take her medication.

Now that she was alone in the quiet and solitude of her home, it seemed clear that her strange connection to Anna Sun could easily be explained by her medication or the lack thereof. A sort of withdrawal symptom. It made so much sense, yet Iris couldn't help but feel a little disappointed. She laughed at her silliness and proceeded to distract herself from this reality by planning how she would get away with not taking her medication for the next day. When her parents got home, she would have to force herself to wear her glasses, or they would immediately suspect something.

As she was putting the last of the vegetables away, the phone rang.

She picked up the receiver. "Hello?"

"Iris." It was her mother. "We have a community meeting to attend after work, so go ahead and have dinner without us. And don't forget to take your medicine."

Iris jumped a little at that last part. The guilt gnawed at her. She had never deceived her parents before. Not like this. At least she wouldn't have to lie to their faces tonight.

She prepared the rice and vegetables, set aside a portion for her mother and father, and sat down with a pair of chopsticks to eat. She touched her face again, feeling the missing glasses, still not believing it. So far, she had been fine. She decided she would wait and see how the next day went.

In the morning, Iris awoke to her mother shaking her awake with a frantic voice.

"Iris! Iris! Your alarm clock didn't ring!"

"It's OK, Ma Ma," Iris said sleepily. "I woke up ten minutes before the alarm went off. I already took the pill and set the clock."

Her mother grabbed the clock, verifying the set alarm. Then

she pulled open the drawer, poured out the contents of the medicine bottle, and counted the remaining pills. She put the pills back in the bottle. The strain in her face softened.

"You scared me," her mother said.

"I told you I'm capable of managing my medicine."

"I'm sorry I doubted you." She left the room.

Iris unclenched her fists from under the blankets. Her heart was beating fast with her deception. She willed herself to calm down so that she didn't cause an episode right then and there and expose herself for the liar that she was. She glanced at the aspidistra, the multitude of stems hiding the recently disturbed soil. That plant was supposed to be able to survive anything, or so her mother told her. They didn't call it the cast iron plant for nothing.

Staying in bed late wasn't unusual in and of itself. Especially in the summer, Iris often called out her goodbyes to her parents as they left for work. Once she was alone, she got up sans glasses and got dressed. She had promised her parents she would stay in all day and study, but it wouldn't hurt for her to have a quick stroll outside to test out her eyesight again. She grabbed her keys, locked the door, and walked down the steps to the storefronts below. Everything was so vivid. It was marvelous. *I won't go too far,* she thought. *I just want to see a little more.*

She walked slowly through Chinatown, again admiring the flowers and the array of fruits and vegetables. A block down from the pedestrian-only walkways, cars sped by. Even from a distance, she could see the car drivers and passengers. Captivated, she walked toward the street and stood for a few minutes, watching the cars zoom by, feeling the rumble of their engines deep in her chest and the breeze left in their wake. The mix of intoxicating gasoline fumes and the rhythmic sound of tires rolling over the asphalt had the contrasting effects of exhilaration and relaxation.

As the cars streaked by, they began to bleed together like a watercolor. Iris took a step back and wobbled. She was starting to feel lightheaded. A cold sweat beaded at the nape of her neck. Before she knew what was happening, she was falling toward the ground. Her knees hit the sidewalk, then her face with a dull thud. The sting of the impact barely registered in her clouded mind.

Move, she told herself. She had to get back to her apartment. But her limbs refused to listen.

From her periphery, she saw some cars screech to a halt. Burnt rubber filled the air. Before she lost consciousness, she thought she saw someone get out of a car and rush toward her.

CHAPTER THIRTEEN

Ling
Summer 2000

Ling Guang paced the halls of the hospital, every so often glancing into the room where Nivi slept. When Ling had gotten the call from the hospital, she had thought she was going to lose Nivi. All these years, she had been angry. Angry at her daughter for committing adultery with a Static. Angry for giving up her powers to care for a Static grandchild she didn't know. And after all these years, she was surprised by how much she cared. Even though Nivi was a lowly Static, she was Ling's last living relative.

Ling remembered the night she had brought Nivi to her house. So small. So scared. She allowed herself to cuddle Nivi that night. To shed a few tears at the loss of her daughter and her powers. But then, after that, reality sunk in. For as long as she was Nivi's protector, she'd be a Static.

Despite Nivi having a Shifter mother, Nivi was a Static. She couldn't have powers due to her father. Ling closed her eyes and pushed away the memory of her daughter's infidelity. It had been devastating news at first to know their family line would die out like that. But Ling had to admit, she didn't care about all that anymore. Now that Nivi was in the hospital, she only cared that Nivi was alive. She glanced into the room again where Nivi slept. When Nivi woke, she'd go in. She didn't want to disturb her before then.

A small possibility bubbled in Ling's subconscious. The pattern of burns on Nivi's arms was similar to those with newly emerging fire powers. The descriptions of the fire at the school and the man who had died were not natural. Nivi's hazy memory of the events. Could it be? Could Nivi be...? No. It was impossible. Impossible to have lived ten years with her and not know. The difference between Statics and Shifters was palpable. At least, it was once powers developed. But Ling was a Static now. She had been for the past ten years. Could she still tell the difference?

Inside the room, Nivi stirred. Ling's heart lifted at seeing her granddaughter wake, and she went into the room.

CHAPTER FOURTEEN

Nivi

Summer 2000

NIVI SAT IN a bed in a room that was cool and white. It smelled sterile and a bit stale. She tilted her head slowly to look at her arms, her neck stiff as if from lack of use. Not stiff, sore. From bruising. She touched the tender skin around her throat. Medical dressings wrapped her hands to her elbows, pale against her tan skin. An IV line slowly dripped its cold liquid into her veins. She welcomed the chill.

A hushed cry came from the doorway. "Ai-yo! You're awake!"

Nivi tensed, ready to flee. All she could see were those sunken eyes. When her vision focused, and she recognized the small frame of her grandmother, Ling Guang, she was gripping the sheets of her bed so tightly her fingers were going numb.

"Po Po," Nivi said weakly. She tried to push herself up to a seated position, but pain ripped through her wrists.

Ling rushed to her side. "Don't exert yourself. It's only been a couple of hours."

Nivi unclenched her face as the pain abated. Confusion took its place. Her grandmother's tone held an unfamiliar softness to it, and her words didn't make sense. "A couple of hours?"

"Yes," Ling said and hesitated before continuing, "since the fire."

Nivi furrowed her brow attempting to bring back the memories. There was red. And heat. But that was all.

"Where's Amber?"

"She's speaking to the police."

Nivi's head hurt as she tried to process what her grandmother was saying. "The police?"

Ling looked concerned. She stroked Nivi's hair which had become matted from the hospital pillow. "No need to talk about it now. Rest."

Nivi had a reflexive urge to jerk her head away from her grandmother's touch. She couldn't understand this sudden show of affection, but her exhaustion and the sedatives in her veins kept her from moving. Her grandmother's eyes crinkled kindly, so different from their usual absence of emotion. Even her hair looked more approachable. Usually tied tightly back in a bun and gelled into place, it was in a casual ponytail, streaks of white running through the long black strands. Her brown skin, darkened from years of gardening, shone warmly in the hospital lighting.

Relaxation came over Nivi as the strong, gentle fingers ran through her hair. A tap on the room window woke her just as she was drifting off to sleep. A woman peered in with slender, ice-blue eyes. She was so beautiful and well-dressed, not a typical-looking Yuras resident. For some reason, Nivi felt she'd seen her somewhere before.

"Meng…" Ling murmured.

"Po Po," Nivi said, fighting sleep. " Who is that?"

"An old friend..." Ling trailed off and walked out into the hall.

An old friend? That friend didn't look old. She looked like she was at least half her grandmother's age. Nivi strained against the sedatives to stay alert enough to hear their hushed conversation. She caught a few words as she drifted in and out of consciousness, unsure which were real and which were a dream: It's been so long; why are you here; her parents; the fire; not again.

The warmth started in Nivi's chest, radiating out to her extremities. Her fingers tingled, and her face flushed. The heat rose to a boil, becoming unbearable. She couldn't breathe. She choked and gasped, writhing in her bed for several seconds. Sweat leaked through her hospital gown, lapping into the sheets beneath. The doctor said it wasn't unusual to have perspiration while healing from a burn. Nivi slowed her breathing as she cooled down. The doctor said she was doing well, better than expected, and would not need a skin graft as originally thought.

A couple of police officers came to ask Nivi about the fire. One introduced himself as Arav's brother, obviously unaware of Nivi's dislike for Arav. He looked just as jockish as Arav, only older.

Apparently, the fire had happened at Coastal High, her high school, after the last final of her freshman year. There was a fatality, but Nivi didn't know the man. He wasn't a student. Still, that knowledge shook her. It could've been her, Amber, or someone else she cared about. She reprimanded herself. He *was* someone that someone cared about. Just because she didn't know him didn't mean there weren't people suffering from his death.

Nivi attempted to answer as many of the police's questions

as she could, although she wasn't much help since she couldn't remember anything. In fact, she was having trouble remembering more than the fire. Everything seemed a little out of focus at the moment. The doctor had also said that memory loss after a traumatic event was normal, and that she may start to remember more over time. She lay back down to sleep. Sleep was supposed to help.

Nivi awoke the next morning to two fuzzy blue lights blinking at her through the haze of sleep. As her eyes cleared, she saw they were just lights on her IV monitor, but the look of them sparked something in her memory. Her grandmother's visitor. The Asian woman with blue eyes. She had heard them talking about the fire, and the woman had said, "her parents, not again." Or maybe that was her grandmother. She couldn't be sure who said what, but she knew that's what they were talking about. A chill went across the back of Nivi's neck. Her grandmother had mentioned a fire the other day when they were commemorating her parents' death. Could they have been speaking about the same thing? Did her parents actually die in a fire and not a car accident? Why would her grandmother lie to her? As these questions ran through her head, her grandmother entered the room.

"Po Po," Nivi said, "Who was that woman?"

"Which one?"

"The one you said was an old friend. She was dressed very professionally."

Ling paused before proceeding. She seemed unsure what to say. "That was Meng Zhang."

"Have I met her before?"

Ling drew out the first word as if she were testing it in her mouth. "Maybe... when you were really young."

"Why was she here?"

The questions poured forth from Nivi. She couldn't help it. Her whole life had just been upended, and now the manner of her parents' death was possibly fake. Not that she would've had anything better to do this summer since she had decided she wasn't going to music camp, but she could've had better plans than sitting in a hospital.

"She heard about what happened and wanted to check in on you and me to make sure we were OK."

That was strange. Some woman that Nivi maybe met when she was young wanted to check on her? Nivi had an idea of the reason. "Because of the fire. Because the same thing happened to my parents."

This seemed to catch her grandmother off guard. "What?"

"I heard you both talking outside of the room. One of you said 'the fire' and the other said 'not again.' So what happened? Tell me the truth."

"That's enough!" Ling snapped. Nivi jumped a little, even though this was the grandmother she was used to. Ling immediately softened. "Because you need to rest. As the doctor said, your memory is affected."

Nivi closed her eyes, mostly to hide the tears threatening to form. Maybe she had imagined the conversation. She was too tired to decipher fact from fiction at this time.

Late that afternoon, Nivi was discharged to continue self-care at home. In the bathroom, she cleaned her hands and arms like she was shown in the hospital and prepared to wrap them back up. As she unrolled the gauze, she hesitated before raising her arms to eye level. She hadn't taken the time to look at the damage just yet, and she braced herself for the reality of the situation. There were definitely going to be scars, but the appearance wasn't quite what she was expecting. Instead of melted, putty-like skin, there were raised, purplish lines branching up from her hands as if her veins had pushed themselves to the surface. She turned her hands back and forth, casting shadows in the valleys and rifts of her wounds. If she wanted to keep people at a distance, this would help. Who would want to get close to her like this? For a moment, she wished she could peel off the crusts and return her skin to the smooth, olive tone that lay hidden beneath.

Nivi lingered a few more moments on the twisted tissues, feeling the faintest pang of sorrow, and then averted her gaze and set her jaw. At least she had a reason to avoid the violin now and didn't have to tell her grandmother she wanted to quit. She began to methodically wrap her hands. As she advanced past her wrist, a glint on her forearm caught her eye. Part of the scar seemed to be alight from within, glowing like an ember in a spent log. Startled, she turned off the light in the bathroom and again looked at her arm. Sure enough, that spot radiated faintly, pulsing with the beat of her heart.

"Why are you in the dark?"

Nivi jumped at her grandmother's voice and flipped the lights back on. "I was just finishing wrapping my arms."

"I'll help you."

"No." Nivi turned her back to her grandmother, hastily winding the material around her arms. "I'm OK."

In the reflection of the mirror, she could see her grandmother reaching toward her with her left hand. The movement exposed a bright red scar on her grandmother's left shoulder, a raised disc about a quarter in size. Nivi had never noticed it before, but that was nothing compared to her own wounds, probably just a reaction to a vaccine or something. Her grandmother would never understand what she was going through, let alone accept the possibility that she had seen something glowing in her veins. She told herself she wasn't going crazy and that it was all part of the healing process.

"OK," Ling said after a pause. "Good night."

"Good night, Po Po."

Nivi tucked the final piece of gauze firmly into place. She wasn't sure which was worse: her grandmother's sudden affection or her inability to receive that affection. Nivi had had plenty of bumps and bruises growing up, and even a broken arm, and her grandmother never acted this way before. Something deeper drove her sudden concern, almost like she felt guilty. But Nivi couldn't see any reason why her grandmother would feel that way. It was probably all in her head.

She left the bathroom and went to her bedroom. As she went to bed, she ignored the heat creeping up her arms.

CHAPTER FIFTEEN

Iris

Summer 1955

A TRICKLE OF LIGHT danced through drawn gossamer curtains. Between hazy blinks, Iris saw two backlit figures sitting before her, a young man and woman, speaking in concerned and hushed tones. Iris squeezed her eyes shut, protecting them from the bright flashes that disturbed her sleep. The voices of her visitors floated through her semi-consciousness and mingled with her dreams.

"How did you find her?" the man said.

"She just showed up," the woman said.

"New to the area?"

"I suppose so."

"Does she know?"

"I couldn't say."

"No matter. Keep her close. Find out what you can. I will find out more at the next meeting."

"Are you sure this is the right way?"

"What choice do I have?" the man said. "I thought you wanted to help me?"

"Of course I do," the woman said.

"If she doesn't know, it will be no loss to her."

Iris moaned a little and stirred in the bed. Why were they talking so close by? Couldn't they see that she was still sleeping? The light continued to shimmer before her eyelids, appearing as sparkling stars in the night sky. When she opened her eyes, however, she saw that it was still daylight. The man and woman were gone.

She reached over to grab the clock on her nightstand. Her hand only encountered mattress. Iris felt around and then realized she wasn't in her own bed. This bed was soft and enormous. Nothing at all like the little, firm bed she slept in at home. Even with her arms stretched out to each side, she could barely reach the edges of the mattress with her fingertips. *Where am I?* she thought as the unfamiliar room came into focus.

She sat up, pushing off the crisp white sheet and disturbing the floral quilt neatly folded at the foot of the bed. A glass of water sat on the nightstand underneath a tasseled lampshade. Realizing how thirsty she was, she gulped it down.

She felt her face and realized her glasses were missing. There was a flash of panic. Then she remembered all about her medication and eyesight.

She got out of bed. Her bare feet sank into a large plush rug. Across the room, she was startled to see a girl looking back at her. An inlay of golden roses glinted from the headboard behind her. In the same instant, she realized it was her reflection in a floor-length mirror. Around the room, old paintings of people in fancy clothes and beautiful landscapes hung on the pale blue walls. A fireplace adorned with flowers on the mantle was on the other side of the bed. The botanic aroma added to the ornateness of the room.

"Hello?" Iris called out.

Her voice was soft and shook with trepidation. Why was she in a stranger's home? Why was it so fancy? She couldn't remember how she got there. She approached the window and drew back the curtains. She was on the upper floor. A lawn spread out below, flanked by luxurious rose bushes. They formed rows of alternating colors that ended in a line of tall trees. Servants were setting a table on a circular, stone patio. Iris backed away from the window.

She moved toward the bedroom door and stuck her head out, looking side to side down a long corridor lined with doors. Not seeing anyone, she walked out of the room and then sucked in a breath. The hall led to a staircase that branched into two and curved down toward a circular entrance area. Rectangles of wrought iron flanked the edge of the staircases and second floor. Within each rectangle was the profile of a lily in bloom. Below, an inlay of reddish-brown stone in the shape of a sun lay in the middle of a polished marble floor. A crystal chandelier reflected off its surface. The height made her stomach tingle. Even though she was only one floor up, the height had to be almost double that of her apartment. White walls made the entrance room look even bigger and brighter. It was the grandest thing Iris had ever seen.

A murmur of voices brought Iris away from the railing. She tried to follow the sound, moving from room to room, listening for more voices or movement. At the third door, she heard a rustling within. She didn't know if she should go in or not. What was she afraid of? Someone brought her here, after all. If they wanted to do something bad to her, they wouldn't have tucked her into a nice bed and given her a glass of water. After a moment of internal debate, she turned the door handle and peeked inside.

The room was dark and smelled stale as if no one had been in it for a long time. Iris let her eyes adjust to the dimness and saw two cribs. Above each crib was a silver frame. The first frame contained a black-and-white photograph of a young girl with pale skin, black hair, and black eyes. She looked vaguely familiar.

Iris shifted her gaze to the frame above the other crib. At first, she thought that her vision had regressed back to a blur because she couldn't make out the photo. When she looked around the room and everything else was in perfect focus, she realized the frame was empty.

She shivered. The room was colder than the rest of the house, probably because the heavy curtains were drawn. Every so often, the curtains moved, causing the rustling sound she had heard from outside the door. She approached the window and nudged the curtain aside. The window was shut, so it must've been leaking air. The view from the window was the same lawn, rose bushes, and patio. The table had two place settings and a covered silver platter.

The sound of voices came again, and then footsteps sounded from below. Iris exited the room and closed the door, trying not to make too much noise. She felt she had been somewhere she wasn't supposed to be. Tiptoeing down the corridor, her bare feet silent on the marble floors, she returned to the room she had woken up in. As the footsteps ascended the staircase, she crawled back into bed and pulled the covers to her chin.

The steps grew louder and louder. Closer and closer. They paused just outside the doorway. Then Iris felt it again, the warmth in her chest. The connection. Like someone she knew was near. She turned and saw a woman walk in. Slim figure, petite, black hair, pale skin. And she was glowing ever so faintly. She wore an ivory, silk blouse, buttoned high up her neck and tucked into a forest green skirt. *I've seen her before*, Iris thought. *She's the girl in the photo, grown up. No, not just that.*

Her brain was still fuzzy. She scrunched her eyes, willing the memories to come. They materialized slowly. Like the microscopes they used in biology class, switching from lower to higher magnifications, adjusting the fine focus, until there it was. Anna Sun! The shock of her realization caused her mouth to gape open. Why was she in Anna Sun's house? And the *feeling*. Here it was again. Was it just in her head? Maybe she was dreaming. Or maybe something really was wrong with her. She should've been taking her medication after all. This strange feeling could be a manifestation of her symptoms and the start of something worse.

"Hello," Anna said. Her voice was velvet. "I'm glad to see you're awake."

Iris closed and opened her mouth. Nothing came out. That voice was so familiar. Her thoughts floated back to when she first woke up in the room. Two people were talking beside the bed. A man and a woman. Was the woman Anna Sun? The voice sounded similar, but the confidence and ease with which she spoke now was so unlike the timid and concerned tone she heard earlier.

"Hello," Iris said, forcing the word through her dry mouth. How different her squeakiness was from Anna's fluid cadence.

"How are you feeling?" Anna said.

"Fine. I think. How— why am I here?"

"You fainted. You gave us quite a scare. The doctor was here while you were still asleep. It's not serious, thank goodness. She said you were suffering from heat exhaustion and recommended hydration and rest."

Iris let out an internal sigh of relief. *Only heat exhaustion. Nothing related to my condition and the pills. But what about this funny feeling? And the doctor. Is she the woman I heard talking by the bed earlier? But then, who was the man?*

"I see you've finished your water," Anna continued. "I'll ask for some more. Margaret?" A rosy-cheeked servant appeared at the door. "Margaret, please bring some more water for… I'm sorry. I don't know your name."

"Uh— Iris."

"Please get some more water for Miss Iris." The servant nodded and took the empty glass. "My name is Anna."

"I know," Iris said, then blushed at her blatant adoration.

Anna smiled. "Nice to meet you. I thought you would be more comfortable coming here and seeing our family doctor than going to the local county hospital. That place is over-crowded. You would've waited all day to see someone. I hope waking up in an unfamiliar place wasn't too much of a shock."

"It wasn't. Thank you," Iris said, trying to be polite. "I'm feeling better, so I should probably go home. I don't want my parents to worry. What time is it?"

"It's just about noon. Won't you stay for lunch? It's a lovely day. I believe everything is all set up for us in the rose garden. Some food will do you good, too."

Iris flooded with glee. She imagined how she would tell her friends when they returned from camp. They would gush about their activities and how much fun they had, and then they would ask her what she had been up to. *Oh nothing much,* Iris imagined herself saying. *I just had lunch with Anna Sun.* Their faces would turn green with envy. She would be the talk of their whole school. But none of that would matter if her parents thought she had gone missing. They would never trust her to leave the house again. Her mother still didn't fully trust her with the task of taking her pills, although with the way things were going, she couldn't really blame her.

"May I use your phone first?" Iris said.

"Yes, of course." Anna pointed to a rotary phone on the nightstand on the far side of the bed.

The servant, Margaret, returned with a fresh glass of water. She and Anna stepped out of the room while Iris drank the water and used the phone. The warm feeling faded from Iris's chest, although she was too distracted to notice as she dialed her parents' work number.

"Hello?" came her father's voice.

"Ba Ba," Iris said. "Are you or Ma Ma coming home for lunch?"

"We brought lunch with us today. Did you need something?"

"No. I just wanted to check if I should make extra food for lunch." Her face burned with the fib. Too many lies in a row. She told herself she would stop after today. "I'll see you tonight."

"See you tonight," her father said and hung up the phone.

Iris fiddled with the handset for a few seconds before putting it down. It wouldn't hurt for her to stay for a little bit, and she was hungry.

Margaret reappeared in the doorway. "Will you be joining Miss Anna for lunch?"

"Yes," Iris said, pulling her shoulders back. "I think I will."

CHAPTER SIXTEEN

Meng
Summer 2000

Meng Zhang walked briskly into the Crescent City governmental building. The Northern California Shifter Representative site was a few hours north of Yuras by car. Luckily, Meng did not need to rely on driving and got there in a fraction of the time.

The building hung on the side of a cliff over the ocean, seemingly precarious to any normal person, if any *normal* person were able to see it. Redwood planks created a beautiful and complimentary esthetic to the surrounding nature. A colonnade of thick redwood trunks lined the facade.

As Meng walked through the corridors, clicking from her chunky high heels reverberated off the 16-foot walls, reflecting the pounding in her chest since seeing Ling Guang. Meng had held it together, of course, remaining impassive and professional as always, but she had been unprepared for how much she would be affected. Part of her was furious as well. *Why didn't*

Ling move farther away? How could she think she could hide Nivi's powers? It had been so long, although that term was relative, especially to them. But ten years without her had still felt like a lifetime. Ling had looked just as surprised as Meng had felt. She looked older too, as one would expect in this situation.

As Meng neared a nondescript office at the end of the hall, a high-pitched voice called from inside. "Come in.".

Meng entered. Representative Bai sat behind a very orderly desk. Intense eyes in an otherwise plain angular face scanned the paperwork before her. She had been pretty once, but it seemed work had taken a toll on her. Meng wasn't surprised based on the decades she had known the representative. Still, the change was dramatic.

Without looking up, Representative Bai raised a skinny wrist encircled with a delicate gold bracelet and motioned for Meng to approach. Light scattered from thin strands of gold that embellished each finger. She set her dark, penetrating gaze on Meng, the sharpness of her face heightened by hair pulled tightly back.

"How may I help you, Vice Chairperson Zhang?" Representative Bai said in a mock tone of deference.

Meng raised an eyebrow. She had dealt with surly representatives before. It was the nature of the job, though she had tried to maintain minimum interactions with Representative Bai in particular.

"I am here to investigate a deadly incident that may have deeper implications for our community," Meng said.

Representative Bai tapped a fingernail on the desk. "I don't really understand why the Council sent *you* here. We've handled incidents like this in the past, and the Council didn't see the need to send anyone then."

"Audits of this nature are simply standard protocol. We

can be sure to finish more expediently if we work together. As you know, our population is dwindling. The birthrate of new Shifters is abysmal. Thus, the need for a more vigilant response when the possibility of previously unknown Shifters arises."

"You would think, in that case, the Council would relax their anti-integration protocols. Maybe it would help the birthrate."

Meng sighed inwardly. She didn't disagree, not since her separation from Ling, but she had to maintain a professional and united front. So, she recited the same points always used in these debates. "We've tried that in the past. Always with deadly results for both parties. In this country alone, there have been witch hunts, massacres such as the 1871 Chinese massacre in Los Angeles, McCarthyism, internment camps… Shall I go on?"

Representative Bai rolled her eyes. "Times have changed. Maybe it's time for you and your fellow anti-integration council members to step aside for a more modern approach. Even our chairperson agrees."

"Your *modern* approach will not solve anything. A Shifter and Static pairing still produces a Static child. And our organization is still a democracy, not an autocracy, so unless the votes are there, the change won't happen."

"All I know is that the anti-integration protocol took effect after World War II, and in the fifty years since, the Shifter population growth rate has declined. Coincidence?" Representative Bai crossed her arms and leaned back in the chair.

This was a waste of time. Meng needed to steer the conversation back to their current concerns. "Correlation is not causation. There are so many other possibilities, all of which we are currently investigating. Pesticides, chemicals, nuclear energy, et cetera. Even Shifters are not immune to everything.

Besides, we are getting off-topic. If you truly desire an audience with the Council, please schedule a meeting."

"I plan to."

"Now that that's settled, let's get back to why I am here."

Representative Bai didn't respond for a moment. She continued to stare at Meng while tapping her nails on the desk. If Representative Bai's face hadn't looked so stern, Meng would've thought she was nervous. Finally, the representative spoke.

"Was I correct?"

"Correct?"

Representative Bai's tone became impatient. "About the girl. In relation to all this, you should be excited about the possible discovery of a previously unknown young Shifter."

"At this time, it appears she was a victim." This was true, just not the whole truth. The representative's agitation seemed to increase, so Meng directed the conversation back to her. "Tell me again what you know."

"Only what was reported in the news. I haven't had a chance to go to the scene myself yet. There was a fire at the high school, and there was one fatality and one survivor. And if the fire is of the nature you say it is, it must mean the girl–"

"It's important not to draw conclusions before the investigation is complete."

"Uh-huh. Right," Representative Bai said, drumming her fingers on her desk. "Again, I'm surprised the Council was monitoring the little community of Yuras. I mean, I guess it's good you don't focus only on large cities." She didn't sound sincere.

"We have monitors performing random observations all over. It's important for the protection of all. We are fortunate that one happened to be in your area at the time of the fire."

"Yes. Fortunate..." Representative Bai trailed off.

"Have you heard any small-town talk from the locals? Do they have any insight?"

"None."

Meng nodded, pondering on the situation. "When will the local representatives be meeting again?"

"In about a month. We just had our meeting last week."

"I hope we can settle matters ourselves far before then."

"Of course."

"However, if this requires more effort than we can muster, we will need to convene the representatives sooner. And potentially the Council authorities. For now, the Statics don't seem to have an inkling. However, one can never be too certain. Let's hope this was an isolated incident. In the meantime, I will continue my investigation with all those involved." Meng moved toward the door. "I know I don't have to remind you that we don't need a repeat of ten years ago when we lost three of our own in this area."

Representative Bai stiffened. "Of course not. You should get going. You must be tired after your travels. Maybe you should get some rest."

"Are you forgetting something, Darling?"

Representative Bai wrinkled her nose at the last word. She opened a drawer in her desk and pulled out two vials, which she slid across the desktop.

Meng took the vials. "I'll be in touch. Please come to me with any new information. You know where I'm staying."

She left the office just as the representative's phone rang.

CHAPTER SEVENTEEN

Representative Bai
Summer 2000

"Like I said, I will have the shipment ready."

Representative Bai gritted her teeth, waiting for the chairperson to hang up the phone first. As soon as she heard the line disconnect, she slammed down her office phone, striking it a few times against the receiver for good measure, then left it lying on the desk. The dial tone droned in the background while she rubbed her temples. She wouldn't be in this position without him. Whether that position was good or bad was hard to tell. It was no coincidence that her promotion to local representative came soon after he became chairperson. He had helped her when she needed it, and she had been grateful at the time. Somewhere along the way, it didn't feel like help anymore. It felt like retribution.

The chairperson was haughty, demanding, and tended to leer. And although her repugnance of him had only increased in the years they had worked together, she had to admit that she wouldn't have made it this far without him. *I've been through worse,* she thought. It didn't help that Vice Chairperson Meng Zhang was investigating her area in the middle of their biggest shipment. *This high school fire was such bad timing. How did Allen even get out? Was it just him?* With all the commotion, she hadn't had a chance to check if anyone else was missing. She would be able to head down to the mine tomorrow with a couple of days to spare before the chairperson arrived.

She rubbed the gold bracelet around her wrist, as she often did in times of stress. Feeling the textured gold surface, running her fingertips around and around, calmed her.

This shipment should be the last, she thought. *Then I'll be free.*

CHAPTER EIGHTEEN

Iris

Summer 1955

MARGARET BROUGHT IRIS her shoes and led her out into the garden. The yard was warm in the noon sun, and Iris felt the chill leave her body. There were roses everywhere, full and ablaze in almost every color of the rainbow. The view from the room was nothing like being immersed among the rows of flowers. Each breath brought in plumes of sweet fragrance.

She followed Margaret down a stone path through the middle of the lawn and onto the round patio she had seen from above. Anna sat at a wrought iron table, drinking a glass of white wine. As before, she seemed to glow. The more Iris focused on it, the more confused she was. Was the glow from her mind or through her sight? The sun was very bright. That could also explain it.

"Glad you could join me," Anna said. Before her, the silver platter had been uncovered, revealing a stack of sandwiches and fruit.

"Thank you," Iris said, not knowing what else to say. She sat at the table across from Anna, feeling shy again.

"Enjoy your lunch," Margaret said and returned to the house.

Anna gestured toward the platter. "Help yourself."

Iris took a sandwich and bit off a corner, trying not to drop any crumbs or get anything on her face. It was egg salad, something she did not often have since they usually had Chinese food at home. She enjoyed it.

"Tell me about yourself," Anna said, relaxed and informal. She cut a piece of watermelon with a knife and fork. "You're Chinese, no?"

"Yes," Iris said, wiping her mouth with a fancy embroidered napkin. She felt bad for soiling such a pretty piece of fabric. "My parents are from China. I was born here in Los Angeles. We've lived in Chinatown all my life."

Surprise seemed to flash across Anna's face, but then it was gone. "Do you speak Chinese?"

"Yes, Mandarin. Probably not as good as my parents want me to. What about you?"

"Oh no." Anna laughed. "My family has been in America for three or more generations. I'm not quite sure exactly. The film industry would love it if I could. They're always trying to cast me in stereotypical roles. They still can't believe that someone who looks like me can't speak Chinese." She rolled her eyes.

Iris reddened, feeling embarrassed from her presumptions. "I'm sorry."

"Don't be. It's not a big deal. Anyway, I'm the one that brought it up."

"How long have you been acting?"

"A few years now."

"And you grew up here?" Iris glanced back at the mansion.

The corner of Anna's lip quirked up. "I did. I know it's a lot. It's been in my family since they first came to California. They made their money in snacks and beverages. My father still works in importing and exporting."

"Oh." Iris slumped down in her chair and took another bite of the sandwich so that she wouldn't have to say what her parents did in comparison.

Anna asked anyway. "What do your parents do?"

Iris swallowed. "They— uh, own a laundromat."

Anna seemed to sense Iris's embarrassment. "That's wonderful. They started their own business just like my family did. There is no shame in hard work."

Iris smiled and sat up a little straighter. "They work really hard so I won't have to when I'm older."

"They must love you very much."

"I guess so." It was something Iris knew in the back of her mind, but hearing Anna's words brought it out into the light. She realized she didn't always take the time to appreciate that fact.

They sat in silence for a few moments before Anna spoke again. "Do you have any hobbies or– special talents?"

Iris snorted. "Not unless you count going to school, working for my parents, and being very punctual in taking my–." She quickly took a sip of water before she could say more.

She couldn't believe she was about to tell Anna Sun about her condition. Something about Anna made her feel so comfortable. So drawn into her words. Even though they had just met, Iris already wanted to be Anna's best friend. To be able to share secrets and laugh about private jokes. But did she really want Anna to know her condition? To think less of her?

Anna raised her eyebrows. "Taking your…?"

Iris thought fast. "Uh– my groceries home to make dinner." She tried to smile. It felt more like an awkward grimace.

Anna studied her with a strange, cool expression like she was searching for something more. Iris picked up her glass of water and stared out at the roses. She tried to change the subject.

"Uh– the roses here are amazing."

"Yes." Anna's voice was sweet but distant.

She continued to watch Iris as if she were trying to determine something. Iris felt like she was going to break under the pressure. She had been lying so much recently to her parents and now to Anna Sun. The glass quivered in her hand. Maybe she should come clean with the truth. Maybe Anna would understand. She set the glass down and turned back to Anna. Her lips pressed together. Her tongue was in position. All she had to do was say it.

Anna spoke first. "Do you have any siblings?"

Caught off guard, Iris let out a mix between a choke and a laugh. "Um, no. I'm an only child."

"Me too."

They looked at each other and smiled. Iris was thrilled to have something in common with Anna.

"So you live here with your parents?" Iris said.

"It's just my father and me. My mother died when I was a child."

"Oh. I'm sorry."

"It was a long time ago. I miss her, of course, but time goes on."

Iris nodded and finished her sandwich. She wished she could sit here all day with Anna Sun, but she couldn't chance getting home too late. "Thank you so much for everything today. Your home is so beautiful, and you've been so nice, but I need to go home. I don't want my parents to worry."

"Yes, of course. Thank you for the company. This house can be pretty big and lonely at times." Anna stood up from the table. "I'll have our driver, John, take you home."

Iris followed Anna back into the house, through the living room and circular entrance area, and out the front door.

"I'm done filming for the next couple of weeks," Anna said while they waited for the car to be brought around. "If you have time, would you like to come visit again? Maybe you could even teach me a little Chinese to impress the filmmakers." She winked.

"I would love to," Iris said, almost cutting off Anna before she finished her sentence.

"Great. Why don't you come back for lunch again? Let's say noon this Thursday?"

"Sure!"

A sleek black car pulled up to the front of the house. The driver got out and walked around to the back of the car. He was short and thick with muscles that flexed through his fitted black shirt as he opened the door for Iris. Anna hugged her. Her embrace was firm yet gentle, and her hair smelled like the roses in the garden.

"Tell John where you want him to drop you off. And arrange where he will pick you up on Thursday as well."

"Thank you again." Iris got into the car. Her chest fluttered. It could've been that strange feeling she kept having around Anna, or it could've been the exhilaration of the day. It all blended together now.

John closed the door behind her and returned to the driver's seat.

"Where to Miss?"

"Broadway and Alpine, please."

Iris watched as they pulled away from the white stone mansion. Arched windows and balconies dotted its facade, and an expansive lawn stretched to either side. Anna Sun waved in the distance. Iris waved back until Anna became indistinguishable from her surroundings. Trees popped up along the sides of the road, obscuring the view of the house. Iris settled into the seat and ran her hands over her face in disbelief. Her heart rattled like a snare drum, overshadowing the sensation that faded as they left Anna behind. A squeal bubbled up her throat. She suppressed it, not wanting to seem childish in front of John. *I can't believe I had lunch with Anna Sun,* Iris thought. *And I'm going to have lunch with her again!*

These thoughts danced through her head and twirled with her heart as they drove out of the hills and back toward Downtown Los Angeles. They occupied her mind with promises of excitement and friendship with Anna Sun. There were other thoughts, too, smothered deep beneath. Percolating, not yet fully formed. The abandoned children's room with the two cribs; one with a child photo of Anna and one with an empty frame. A room for two children, even though Anna was an only child. And the unknown voices while she had been sleeping. One asking the other to *Keep her close.*

CHAPTER NINETEEN

Meng
Summer 2000

MENG REMOVED A vial from a hidden pocket in the skirt of her skin-tight, black dress. In most situations, her natural beauty was enough to get her way, but she couldn't risk it today. She opened the vial and dabbed a drop of the purple liquid onto her forehead.

Meng entered the police station and approached the information desk. A young, blonde man in his early twenties sat there slouched and looking bored. When he spotted Meng, he almost fell backward in his chair. He jumped to his feet and straightened the front of his uniform.

"H-How may I help you?"

As Meng drew closer and the full effect of her allure tincture took hold, the young man's eyes became round and glossy, and his jaw slackened. A dreamy smile spread on his thin lips.

Meng didn't waste any time getting down to business. "Who is in charge of the high school fire case?"

"What an accent," the young officer said. "Are you from England?" He put his elbow on the countertop and cupped his chin in his palm.

"I've spent a lot of time there," Meng said, plastering on a patient smile. "Now, if you wouldn't mind pointing me to who's in charge of the high school fire case?"

"Sure thing." He pointed to an office with a large window where two women spoke. "There's the chief speaking with the lead officer on the case."

Meng assumed by her posture that the police chief was the shorter officer with curly black hair. The taller one with cropped, brown hair nodded intently as the first officer spoke.

"Thanks, Darling."

Meng strode toward the office, needing to be quick. With increased distance, the power of her tincture would fade. She pulled out another vial from her dress pocket. This one contained a black liquid. When she got to the office door, she heard the young officer call out with a tone of hesitation.

"Hey, you can't just go in there."

Meng dabbed a couple of drops of the oblivion tincture onto her pointer finger and pushed open the door.

The chief of police and the head officer on the high school fire case turned with a look of indignant surprise, but then their expressions glazed over, and grins took over their faces.

"Hi," they said, drawing out the word as if they were inebriated and slurring.

"Hello," Meng said. "Would you mind telling that young officer out there that we'll be a few minutes and he needn't worry? And then close the blinds and take a seat?"

The taller officer with the short hair went to the door and called out to the young officer, who looked confused but nodded. Then, she closed the door, pulled the blinds over the window, and took a seat across the desk from where the chief of police had sat down.

Once they were comfortably seated, Meng dabbed each of their foreheads with the black liquid. "I wouldn't want either of you to fall and hurt yourself."

At her touch, each officer slumped into her chair, unconscious. Meng tapped her foot as she watched the clock tick on the office wall. After about a minute, the women woke back up. Their expressions were blank. Meng spoke to them together.

"You will close the high school fire case. The man who died in the fire was a mentally unwell vagrant. He brought in a bomb and attacked the girl when she walked in on him. She was in the wrong place at the wrong time. And you'll tell the officer at the information desk that I was looking for my missing cat."

The two officers nodded. Meng didn't wait for them to say anything else. She hurried from the office. Looking down to replace the vial back into her pocket, she bumped into another officer who was coming from around the corner. Worried that her allure tincture would be wearing off, she smiled her sweetest smile.

"My apologies, Officer–," she glanced at his name badge, "Kabir Markson."

He looked confused at first but then smiled back, his muscular, tan body relaxing. "No problem at all, Ma'am."

Meng nodded at Officer Markson and the young officer at the front desk. "Have a nice day, gentlemen."

She walked out of the police station, tensing a little as she waited for someone to follow her out with questions. When no one pursued her, she let out a breath. She got the job done. The Statics of Yuras should no longer be a problem in the high school fire case.

CHAPTER TWENTY

Davis

Spring 1936

DAVIS CLOSED AND locked the front door to The Housing and Resource Center, then swept and mopped the entryway. Rows of people settled in for the evening on the sidewalk. The number of people in need hadn't diminished in the last couple of months Davis had been in the shelter. For a moment, Davis felt the despair of all those people out there start to overwhelm him, but he reminded himself that he was also in need and was doing his part by working in the shelter.

Once the entryway was clean, Davis took his mop and bucket to the communal restrooms. As he cleaned the toilets, sinks, and showers, he heard two women chatting in the hall: Frances, the woman who had checked him into the shelter, and Doreen, the woman who had given him clothes and showed him around. At first, he didn't pay much attention until a key phrase caught his ear.

"She had to retire because she apparently lost her hand," Doreen said.

Frances gasped. "Is that why she was on medical leave? And you'd think someone with her connections could've had her choice of healers."

Davis poked his head into the hallway before he could stop himself. Could this be the same woman who had caused trouble for his father? If so, he wanted to find out more.

Doreen saw Davis and smiled. "Did you need something, Davis?"

"I'm sorry. I didn't mean to eavesdrop. But I was wondering, who lost a hand?"

Frances turned around with a conspiratorial look on her face. She always seemed ready to gossip. "It was Representative Bai. Can you believe it? I wonder who will replace her."

"This could change everything for the anti-integration vote," Doreen said. "Representative Bai was firmly against integration."

Davis knew nothing about Shifter politics, but this Representative Bai had to be the same woman his father had dealt with. Someone in politics who could influence the way the anti-integration vote turned out. "That's terrible," he said, pretending to know what was going on. He took a chance with his next question, hoping Frances or Doreen would know where Representative Bai's home was. "Does she happen to live nearby?"

"Not far at all," Frances said.

So she knew! Now, how would he get her address without seeming too suspicious? He put on what he thought was his most innocent-looking expression. "Do you think it would be a nice gesture to pay her a visit? Bring her flowers or something?"

Frances wrinkled her nose but spoke in the same patient voice she had used with Davis when discussing anti-integration and the effects on the resource center. "That would be very considerate of you, but Representative Bai is not known for being a particularly pleasant person."

Davis tried again. He didn't want to let this opportunity slip by. "But maybe that could help cheer her up. Let her know she's not alone."

Frances hesitated.

Doreen chimed in with a laugh. "Oh, let the boy bring some joy to that grumpy old bag. A face as attractive as his could make a stone smile."

She nudged Davis, who smiled at Frances as if on cue. He was beginning to realize the effect his looks had on those around him, although he was still not used to the attention.

"OK," Frances said. "I'll walk you over to Representative Bai's home once you're finished cleaning. We don't have much here, but I'm sure we can find something to bring her to show we care." She said the last words with a hint of hesitation.

Careful not to show too much excitement, Davis nodded and hurried about his chores. When he was finished, he met Frances at the door. He put on a gray wool jacket over his white shirt both provided by the shelter. Both clothing items were faded and pilled, and Davis cringed, thinking of the impression he would be making at the representative's door. Why couldn't he have thought to grab other clothes from his house? Instead, he had run off into the rain, a scared little boy. He was pathetic.

Frances handed Davis a basket while she put on a jacket. "There's a loaf of bread and some fruit in there. Hopefully, she doesn't laugh in our faces at our meager offerings."

Davis offered a small smile and looked out at the families on the street as they walked out the door. Those families could probably use this food, but this was for a good cause. He was going to help his father, and they could finally be a family again.

As they walked down the busy street, cars whizzing by,

Davis was full of questions about Shifters. How could he phrase his questions so as not to give himself away?

He turned to Frances. "I grew up, uh, in the country. And since my parents weren't in my life for a while, I don't really know much about being a Shifter. How do you know what another Shifter's power is?"

Frances laughed. "Not much secret there. You just ask. Or you get used to seeing people at the meeting areas that Shifters go to to transform. Which you should go to at some point. I'll show you where to go. It's not good to hole yourself up for too long. Can start to make you a bit stir crazy."

"But don't they need to keep track of people?"

"They?"

"I don't know. The government?"

"Hmm, the government. I'm sure you'd have to register your powers if you got involved with politics. And I wouldn't be surprised if they tracked people for their own purposes, especially with their anti-integration agenda."

Belatedly, Davis realized if he told Frances what his power was, it could change later when he had to use another transfer stone. So he quickly changed the subject, asking where she grew up and how she became involved with The Housing and Resource Center, hoping she wouldn't ask. It worked. Frances seemed happy to talk about how she was a Los Angeles native, how she grew up in a middle-class family and saw how many of her peers fell into destitution with The Great Depression, and how that motivated her to start working at The Housing and Resource Center. Davis nodded enthusiastically as they walked for two more blocks. They turned onto a pedestrian street lined with stores on the street level and apartments above. A lot of the storefronts were shuttered. Davis hadn't been to this area before, but he figured it was part of Los Angeles Chinatown based on the signs with Chinese characters and red lanterns hanging from building to building.

Frances stopped in front of a bakery, one of the only stores still open, and walked up a staircase to an apartment just above. Davis followed. The representative lived here? How could someone in the Shifter government live in such low conditions? Davis had naturally assumed all Shifter government officials lived in estates as big as his own family's. Maybe this would make it easier for Davis to work his way up in Shifter politics since he wasn't currently living in the most glamorous place either.

Frances handed the gift basket to Davis as she knocked on the door. A moment later, a man came to the door. He was an Asian man who looked to be in his thirties, stout and well-built, with a stern look on his face.

"Yes?"

Frances smiled and spoke in her usual bright manner. "Hello. You must be Mr. Bai. I'm Frances, and this is Davis." She gestured toward Davis. "We're here from The Housing and Resource Center to see Representative Bai and bring her a gift basket to show we're thinking of her."

Mr. Bai looked from Frances to Davis and back. His expression didn't change. "She's not a representative anymore."

"Yes, of course," Frances said. "And we're very sorry to hear that. Please give her this gift from us." She nudged Davis, who held the basket forward.

Mr. Bai took the basket, nodded, then closed the door.

"Well," Frances said with a shrug, "I guess that's the best we could expect."

"It was still good of us to come here," Davis said. And he meant it because now that he knew where the former representative lived, he could keep track of her for his father.

CHAPTER TWENTY-ONE

Amber

Summer 2000

AMBER SU SAID bye to Arav and hung up the phone. She wanted to immediately go to his house, to see what his brother Kabir had to say, but she knew she should talk to Nivi first. Nivi was sure to have a reasonable, science-based explanation for what Amber saw. It was probably all a misunderstanding.

She picked up the phone and stared at the numbers on its base. Her hand trembled, and she let the receiver fall. It landed silently on a pile of dirty clothes. *Tomorrow,* she thought, allowing the exhaustion to sweep her off to sleep, not bothering to change out of the clothes from that morning.

The next day came, and the next, and the next. Amber knew why she was avoiding Nivi, and Arav for that matter. She couldn't face Nivi knowing what she saw and didn't want Arav to give her the same sympathetic pity as Kabir. But why hadn't Nivi reached out to her?

Finally, she couldn't take it anymore, wasting away the prime summer days lying in bed when she knew her friends were on the beach every day and that music camp was starting soon. One crazy incident shouldn't keep her from her summer break. *And it was crazy, wasn't it? Maybe I just made it all up? Like my mom said, maybe it's from my heated emotions or the traumatic event.* She willed herself to believe that as she packed a beach bag, threw on cutoff shorts and a halter top, and headed out the door. Her parents heaved a visible sigh of relief when they saw her emerge from her bedroom.

"I'm going to the beach," Amber said without pausing to explain. Her parents waved and smiled as she left.

Ten minutes later, she found herself pacing in front of the beige house with white shutters, the one she used to enter without knocking. She kicked at stray maple leaves, trying to decide what she would say.

"Are you looking for Nivi?" A voice called out.

Amber jumped. She had been so lost in her thoughts she didn't notice anyone around. Ling Guang sat on the porch, reading an ancient-looking tome.

Amber spoke quietly, hoping Nivi wasn't close enough to hear her. She wasn't ready to see her yet. "Oh. Hello, Grandma Ling."

Maybe she should leave and come back later. Yes, that's what she would do. It wouldn't make a difference if she waited another day to see Nivi. Too late. The front screen door opened. Nivi came out, rubbing her eyes with her bandaged hands.

"Hey," Nivi said, her words tinged with sleep.

Amber stood frozen and speechless. All the words she had practiced suddenly escaped her mind. Fortunately, Nivi had a far-off look in her eyes and didn't seem to notice Amber's awkwardness.

"Um," Amber managed to blurt out. What was wrong with

her? She was usually the fearless, outgoing one, and Nivi was the socially awkward one who didn't know what to say.

Ling motioned for Amber to take her seat on the porch while she picked up her book and moved indoors.

Amber inched up the front steps and sat on the porch bench on the far end from Nivi. Nivi seemed lost in a world of her own. She took a seat on the other side of the bench from Amber. Silence stretched the four feet between them.

"I'm glad you're here," Nivi said eventually. "I'm sorry we haven't talked much since… I haven't been myself."

"Me too." Amber hesitated before continuing. "How are you doing?" She gestured toward Nivi's arms and neck. The neck marks had turned a deep purple and green.

Nivi stared down at her bare feet. "I'm OK."

Amber wrung her hands, finding the words she had been practicing. She meant to say it quickly, rip off the bandaid, but her words came out falteringly.

"What happened– in the school that day?"

Nivi looked at her with furrowed brows. "You mean the fire?"

"Yes, but…" Amber wasn't used to having this much difficulty talking. "What happened– just before?"

Nivi returned her gaze to the ground. "I don't know. I can't remember."

That was surprising. Nivi seemed to be telling the truth. Could she have blocked out what happened?

"Nothing?"

Nivi shook her head. "Every time I try to remember, it's just a jumble of images. And then I feel like I start seeing *things*."

Amber scooted a little closer to Nivi. "What kind of things?"

Nivi opened her mouth, then closed it and looked away. "It doesn't make sense."

If Nivi couldn't remember anything, she wouldn't be able to verify what Amber saw.

"Can you remember anything about who did this to you?" She pointed to the marks on Nivi's neck.

Nivi shook her head.

"At the police station, they told me he's unidentified. He's not from around here. No one knows who he is. No one has claimed his body."

"He's the one who died?" The last word was almost a whisper.

Amber nodded.

Nivi moved to the edge of her seat and rested her elbows on her knees. "I wonder…"

"What?"

"If he's unidentified and unclaimed, is he still at the morgue?"

"I guess?" Then Amber realized what Nivi was thinking. "You can't be serious."

"I have no memory. Maybe if I see him… I need to know what happened."

"You can't just go in there."

"Why not? You're the one who always says no one locks doors around here."

Amber was dumbstruck. Nivi was going to break the rules? And why didn't she support Nivi in this idea? "But…" She didn't know what else to say.

"Will you come with me? It'll be an adventure." A glimmer of a smile touched the corner of Nivi's mouth.

"I can't."

"Why not?"

"I just– it's dangerous." Or did she want to say *you're dangerous?*

"It can't be more dangerous than going to an abandoned mine in the middle of the night."

"Yeah, but…"

"Come on. I've always gone with you whenever and wherever you've asked me to. You owe me."

"I know, but–"

"But what?" Nivi's smile was waning, and she was starting to sound exasperated.

Amber shuffled her feet. She had to tell Nivi what she saw. It would be fine if she could just tell Nivi. Nivi would tell her what really happened, and they would laugh it off. Then Amber could join Nivi at the morgue without any worries. But what if Nivi couldn't remember anything?

Nivi stood up. "Fine. I'll go without you." She turned and headed back toward the house.

Amber got up and followed her. She didn't believe Nivi would go by herself to the morgue. Nivi was terrified of strange places, not to mention rule-breaking. That was why seeing Nivi set a fire at the school was so strange. It didn't fit with Nivi's character. Amber had to find out the truth but didn't know how to bring it up. She just needed to keep Nivi from leaving until she could figure out how. "Wait. What about music camp?"

Nivi turned around. She seemed genuinely happy when she held up her bandaged hands. "I guess I don't have to worry about violin or going to music camp anymore."

Amber's stomach turned. Someone in a terrible accident wouldn't be that happy about her injuries unless she planned them. After all these years, maybe she didn't know Nivi at all. "Oh my god, you did do it, didn't you?"

"What are you talking about?"

"You set the fire. To get out of music camp."

Nivi's face reddened. "Are you crazy?" Her tone was

indignant, but she averted her eyes from Amber's gaze. "I have no idea how the fire started. And if you forgot, I was attacked."

Amber continued talking quickly. Now that it was out, she couldn't stop herself. "I saw you. I saw you light a fire. Maybe you just meant to injure your hands a little, but then it got out of control. And the guy who died. That was an accident, too. Maybe he grabbed your neck to stop you from setting the fire. You didn't mean to set the whole place on fire. You didn't mean to kill him. I don't blame you if it was an accident. Just tell me what happened. We can figure it out together."

"You can't be serious." Nivi's voice was weak, and her brown complexion became red and blotchy.

Shame shot through Amber's body. Her palms perspired. She needed to slow down and think. "I'm sorry. I know it sounds crazy."

Nivi's voice grew louder. "It is crazy!"

Amber was stunned. Even with her harsh accusation, she hadn't expected such a forceful response, especially from Nivi. "I didn't mean–"

"So what did you mean?"

"I– I'm not sure. It's just that I thought that's what I saw."

Nivi sounded frantic. "You *thought*? Did you tell the police what you *thought* you saw?"

Amber looked down. "They didn't believe me."

"Wow. I can't believe you told the police. I thought you were my best friend. At least they didn't believe you because it's crazy."

That last part felt like a personal attack. "I'm not crazy."

"I didn't say that." Nivi's voice took on a diplomatic tone. "Look, I was attacked, and there was a fire. I'm sorry you thought you saw something, but it wasn't real. We're both going through a lot right now."

Amber closed her eyes. The image of Nivi with the fire was so clear. "But, I did see something…" Her voice trailed off. Why was she still pushing this? The police didn't believe her, her parents didn't believe her. There was no evidence except her memory, which was most likely faulty. She could barely remember enough to pass her classes, how could she be so sure she saw what she saw? Plus, she was alienating Nivi in her time of need. She should support and believe her best friend.

"Wow." Nivi paused as if she was going to say something else but instead turned and stormed into the house. There was a click as she closed and locked the door. It was probably the first locked door in all of Yuras.

Amber stood with tears in her eyes. She paced back and forth, unsure if she should try knocking on the door. The image of what she saw burned so brightly in her mind. She should've let it go. She should've believed Nivi.

Amber stared at the front door, hoping it would unlock. When it didn't, she slowly headed home. Clouds gathered overhead and a cool breeze broke through the summer heat. Amber shivered. She no longer wanted to go to the beach anyway. She turned onto Main Street as light sprinkles dotted the sidewalk.

When she arrived at Maple Lane, she surprised herself by continuing on past it. Maybe what she saw was all in her head, but maybe Arav's brother Kabir would have more information that would explain everything. She picked up the pace toward Forest Lane as the rain came down harder, hoping that Kabir could tell her something that she could use to repair her friendship with Nivi.

CHAPTER TWENTY-TWO

Iris

Summer 1955

IRIS SAT WITH her parents, silently eating dinner, lost in her thoughts. Their chewing and the whirring of the ceiling fan were the only sounds between them. The night air was hot, and her parents sat in sleeveless shirts. Matching, circular, bright red scars stood out on their left shoulders. The result of childhood vaccinations, they had said. Iris wondered why she didn't react similarly when she had had her vaccinations.

"Where are your glasses?" her mother asked. Her father was reading a newspaper and not fully paying attention.

Iris jumped. She had been so distracted that she had forgotten to put them on.

"I—have a headache. I'm just taking a short break from wearing them." Worried that her mother may be catching on, she squinted her eyes and pointed across the table. "Can you pass me the broccoli?"

"Hmph. If you keep squinting like that, you'll worsen your

headache," her mother said. She passed the bowl, and Iris took it, keeping her eyes downcast.

Her father put down the newspaper he was reading. "We have some good news, Iris."

He looked over at her mother, who put her bowl aside and placed both her hands on the table.

"It's about the cure," she said. "There is a good chance it will be ready in a week or two."

Normally, Iris would just nod and say nothing, as she had heard this so many times before, but now she wasn't so sure she wanted a cure anymore. The questions spewed forward.

"Who told you this?"

Her mother raised her eyebrows. "Our local representative, Mr. Davis. He keeps us informed with any updates."

"What exactly does a cure mean?"

"It means you don't have to take your pills anymore."

"So," Iris said, "I won't have any more episodes? No more seizures?"

"That's right," her mother said.

"And what about— my eyesight?" Iris was not sure if she should bring attention to it, but she had to know. She squinted again for effect. "Will I still have to wear glasses?"

"Of course," her mother scoffed. "Why would you think otherwise?"

"I— just thought they might be related."

"Having the cure will be a blessing enough."

Iris looked to her father for feedback, but he nodded in agreement with her mother and picked the newspaper back up. They finished their meal in silence, after which Iris went to her room.

What good is a cure if it takes my eyesight away again? she thought. Ever since she had stopped taking her medication, she felt so much more energetic, so free. She hadn't even had an episode. Just heat exhaustion that one day, but it was unrelated. She was starting to think she had maybe outgrown the condition. It was probably a coincidence, but everything seemed to be going right ever since she stopped taking the pills.

The clock ticked by her bed. The alarm would go off soon. Iris opened the medicine bottle, took a pill, and placed it on the nightstand. She had told herself earlier that she would stop these lies. She stared at it: the pill that was smaller than her pinky nail; The pill that made her miss so many lunches at school with her friends; The pill that took away her eyesight.

In a fit of indignation, she grabbed the pill and pressed it into the soil of the aspidistra plant just as the alarm clock rang. Raising the glass of water to her mouth, she gulped it down as her mother stuck her head in to check on her. She even put on her eyeglasses to say good night, attempting to look as natural as possible even though her head spun through the strong blur of prescription lenses.

As she floated off to sleep, she dreamt of her next lunch with Anna Sun. They sat in the garden as they did before. Anna sipped white wine, and they ate egg salad sandwiches. A rose bush rustled to Iris's left, and another rustled behind her. All of a sudden, all the bushes were shaking. Snakes emerged from the foliage. Hundreds of them. They slithered over the grass and approached their table. Anna Sun continued to drink her wine, seeming not to notice or care. For some strange reason, Iris was not scared. She watched the snakes approach, and as they did, she felt a power surge through her body. The closer they came, the more powerful she felt. Her body became neon white. Her dark brown eyes gleamed burgundy.

Iris awoke with a start, gripping the sides of the bed with the force of energy she had felt in the dream. With wide eyes, she glanced around the room. Everything was red. She blinked several times. Maybe the sun was rising, and the dawn cast a crimson glow through the window. She got out of bed and shuffled over to the window to close the curtains more tightly. As she drew the curtains together, she caught a glimpse of her reflection in the glass. Staring back at her were two glowing red eyes. She gasped and jumped back. The curtains fell from her hands and swung side to side, covering her reflection. She clasped her hands to her face and felt around. Nothing felt different. Bracing herself, she took a step forward and pushed the curtain aside. Her regular brown eyes stared back.

I must've been half asleep, she thought.

The sky was still dark. She looked at the clock. The sun wouldn't rise for another few hours. She rubbed at her neck and then rubbed at it again. She could've sworn her skin felt rough, like reptilian scales.

CHAPTER TWENTY-THREE

Nivi

Summer 2000

Nivi flew past her grandmother, who was sorting books at the dining room table and went straight into her room before any questions could be asked. A moment later, a knock came at her bedroom door.

"Nivi?" came Ling's voice.

Nivi didn't respond, and when the knock came again, she blurted out, "Leave me alone!" She had never spoken to her grandmother or Amber like that, but at the same time, she was too mad to care.

Nivi paced the room. Amber was crazy. How could she have accused her of something like that? Nivi paused to look down at her arms. *But maybe I'm crazy, too.* The bandages were almost daring her to take them off. In a fit, she ripped at them, unraveling around and around. They fell on the beige carpet in a long, lifeless strand, like the discarded skin of a snake. She braced herself for what she was about to see. There were the raised purplish, branching scars extending from her hands to her forearms, but no sign of glowing or whatever it was she thought she saw before. Hysterical giggling burst from her mouth. *See,* she thought, holding her arms out in front of her, *It's just the stress of it all. It's making us both crazy.*

The laughter didn't last long, and soon, a mixture of sadness, anger, and guilt replaced it. She let her arms fall beside her, then gingerly touched the healing bruises on her neck. Could she have started the fire? She didn't remember anything after all, so it *was* possible. Even the night before the fire, she had blacked out in the cave. Was she becoming one of those people who blacked out and committed crimes like she saw on TV? But she hadn't done anything bad in the cave. And even if she had wanted to start a fire in the school, she had nothing to start a fire with. No, it didn't make sense. Nothing did. She had no one she could talk to anymore. Her grandmother shut down her questions. And Amber thought she was a criminal. How was she supposed to get any answers?

The unidentified body is still in the morgue. The thought percolated through her head, repeating itself over and over. She let it gain steam. The morgue terrified her. She hadn't been fully serious when she had suggested it earlier. Then, she only pushed it because Amber was being so reluctant. Could she actually go by herself? Would she get in trouble? *It's not like I'd be doing anything wrong by just going in. I'll take a quick look and then leave.*

Nivi lay down in her bed. The mental debate continued while she stared at the popcorn ceiling. She counted the recessed spots on the textured surface, unfocusing and refocusing her eyes. Eventually, she got up and went to open the window. The air was crisp, like the feeling before the rain. In the distance, clouds were gathering, blotting out the sun and darkening the forested hills. She could do this. She would do this. Nivi put on a gray sweatshirt, looked back at her bedroom door, and threw a leg onto the sill.

Gusts of cool wind broke through the summer heat and rustled the maple trees that lined the streets. Nivi turned left onto Main Street and then right onto Peninsula Street. Peninsula Street was where all the official buildings of Yuras were located, including the morgue, probably because it was also where the 101 Freeway entrance and exit were.

As she went, Nivi practiced reasons for visiting the morgue in case someone asked. Raindrops began to speckle the brick sidewalks as Nivi arrived at the morgue. The cool summer rain grew quickly, streaming down the colonial grid windows that lined the front of the boxy, wooden building. Nivi jogged forward and pulled open the heavy wood door. She caught it before it clanged shut behind her. With a racing heart, she let the door close gently and turned with her prepared story for being there. The security counter was empty.

Rain coalesced on the windows into rivulets that obscured the gray sky beyond. Nivi crept further in, not certain which direction to go. In the background, she heard someone laughing and talking behind a closed door. Maybe it was the security guard taking a break, talking on the phone, or watching TV. Off to the right was a room lined with silver freezers. Stainless steel gurneys sat empty on the cold concrete floor under wood beams and rafters. A half-eaten sandwich sat off to the side on the counter. Nivi wrinkled her nose. Who could eat in a place like this?

Panic built up inside her. She leaned against a wall outside the freezer room and took deep breaths. She could leave before the security guard returned and no one would know the difference. But where would that leave her? Back home with no answers. She had to do this.

After another deep breath, she tiptoed into the room and began scanning the freezers as fast as possible. She wasn't sure what she was looking for, but she figured there couldn't be that many dead bodies stored here based on their small population. Every few seconds, she stopped to listen for approaching footsteps. All was quiet except for a soft electric hum accompanying the flickering fluorescent lights.

On the front of the freezers were plastic pockets. Some of the pockets displayed note cards with names, dates, and ID numbers. Nivi read each note card until she came across a freezer labeled "John Doe." *This must be it.* She touched the cold, metal handle. Her pulse quickened and throbbed through her hand as she tightened her grasp. *I can do this. I can do this.* Holding her breath, she pulled on the handle, releasing a gust of icy pressure. The cold hit her face and sent a shiver down her spine.

She breathed slowly, maintaining an outward appearance of calm and composure. Other than this morning with Amber, it was rare for her to display strong emotions, even in times of stress. Inwardly, however, she felt like an unsteady surface trying to keep apart a lit match and a stick of dynamite. Balancing her nerves, she bit her lip and slid the platform out. The body on the platform was fortunately sealed in a black body bag. Still, just the knowledge that a dead body was in there was enough to make Nivi's legs wobble. She reached for the zipper and then retracted her hand. She felt like she was going to be sick.

Resting her back against the freezer wall, Nivi leaned over until the nausea passed. She couldn't do this. It was too much. She couldn't do anything like this without Amber. What would Amber say if she could see her now?

Poor Nivi, such a goody-two-shoes. She always has to follow the rules or she'll just fall apart. See, I told you it was too dangerous. For you, that is.

Nivi scrunched her eyes. She would show Amber that she didn't need her. She didn't need anyone.

Standing up straight, she pulled down the zipper on the body bag before she could hesitate again. A clump of matted, dark blonde hair came into view. She recoiled, jumping back a few steps. There was something about seeing the hair that made it much more real.

Steeling herself, she approached again and uncovered a sallow face and sunken eyes. Those eyes. She had seen those eyes when he was blocking the doorway in the school hall. It was working. Her memory was coming back. There was something else, something that seemed familiar about the man. The freezer fan kicked on, emitting an eerie murmuring sound. That was it! The man had been murmuring as he approached her. It was the same murmuring she heard in the oceanside cave with Amber. He must've followed her from the cave. But why?

More memories came back. She realized she was wearing the same sweatshirt she had worn the night of the cave. In the pocket, there was a stone. She pulled it out. The stone was translucent and dark inside as if it had been charred. That didn't seem right. Nivi remembered a lighter-colored stone that had some movement inside. Swirling clouds of gray. This stone was devoid of movement as if life had been burned out of it. Not knowing what to make of it, she put the stone back in her pocket.

Returning her attention to the freezer, she dragged the zipper further down and gasped. The torso of the corpse was melted, the flesh charred and peeled away, exposing several ribs and a pit scorched through the heart. The blood drained from her face and continued down until her whole body felt cold. She leaned up against the side of the freezers to support herself. The smell of burnt, decomposed flesh wafted up her nose, causing her to gag.

It was horrific, yet part of her felt relief. There was no way she could've started a fire that caused this type of damage. This was like a bomb had exploded in his chest. Maybe what Amber saw was the aftermath of the bomb. If Nivi had put her hands out to shield herself, her hands would have caught fire. That was probably what Amber saw.

A noise to Nivi's left caused her to jump: footsteps and rustling muted behind a wall. Nivi jumped into action, pulling the zipper back into place and replacing the body in the freezer as quickly and quietly as possible. She tiptoed toward the door, thankful the concrete ground did not creak like a wood floor would. Before she reached the doorway, a voice came from behind her.

"Can I help you?

Nivi froze. She had endured as much composed stress as she could for one day, and her hands trembled openly. As she turned around, she saw a woman with short black hair, wearing a blue lab coat, standing in front of a doorway at the end of the freezers. She looked like a mad scientist with a tall, lithe figure and disheveled hair that bore a prominent gray streak by her forehead.

"Um, I'm looking for someone," Nivi stammered, realizing how silly that sounded.

"In here?" the woman said.

Nivi looked down at the floor, wishing she could crawl into herself. Why did she think this was a good idea again?

The woman softened. "People deal with loss in different ways. What's your name?"

"I'm Nivi. Nivi Dawan." She belatedly realized maybe she shouldn't have used her real name. She was too used to responding obediently to authority figures.

"I'm Ji." She gave Nivi a sympathetic smile. "Let me see if I can help you. Are you looking for a friend or family member?"

Nivi stood there, shifting awkwardly. "A, uh, friend."

Ji went to a computer next to Nivi and brought it out of sleep mode. At her closer proximity, there was a musty, unwashed smell. A mix of mold, dirt, and sweat. There even seemed to be muddy smudges on her hands and face. Nivi wrinkled her nose. She shivered to think of what substances must have rubbed off on this mortician's body.

"What's your friend's last name?" Ji said.

"I, uh, don't know."

"First name?"

"I'm sorry, I–" Nivi began, then ran from the room before finishing.

She ran toward the front door, where the security guard had returned to his post.

"Hey!" he exclaimed, obviously startled by her presence.

Terrified and humiliated, Nivi didn't stop. She ran out into the rain and kept running until she was out of breath and sure no one had followed her.

CHAPTER TWENTY-FOUR

Iris

Summer 1955

Thursday morning arrived without any hiccups. Iris sat at the dining table wearing her glasses and trying to eat her green onion and egg pancake. Her father had left early as usual. As her mother got ready for work, Iris watched from the corner of her eye. If her mother planned to come home for lunch today, she would have to tell John to cancel her visit with Anna Sun when he came to pick her up. Over and over, she missed the thin crepe due to her blurred vision, so she resorted to chewing on her chopsticks instead. She closed her eyes and willed away the impending throb from her headache-inducing eyewear.

"What's wrong with you?" her mother said.

Iris's eyes shot open. "Nothing." Her voice was a tad too high-pitched.

"Then why aren't you eating?"

"I was thinking— about my studies."

"You need to eat to feed your brain."

Iris lifted the plate and shoveled the pancake piece into her mouth. Her mother turned to the refrigerator and took out a couple of zongzi; pyramid-shaped glutinous rice and pork wrapped in bamboo leaves. Iris sat up straight. Her mother was taking lunch to work.

"You won't be home for lunch?" Iris said, peering over the top of her glasses.

"No. Too much work today. And you've been managing your medication. I don't need to come home to supervise anymore."

Iris's cheeks heated. She swallowed too quickly, and the food stuck in her throat. She coughed.

Her mother sighed and shook her head. "You need to chew your food."

"Yes, Ma Ma." Iris cleared her throat and away wiped tears.

"Lock the door after me?" her mother said as she left.

Iris immediately took off the glasses. She put them in their case and tossed them into a cloth bag in the kitchen on her way to lock the door. She was sick of pretending she needed them.

"Better," she said, rubbing her temples.

What was she afraid of? She should tell her parents that she didn't need her medication or glasses anymore. It had been several days since her last pill, and she was fine. Better than fine.

I don't have time to think about this right now, she thought. *I have to get ready to go to Anna's.* Go to Anna's. So informal. They were basically best friends already.

Iris undid her braids. Her hair fell in long waves of black. Her thick, straight hair never held a curl for long, but she enjoyed it for the moment, spinning around and flipping the strands over her shoulder.

I should bring a gift. She didn't know what she could bring, so she went to her bedroom and took out a tin box she kept in the nightstand drawer. From inside, she took out a few dollars from the stash she had made from doing chores and helping her parents at their business. She grabbed the cloth bag from the kitchen and went to visit the vendors below.

When she reached the bottom of the staircase and looked into the Chinese bakery, she immediately knew what she should get. Fresh-baked pineapple buns. She counted the few dollars she had. It should be enough.

John met her at the same corner where he had dropped her off last time. They drove through the city and up into the hills. Iris watched with excitement as Anna's mansion emerged through the trees, the white stone facade gleaming in the sun. John pulled up to the front door, and Iris exited the car, carrying her bag of pastries. John closed the door behind her and drove away to park the car. Margaret stood on the front steps, prepared for her arrival. She showed Iris into the grand entrance, through an archway to the left, and into the living room. Anna Sun sat on a sofa in front of a row of floor-to-ceiling windows that looked out onto the garden. She stood as Margaret and Iris approached, her yellow dress cascading around her knees. Iris felt the warmth in her chest as usual. In her yellow dress backlit by the sun, Anna glowed more brilliantly than ever.

"Welcome back," Anna said. "It's a bit hot out today, so I hope you don't mind if we sit inside. At least here, we still have a view of the garden."

"This is perfect. Thank you," Iris said.

Margaret poured Iris some water as she and Anna sat, then bowed her head and left the room.

"How are you doing? How are your parents?" Anna said while looking over Iris's head as if she were expecting someone.

Iris glanced behind her and didn't see anyone. "We're all very good. How are you?"

"Just fine. Thank you." Anna leaned forward, hesitating before continuing. A shadow from the gridded windows fell across her eyes. "We'll have company joining us today."

Iris looked around again. They were going to have company? Was it another celebrity? Or a member of Anna's family? She felt anxious about the possibility of either, and the way Anna was acting made it seem she felt the same. Before she could say anything, Anna spoke again.

"There's no easy way to say this, so I'll just ask you straight. Do you know what a Shifter is?"

Iris furrowed her brow. "No. What's that?"

"Oh, nothing." Anna laughed and leaned back as if she were relieved. "It's— industry-related."

Iris assumed the term had something to do with the movies but didn't understand why Anna would be nervous about it. Maybe there was a big celebrity joining them, someone even Anna was intimidated by. Her palms began to sweat. She wiped them on the bag in her lap, then remembered the gift.

"I brought you something."

She took the pastries out of her bag and put them on the coffee table. She placed the empty bag under the coffee table.

Anna looked surprised. "You did?"

"They're called pineapple buns— because they kind of look like pineapples. There's no pineapple in them, though. They're from a Chinese bakery near my home. I hope you like them."

"How wonderful. Thank you." She tore off the edge of one piece and put it in her mouth. "They're very good."

"I'm so glad you like it." Iris sat back and glanced around again. "So, who is coming to join us?"

Anna swallowed her food and gazed at Iris for several seconds without speaking. Her closed mouth still curved up in a smile, but her eyes looked sad.

"This isn't right," she said after a moment.

"The pineapple buns?" Iris said.

Anna didn't respond to her and instead called out for Margaret. "Have John bring the car up front."

"Is something wrong? Did I do something—."

Before Iris could finish, Anna stood up and took her by the arm. "You have to go. Now." She pulled Iris toward the door.

Iris felt her face flush. "I don't understand."

They exited the house as John was pulling the car around. Before John could get out of the car, Anna opened the back door and pushed Iris in.

"John, take Iris home," she said, leaning into the car.

She slammed the door, and John took off. Iris turned to look out the back window and saw that Anna had already gone into the house.

"Excuse me, John," Iris said. "Do you know what's going on?"

"I just follow my orders, Miss." His words were polite and professional but also with a finality to them.

She sat silently in shock. Her hands trembled, and she gripped them together to stop them. When they arrived back in Chinatown, John opened the door for her.

"Miss," he said with a nod.

"Thank you, John," Iris mumbled.

She returned to her apartment, each step as heavy as her heart. Not wanting to make eye contact with anyone, she kept her eyes on the ground. She dragged her feet up the steps to her apartment, went inside, and flopped on her bed. Confusion and embarrassment wrenched her gut. She wanted to cry but resisted the urge.

How could I be so stupid as to think I could be friends with a moviestar? Iris ran the events through her head again. She had arrived at the house. Anna had seemed happy and nice as usual. It wasn't until she had eaten the pineapple bun that she had suddenly switched. Maybe she didn't like it? Or she was allergic? But did that warrant such a strong reaction? None of it made sense.

She lay in bed a while longer. For a moment, she considered starting her medication again. Maybe if she hadn't stopped, none of this would have happened. No, she needed time to think. She wouldn't let this one event sway her so quickly. She got up to do her chores and studies. Her mother was right. She shouldn't dwell on something as silly as a movie star. What would her parents think if they knew how twisted her priorities had become?

In the living room, Iris pulled out the precalculus and physics books she had requested early for the next school year and flipped to the bookmarked pages. She took a deep breath and began the practice problems. From the open window, she could hear the pigeons cooing. The rhythmic sounds had a calming effect on her, and she could feel her shoulders start to relax as she became engrossed in finding the angles of a triangle. After completing several precalculus problems, she switched to physics. The first problem asked her to find the focus point of a convex lens. *Lens.* Iris touched her face. *My glasses. Where are they?* She glanced around the room. Suddenly, she felt a strong pull toward Anna. A vision of Anna's living room and coffee table flashed in her mind. It was so vivid it was as if Iris were standing in Anna's living room. *How is this happening?* She could see the fabric bag under the coffee table, and she could see her glasses through the bag.

Oh no. The vision faded. Iris cupped a hand over her mouth. The fear of telling her parents she lost her glasses overshadowed her surprise at having a vision. She paced back and forth in the kitchen. *What should I do?* Should she forget about them? She didn't need them anymore after all. But she wasn't sure she was ready to confront her parents about her medication, especially after a strange and draining day like today. And what if she needed to start taking her medicine again? Her parents wouldn't be able to afford a new pair that easily.

The answer was clear. She needed to go back to Anna's house and get her glasses. But how would she get back to the house? She didn't have Anna's phone number and hadn't paid enough attention to know how to get there. Again, as she thought of Anna's house, a vision appeared showing her the way. Not only that, she felt drawn in the direction of Anna's house. *Maybe I did pay enough attention.* She didn't know how else the directions would have come so clearly into her mind. Would Anna be mad to see her back so soon? Maybe she could ask Margaret to bring the bag, and she wouldn't need to go in the house.

She went to her bedroom and pulled out the tin box from her nightstand drawer, wincing as she counted out more of her money. She had worked hard for that money, but better her money than her parents discovering her lies. Back in the kitchen, she found a large yellow pages book. She flipped the pages until she came to the local taxi section.

CHAPTER TWENTY-FIVE

Ling
Summer 2000

Ling Guang rummaged through the stack of musty library books she had been accumulating all week. The books made a dull thud on the solid wood surface of her oval dining table. Ling froze, afraid to wake Nivi, whom she assumed would be asleep by now. She took a breath and looked up. An antique bronze chandelier illuminated the table. Real candles once lined its curved arms. The cauldron-shaped porcelain center was painted in a Chinese style, depicting a blue dragon among the clouds. Ling smiled as she admired it, reminded of times long past, although she much preferred the electric light, which was brighter, safer, and didn't create a mess.

Since returning from the hospital, Ling had buried herself in research. Over the last ten years, she had gotten used to a simple life with Nivi, and she had let her guard down. The fire and Meng's arrival had brought her back to reality.

Meng Zhang, Ling thought, closing her eyes and shaking

her head. She was confused. A mixture of fear, resentment, and hope collided in her mind. Meng looked as beautiful as ever. Ling tried to push the thoughts from her head. That was over now. Nivi was her top priority. Yet she kept mulling over their conversation.

"Why are you here?" Ling had asked at the hospital, even though she already knew the answer.

She had hoped there could be another reason, but Meng's expression told her all she needed to know. She answered her own question. "The fire. Not again." Whoever had set the fire that killed Nivi's parents was back to finish the job. A pit formed in her stomach as she remembered the events a decade prior. She looked at Meng and realized she shouldn't be able to recognize her like this. "Why aren't you camouflaged?"

"Because," Meng said, "I need you to know I'm investigating this case. That you have someone you can trust."

Ling glanced around. Hospital staff went about their business in the background. No one seemed to be paying them any attention. "You're taking a risk. Please tell me you traveled here by ordinary means." Ling lowered her voice to a whisper. "As you know, the camouflage pendant doesn't guarantee coverage in your Shifter form."

Meng pressed her lips together. "I can handle myself. But you. You still haven't told *her*?"

Shame crept up Ling's cheeks. "I was hoping—"

"That she'd be a Static?"

Meng didn't know about Ling's daughter's infidelity. No one did. Now that her daughter was ten years dead, there was no need to reveal that Nivi had Static blood. That she shouldn't be able to have powers. "I was hoping she could live a *normal* life."

Meng let out a bitter laugh. She reached out toward Ling

and lifted the capped sleeve on her left shoulder, exposing the raised red scar. "This isn't normal."

Meng's touch was electric, and Ling longed to melt into it, but instead, she pulled her shoulder away. "We both gave up a lot that day."

Meng sighed. "I know."

Ling tore her eyes away from Meng. There was no use dwelling on things that couldn't be changed. "Look at Nivi. Is her aura present?"

Meng looked in the hospital room window where Nivi lay sleeping. "No. She's at the age where she is just starting to develop her powers. That will buy us some time from detection from other Shifters. Those that may wish to harm her."

"What now?"

"I will meet with Representative Bai and go from there."

Ling wrung her hands. "How has it been ten years, and we still don't have any answers?"

"I'm sorry." Meng averted her eyes. "I truly am. Everything has been quiet until now. But I believe we are close to a breakthrough. Be patient. Give me a little more time. And please, you must tell Nivi."

Tears glistened in Ling's eyes. "I don't know how. She will hate me."

"Would you like me to?"

"No. It must come from me."

"She will understand, eventually."

All week, Ling avoided the inevitable conversation with Nivi, focusing instead on her research, and thinking that the more information she possessed, the more of a segue she would have.

At the bottom of the pile of books, she found what she was looking for. The leather-bound tome was relatively old, though far from the original written a couple of millennia ago. Ling guessed this edition was at least fifty years old. Embossed Chinese calligraphy swept down the center of the dark leather cover.

She traced it with her finger, translating the title in her head. *Shan Hai Jing. The Classic of Mountains and Seas.* She positioned herself in the upholstered dining chair, sinking into the floral earth tones as she opened the book. With great care, she turned the stitch-bound, frayed, and curled pages. Colorful watercolor depictions of various beasts adorned the yellowed pages. Vertical columns of Chinese characters lined the upper right margins. The book was considered a compilation of mythical animals and places in ancient China, but Ling knew better. It was a record.

She flipped through the pages, noting anything that stood out. There were sea creatures, land creatures, and creatures of the air. Fish people and snake people. Rabbits with human heads that spread lies. Winged lions and celestial dogs. All variations of the more common dragon, and many less common. Creatures with many heads. Some had no heads. There was Di Jiang, the six-limbed, pink fur creature with four feathered wings in place of a head. There was Sheng Huang, a white fox with antlers that sprouted from its back. Some had many tails, like Huli Jing, the nine-tailed fox, and Huan, the three-tailed cat with one eye and four ears. There was Kui, a one-legged ox with a howl like thunder. Some had aspects of many animals in one, and some had no modern-day descriptive equivalent.

Ling lingered on one page in particular. A majestic blue-green dragon with a long serpentine body and four taloned feet glided across the page. Two horns protruded from its silvery mane and long whiskers whipped back from its toothy snout as it flew, wingless, through the air. Ling gently touched the dragon's body, sighed, and turned the page.

A few pages later, Ling paused again. More nostalgia filled her heart. The vermillion bird, covered in fiery red feathers that trailed into a long, flame-like tail. She turned the page before the tears could begin to well up.

The next page also gave Ling pause. In the center of the finely textured paper was a beautiful and strange beast, with a body and hooves like a horse, completely covered in prismatic scales that appeared to glimmer between green and rainbow. The head was like that of a traditional Chinese dragon with long, flowing whiskers, except with a narrower face and snout, giving it a delicate yet still fearsome appearance. Tufts of fur sprouted from the end of the long, scaled tail and trimmed the hooves and chin. Two great, branched horns swept back from the head. The horns and hooves gleamed of gold. All around the extraordinary creature, emanating from as well as encompassing, was fire. Next to the dragon-horse hybrid was an inscription. *Qilin.*

"Chee-Ling," Ling said aloud, feeling the word on her tongue. She was well acquainted with what a qilin was, a mostly benevolent creature that could become fierce to protect against malicious intent.

There hasn't been one of these in a hundred years, she thought.

As she turned the page, a gust of wind kicked up from the kitchen window she had left open after cooking. It flipped the page back to the qilin. Ling looked up at the window and back at the page with a furrowed expression.

It's a sign. But she knew from experience not to conclude anything prematurely, as signs could be obscure and imprecise.

She stared at the page, then walked over to Nivi's bedroom

and put her ear to the door. She waited with her ear on the door a moment longer, and not hearing anything, she retired to her own bedroom. If Meng knew Nivi's true heritage, she wouldn't be so sure of Nivi's powers. But Meng seemed to think the incident at the school was due to Nivi's emerging powers. Could it be that Ling had been wrong all these years? That Nivi's mixed blood could still give rise to powers?

Tomorrow, she thought, *I will talk to her tomorrow.*

CHAPTER TWENTY-SIX

Davis
Summer 1955

Davis gazed upon his mother's tombstone.

Xiang Liu Sun
Beloved Daughter, Wife, and Mother
September 14, 1898 - January 20, 1935

It had been over twenty years since Davis's mother's death. Twenty years. He had accomplished a lot in that time, but it wasn't enough. He placed a bouquet of white roses on the headstone and stepped back. A large maple tree shaded his mother's grave on this warm summer afternoon. It was a peaceful and beautiful place. A place Davis often visited, especially when something was on his mind.

Despite his careful efforts to minimally use his powers, he could sense a change in himself. He was losing his powers, and he was afraid. Over the years, he had built a life for himself in the Shifter community, something he wouldn't have been able to do without his mother's help. He touched the two stones in his pocket. It was time to finally put them to use. Time to nullify his father's enemy. Time to prove himself to his father.

Technically, Mrs. and Mr. Bai were no longer a threat, having given up their powers of their own accord after his father's henchman cut off Mrs. Bai's hand. But they still had a daughter. A daughter who was just coming into her powers. Davis palmed one of the stones from his pocket in his left hand and brought it out. It felt sticky with his sweat. He imagined back to the day his mother had given him her powers. She had held out the stone and asked him to touch it, so all he had to do was touch it to Mrs. Bai's daughter, and it would be done.

It wasn't like she needed her powers. Mrs. and Mr. Bai had been attending all the meetings about the *mark*. A mark that would take away powers from Shifters who wished to assimilate with Statics. They wanted it for their daughter. So he was really doing them a service. They didn't have to wait anymore.

So far, Davis had avoided questions about his powers. Fortunately, it was only recently that an official list was started for Shifter powers, and even then, it was only for the young Shifters who were starting boarding school after coming into their powers. He could take Mrs. Bai's daughter's powers, and no one would know that his powers had changed. From what he gathered, Mrs. Bai's daughter didn't even know she was a Shifter, and Mrs. Bai wanted to keep it that way.

As he walked away from the grave, a sense of dread grew. What if his sister didn't hold up her end of the plan? His powers would fade, and he'd be seen for what he truly was. A charlatan. A fake Shifter. At least he had somewhat of a backup plan. That night, he had an appointment with the Bai's to offer their daughter the mark. If he had to, he could take her powers under the guise of placing a mark on her. It was riskier, especially since Mrs. and Mr. Bai would be present, but it was still something.

At the street corner, he hailed a cab and directed it toward the hill of his family home. The sky grayed as the taxi drove up the winding road. He had the cab stop just outside the property and got out by a row of trees lining the backyard. Before he could enter the rose garden, his sister saw him and ran toward him from the house.

"Where is she?" Davis said, breathless from excitement. This was really going to work. He had his doubts from the beginning, but Anna pulled through. His annoying, perfect sister. His father's favorite. But she had been loyal to *him*.

Anna scrunched up her face and shook her head. "I couldn't do it. She deserves to keep that part of herself."

Rage flew through Davis so quickly that his body reacted before his mind caught up. He raised a hand over Anna, who shrank back.

A deep voice yelled from the garden, stopping Davis's actions. His father rushed over, cane in hand.

"What are you doing? Get away from her!"

The tone of his father's voice struck him hard. It was as if his father were addressing a monster. Perfect Anna. His father's favorite. There was only one thing that differentiated them. One thing that kept him from being his father's favorite. Davis reached into his pocket, grabbed a stone, and shoved it against Anna's arm. A bright white flash followed by a surge of energy through Davis's body. Anna dropped to the ground with a cry. Davis inhaled deeply. He felt good. Restored. Powerful. Not only that, but his mother's water power felt stabilized. He would still be able to use it for a while.

A light sprinkle of rain dusted Davis's face as he looked at his father. His heart raced. It didn't matter that he was now taller than his father or that his father limped more than he used to. He was still a scared little boy in his presence, unfit to be part of the family. That was why he had to do this. To prove to his father he could be the strong one and take care of the family. Ever since Davis's mother had passed, his father had faded from Shifter society. No one spoke about him anymore. No one knew they were related. But his father was still in danger, dealing with people like Mrs. Bai behind the scenes. And Jackson Dawan was still out there. But Davis could keep his father safe. Yes. That was what he needed to do. He would take on the burden his father had borne all these years. He removed the other stone from his pocket, keeping it concealed in his hand.

"What have you done?" His father's voice carried the calm force of a wave that was about to break.

"I–" Davis's voice croaked.

The rain fell harder. His father kneeled by Anna, comforting her. How could he still care for her? She no longer had any powers.

Davis trembled, and his eyes burned. "She planned this." He pointed down at Anna. "She has been helping me all these years."

His father looked at Anna with shock on his face and stood up.

"Davis, please," Anna said.

"I'm helping you, father." Davis stepped forward. "I'll show you. I will be the most powerful Shifter there ever was. And I will keep you safe that way. No one will ever bother our family again. With these powers, I will take down Jackson Dawan for killing Mother!" He took another step forward and pressed his hand to his father's.

Another flash of white light. His father went limp, but Davis supported him and kept him from falling to the ground.

Energy ripped through his veins. Swelled through his muscles. His father felt light and frail. Inconsequential. Davis needed more. More of this invincible feeling. He had to be as powerful as possible to defeat Jackson Dawan.

"Tell me, father. Where did you get the stones?"

His father groaned. "What have you done?" He shoved Davis away. Anna tried to approach their father, and he shoved her away as well.

Davis tried again to ask his father where he got the stones.

His father laughed and spat into the rain. "There are no more." He continued to laugh.

That couldn't be. There had to be more stones. There had to be a way to find or create more. Maybe there were more in his father's storage room where he had found the original three. Davis stood and ran down the path to the storage room under the arch. With his new powers, he transformed into a grizzly, feeling the strength and power as he crashed through the locked door. He ripped apart boxes. Shook out clothing. Pulled apart frames and lamps. Nothing. No transfer stones anywhere.

Davis emerged from the storage room, chest heaving, covered in debris. There must be more. There must be. The sound of a car coming up the driveway startled Davis out of his thoughts. He didn't worry about his father or sister approaching Shifter society to disclose his illegal use of transfer stones. Their pride would keep them away. But he couldn't be seen by someone else that could turn him in. He had to leave. And he had an appointment to get to. With the powers that were previously his sister's, he transformed into a hummingbird and darted away through the rain.

CHAPTER TWENTY-SEVEN

Iris

Summer 1955

Iris guided the taxi driver toward Anna's house, following the tug of the map in her mind. In no time, they were pulling up to the driveway in front of the mansion. The taxi driver gave Iris a questioning eyebrow raise as he parked the car.

"Can you wait for me here?" Iris said. "I'll only be a few minutes."

"OK, but I've heard that before. You can pay me for the first part of the ride now. If you take more than a few minutes, you'll have to call another cab."

Iris nodded and handed over the money, then rushed to the front door and knocked. Ribbons of cold air broke through the day's dry heat, sending a chill up her spine. It was the kind of strange mix that felt like the approach of a storm. She looked around the clear sky. Soft, white clouds hung at the edge of the horizon. It was not likely to rain, especially in Los Angeles in the summer, although it was always possible. Her skin prickled with another gust of icy air. Then the summer heat engulfed her again.

She waited, cocking an ear and listening for footsteps, expecting to see the curvy and solemn Margaret open the door at any moment. The steps didn't come. Iris knocked again, a little harder. The door cracked open. She poked her head into the grand entrance room. There was no one around.

"Hello?" she called out.

She glanced back at the idling cab, and, not wanting him to leave, decided to push ahead into the mansion without anyone coming to greet her. She scurried across the marble floors into the living room. No one was around. All was quiet. She rushed over to the coffee table and saw her cloth bag underneath. She grabbed it and was relieved to find her glasses inside. Turning, she prepared to race out the front door before anyone could see her. A soft sob stopped Iris from leaving the room. She turned toward the noise and saw Margaret on the ground in a corner.

"Oh no." Iris ran over to her. "What happened?"

Margaret's usual pulled-back hair was loose and disheveled about her shoulders. Her eyes were red and puffy. "I couldn't stop him," she sniffed.

Iris's heart pounded. "Stop who?"

Just then, cries came from the garden. Margaret covered her face and continued to cry. Iris felt the urge to run back to the cab and go home. If something bad was happening, there was little she, a young girl all alone, could do to stop it. The cries came again. It was Anna.

The hair rose on the back of Iris's neck. She couldn't just leave if Anna were in trouble. She ran over to the patio door and pushed it open. Dark clouds gathered in the sky. A sprinkle of moisture hit Iris on the forehead. She had been right. The weather had felt like a storm was coming.

There was no one in the garden. Iris scanned the yard, looking for the source of Anna's cries. There was movement beyond the trees at the perimeter of the garden lawns. She broke into a jog, passing fragrant roses as a light rain started. The water coalesced, slowly at first, as if it were as thick as blood. It flowed down the stems, dripping from the thorns.

Another cry. Iris picked up her pace. Her feet squished in the wet grass. Reaching the garden's edge, she ducked behind a tall, evergreen tree. The pine needle aroma prickled her sinuses. A scream pierced the air. Iris clung to the tree trunk, afraid to move. Drops of rain tapped at her head. She wiped her face and blinked the water from her eyes. Her hair dragged down with increasing weight as the rain intensified. The clouds thickened, blotting out the sun and darkening the land. Then, a flash of lightning illuminated the sky.

Iris jumped as thunder rumbled through her bones. She took several deep breaths, then inched around the tree just enough for her to see. Before her were two people. Anna on the ground holding her hands above her head. Her beautiful yellow dress was soaked and muddy. A tall man with a thick, graying mustache stood over her, a cane raised in his hand. Iris craned her head forward, trying to hear what they were saying.

"You're just as useless as your brother now," the man said.

Brother? I thought she said she was an only child. Iris thought back to the children's room with the two cribs and the empty frame and shuddered. What happened to a useless brother?

"How could you be so dimwitted," the man continued. "So unaware and vulnerable. You were supposed to be the powerful one. The one our family legacy would be based on. Now we're left with nothing. Nothing!"

"Father, please," Anna whimpered. "I didn't know."

"You *didn't* know!" her father bellowed. "Was it not you

who has been conspiring with him all this time?" He brought the cane down on Anna's shoulder, and she yelped. Iris recoiled and clapped her hands over her mouth to prevent a scream. She had to help Anna. But how?

"I didn't know he was going to do *this*." Anna climbed to her feet and backed away. "How could I have known? You weren't the only one affected, you know. He took *it* from me, too."

"How do I know you didn't willingly give it to him like your mother did?"

Anna's eyes widened. "You knew this whole time? Then why did you force him to leave?"

"Because he's the reason she's dead."

"That's not true. You know that's not true. All this time, you led me to believe he was the evil one. But did you think I didn't realize what *you* were doing? All the conspirators that visited you in the middle of the night?" Anna's father's brow furrowed at her words. "That's right. You thought I was too young to understand, that I was always sleeping through everything. But I know a lot more than you give me credit for. I know that you and Mother had different political views. That you were pressured to change her stance on integration. In fact, if I had to guess, I'd wager *you* were the cause of Mother's death. Not Davis," she sneered. "You always told me you loved me, but that was only while I was useful. Now that I'm no longer useful to you, you have no hesitation to hurt me, just like you hurt her!"

"That's enough!" He raised the cane over his head again.

Anna flinched and put up her arms. Something ignited within Iris's being. She couldn't stand by any longer while this man hurt Anna. Without thinking, she jumped forward from behind the tree trunk and the protective awning of pine needles. Rain pelted down.

"Stop!" Iris put herself between Anna and her father.

Anna's father withdrew in surprise.

"Iris! What are you doing here?" Anna said.

Anna's father focused his beady eyes on Iris and scoffed. "Iris, is it?"

"Uh, yes." Iris suddenly realized the futility of her actions. She tried to maintain her defiant composure. "Who are *you*?"

He smirked. "Oh, we're going to play that game, are we? Just pretend you're not another one of Anna's co-conspirators?"

"I don't know what you're talking about," Iris said.

"She's telling the truth, Father," Anna said.

"Well then, my name is Randall Sun." He stepped toward her, towering over her, his face twisting. "And you're too late! It's all gone already. All of it!"

Iris blinked several times. Her pulse raced in her ears, and her heart thudded in her chest. No one had ever spoken to her in this way before. It wasn't so much the words he said. She was used to sternness from her parents and teachers, but this was different. There was something derogatory to his tone. Maybe if she had been taking her medication as she should have been, she would be more hesitant to stand up to a scary, angry man. The sedative effect would have kept her from reacting. Instead, she was infuriated. She stood her ground and glared into the tall, thin man's eyes. In the stormy weather, his eyes were as black as night. His mustache drooped in the rain, emphasizing his scowl. Although he towered over her with a frightening countenance, her fear dissipated, replaced with a fury of her own. How dare this man hurt Anna and threaten her?

Randall reacted to her defiance by lifting his cane over his head, preparing for a strike.

"Father, don't hurt her. Iris, run! Get out of here!" Anna cried.

He brought the cane down with powerful speed. Iris stepped forward and met the cane with her outstretched hand, stopping it with a loud crack.

"No," she hissed. Her voice resonated within her chest, sounding like two voices speaking at once.

Randall's eyes widened as he struggled to remove his cane from her grasp. It didn't budge. Iris clenched her fist. Her palm felt hot. The skin on her hand began to glisten. Raised marks appeared across her skin, forming diamond-shaped, iridescent scales. Her eyes and throat burned. She surged with adrenaline and strength. Fracture lines appeared on the cane, splintering to either side of her constricting fist. She squeezed, and the wood shattered.

Randall no longer appeared tall and menacing to Iris. He looked smaller, especially as he began to cower. In fact, he *was* smaller. Or she was larger. Everything was shrinking around her. She grew up until the tops of the trees were at her eye level. When she looked down on him now, he fell back and pulled himself through the puddles away from her. The build up of pressure within herself grew and grew. She felt like she was going to burst. She drew back her head and opened her mouth. A torrent of flames spewed forward, sizzling through the wet air and hitting the ground in front of the man. Steam rose up from the puddles at his feet. She drew back her head again, readying for more fire.

"Wait, please!" Anna said, waving her arms up at Iris. "I know he's not a good man, but he's still my father."

Iris paused. In the heat of the moment, she had forgotten about Anna. She looked down at the small, pleading figure, and her eyes came to a rest on her own reflection in a puddle at Anna's feet. The rain had stopped, and the water's surface had a mirror-like sheen. Two blazing red eyes stared back at her from a white, scaled and horned head. Smoke curled from between rows of long, pointy teeth that rested atop a long, serpentine body. It was a giant snake. *She* was a giant snake.

The rage left her body. The red cleared from her vision. Her skin and muscles constricted while her viewpoint descended until she regained her normal height. Arms separated from her torso and her tail split into legs. She held her hands out before her and saw the scales melding back into her skin. In disbelief, she patted her head, chest and shoulders. The horns and spikes were gone. She ran her tongue over her teeth. They were no longer long and sharp. Her body had returned to normal. All her limbs were accounted for. Even her clothes had reformed, unscathed by the transformation.

Anna looked relieved, and there was something like awe in her eyes when she glanced at Iris. Randall walked up to Iris but stopped a few paces away. He pointed an accusing finger.

"So, Shifter. You think you're better than us now that we're powerless? Don't be so smug. *He* may come for you next."

Iris didn't respond. She held her ground, staring at him with her hands clenched at her side until he dropped his arm and backed away. He no longer looked tall and menacing but thin and frail. He turned to Anna and spoke with a wavering voice.

"I loved your mother more than anyone in this world. This wasn't supposed to happen. None of this was supposed to happen. They were only supposed to scare her. Scare her into changing her mind, her policies…"

He trailed off and put a hand over his mouth as if he knew he'd said too much. Without another word, he broke into a quick, uneven walk toward the house. When he was gone, Iris relaxed her hands. Her legs wobbled. Her fatigued muscles ached like she had been running a marathon. Anna ran to help her to the table where they had lunch before. Margaret met them there and wrapped them in towels.

"It's alright, Margaret," Anna said. "I'm alright. You may go back inside."

"Yes, Mistress." Margaret sniffled and went back into the house.

"Iris," Anna said, putting a hand on hers. "You truly didn't know? About your powers?"

Iris shook her head. Exhaustion coursed through her body, and she put her head on the table.

Anna gently patted Iris's back. "The first transformations are very tiring. But it will get easier."

Iris lifted her head and looked at Anna through weary eyes. "You knew?"

"I knew that you were a Shifter. Not what kind."

"Shifter?" That was the word Randall had called her.

"That's what we are." Anna sighed. "At least that's what I was. We can shift into another form. We can sense each other when we are close." She put her hand to her chest. "Here."

Iris remembered the strange sensations she had felt in her chest when she was near Anna. The warmth. The glow that surrounded Anna. Then she suddenly realized that she no longer felt it. For some reason, she felt alarmed.

"It's gone. I— don't feel it anymore."

"Yes," Anna said with downcast eyes. "My powers were taken from me, as they were from my father." She brushed a tear from her cheek.

"By your brother?"

Anna nodded. "My father had a right to be angry with me."

"No. Not like that." Iris put her head back on the table to rest, then lifted it again. "Why did you say you were an only child before?"

"My father disowned my brother when I was very young. I wasn't allowed to see him or mention his name." She put her head in her hands. "I should have known what he was up to. What he was capable of." She looked up at Iris. "You have a gift. Don't let anyone take it from you like it was taken from us." Tears fell from her eyes. "It's over. It's all over."

"What's over?"

"My career. Without my power, I'm nothing."

Iris leaned forward. "That's not true. You're amazing."

Anna smiled through her tears. "Don't you feel the difference?"

Iris bit her lip, not wanting to answer. The glow was gone, but there was something else missing too. Something she didn't know how to name.

"My power– it was allure. I could make anyone like me. I could sway their thoughts and actions. That's how I became famous."

Iris shook her head again. She felt like crying, too. "No. You're amazing as– just you."

It was an honest statement, but something else was bothering Iris that she couldn't quite figure out. She sat silently for several moments, allowing her mind to make sense of her time with Anna. Eventually, another memory surfaced: the figures talking by the bed when she was first brought to Anna's house. The hair on her arms prickled as she realized who they were.

"It was you and your brother that day."

"What do you mean?" Anna said.

"After I fainted on the sidewalk, you brought me here. I heard you and your brother talking. You were planning to take my powers from me."

Anna's face paled. For the first time, her speech was broken. "I— No— I wasn't going to let him."

Iris frowned. It wasn't safe here. The desire to leave as soon as possible crept up her spine. She got up from the table and started to walk away. Anna followed her, speaking rapidly.

"That's why I made you leave so suddenly before *he* arrived. I decided against it. It wasn't right. He was furious with me. That's why he took my power and my father's power instead. Please believe me. I'm so sorry I brought you into this."

Iris stopped and turned back to Anna. She didn't know what to think anymore. "Was it a coincidence that you were the one that found me that day?"

Anna hesitated. "No."

Iris swallowed hard, a lump growing in her throat. "What's to stop you from taking my power from me right now?".

Anna looked taken aback. "I can't. It doesn't work that way."

"That didn't seem to stop your brother." Iris continued walking again. She needed to get out of here. Didn't Anna's father say her brother would be coming for her next?

"I promise. I couldn't take your power even if I wanted to." Anna reached toward Iris's arm. "I'm so sorry."

Iris pulled away. "I have to go home."

Anna's hand fell to her side. "Yes. Of course. John can take you."

Iris didn't want anything more to do with Anna or her household. She walked through the house and to the front door, hoping to still see the taxi idling. It was gone as expected after so much time. She reluctantly accepted the ride from John.

Once in the car, Iris realized she still didn't have her glasses. She must've dropped them in the garden when she ran out to look for Anna. Tears welled in her eyes as she began to laugh. She wondered if she should go back, but it didn't matter anymore. Now that she knew the truth. Her laughter faded. How could her parents have kept this from her? Maybe she should go back to taking her medication and pretend none of this ever happened. Even as she thought it, she knew she would never go back to how things were before. As crazy as it all seemed, she didn't want to give it up. She had never felt so alive. So power-ful. So free. Like Anna said, she had a gift.

John started the car. Iris eyed the back of his head. Did he know about Anna and her family? About Shifters? If what Anna said was true, he wasn't a Shifter himself. Iris didn't feel anything in her chest when she was near him. She decided not to ask. She doubted he would tell her anyway.

She looked over at Anna, who was standing by the front steps. A breeze had picked up, lifting damp tendrils of Anna's hair and holding them aloft. Even in her wet clothes, she held herself with such poise that it was a shame that there weren't any cameras at that moment to film her. Anna was wrong. She didn't need her power of allure to draw an audience. She had that power naturally.

The clouds were parting, and rays of the setting sun cast everything in a golden glow. Anna put up a hand in farewell, and Iris returned the gesture. They stayed that way for what seemed like several minutes, a moment frozen in time, until the car drove away. It was like the end of a movie where they knew they would never see each other again.

CHAPTER TWENTY-EIGHT

Representative Bai
Summer 2000

Representative Bai stood on the edge of the cliffs outside of downtown Yuras, watching the delivery of the box full of smooth gray stones. The half a dozen people who carried them, if they could still be called people, stood waiting for instructions, dripping from the rain. Their haggard, thin frames were deceptively frail, as they had easily hoisted the heavy box into the cart that was waiting for them.

"I almost feel sorry for them." The chairperson stood next to the cart. His black hair, wet from the rain, was matted over his forehead like a splayed-out spider.

"You should feel sorry for me," Representative Bai said, her teeth chattering from the cold. "They can't feel anything."

"Oh, I do."

Representative Bai glared at him. "Don't mock me."

"I would never." He smiled his suave smile at her.

Her heart fluttered for a split second before she squelched

it down, repulsed. It wouldn't work on her. At least for the most part. "How much longer? I've gotten you the amount you asked for. I even made the deadline even though I was down two helpers."

"We're getting close. Real close." He moved toward her and placed his hands on her shoulders.

He was much taller than her. The height difference caused rain to drip from his head onto her face. He brushed her cheek with the back of his fingers. Representative Bai's vision turned red. A single flame slipped through her lips. The chairperson's finger sizzled from the heat, and he snapped it back with a look of rage and pain. His face contorted, bulging with bones that formed and reformed, as his body attempted to transform in response to the assault. Eventually, he settled down and back into his human form. Representative Bai watched him with a look of satisfaction.

"Don't forget who's helping who," he said, holding his hurt finger in his hand. "I was there for you when no one else was."

A strange feeling washed over Representative Bai. A sudden bout of attraction and desire. It was how she used to feel toward him all the time, but it was just as quickly gone.

"I have enough problems right now. Meng Zhang is here to investigate. She's your vice chairperson. Can't you reign her in?"

The chairperson spread his hands. "The Council sent her. Not me. And it's too early. I don't want to draw attention before I'm ready. I'll meet you at your office in two days to plan our next move. Are you ready to be a senator? Or even the vice chairperson?"

Representative Bai smiled tightly and nodded. The chairperson turned and wheeled the cart back toward town over large branches along the way. Stones bounced precariously toward the edge of the overfilled cart. She winced. He needed to be careful. If any fell out, the whipping wind and crashing waves would have drowned out the gentle thuds in the pine needles.

Ugh, the nerve! Representative Bai thought, shaking off the feeling of his fingers grazing her face. She wished she didn't need his help anymore. That she could take the stones for herself. But he had thought of that too and must have cast some spell that didn't allow her to touch them. Every time she tried to reach for one, she wasn't able to. It was as if there was an invisible barrier.

The helpers shuffled back down the cliff ramp and into the tunnel. Representative Bai remained at the edge of the cliff, looking out at the ocean. Just a couple of days, he had said. And then she would finally get that promotion. A real smile spread across her face.

CHAPTER TWENTY-NINE

Iris

Summer 1955

IRIS RETURNED HOME and closed the door behind her. She leaned against it, closed her eyes, and sighed.

"Where have you been?"

The unexpected sound of her mother's voice jolted her eyes open. She jumped and swallowed hard. Could this day get any worse? She knew she would have to confront her parents at some point, but all she wanted to do right now was sleep. She only had the energy to state the obvious.

"You're home."

Without waiting for a response to her first question, her mother fired off another accusatory question. "Where are your glasses?"

Iris threw her hands to her face as if covering it would solve the problem. She tried to think of possible excuses she could give her mother, everything from losing the glasses to having them stolen to just having forgotten them at home. Nothing seemed plausible enough. Nothing would explain where she had been for so long. Her heart thumped loudly, and then she felt a sudden burst of defiance. She didn't need this after everything she had already been through today. She had been taking care of herself this whole time. Chores and studies in the home, cooking meals, walking to and from places by herself. She didn't need to be treated like a helpless child anymore. She straightened her posture and lifted her head.

"I don't need them anymore."

Her mother raised her eyebrows. Iris could see the whites of her eyes gleaming in the light. She felt a little tremor of fear but forged ahead.

"Ma Ma, I know."

Her mother shook her head as if she didn't understand.

"I stopped taking my medication." Iris let out a hysterical laugh as she said it. She spread her hands out to the sides. "See, I'm fine. I've been fine. For weeks."

Her mother's face became very serious.

"You will resume taking your medication at once." Her voice was calm, but the intensity of her eyes felt like they could burn a hole through the wall. Iris cowered ever so slightly.

"No," Iris said. "I won't. I'm fine."

"You are not fine. You are in danger. You are putting our whole family in danger. Go get your medicine. Right now."

Doubt crept into Iris's resolution. It couldn't be true. Her mother was overreacting. This was about control, not danger. Iris shook her head and stepped back, bumping into the front door. Tears began to gather in her lower lids. Her mother stood up and took a step forward.

Iris spoke through gritted teeth. "How could you hide this from me? All this time, I thought I was– sick."

Her mother took another step forward. Her steps seemed

slow and deliberate as if she did not want to startle her. Iris pressed her back to the door. She felt around with her hand until she detected the round, cold metal of the doorknob.

Her mother continued forward. "You need to take your medicine right now. This is dangerous."

"I want you to explain everything right now. Why have you been lying to me?" A tear slipped out of her eye, trailing down her cheek to the corner of her mouth.

"Take your medicine first, then I will explain."

"No. Explain now." Iris grasped the door knob.

Her mother took another step toward her. She was almost within reach. Iris pulled the door open and ran out before her mother could stop her.

"Come back!" her mother cried.

Iris raced down the stairs, turned the corner, and smacked right into her father. He grabbed her firmly by the shoulders.

"What's wrong?"

Iris sunk her head into his chest, tears flowing from her eyes.

"Ba Ba, I—" she said, then stopped when she realized he wasn't alone.

A tall, imposing man was beside him, dwarfing her father's modest height. He stood very straight, with an air of importance in the way he scanned his surroundings. His black hair gleamed under the apartment lights, framing youthful, chiseled features. By the way he held himself, he seemed like a man of experience, maybe in his thirties. Iris sucked in a breath, not just because he was very attractive but because her chest was abruptly filled with the warmth and light that she had come to know around Anna. He was a Shifter.

"Iris," her father said. "This is Mr. Davis, our community representative."

"Hello, Iris," Mr. Davis said.

"Let's go back upstairs," her father said. "He has some exciting news."

Iris returned to the apartment where her mother sat at the dining table. Her mother looked like she would reproach her, but her expression changed when she saw her father and Mr. Davis enter shortly after.

"Mr. Davis," her mother said. She stood up with a large smile and bowed her head. "Welcome."

"Thank you, Mrs.—" he began, but Iris cut him off.

"What is this about?"

"Iris! Watch your manners," her father said. "Sit down."

Iris joined her mother at the dining table, sulking. Her father and Mr. Davis sat across from them. Mr. Davis looked at her and gave her a little smile and nod. Iris's heart fluttered from his attention, but she stared back without smiling. For some reason, she felt drawn to Davis, maybe because he was a Shifter like herself. At the same time she didn't trust him. She didn't trust any of them. They all knew this whole time and kept it from her.

"You're a Shifter," Iris said.

Her father shot a wide-eyed glance at her mother, who shook her head.

Mr. Davis raised his eyebrows. "So you *are* aware."

"Iris stopped her medicine several days ago," her mother said, drumming her fingers on the table. "She just informed me."

"I see," Mr. Davis said, unperturbed.

Her father's disapproving stare bore into her.

Iris tried to ignore him. "Can someone tell me what's going on?"

"We were trying to give you a good life," her mother said. "Keep you safe."

"By drugging me?" Iris said.

Her father slapped his palm on the table. Iris jumped. She looked down at her lap, avoiding his gaze.

"We kept you from sticking out," he said. "From becoming a target. You were doing fine. Everything you achieved was on your own merit."

"I didn't have my sight," Iris mumbled, still looking at her lap. "And for years, I missed lunch with my friends.

"But you were safe," her father said.

"Iris," her mother said with a heavy sigh. "I didn't lose my hand in a work accident."

Iris looked up at her mother. "What do you mean?"

"When we first moved here from China, Shifter communities were still out in the open. Ba Ba and I lived in one such community for many years before you were born. We were happy there." She exchanged a glance with her father, and her father winced as if bracing for something painful. "There were some Statics, those without powers, that were threatened by us. They attacked one night while we were asleep and…" She raised her left arm, showing her missing hand, but didn't continue speaking.

Mr. Davis had raised his eyebrows while listening to her mother speak. Her mother once again exchanged a glance with her father. Iris was starting to get the feeling that she wasn't hearing the whole truth.

Her father jumped in. "After that, we lived on the run for years and years, never knowing who we could trust, which Statics were friendly, or if a rogue Shifter would give us away to the Statics for personal gain. Then, one day, the Shifter council members found a way to combine their powers and create a special mark. They needed volunteers to test the mark." He pulled up his left sleeve to show his scar, which Iris had thought was from a vaccine. "When this mark is placed on a Shifter's left shoulder, all his powers cease. In all aspects, he would be a Static from then on. No other Shifter could identify him unless she was looking for the mark. Of course, your mother and I seized this opportunity, and we have lived in peace ever since."

Iris felt like her head was going to explode. The questions burbled out nonstop. "You gave up your powers? People were hunting you? That can't still be happening, can it? If Shifters live out in the open, how come I've never heard of one?" She stopped to take several breaths. Things were not adding up. Then she thought of another question. "So, when exactly did you lose your hand? And when did you get your– marks?"

"I lost my hand in 1692," her mother said. "And we got our marks in 1935 when I was pregnant with you."

Iris's jaw dropped. Did her mother misspeak? "Uh, did you mean 1892…"

But her mother was only in her mid-forties now, so that wouldn't add up either.

Mr. Davis cleared his throat. "Allow me to explain some things. Shifters don't age as quickly as Statics do, at least after a certain point. In their first thirty-some years, they age at the same rate as Statics, give or take a couple of years. We think this corresponds to when the brain fully develops. After that point, the aging rate for Shifters slows down tremendously."

Iris counted her fingers. "Wait, so are you telling me you're around 300 years old?" She looked back and forth between her parents.

Her parents took a deep breath and answered in unison. "Yes."

"How old are you?" Iris said to Mr. Davis.

"I'm actually just thirty-three."

"Can you live forever?"

Mr. Davis chuckled. "Shifters are not immortal. We can be hurt and killed, so it is not known exactly how old the oldest Shifter is or was. But a good estimate is a couple of millennia."

"Millennia!" Iris said. "So what happens if you get a mark?"

"In Static years, we looked around thirty when we got the marks," her mother said. "Once we got the marks, we began to age like Statics."

Iris rubbed her temples. Her mind was spinning.

"We hoped," her father said, "that we had gotten the marks in time to prevent you from becoming a Shifter. But as you now know, that wasn't the case."

"We just wanted to keep you safe," her mother said. "We didn't want you to fear being hunted like we were."

"So, why is Mr. Davis here?" Iris said. "Are you going to put a mark on me too? Why didn't you just put one on me when I was a child?"

"There had been some political changes in the Shifter Council after your parents got their marks," Mr. Davis said. "From then until now, marks were kept only for delinquent Shifters for several years. Last week, the Council of Shifters passed a remarkable new anti-integration policy between Shifters and Statics due to misunderstandings that kept occurring. With the new law, Shifters that retain their powers may no longer integrate with Statics. You have the option. You can choose to have the mark and continue life as you know it, or keep your powers and attend the boarding school mandatory for all burgeoning Shifters. There you will learn how to control your powers and how to live life in the Shifter society."

"Will I be hunted if I keep my powers?" Iris said. "Like my parents were?"

"Things are much safer these days," Mr. Davis said. "For one, as you noted, the existence of Shifters is kept secret nowadays. Most Statics do not know we exist. And education at the boarding school will train you in the expertise of your primary and secondary powers, which is a protection when used wisely."

"Primary? Secondary?" Iris said.

"A Shifter's primary power is the ability to transform into another creature," Mr. Davis said. "The secondary power is often related to the primary. Some examples are the ability to manipulate water or fire or the ability to fly."

Mr. Davis took something from his pocket and handed it to Iris.

Iris looked at the object in her hand. "It's a rock." She was confused and unimpressed.

Davis took the rock back and, holding it between the fingers of both hands, made a motion as if to pull it apart. The rock stretched between his fingers, bending and curving with Davis's hand movements until it formed a circle. He handed it back to Iris.

Iris's mouth gaped. "That's amazing."

Mr. Davis smiled at her. Iris's heart fluttered, and she averted her eyes from his handsome face before she blushed.

"Do you know what your secondary power is?" he asked.

Iris thought for a few moments. She remembered the fire that spewed forth from her mouth. "It must be fire—"

"Finder," her mother said at the same time. "That's what she exhibited when her powers started to manifest five years ago."

They looked at each other, confused.

"Interesting," Mr. Davis said. "Fire and finder. It is not unheard of to have more than one secondary power, but it is unusual. And also admirable. I used to know someone with two secondary powers. Just like him, you will be poised to rise in the

Shifter ranks if you choose to. If you choose to enter the boarding school, your powers will be recorded in our records. These records are not public. They are for our government to maintain order if foul play is suspected. So you are free to divulge your powers if and when you choose."

Iris thought for a while. She realized now what her visions were and why she was able to find her glasses and Anna's home. She weighed her options some more.

"Will I be able to see my parents?" Iris said.

"Yes," Mr. Davis said. "There are special rules for marked Shifters in good standing, especially when they are the family members of current Shifters. There are special days and times they may visit the boarding school, and when you graduate, you can visit them."

"Iris. No!" her mother pleaded. "You can't seriously be considering this. Please. Take the mark and live a normal and simple life with us, your family."

"How long do I have to make my decision?" Iris asked.

"Until the end of the week," Mr. Davis said.

"And what happens if I don't take the mark and I don't go to the boarding school?"

"Then the choice will be made for you. Forcibly."

"Iris, please. Just take the mark," her mother said.

Both her parents' eyes were large and shiny, imploring her. Iris closed her eyes and furrowed her brow.

"I will be back in a week," Mr. Davis said. "You can think about it until then."

Iris was sick of all the lies. She was sick of having to hide. She opened her eyes. "I don't need that long. I've made my decision. I want to go to boarding school."

Her mother gasped. Her father frowned and bowed his head.

"Iris, please," her mother whimpered.

Iris swallowed, trying to keep her emotions down. She kept her eyes on Mr. Davis. "When do we leave?"

"If you are sure of your decision, I can take you to the local representative office to register, and then we will head to the boarding school in the morning."

"I'm sure."

CHAPTER THIRTY

Meng

Summer 2000

THE SUMMER RAIN danced on the brick sidewalk as Meng Zhang walked through Downtown Yuras. She pulled her black hooded cloak over her hair to prevent the cold wind from sending droplets into her face. She had spent the day trying to find out more about the fire before the trail went cold. So far, there weren't any leads, and no indication that anyone had tried to attack Nivi again. Without anything else to go on, Meng booked a room at the Bluefish Inn, a modest local establishment, hoping that some time spent in town would lead to more information. She kept her camouflage pendant off because she needed to be able to interact with the local Statics, in case they had any information.

As she turned into an alley that led to her lodging, the smell of newly rehydrated fish residue filled the air. Meng wrinkled her nose. She should have thought twice before booking a room next to a fish market where the cleaning and gutting of fish left daily drippings. Despite the smell, the little alleyway was quite quaint. Cobblestones glistened in the rain, collecting scattered pools in their depressions. The backs of brick buildings flanked each side of the alley, each with its own wooden signage hanging from a horizontal metal post. Black lamp posts cast golden halos through the misty air. It reminded her of some of the medieval towns in England.

She continued on, and soon the smell of fish was replaced by that of beer and urine. She was surprised to find that she preferred the former. The smell emanated from a bar to the right, where a couple of patrons swayed outside the back door, engaged in a lively conversation. They didn't seem to mind the drizzle. They sipped beer and leaned against the wet bricks of the bar's wall. Both men had obviously overindulged. The burly one in a flannel shirt stared down with a melancholy look, while the skinny one in a plastic poncho, oblivious to his friend's mood, laughed a little too heartily and patted him with a little too much force between gulps and burps.

Thinking nothing of them at first, Meng picked up her pace, her boots sending water leaping in all directions. The glint of something on the burly man caused her to slow back down. Around his thick pale neck, ruddy from the alcohol, he wore a polished, gray stone, a couple of centimeters in diameter, or a little less than an inch, depending on which system one used. It appeared to have some wire wrapped around it and was hung on a simple string. The stone sparked something in Meng's memory, which caused her to reluctantly approach the two drunk men just as the skinny one excused himself to go "take a leak."

"Excuse me, sir," Meng said to the burly man, who was now alone with his beer. "I noticed you have quite a unique pendant there. May I inquire as to how you obtained it?"

The man looked at her with unfocused eyes. Once his eyes settled on her face, he stood up a little straighter and puffed out his chest.

"Hey," he slurred, putting his beer aside and linking his thumbs into his belt. "You like my necklace?" He chuckled to himself.

Meng gave a polite smile and tried again. "Yes, it's very nice. How did you come by it?"

"Made it, wire and string." He wiped his mouth with his hand, then wiped it down his flannel shirt.

"I see that." Meng controlled her annoyance with slow breaths. "But how about that stone?"

"Found it."

"Where?"

"On the ground."

Meng gritted her teeth through her smile. "So you're telling me you were walking along and just happened to find this stone on the ground?"

He waved the pendant around and looked off to the side. "Must've fallen off something."

"So, you stole it?"

At this point, the man's friend returned, stumbling into place next to him, not seeming to notice Meng right away.

"No," the man burly said. "Found it, square 'n fair."

"I believe you mean fair and– oh, whatever. *Where* did you *find* it?"

"Cliff Trail. Monster people… out there."

The skinny man elbowed him. "Not supposed to talk about– that."

Monster people. So, these two were in on the local conspiracy theories. Little did they know they were talking to one now. If Meng could, she'd use oblivion tincture to wipe these silly thoughts from all the locals, but the Council wouldn't approve of that. It was an irresponsible abuse of power, they said. They had principles. Oblivion tincture was used only in cases of known contact with a Shifter or observation of Shifter powers.

"Did you *find* one, too?" Meng asked the skinny man.

The skinny man's smile faded, and he narrowed his eyes. "Why do you care so much anyway? Who are you?"

Meng thought fast and tried to sound as nonchalant as possible. "I was just admiring this unique stone. It's my mother's birthday coming up, and I was hoping to get something like it for her." She smiled sweetly at the skinny man. "Can you point me in the direction of this Cliff Trail?"

The skinny man relaxed and returned the smile. "Oh, in that case, it's just down the street. Can't miss it." He pointed at a street that led into a neighborhood.

Meng looked down the street, then turned back to the men. "May I see it?" She pointed at the pendant.

"Sure." The burly man took a step toward her, smelling of beer and onions, a half smile on his lips.

"Hey, look at that!" the skinny man laughed. "I haven't seen Frank smile in ages!"

Meng ignored them as she focused on the stone, taking it in her hand. As she touched it, she felt a strange tug, as if something within the stone were calling to her, or not exactly her, but her power. Out of curiosity, she allowed the pull to contact her powers for the briefest instant, and the interior swirled with a frosty blue. She could feel her eyes lighting up with the transfer of her power into the stone and immediately let go, stopping the transfer. Fortunately, she was fast enough that the amount she lost was barely noticeable.

The burly man, whose name was apparently Frank, opened his eyes wide. "Whoa. Your eyes. How did you…?"

Meng closed her fingers over the pendant. *How did he get one of these? This doesn't belong in the hands of a Static.* She believed she knew what the stone was, but it had been a very long time since she last saw one. *Ling would know. I will need to show it to her.*

"Pardon me," she said with a sudden jerk, snapping the string off Frank's neck. "I'll be taking this now."

"Ouch. Hey," Frank said.

Meng took off in a brisk walk. The skinny man laughed behind her, apparently finding it funny that Meng had stolen his friend's necklace. Frank didn't sound amused. In fact, his tone became menacing.

"She's one of *them*."

"Hey, where are you going?" she heard the skinny man say.

"After her," Frank replied.

Meng hurried down the alley toward the neighborhood street that led to the Cliff Trail. Footsteps followed her. She had thought the inebriation would slow him down, but he was gaining on her. Dodging maple trees on the sidewalk, she hurried past the darkened neighborhood houses and toward the forest beyond. Her heart raced. It was irresponsible of her to have left her camouflage pendant in her room. If she had it now, it would have solved this little conflict. She mistakenly thought she didn't need it in a safe, small town. And she had utilized all the oblivion tincture authorized by the Shifter Council on the officers, so that wasn't an option.

As soon as she hit the treeline, she broke into a run. Frank's pace also increased. The trail branched. She followed it to the right. Wrong turn. An old rock wall covered in moss and vines blocked her way. Her boots skidded to a stop in the muddy pine needles. Frank arrived shortly after, breathless.

"Hey," Frank said. He was little more than a silhouette in the forest, but she imagined a grimace on his face. "You remember a woman named Fatima?"

"I'm sorry. I don't know what you're talking about."

Frank continued as if she hadn't spoken. "About this tall." He raised his hand to his shoulder. "Dark brown, curly hair. Brown skin. Large, beautiful eyes. The most perfect woman." His voice cracked with the last phrase. He took a couple of steps toward her.

Meng stepped back into the wall. *He's drunk. He doesn't know what he's saying. It would be too easy to take care of him.* Her eyes burned with her internal power, and she knew they were starting to glow in the darkness. She wouldn't be able to explain it to the Council, though, and would risk grave consequences. Not to mention complicating the matters she was already investigating. The burn faded from her eyes for a moment as she reasoned with herself, but then the man moved toward her.

"Now, sir, I don't want any trouble." Her eyes lit up the man's face and the nearby trees like sunrays through blue ice.

Frank gasped and jumped back. "I knew it. Everyone thought I was crazy, but… why'd you do it? Why?" Tears formed in his eyes, reflecting in the blue light.

This wasn't good. Meng would have to expose more of her powers than she already had. Perhaps no one would believe an intoxicated Frank, if he even remembered anything in the morning. It seemed he already suspected the existence of Shifters, or what this area called monster people, so maybe people were used to his ramblings and wouldn't think anything of another story. She doubted the Council would authorize more oblivion tincture for a man who probably wasn't taken seriously in town.

He approached her warily. She looked side to side. There was no way out. Her back was against the wall, and there were overgrown bushes and brambles to either side of the path. Frank easily blocked the path back to town with his body. The only way was up.

Frank lunged forward.

Before Meng could react, there was a rustle like an animal had been startled, and a flash of white came from between the trees. The animal leaped over the bushes, knocked into Frank, and disappeared into the brush. Meng flattened herself against the wall and was left unscathed. Frank collapsed, cursing and slipping in the mud. He tried to get up but slipped and fell again. Meng took advantage of the distraction to run around the fallen man and back down the path into the darkness. Her cloak should've blended in with the shadows, making her nearly invisible. She hid behind a tree and listened for Frank's departure.

"Damn deer," Frank said.

His footsteps went back and forth a few times before they headed back down the path that led out of the forest. All the while, he muttered to himself, swearing revenge. Meng waited in the shadows, processing what she had seen. Could it really be her? Frank thought it was a deer. He hadn't seen what she had: the pure white fur tipped in black at the tail and ears and the splendid, silver horn that arched back from the creature's forehead.

CHAPTER THIRTY-ONE

Davis

Summer 1955

DAVIS AND IRIS got out of the taxi in the Sierra Nevada Lodge parking lot in Sequoia National Park. He led her around the back of the wood-faced lodge and down a trail through the forest of pines and giant Sequoias. Iris stared up with an open mouth at the redwood giants. It was obvious she had never seen anything like them. Of course, she wouldn't have, coming from a lowly, laundromat-owning family. She would've spent all her free time working in her family's business. But now she had the chance to actually become something special with her multiple powers.

Having two secondary powers probably helped his father to achieve his position and influence as well. With all his and Anna's powers, Davis was also primed for greatness. He just had to figure out a way to keep his powers or find more transfer stones. If only Davis had been more patient, he could've used a transfer stone on Iris. How could he have been so stupid?

So impatient? So weak. But he couldn't have known. And his powers had been fading rapidly. Now, he needed to figure out how Iris could use her finder powers to help him find more transfer stones without her knowing. He mulled over the best way to broach the subject as they walked.

Wooden posts with embedded green camouflage stones lined the path and the perimeter of the school. They approached a dense line of sequoias woven together with natural fiber rope and intricate knots so that they formed a fence of about ten feet tall. The trail led through the burnt-out center of one of the sequoias. As they walked through the sequoia, Iris made the first noise she had made since leaving her home. An awe-filled gasp.

The wall of sequoias opened up into a sunny, grassy glade. It took around ten minutes to jog the perimeter of the glade. The school was only fifteen years old, so Davis hadn't attended the school, but he had sometimes joined in on morning exercises when he dropped off new students. An imposing building made of large, monolithic stones stood in the middle of the glade. The stones were locally sourced and beautifully placed to mimic the naturally occurring monoliths in the forest.

"You should see this place in the Spring," Davis said, exuding the allure that was previously his sister's power. "The glade is filled with flowers. Poppies, Wild Hyacinth, tickseed. Oranges, purples, yellows. It's beautiful."

Iris only nodded. Her eyes rounded when she looked at Davis, so he knew his power was working, but she maintained the stoic expression she had worn the entire car ride. It must've taken a great deal of will to fight against his allure. He didn't blame her for not trusting him. She had been lied to her whole life, so gaining her trust would take time. Interestingly, Mrs. Bai had continued to lie to Iris last night. She hadn't divulged her involvement in a gang against Davis's father or how she really lost her hand. Davis knew why Mrs. Bai had chosen the date of 1692. It was a historically known time of persecution for Shifters, or witches as they were called then. If Iris researched it, she wouldn't question her mother's account.

They had left Los Angeles at eight that morning, so it was now almost noon. Sure enough, the bell in the building's tower began to gong. Dozens of teenagers streamed out of the building. Some sat on benches to eat in the shade of a pine tree. Some sat in the grass in the sun. Others ran around the back of the building, shifting into all sorts of creatures, flying, galloping, slithering. This gave Davis an idea.

"When you enter the school, they will want you to demonstrate your powers to verify them before they record them. So we should practice now before I drop you off. Let's start with your Shifter form."

Iris gazed at Davis, expressionless except for a tenseness in her jaw and a slight tremor in her hand. Davis realized that not only was Iris distrustful, she was nervous. Davis tried to think back to his first experiences in Shifter society. Was he that weak-minded? At first, Davis was worried Iris would refuse or question his directives, but then she took on a look of concentration and grew and elongated until she became a giant white snake. Davis was impressed. Sparkling white scales, fangs glinting in the sunlight.

"Very good," Davis said as if he were used to testing students. "Now, let's see your fire. Make sure to aim away from anything flammable."

Iris turned her serpentine head back and forth, then lifted it up to the sky and blew forth a stream of fire into the open air.

Davis nodded in approval. "OK. Now transform back to human form, and we'll practice your other secondary power."

Iris shrank down in height and length until she resumed her

human form. Long black hair in two braids. Plain white t-shirt and cropped blue pants. She looked at him, still without smiling, but her face was flushed as if she were exhilarated.

Davis thought about his next directive. Should he present one of the defunct transfer stones and simply ask her to find more of them? No, too dangerous. She could easily tell other students or teachers what he had asked her to do, and that could bring suspicion upon him, even if she didn't know the name of the stone. He needed more information about transfer stones without making her aware that that was what he wanted.

"Before we practice your last power, can you tell me how your finder power works?"

Iris looked at him and then looked at the ground. Her voice was quieter and less defiant than it had been last night. "I think about something I want to find, and then I feel a pull toward a direction."

This was more problematic. If Davis asked Iris to find transfer stones and they were halfway around the world, they couldn't just up and go there. He had to think of something close by that could give him more information. Something that could get him close enough to transfer stones that if he needed to use Iris's powers in the future, they would be within walking or driving distance already. In the meantime, he would try to find them himself, learn more about Jackson Dawan, and work on gaining Iris's trust. He wasn't in the biggest hurry. He judged he had at least a few decades of power before he needed to replenish it, more if he used the powers more sparingly, but he still had to be careful to use that time wisely.

The boarding school had a massive library. Davis had perused it in the past but hadn't found anything of use. Maybe more books had been brought in since he last checked. Or maybe he hadn't known where to look. All he could do was try. If this was a fruitless effort, he would just have to try again later.

"Let's get you registered first. Then I'll give you a tour of the school, and we'll practice your finder power during the tour."

They walked up to the school and entered through two large wooden doors. Inside, light streamed in from all angles through glass-filled crevices between the monoliths of the atrium. Lush ferns bordered a wooden staircase and hung over the sides of the second-floor balustrade. Doors and hallways lined the edges of the atrium on the first and second floors. Davis led Iris to a room to the left where a thin man with a scraggly beard sat behind a desk.

"Hi Bernard," Davis said, shaking the man's hand. We have a new student.

Bernard smiled at Iris, his eyes large behind thick glasses.

"Nice to meet you, Iris. I'll need all your information. Then I'll get you registered, and we'll get you a class schedule and ID card."

Once the registration was complete, Davis and Iris went to a room next door where Iris received an allocation of school uniforms. T-shirts, sweatshirts, shorts, and pants, all forest green in alignment with the school's desire to harmonize with the surrounding nature.

Davis showed Iris the cafeteria on the first floor, where some students were finishing up their lunch. They walked by all the classrooms, which were all on the first floor as well. Down a hallway to the right of the atrium, Davis showed Iris the indoor pool and gym, and then he walked her into another high-ceiling room with rows and rows of books.

"Here we are at the library," Davis said.

Iris turned around, looking up at the stacks of books. Her

expression was softening more and more, being replaced with a look of wonder and excitement.

Davis's heart raced in anticipation. Would this work? "Let's practice your other secondary power now. Can you find me a book about the discipline of combining Shifter powers into stones?"

Iris gave him a questioning look, then closed her eyes. She opened her eyes, her face back to an expressionless mask. It must not have worked. There was nothing here. But then Iris raised a hand and pointed.

"Over here."

Davis followed Iris down the rows of books to the back of the room. She stopped in front of a rock that was slightly taller and wider than him and placed a hand against it.

"It's behind here," she said, patting the wall.

Davis tried to hide his surprise. "Very good. You're ready to join the other students now."

He led her back to the main atrium and up the stairs to a second-floor hallway where the bedrooms were. He waited outside the room while Iris changed into the school clothing, then took her downstairs to her first class of the afternoon. Pre-Calculus.

"They'll give you a textbook in each class you go to," Davis said as they stood in front of the classroom door, "and they'll provide you with notebooks and pencils as well. You'll do great..."

Iris went into the classroom before Davis finished his last word. She was going to be difficult to win over, but he had time. And now, thanks to her, he might have more information.

The school bells clanged to signal the end of lunch. Davis waited a moment while students returned and filled the classrooms. Once everyone was seated and quiet and classes had begun, he quickly made his way back to the library.

The afternoon light shone brightly overhead, scattered into prismatic rays between crisscrossed monoliths and wooden beams. Leather-bound volumes filled the air with their earthy aromas. Davis inhaled deeply, almost trembling with anticipation. He made his way down the center aisle toward the stone that Iris had indicated at the back, most likely a hidden door. The stone was the same gray granite as the rest of the building, wedged between wood studs and more stone. Davis ran his fingers around the edges. He pushed on it. Pulled at the edges. Looked for a secret button or latch or handle. There was nothing. It was most likely a magically sealed door.

It was OK. It was all coming together. He hadn't been too hasty after all. This was how it was meant to be. He was meant to take his father's and sister's powers instead of Iris's. His sister's allure would help him win friends in Shifter politics and eventually win over Iris as well. Iris would continue to assist in his search for transfer stones. And his father's stonemasonry would help him now. Placing a finger on the rock, he tested his ability to melt away and re-form the rock, making sure he would leave no trace of his coming and going. Then, he moved his fist through the stone until he encountered space. He peered through the hole and saw a bookcase with large tomes facing him, about two arm-lengths away.

Davis opened up a hole in the rock wide enough to climb into the space in front of the bookcase. He summoned a small ball of fire in his left hand to illuminate the book titles, again praising himself for taking his father's powers. There were maybe fifty books behind this wall. He wondered who had put them there and how many people knew of their existence. Running his right hand over the embossed gold lettering on each book spine, he read the titles of the top row under his breath.

The Anatomical Exercises of Dr. Henry George Fletcher
A Collection of Preserved Rarities
The Partitions of Sciences of Shapeshifter Anatomy

None of these sounded like what he was looking for, but he gingerly flipped through a few books to make sure. He had to place the books on the ground so that he could use his right hand to turn the pages while keeping his fiery left hand close enough to see but far enough away to prevent any unintentional singeing. The books seemed to document gruesome experiments performed on Shifters and potential magical and herbal uses of various Shifter body parts. Interesting, but not his cup of tea. Maybe his father would've enjoyed some of these techniques or at least directed his henchman to perform them. He skimmed through the remaining titles on the top row and moved on to the next row.

Alchemy of Gasses
Alchemy of Liquids
Alchemy of Solids

This seemed more promising. He took the third book out and spent some time perusing it. There was a lot of documentation of combinations of various Shifter powers and solid substances: stones, glass, metal, wood. It seemed very complex, and even if Davis found the recorded formulation for creating transfer stones, he doubted he'd be able to execute it. The sheer number of powers required at a particular location, a particular time of year, particular weather, particular star alignment, particular words to be spoken, even what insects might be present. His hopes fell. This must be the information Iris had led him to, but this wouldn't get him any closer to finding or creating more transfer stones. He kept the *Alchemy of Solids* out as he skimmed through the remaining titles to make sure there wasn't something else. There wasn't.

Davis sighed and turned back to *The Alchemy of Solids*. He may as well find out if there was a recipe for transfer stones. Even if he couldn't replicate it, maybe it would tell him something. He turned page after page of the enormous tome. The old handwritten script began to blur together. He closed his eyes for a moment to reset his vision.

A sudden loud clang of the school bells caused him to jump, and he instinctively extinguished the ball of fire in his hand. Cocking an ear, he listened to the students heading to their next classes. It didn't sound like anyone was approaching the library. He peered out from the hole in the wall, and, not seeing anyone, reignited his fire and continued his search through the tome. He didn't have much time. There was another hour of classes before school would be done for the day and students may come into the library to study. He thought about taking the book but didn't know who else had access to this hidden room or what kind of alarms might be set off if this book was found missing. Best to leave the book where it was. If he didn't finish today, he'd have to come back another day, and he worried how much of his stonemasonry powers he'd use up in this search.

Finally, two-thirds of the way through the book, he came across what he had been looking for: *Transference*. As all the other recipes, this one was elaborate, spanning over a dozen pages of tiny script and hand-drawn diagrams. Davis could not make any sense of it. He was turning the last page of the entry, ready to give up, when the page came out in his hand. An inserted page, not part of the original binding, folded in half to fit the dimensions of the rest of the book. A handwritten journal entry.

In the sole attempt in which the success of transference imbuement was achieved, it was not easy to determine by what rule of magic would produce the desired result. Pertaining to the arts to which alchemy of solids relate, the previous acts upon a singular stone were uneventful, and since furthering of the imbuement could not be generally derived from past observation, the necessity of novel techniques were to be implemented. In the course of a series of trials, the discovery that transference must be created as a whole instead of a singular furthermore led to the Northern Coasts of California, a small and little known town by the name of Yuras.

Yuras! It could not be a coincidence that Jackson Dawan had his family home in Yuras. He must know of the transfer stones there. He probably used them for his own benefit.

With excitement and unease at his discovery, Davis folded the paper and inserted it back into the tome. On second thought, he removed it and held it up to the fire in his hand. No one else needed to know the location of the transfer stones. Once the paper had burned to ash, he replaced the book and extinguished his fire. He climbed out of the hidden book room and re-formed the stone wall. Just in time. The school bell rang to end classes for the day. He made his way back to the front and entered the school administrator's office. It would take some time, but he had to befriend Iris, get her to trust him so that she would help him find the stones without question.

"I'll be sticking around a while longer," Davis announced to Bernard. "You know how I love to help new students get situated."

CHAPTER THIRTY-TWO

Iris

Summer 1990

IRIS STOOD BEFORE her parents' home, holding her overnight bag, and readied herself for the criticism that was sure to come. When she had left her parents' home for the Shifter boarding school over thirty years ago, she wasn't sure if her parents would want to see her again. After all their lies, she wasn't sure if she'd want to see them again either. But they came to all their allowed visits at the boarding school, and their relationship continued throughout the years.

Light streaked through the tall coastal redwoods surrounding the quaint cabin in the peninsula-based town of Yuras, California, an hour's drive from the Oregon border. As they got older, her parents had wanted to escape the traffic and crowds in Los Angeles. Iris had relocated to San Francisco twenty years prior to pursue her political aspirations and couldn't help them as frequently in Los Angeles anymore. In passing, Iris had mentioned this to Vice Chairperson Davis, and he suggested her parents move to Yuras.

Fifteen years after she'd moved to San Francisco, her parents retired and moved to Yuras. Yuras had everything her parents wanted; Northern California coastline, nature, quiet, small-town charm. It wasn't any closer to San Francisco than Los Angeles, but the fact that it was the primary residence of Chairperson Dawan and his family when he wasn't in San Francisco was a bonus. Having a reason to be within proximity to the chairperson's family would only help her political ambitions.

Pine needles crunched under her feet as she walked up the paved driveway and knocked on the door. The door opened. Iris found herself averting her eyes from the wrinkles and gray hair of her mother. Seeing her parents age as quickly as they were was still strange.

Her mother looked around with a confused look and began to close the door.

"Oh, I always forget," Iris said. She lifted the quarter-sized green pendant and chain over her head and tucked it into her pocket.

As soon as the pendant was off, her mother jumped at what must've looked like Iris's sudden appearance out of thin air. Then, she quickly regained her composure. "Must you always startle me like that? At least you finally came to visit. It's been so long that I thought our only daughter had forgotten about us. And with your father's... you know. Remember not to mention it to him."

"Hi, Ma Ma. It's good to see you too." Iris walked into the house, closed the door, and removed her shoes. She hung her jacket by the door, set her bag down, and followed her mother into the recessed living room. In the corner, a fire crackled in a wood-burning stove. Iris took a seat on the orange fabric sofa.

"Where is Ba Ba?" Iris said.

"In the bedroom. Resting."

"Why can't I speak to him about his health? If it's serious, he should know."

"No, no. There is no point worrying him." Her mother walked into the kitchen and spoke to Iris through the cutout in the kitchen wall. "Do you want some tea?"

"Sure." Iris stared out at the darkening forest, listening to the clinking of cups from the kitchen.

Her mother brought her a cup of hot green tea and set another cup on the coffee table for herself. She put another log into the wood-burning stove and joined Iris on the couch. They sipped their tea in silence as the sun set. Light from the fire danced across their faces. Her mother stood up and turned on the living room light. She looked down at Iris's overnight bag.

"Such a small bag for your visit."

"I can't stay long. I have to be back for the election results."

Her mother sat back down on the couch and took a sip of her tea. "Hmph."

"I think I have a pretty good chance this time."

Her mother finished her tea and took the empty cup to the kitchen to wash. Iris repeated herself louder over the sound of the water.

"I think I have a pretty good chance this time."

Her mother turned off the water. "Why do you need to keep running for office and bring attention to yourself? Just live life and blend in."

"You were the one who taught me to have ambition."

"Yes, to become something like a doctor. Not a politician in Shifter society. It's too dangerous."

"Ma Ma, it's been over two decades since I graduated from the Shifter Academy. Nothing has happened to me."

Her mother returned to the couch. "I need to tell you something."

"OK." Iris took a sip of tea to hide her discomfort. Her mother was being weird.

"I didn't tell you the truth about how I lost my hand. I lost it because I was involved in Shifter politics."

Iris choked. Another lie. Insecurities from her childhood rose to the surface. How could she trust that her mother was telling her the truth now? How could she trust anyone? More reason to only trust herself and stick to her plans.

Her mother continued. "When you are in politics, you get involved with some bad people. Some of them will do things to intimidate you."

"I– don't know what to say."

"Say you'll drop out of this election."

Something hardened within Iris. Maybe her mother had failed in her political aspirations. Maybe she suffered for it. But Iris was different. She was stronger. She wouldn't quit what she had worked so hard for.

Her voice took on a rigid tone. "I'm sorry that happened to you, but I can assure you I am not getting involved with people like that. I don't know what you got yourself involved in, and I don't want to know."

"Please. Reconsider. I also thought I knew what I was doing before Randall sent his goons to *punish* me for veering away from his political ambitions."

Randall. For some reason, that name rang a bell. It was probably nothing. "I'm still going to run. I want more in life. I want to be respected. I want to make a difference."

"What kind of difference?"

"For you. For us. So we don't have to live so separately like this. I can make sure things stay safe for you. So you don't have to grow old and sick."

"This is the life we chose. We are happy. If you worry about our health, you could have been a doctor."

Iris rolled her eyes. "You know that wouldn't have made a difference in your longevity."

Her mother sighed and shook her head. She returned to the kitchen, turning the water back on to continue washing the dishes. Frustrated, Iris got up and left the living room. She walked down the short hall to her parent's bedroom and peeked in. A fit of hacking came from within. Her father was awake, sitting up in bed.

"Ba Ba?" Iris said softly.

Her father looked up and waved to her. "Come in. I just woke up." He broke into another fit of coughs.

"How are you…?" She trailed off, mindful of what her mother said. She didn't want to upset him.

With shaky, spotted hands, he took a sip of water from a glass on the nightstand. He looked even older than her mother. His hair was almost completely white. And he was thin. Gone was the round tummy she knew from her youth. Her heart ached to see him so frail.

"I'm fine. I'm fine," her father said after clearing his throat.

Iris sat down on the side of the bed. She tried to relax her furrowed forehead and managed to smile. "So, what's new?"

"Iris, you don't have to pretend. I know."

She began to raise her eyebrows in feigned ignorance.

Her father put up a hand. "I know about the cancer." He lifted a handkerchief to his mouth and coughed into it again. "The doctor says I don't have much time."

"Oh, Ba Ba." Iris took his hand in hers. "Ma Ma didn't tell me it was that bad."

"I don't know if she let herself fully absorb the facts. She's tough, but she will need the support of her daughter."

Iris held back tears. "You'll be alright, Ba Ba. Things will be changing soon. The election results are next week. If I win, I'll change things. I'll make it so we can heal you."

Her father waved a hand. "I am at peace with my path. Just know that we've only ever wanted the best for you and to keep you safe. Try not to hold that against us. Against Ma Ma."

"You'll be alright. I know you will."

He pointed to a small, wooden box on the nightstand. "That's for you. It was your mother's, but she hasn't worn it since she lost her hand."

Iris picked up the nondescript box and opened it. Inside was a simple gold bracelet. She didn't know what to say. Her parents were never sentimental or the gift-giving type. She wanted to ask about its history, but this didn't seem like the right time. When she looked up at her father, his eyes were closed.

"I am tired. I need rest now."

Iris put the box into her pants pocket and tucked her father in. She returned to the living room and put on her jacket and shoes.

"Where are you going?" her mother said from the kitchen.

"For a quick walk."

"Don't be too long. Dinner will be ready in thirty minutes."

"I won't."

Iris stormed out the front door and put her pendant back on. She didn't need it for where she was going, but she figured she should be in the habit of always putting it back on as soon as she was in public. Tears fell freely now that she was alone. She wiped them away with a sleeve. How could they say they were keeping her safe in her childhood only to let themselves get old and sick? If her parents wouldn't help themselves, she would do it for them.

She got in her car and sped down the narrow forest road. Densely packed redwoods danced into view as her headlights illuminated them. After a couple of miles, she pulled into the driveway of a one-story white house with an especially broad redwood in front. She turned off the car and sat for a few moments without moving. Her pounding heart flooded her ears. The house and tree before her turned red. White scales appeared on the backs of her hands. Iris forced herself to take several deep breaths. So much about this was unprofessional, especially if she lost control of her powers. As her breathing steadied, her vision returned to a normal hue, and the scales dissipated. She set her resolve and got out of the car. The aroma of pine mingled with fireplace smoke in the air. She passed the large redwood to her right, walked up a few steps to the door, and knocked before more hesitation could stop her.

A woman with shoulder-length black hair, a few inches shorter than herself, answered. "Yes?"

"Sorry to bother you so late, Mrs. Dawan."

The woman peered closer at her. "Iris? Shouldn't you be in San Francisco for the election?"

"I'm in town visiting my parents. My father's not doing too well."

"I'm sorry to hear that. Come in. Come in. Don't worry about whispering. Our daughter is a sound sleeper."

Iris removed her shoes at the door. Mrs. Dawan led her into the cozy home and motioned for her to sit on the leather couch in front of the fire.

"Actually, that's part of why I'm here," Iris said as she sunk into the couch.

Mrs. Dawan paused in her movement toward the couch. "Oh?" She turned and walked toward the kitchen instead. "Can I get you something to drink?"

"No, thank you."

Iris waited on the couch for Mrs. Dawan to return from the kitchen. She fidgeted with her fingers and tapped her toes on the Persian rug. Mrs. Dawan returned carrying a glass of water. She sipped it, set it on the coffee table, and sat next to Iris.

"So, how can I help you?"

"I know this is unconventional, but my father– he's very sick. The doctors say he doesn't have long."

Mrs. Dawan nodded, listening. Her face was compassionate and solemn. Iris continued.

"I had to take this chance to ask– if you could help him? Just this once. I wouldn't chance it if it weren't serious."

Mrs. Dawan picked up her glass of water, took a sip, then set it down. "I'm very sorry about your father. I truly am. But the law is the law. I have a duty to enforce it. Can you imagine what would happen to my husband– to my family– if I were caught?"

Iris lowered her head. She squeezed her eyes and fists shut, then relaxed and looked up. She tried to answer in as calm of a voice as possible. "Of course. This was so inappropriate of me to ask. I was– desperate."

Mrs. Dawan laid a hand on hers. "There's still the election next week. And the upcoming ballot measures after that. Things could change. Think positively." She patted her hand and gave a small smile.

"Yes." Iris stood up. She bit her lower lip so it wouldn't quiver. "I better go. I have a six-hour drive back to the city in the morning. Thank you again for seeing me so late."

"Of course."

Iris rushed to the door and put her shoes on. She said goodbye and got into her car. A lump stuck in her throat. She wanted to scream, but she held it in. All these years she had been working to change the system, and nothing had changed. Now, her father was dying, and there was nothing she could do about it. No one would help. Her parents wouldn't even help themselves.

She had no choice but to wait for the election results on Friday and the ballot measure votes the following week and hope that her father would hang on until then. That was all she could do.

CHAPTER THIRTY-THREE

Amber

Summer 2000

AMBER ARRIVED AT Arav's home at the end of Forest Lane. It was strange to think it had only been about a week since she and Nivi came this way to see the cave. She wrapped her arms around herself, feeling a chill as she hurried through the rain toward the house. Tall pines loomed overhead, swaying ominously in the wind. Arav opened the door as she ran up.

"Are you OK?" he asked, putting his hands on both her shoulders.

She nodded, and he hugged her. It was warm and strong and comforting. Before she could let herself fully relax into his embrace, he ushered her in, out of the rain. In the living room, a wood-burning stove crackled with a cozy fire. Amber removed her shoes and hung her jacket by the door, leaving it to drip onto the wood floor.

"Is your brother home?" Amber said.

"Yeah, he's in my room. We were hanging out. Why?"

"I was wondering if I could talk to him about some things if he wouldn't mind."

"I'm sure he wouldn't. Come on."

Inside Arav's room, Kabir was sitting on the perfectly made bed. The room was spotless. In fact, there wasn't an out-of-place item in sight.

"Wow. You've really cleaned up. You're worse than Nivi," Amber joked, trying to seem more lighthearted.

Kabir stood and put his hands up. "Don't look at me. This was all Arav."

"Alright, alright," Arav said. "I just thought it was time to get my act together. That guy who died in the fire really spooked me. I started thinking, 'what am I doing with my life?' You know?"

Amber nodded but was internally taken aback. It wasn't that she thought Arav wasn't capable of organizing his life, but that her actions in the past week were such a stark contrast to his. That was it. She wouldn't wallow away in her bedroom any longer. She would follow Arav's lead and get her life in order. And today was a start, wasn't it? Even though her interaction with Nivi didn't go quite according to plan, at least she was trying to get to the bottom of things. That was why she was here now.

Arav pulled the chair from his desk and motioned for Amber to sit, then sat on the bed next to his brother. Sitting side-by-side, Arav looked very similar to Kabir. Both had the same brown skin and lean muscular form, except Kabir was a little taller and broader in the chest. If Amber remembered correctly, his eyes were like his mother's, larger and wider-set. He kept his curls cropped on top and shaved on the sides. Arav let his hair grow longer and more wild.

"Anyway," Arav continued, "Amber didn't come here to admire my organizational skills. She wanted to talk to you."

Kabir raised one of his thick eyebrows.

Amber cleared her throat. "About the fire. If that's allowed since you're still investigating and all."

"Actually," Kabir said, "the case was closed already."

Amber leaned forward, a bit of hope energizing her voice. "So, you know who set the fire?"

Kabir's face darkened. "Apparently, the man who attacked Nivi had some kind of explosive. And, when it went off, it killed him and set the school on fire."

"You don't look like you believe it," Arav said.

Kabir rubbed his palms on his knees and lowered his voice. "This stays between us, but the evidence doesn't add up."

"Does it have anything to do with what I told you at the station?" Amber glanced at Arav, who gave her a questioning look.

Kabir shook his head. "The whole thing doesn't make sense. If there was an explosion, there would have been evidence of it on both the unidentified man and Nivi. Marks on the face and singed hair, for instance. But only the man's chest was burned, and burned with a hole right through it. A simple fire wouldn't have caused that either. It had to be something hot and concentrated. Nivi's burns were localized to her hands and arms, and her burns didn't look like any kind of burn I've ever seen."

"What'd they look like?" Amber asked.

"I'm not sure how to describe it exactly," Kabir said. "They almost had a pattern to it, like they followed her veins."

Amber chewed her lip. More doubt shrouded her memory of that day. If what Kabir said was true, then Nivi really didn't start the fire. Amber felt terrible for her accusations, and yet she still felt uneasy about the whole situation. Nivi was the one who went through trauma that day. She had a legitimate reason for a faulty memory. Why would Amber have seen something that didn't actually occur?

Arav's voice drew Amber out of her thoughts. "Did you notice anything else strange?"

"What do you mean?" Kabir said.

"I don't know. Anything that could explain the fire or why they would close the case so quickly? Are they trying to hide something?"

Kabir rubbed his chin. "There was this woman at the station that day."

"A woman?"

"Yeah. She came out of the chief's office and almost bumped into me like she was in a hurry. After she left, the chief and Officer Clayton came out and told me the case was closed. When I asked who the woman was they said it was someone looking for her cat, but she didn't look like someone from the area."

"Why not?"

"She was dressed really fancy, in a sexy but professional way. And she had a British accent. Oh, and these really intense light blue eyes."

Amber perked up. "Was she Asian?"

"Yeah. How'd you know?"

"I think I saw her too. I remember those eyes. She was coming out of the hospital the day of the fire." Amber continued, thinking out loud. "Why would she go to the hospital right after the fire and then the police station? And then immediately after the case is dropped."

"Maybe a coincidence?" Arav suggested.

"In my line of work, things aren't usually just coincidences," Kabir said.

"You know what else is a weird coincidence?" Amber said,

remembering something. "Right before the high school fire, Nivi mentioned the possibility of a deadly fire around ten years ago. That's weird, right? She happened to mention a fire, and then right after there was a fire. I told her I'd ask my parents because they love reading the news and might remember something like that."

"Did you ask them?" Kabir said.

"No. With everything going on, I forgot. But I will now."

"So what can we do?" Arav said. "If the case is closed already, is there a point in worrying?"

The image of Nivi lighting a fire once again appeared in Amber's mind. She knew she should drop it but she couldn't let it go just yet. Maybe if she framed it from exploring all angles, she wouldn't seem so fixated on one possibility. "What if there's someone still out there trying to harm Nivi or other people in our town? Or worse, what if it's–"

The front door opened and slammed shut, disrupting Amber. It was probably better that way, so she didn't come off blaming Nivi again. What did she hope to achieve anyway? Did she really want Nivi to go to jail, or was she just mad because of their fight?

Heavy steps sounded from down the hall, followed by the sound of the fridge opening and something falling to the floor. Kabir got up and went to the doorway.

"Dad?"

There wasn't any answer. More items sounded like they were falling on the floor.

Arav sighed. "Do you think he's been drinking again?"

"Maybe." Kabir looked grim as he left the room.

Arav turned to Amber. "I'm sorry you'll have to see this. I told you my dad drinks, right?"

"Yeah, since your mother died."

"I didn't tell you this before because it's pretty crazy

sounding, but you'll probably hear my dad say something about it. My dad is obsessed with the idea that a monster person killed my mother."

"Really?" What happened to Arav's mother was a terrible family tragedy, but Amber couldn't help getting a little excited by the idea of a monster person.

"You don't believe those silly stories, do you?"

"Uh–" She tried to redirect the conversation. "How did she die again?"

Arav fiddled with his fingers. "She jumped from the cliffs. They found her body on the rocks below. It was ruled a suicide, but my dad swears he saw someone or something push her, that she would never willingly do something like that. Especially because she had these strange marks across her back, almost like claw marks. The police said they could've been from the rocks, but my dad…" Arav shook his head.

Amber put an arm around Arav. "I'm so sorry."

"Anyway, if he says anything to you tonight about monster people, don't encourage him. It just makes things worse."

"I won't." Amber kept telling herself she wouldn't say anything, but part of her hoped Arav's dad would say more about monster people.

They walked out to the kitchen, where a large man wearing a mud-covered flannel shirt, dripping from the rain, was rummaging through the fridge. A loaf of bread, a jar of peanut butter, and a butter knife lay at his feet.

"Hey, Dad," Kabir said. "You OK? Did you fall?"

Frank Markson turned from the fridge with a stick of string cheese sticking out of his mouth and a can of beer in his hand. His eyes were red and bleary, and he reeked of beer.

"I saw one. I know it." Frank muttered to himself, then turned back to the fridge.

Arav filled a glass with water from the kitchen sink and tried to hand it to his father. "Here, Dad. Drink this."

Frank turned to face Arav, his eyes taking a moment to focus. When they did, he clapped Arav on the shoulder with his free hand, almost causing him to spill the water. "I knew it, Son. I knew it. Didn't I tell you? All this time?"

"What are you talking about?"

"I saw one. One of those monsters. A woman. She'll pay. She'll pay for your mother's…" Tears filled his eyes. "She'll pay."

Arav looked uncomfortable and glanced at Amber. Amber kept her promise and said nothing, although she was dying to know more. Kabir took the beer from his father and set it aside. He put his arm around his father's shoulder.

"Come on, Dad. Let's get you to bed."

Frank pushed Kabir away. "No. I need to find her. Make her pay."

Kabir sighed. "OK, first drink some water." He took the cup of water from Arav and was able to get his father to drink a couple of sips. "Now, tell me what you saw."

Frank swallowed and wiped his chin with the back of his hand. "A woman. Beautiful. Her eyes. So blue. Like ice." He rubbed his face.

Amber couldn't hold in her anticipation any longer. This couldn't be another coincidence. She stepped forward, her heart racing. "Black hair? Pale skin? A British accent?"

"Amber, don't." Arav muttered.

Frank's eyes focused on Amber. "Yeah. How'd you…?"

Amber turned to Kabir and spoke in a hushed tone. "Don't you see? It's the same woman. We need to find her."

"Where'd you see this woman, Dad?" Kabir said.

"In town."

"Is she still there?"

"No. The forest."

"She's in the forest?"

"Yeah. I chased her."

Arav threw his hands up. "Geez, Dad," he said with an exasperated voice.

"Arav, get Dad to bed. I'm going to go check it out." Kabir pulled on a coat, took a flashlight from a drawer, and then left through the front door.

After a little bit of persuasion, Arav was able to get his father to bed. He came back to the kitchen, where Amber waited.

"I'm really sorry about that," he said.

"It's OK." She gave Arav a hug and a kiss on the cheek. "It's getting late, but I can stay a little longer if you want me to."

"That's alright."

They walked out of the kitchen, holding hands. Arav opened the front door for her. It had stopped raining, and a dense fog hung in the air.

"You want me to walk you home?"

Amber laughed, trying to seem carefree. She had always prided herself on being a fearless dare devil and didn't want that to change now. "You think this town is unsafe now?"

"Just with everything going on."

"I'm fine." She kissed him and walked out to the sidewalk. Arav called after her.

"Maybe we can go hiking tomorrow? I'd like to go back to that cave of stones. Low tide is about 7:30PM tomorrow."

"OK, I'll meet you here at 7."

"Sounds good."

She glanced toward the forest where Kabir's flashlight shined from between trees. A moment later, he emerged and shook his head.

"Nothing."

Amber shrugged. "I'll let you know if I see that woman again."

Kabir nodded and went back to the house, where Arav stood in the doorway. They waved to her as she walked down the street. She tried to remain relaxed, but it took all her power not to keep glancing back at the forest.

CHAPTER THIRTY-FOUR

Iris

Summer 1990

ON THE SURFACE, that Friday morning was like any other. The San Francisco rush hour traffic was diminished compared to the rest of the week. The sidewalks and restaurants were filled with people ready to enjoy the weekend. Inside, anxiety and anticipation accompanied Iris to her destination. She wondered how many others she passed were also filled with emotions that did not mirror their outward appearance. Two questions weighed heavily on her mind. At least she would get their answers today.

She got off the public transit a few stops early so she could walk, relax, and think. The cool weather and overcast sky made walking comfortable, even in a suit. As she approached the jade-shingled roofs of San Francisco Chinatown, she paused and took a deep breath. The memories of her Los Angeles Chinatown home flooded back. Guilt pecked at her subconscious. She'd been avoiding her parents' calls by purposefully not answering her phone and cutting them short when she did pick up. Part of that was because she had been busy with the election. Mostly, it was because she didn't want to acknowledge the fact that her father was sick and getting worse. Hopefully, she would have good news to report by the end of the day. She continued walking and turned a corner, almost bumping into a middle-aged woman in the process.

"Excuse me," Iris said, making her way around the woman.

"Iris?" the woman said.

Iris turned back, expecting to see a fellow Shifter, but found she was looking at a Static. She felt her neck and realized the camouflage pendant was not there. In her distracted state, she realized it was still in her jacket pocket. But she couldn't put it on midconversation with a Static that had recognized her. That would cause too many questions.

"It is you!" the woman continued. "Do you remember me?" She patted her chest. "Stephanie Chu. We were in high school together."

"Oh, Stephanie," Iris said, flustered. She was embarrassed at her lack of professionalism with the camouflage pendant. At the same time, the ridiculousness of having to hide herself in plain sight increased her frustrations with the current Shifter system. "How are you?"

"I'm fine. I'm fine. How long has it been? Thirty-five years? The last time I saw you was the summer you left for some special private school, right? The summer that Anna Sun was filming in our neighborhood!"

Stephanie's cheeks still flushed with excitement when she spouted off her knowledge, cheeks that now sagged with age as any Static's would have by this time. Iris stepped away and turned her face as she felt Stephanie's eyes scrutinize her. It didn't work.

"Oh my," Stephanie said. "You look amazing. You don't look a day older than thirty. How do you do it? You'll have to tell me your secret."

"You're too kind. It's probably just the lighting. It was really good to see you, but I must be going. I'm late for a meeting."

Before Stephanie could say anything else, Iris took off with a wave and as friendly of a smile as she could muster. *That wasn't good,* she thought. She glanced around to check if there were any other Shifters present who could report her unprofessionalism. Fortunately, she didn't see any. Stephanie began to follow her, apparently wanting to catch up some more. Iris quickened her pace. She stuck her hand into her pocket and pulled out the pendant, slipping it over her head as she turned a corner. Stephanie rounded the corner a moment later. She stopped as she looked past Iris at the other people around her. Confusion furrowed her brow. Iris was no longer recognizable to her.

Iris walked toward the Embarcadero, the northeast waterfront border of San Francisco. Palm trees lined the large median divider between the two-lane streets adjacent to the piers. She crossed the street to Pier 19, a large white, warehouse-type building on the water. She wasn't sure what it was originally used for, probably something to do with receiving ship cargo. On the right side of the building, she approached and held up her mottled green pendant to a solid metal gate. People walked by on the sidewalk, paying no attention to her presence or the presence of the gate. In addition to the camouflage magic, the stone was also imbued with the ability to unlock certain doors. This access was dependent on a Shifter's political rank, of course. Shifters could accomplish incredible things when they used their powers together, like this camouflage and key magic, and the creation of the marks that took away her parents' powers. Iris wrinkled her nose at this last thought. The gate opened. She went through and it immediately snapped shut behind her.

She descended the steps down toward the water. Gray ocean mirrored the gray skies above. Seagulls squawked overhead. Seaweed and fish aromas filled the air. At water level, Iris walked along a floating deck by the building. She lifted the pendant from around her neck and held it to the wall on her left. The outline of a door appeared in the white stone, glowing faintly. With a groan and the scraping of stone on stone, the door slid back and to the side, allowing her to pass. Once she was inside, the door slid back into place. The outline disappeared, leaving no trace of the door.

A flight of stairs led down to a brightly illuminated hallway. White travertine lined the floor and the wall to Iris's left. To her right, underwater windows hung like art in a gallery. Bubbles and pieces of kelp drifted by in the gray waters of the Bay. Rays of light sparkled down from above. Here and there, the silvery flash of a fish darted by. Even after all these years, Iris still loved the Shifter City Hall's magical feel. She longed to become an elected official to have more opportunities to visit this building. Her anticipation and anxiety grew as she walked down the hall.

The hallway opened up to a wide reception area where a crowd of people in suits had gathered; those that had already found out if they had been elected to their representative positions or not. Champagne flowed from bottles into glasses. Iris surmised that those who chugged their glasses down with a grimace were not the victors. A large screen hung over the room, showcasing the California Representative and National Senate results. Every so often, the screen flashed through the results of other state representatives elections. Iris looked over the current California results. One progressive and one conservative were elected for the senate. The representative results for the Desert, Central, and Bay Area were all progressives. She sucked in a breath. The Southern, Central Coast, and Northern—the representative region Iris was running for—results were pending.

As she watched the monitor, the results for the Central Coast region updated: conservative. On the far side of the room, the elevator doors opened, and several of the newly-elected officials emerged. People clapped and toasted their victories. Iris forced herself to appear calm and collected. If another conservative won the Southern California region, it meant Iris would have to win if there was any hope of changing the law in time to help her father.

Several people approached her.

Newly-elected Bay Area Representative Anwar Johnson, a balding man with glasses and kind eyes, shook her hand. "Good luck, Iris."

"Thank you. Congratulations to you, Representative Johnson," she replied.

He raised his glass of champagne to her and continued mingling with other people in the room.

Kris Springston, one of the newly-elected California Senators, patted Iris on the back. "You've got this." Her tightly pulled-back blond hair gave her a severe appearance, but she winked and quirked up the corner of her mouth.

"Thank you, Senator."

A raspy voice came from behind Iris. "The white snake."

Iris turned and saw Mindy Le, the conservative candidate for Southern California Representative. In a sea of black and gray suits, Mindy wore a bright red dress. Some thought her raspy voice was sexy, but it made Iris want to clear her throat.

"Hi, Mindy," Iris said.

Mindy wagged a finger at Iris and pointed to the screen. The Southern California Representative winner had updated— to Mindy Le.

Iris forced a smile and shook Mindy's hand. "Congratulations, Representative."

Mindy met the shake with a limp hand. "It seems the people have spoken. Your pro-integration ideas are dangerous and irresponsible."

She lifted her hand from Iris's grasp and wiped it down the side of her dress.

Iris clenched her teeth but kept a smile plastered on her face. "Anti-integration is dangerous and irresponsible. The Statics' technology is advancing at a rapid rate. Who cares if we have powers and longevity if the Statics can bomb us with heat-seeking missiles? And half of us are no match for handguns, for that matter."

"You're misinformed. And the people agree."

"The election isn't over yet."

"You know, some people just have what it takes to be politicians, and some..." Mindy looked Iris up and down.

"No need for rudeness," Kris said."We're all comrades here."

Mindy feigned a look of innocence. "Is speaking the truth rude?"

Kris rolled her eyes and exchanged a look with Iris. "I'll see you down there, Iris." She turned and walked toward the elevators.

A chorus of murmurs hummed from the far side of the room. Iris and Mindy turned to look as Vice Chairperson Davis exited the elevator.

"Now there's a prime example of a great politician and leader," Mindy said. She pursed her lips and gravitated toward the vice chairperson.

"Yeah. Nice chatting with you, too," Iris mumbled under her breath.

Her cheeks heated as she looked over at Davis and caught

his eye for a split second before the back of Mindy's head obscured her view. After all this time, she hated how she still felt her stomach jump when she saw Davis; how she and everyone else in the room seemed so drawn to him. It meant that Mindy was right, that some people just had what it took to be admired and respected.

The crowd thinned around Iris. She made her way toward a gold desk by the elevators, pushing through the throng that congregated around Davis.

"Hi, Marcus," Iris said to the man sitting behind the desk. "I'm here for the final tally—"

"They're waiting for you downstairs," he replied curtly without a smile. He pressed a button, and a door slid open in the stone wall behind him.

"Thanks." Iris walked into the elevator.

A low rumble vibrated the walls as she descended. She was nervous, she admitted to herself. Her surprise run-in with Stephanie hadn't helped her confidence. It proved how she continued to be unprofessional after propositioning the Chairperson's wife to break the law to help her father. Even though she had worked hard for this position, maybe she didn't have what it took after all. If Mindy could see that, the constituents probably could as well.

The elevator door opened, and Iris stepped out into a circular chamber. Floor-to-ceiling glass windows encased the room in an underwater capsule. Rows of desks were aligned in concentric semicircles on either side of a central aisle. The chairperson, the vice chairperson, and the fifty state senators of the Shifter Council filed back in from break. The sea water cast a bluish-gray hue over the two people who sat at the long desk at the front of the room: Chairperson Dawan and Vice Chairperson Davis. The room glowed with all the Shifter auras in one place.

The other Northern California Shifter Representative candidate was already in the room: Ariana Peters, a stately woman with a similarly thin and tall physique to her own. Iris exited the elevator at the center back of the room and walked to the left to shake Ariana's hand.

"Good luck," they said to each other with professional courtesy.

Stoic expressions masked both their faces. Then, the sides of Ariana's jaw flexed and wavered, an indication she was clenching her teeth. Iris smiled to herself. At least she wasn't the only nervous one.

"Good morning, Senators and Northern California Representative candidates," Chairperson Dawan said in a loud, deep voice that took command of the room. He stood up, an impressive figure. Tall, broad chest, chestnut skin tone, a head of cropped, thick, curly hair. "Thank you for joining us. Representatives, please approach."

Iris's heart leaped. She and Ariana walked side-by-side down the center aisle. As they approached, Vice Chairperson Davis also stood. He was taller than the chairperson, but his leaner build made him seem almost diminutive compared to Chairperson Dawan's broad chest.

"Today is a big day for you both," Chairperson Dawan continued once they stood at the front of the room, "As this will be your first time running for the position of senator. This is a position with a commitment of thirty years. You have both shown great promise through the years in leadership and skill. Before I announce who has been elected to the position of Northern California Representative, I want to say how appreciative we are of everything both of you have done for our organization and people. No matter the results of this election, I hope you both will continue to be as involved. About 70% of the 1.1 million shifters in California voted; a good turn out." A member of the senate handed Chairperson Dawan an envelope. "And now, I am pleased to announce our new Northern California Representative…" He opened the envelope. Iris clenched her fists and dug her nails into her palms to keep from trembling. "With 67% of the votes, Ariana Peters!"

Ariana broke into a wide grin. Iris sucked in a breath and dug her nails deeper into her flesh. The room blurred and tilted before her. She managed to release her fists to shake Ariana's hand. Everyone in the chamber stood up and clapped. Iris followed suit, a smile plastered on her face.

One by one, the Senators filed out from behind their desks and made their way to the front of the room, shaking hands with Ariana and Iris and offering words of congratulation and encouragement before exiting the chamber down the center aisle.

"Thank you. Thank you so much," Ariana said.

Iris echoed the thanks over and over again, like an assembly-line robot.

"Congratulations, Representative Peters," Chairperson Dawan said, shaking Ariana's hand. He continued to Iris. "Thank you for your service to our community, Iris. Please don't let this be a discouragement."

Iris gripped Chairperson Dawan's hand. She wanted to beg him to help her father. Beg him to make his wife use her healing powers on a Static. But she already knew what his answer would be. Any attempt she made would be political suicide, and she would lose any ability she had to run for office and make a change in the future. She let go of his hand and watched him walk out of the room, chatting and laughing with newly-elected senators.

Vice Chairperson Davis came next, congratulating Ariana.

Then he turned to Iris, pausing while shaking her hand to whisper in her ear. "I voted for you."

He let go of her hand, winked, and walked to the elevators. Iris's heart thudded in her chest. Even in her distressed state, Davis's words had the power to lift her mood. A jumble of emotions collided through her body. Despair, anger, and that annoying giddiness that Davis caused. The giddiness subsided once Davis was out of the room, but her mind was still turbulent.

As the chamber cleared out to join the party upstairs, Iris followed numbly. The whirring of the elevator mirrored the buzzing in her head. When the elevator door opened, someone handed her a glass of champagne. There were claps on the back. Clinks of glass. Laughter. Iris downed the champagne with a grimace, just like all the other losers. She waded through the crowd, setting her empty glass down on a window sill. The grandeur of the underwater room that had wowed her from the first moment she saw it now seemed frivolous in the face of her father's impending mortality. She needed to get out of here. No one seemed to notice as she dashed down the hall, up the stairs, and out into the sun.

She walked the entire way home, the day's events spinning through her head. Her legs ached when she finally reached her Golden Gate Park adjacent apartment three hours later. This side of town was quieter, filled mostly with families and medical and dental residents. She welcomed the calm. Unlocking the exterior apartment door, she climbed an internal flight of stairs and unlocked another door off the landing to enter her apartment. She kicked off her shoes and threw her keys onto the dining room table, then poured herself a glass of red wine and sank into the couch.

The numbness faded and a surge of anguish expanded in her chest. She set aside the wine and grabbed a decorative pillow. Pressing it to her face, she screamed out her frustrations.

She threw the pillow across the room and collapsed back into the couch, heaving. After a moment, she picked up the wine glass and gulped down the contents. The warmth of the late afternoon sun streaming in the window and the wine flowing through her veins relaxed her. She remembered a similar feeling when she used to take the sedatives that repressed her powers. That seemed so long ago now. She shook her head. What would her life be like if she had given up her powers? Would she be fighting for her life like her father was?

The last time she had spoken to her parents, her mother finally admitted that the cancer had spread. It was only a matter of time. Anger clouded Iris's face. Her parents had been Shifters for hundreds of years before becoming Statics. Shouldn't that count for something? Mrs. Dawan could have helped if she had wanted to. The more Iris thought about it, the more she was convinced that Mrs. Dawan must have told her husband about her request, which meant the chairperson was complicit in her father's sickness as well. He could have made an exception. Especially with the ballot-measure vote coming up. But now they had to wait. If her father could just hold on until after the vote, then maybe there was still hope.

Iris set down her glass of wine and hugged her legs to her chest, looking out the window behind the couch. The street was full of cars; people trying to get out of town for the weekend. Beyond, the trees of Golden Gate Park wavered in the breeze. She felt the urge to escape as well.

The phone rang from the side table, startling her out of her thoughts. She hesitated, then picked up the receiver and untangled the phone cord.

"Hello?"

"Iris," her mother's voice said in a tone that made her stomach drop. "It's Ba Ba… You'll need to come home."

CHAPTER THIRTY-FIVE

Meng
Summer 2000

ENG WATCHED FROM behind a tree as Frank entered a house that bordered the forest. She pulled her wet cloak around herself and waited to ensure he wasn't coming back, shivering in the dark.

Something rustled behind her, and she spun around, hoping to see the creature again, but nothing was there. While the creature was similar in size, it had not been a deer. The white fur. The large, black-tipped ears and fluffy tail. The narrow canid face. All were those of a fox. And not just any fox. The gleam of its curved, silver horn proved that, as did the warm glow Meng felt in her chest. That was a Shifter. But the only Shifter she knew like that was dead. So who did she see? She needed to go see Ling first thing in the morning. Maybe she would have some insight.

When there was no movement from the house, Meng breathed a sigh of relief and began to emerge from behind the tree, but a moment later, the door opened. Meng ducked back behind the tree. A young man walked out of the house and headed to the forest with a flashlight. He looked familiar. As he neared, she realized where she had seen him before. He was the officer she had run into while coming out of the police chief's office. She closed her eyes and tried to picture his name tag. Kabir Markson. That was it. It seemed that Frank may be related to Officer Markson. That was problematic. If Frank got this officer's suspicions aroused, she'd have to explain to the Council why she needed more oblivion tincture to prevent the whole police force from investigating Shifter business again.

Kabir trudged into the forest, shining his flashlight around. Meng kept a tree between him and her and remained very silent. After five or ten minutes, Kabir turned around. Meng got the feeling he wasn't seriously looking for anything.

A girl with long black hair walked out of the house at the forest's edge. Meng knew from her observations of Nivi that this was Amber, Nivi's friend. She supposed she shouldn't be so surprised that several people's paths would cross in a small town. A boy stood in the doorway and called out to Amber.

"I'd like to go back to that cave of stones. Low tide is about 7:30PM tomorrow."

"OK, I'll meet you here at 7."

Kabir walked out of the forest to Amber, and they said some things she couldn't hear. Then Kabir went into the house with the other boy, and Amber walked away.

When Amber had gone, and the house remained quiet, Meng came out from behind the tree and walked back to her hotel, keeping to the shadows in case anyone looked out from the house windows.

A cave of stones?

She fingered the stone in her pocket. First, she had taken

this stone from a man who lived in that house, and then a boy from that same house, presumably the man's son, spoke of going back to a cave of stones. That's probably where Frank got his stone, to begin with. If the stone was a transfer stone, as she suspected, this was very serious indeed. Not only were they illegal in Shifter society, but who knew what Statics could be getting up to if they discovered what the stone could do? She would have to go back and investigate. When Amber and that boy went hiking tomorrow evening, she'd be waiting for them.

CHAPTER THIRTY-SIX

Amber

Summer 2000

AMBER TOSSED AND turned all night. There were too many strange things going on, and she felt if she could get at least one question answered, things would start to make sense. When she heard her parents come out of their room, she jumped out of bed, dressed, and ran to the kitchen, where they were microwaving mugs of water for their instant coffee.

"Mom! Dad! I have a question," Amber said.

Her parents jumped at her outburst.

"Good morning, Amber," her father said. "Glad to see you so energetic this morning." He sat at the kitchen counter with his mug, put on some reading glasses, and opened a newspaper.

Her mother smiled sleepily. "Good morning, Dear."

"Yeah, good morning," Amber said, skimming past the pleasantries. "Do you remember a fire that occurred ten years ago?"

Her mother's brow furrowed. "A fire? What kind of fire?"

"I don't know. Anything that seemed strange at the time."

"Why do you want to know about a fire from ten years ago?"

"I just do, OK."

The corner of her father's mouth quirked up. He spoke without looking up from the newspaper. "You know, the library keeps copies of all newspapers over the years. You could look up the newspapers from around that time.

Amber grimaced. "The library?"

Her father looked up from the brim of his glasses. "You can go to the library and still be cool."

Amber rolled her eyes. "Uh-huh. I thought you guys would've had the answer since you have that photographic news memory you always use when watching Jeopardy." Her parents chuckled. Amber sighed. If Nivi could go to a morgue, she could go to the library. "When do they open?"

Her mother glanced at her watch. "At eight, so in about ten minutes."

Amber grabbed her bag from the kitchen counter. "I'll see you later."

She walked briskly onto Main Street until she came to Cedar Lane, the next street to the left. The library stood on the corner of Main and Cedar, two stories tall, its brick facade seeming to rise as an extension out of the brick sidewalk. She glanced around to make sure no one was looking before she walked up the steps and through the double doors. Even Nivi didn't go to the library.

Stained glass windows cast colorful patches of light across rows of bookcases. A musty smell from old leather and paper filled the air. In the center of the entryway, a librarian sat at a desk in front of a boxy computer. Amber approached the elderly woman whose white hair was currently a rainbow of stained glass light.

The librarian smiled at her and spoke with a soft voice. "How can I help you?"

"Um, where can I find old newspapers?"

"Downstairs in the archives. Do you know how to use the microfilm reader?"

Amber must have had a blank look because the librarian got up from her seat and motioned for Amber to follow her. She led the way down a narrow staircase to a basement with concrete floors and rows of shelves with magazines and boxes on them. They stopped in front of a shelf of small, labeled boxes.

"Do you know what date you want to look up?" the librarian said.

"Um. Let me think." Amber wanted to look at newspapers from ten years ago, but which month and which week? Until recently, Yuras only printed weekly newspapers, so Amber would have to go through fifty-two newspapers at most, but that was still a lot. From what she knew, Nivi had lost her parents shortly before they met in kindergarten, and in their area, all schools started around the end of August, so that cut down on some months. She knew Nivi and her grandmother commemorated her parents' death each year. When was the last time she saw the shrine setup in their house? It wasn't in the winter or the spring. It had to be close to about now. She hadn't been in their house recently, and Nivi hadn't said anything. So maybe it was a little bit back. A month ago?

"I'll start with the beginning of May 1990," Amber said.

The librarian scanned the shelf until she came to a little box labeled "April 29, 1990 to May 5, 1990." She took it to a boxy screen that was more narrow than a standard computer screen. Below the screen were two spools, each with a little handle.

The librarian removed a roll of film from the box and showed her how to wind it around the spools. She flipped a switch that turned on a light between the two spools, and an image of a newspaper cover appeared on the screen.

"You can move through the newspaper pages by turning these handles," the librarian said, indicating the handles on the spools. "Please put the microfilm back in the box and in the proper place on the shelf when you're done. And please ask me if you have any questions."

She went back up the stairs, leaving Amber by herself in the dimly lit basement. At least no one would see her down here.

Amber scrolled through the newspaper headlines: Community programs, city improvements, local elections, school events, births, marriages, and deaths. She got to the end of the first film. No mention of fires. She removed the microfilm from the reader and rolled it back up into the box. She replaced the box on the shelf and took the next one with the label "May 6, 1990 to May 12, 1990." One by one, she scrolled through the headlines. Still no fires. By the fourth roll of film, Amber's eyes were getting dry and her vision blurry. She closed her eyes and took a short break. If she had miscalculated the date, she couldn't imagine going through forty-eight more rolls of microfilm. At least not today. What if there were no mysterious fires ten years ago?

She moved on to the "June 3, 1990 to June 9, 1990" microfilm and half-heartedly scanned the headlines. When she had reached the halfway point, an image clicked in her head, and she scrolled back to the beginning. This time, she scrolled more slowly through the headlines. And there it was. On the front page, just below photos of the graduating high school class, was the headline, "Fire Demolishes Abandoned Home."

Amber read through the short piece and then re-read it

several times. Her hopes of answered questions petered out with each read. It didn't say much. Just that a fire broke out in the night at an abandoned home on Redwood Road. Apparently, locals weren't really aware of the abandoned home until someone spotted the fire and called it in. There were concerns it could cause a forest fire, but fortunately there had been a heavy rainstorm that extinguished the fire by the time authorities arrived. A photo of the house, or what was left of it, displayed a one-story structure with a dark-colored pitched roof, light-colored exterior paint and shutters, based on half a shutter that remained on the left-most window. The roof had caved in, and soot covered most of the house's exterior.

Was this the mysterious fire Nivi was looking for? Even though it didn't answer any questions for Amber, maybe it would for Nivi. Amber clicked on the print button and retrieved the copy from the printer. Just to make sure, she reviewed one more roll of microfilm, and when she didn't see any other fire headlines, she packed up, thanked the librarian, and headed to Nivi's house. When she reached Nivi's home, she considered knocking on the door. But with their fight still so fresh, she instead folded the newspaper printout and pushed it into the seam of Nivi's bedroom window. Nivi would understand what Amber had done for her, and then they could forget their fight and go back to how things used to be.

CHAPTER THIRTY-SEVEN

Iris

Summer 1990

I RIS PULLED THE last of her father's dust-covered boxes from under the bed. She thumbed through a few items, then pushed the boxes off to the side and went to the living room to take a break. Except for the dining table, which was the same one she had grown up with, everything about the house had felt unfamiliar. Without her father, it felt completely foreign.

She touched the gold bracelet on her wrist. Even though it used to belong to her mother, she liked to think of it as a gift from her father. Something to remember him by.

Her mother had kept a brave face throughout the funeral, and, even now, was completely focused and perfunctory in her cleaning of the house and the dishes. The last of the guests had left the night before.

"Have some more food," she said. "You barely ate dinner. You're too skinny."

"I've always been like this."

"Yes, always too skinny."

"And you're always trying to feed me more."

"I'm your mother. It's my duty to feed you."

Iris watched her mother as she prepared a plate of leftovers. She had always been petite, but with age her hunched form made her appear even smaller. Her right hand had a tremor, and she struggled to balance the plate on her left wrist, when before she had done all with ease. She almost spilled some sauce on her sleeveless, pale yellow house dress. The bright red mark glared from her left shoulder.

A wave of anger washed over Iris. "It didn't have to be like this."

"Like what?"

"Like this!" Iris's voice rose. She pointed at her mother and then all around her.

"Iris, calm yourself." Her mother placed the food on the table.

"How can you be so calm? Ba Ba didn't have to die. You didn't have to get old so quickly. You *chose* this."

"Yes. This is the life we chose. The life that made us happy. I accepted that you chose a life different from us. Now, you will have to accept what we chose for ourselves."

Iris clenched her fists together and got up from the table. "I'm not hungry. I'm going for a walk."

Her mother sighed and muttered something under her breath in Mandarin while taking the plate of food for herself. Iris grabbed a gray cardigan from a coat stand and stormed out the front door. She slammed the door behind her and stared at the ground, stifling a sob. The night air was cool and full of moisture, similar to nights in the Bay Area. She wished she were home in San Francisco, sitting on her couch with a glass of wine. Her mother kept a dry home, and nothing was open at 9PM on a Sunday in a small town.

Footsteps approached on the sidewalk. Iris snapped her head up. Vice Chairperson Davis was walking toward her. He wore a suit and carried a bouquet of white lilies. As usual, Iris felt her heart quicken at the sight of him. She quickly wiped her eyes and composed herself.

"Vice Chairperson," she said. "What are you doing here?"

He smiled, looking sincere and almost shy. "Please, call me Davis. I'm sorry to bother you, but I wanted to give my condolences. Chairperson Dawan gave me directions, since he's your parents' neighbor and all. I hope that was OK. I'm very sorry to hear about your father." He handed Iris the flowers.

"Uh– Thank you." Iris looked around, not sure what to do with them. She wasn't in the mood to interact with her mother right now. Eventually, she set them down in front of the door.

"Don't you want to take those inside?"

"Later." She raised an eyebrow at him. "You came all the way here to see me? Or were you here to see Chairperson Dawan?"

"Well, after what happened at the election… you left the party so quickly. And then I heard about your father. I was worried about you."

She was surprised he had noticed her absence at all. Her pulse raced. She kicked herself. Why couldn't she control her emotions around him? He was just a man.

Davis continued. "May I give my condolences to your mother?"

"It's not a good time."

He nodded, watching her with a furrowed brow. Silence hung between them, as thick and uncomfortable as if it were a hot, humid night.

Iris shifted under Davis's gaze and looked at the sky, half speaking to herself. "I really need a drink."

Davis perked up. "I may have just the thing." He pulled out a flask from inside his jacket. "Is this very unprofessional of me?"

Iris hesitated, then shrugged. She strode forward and took the flask, twisted off the lid, and took a swig. Whiskey burned her throat.

Davis took the flask back and raised it. "To your father." He took a sip. "And to you, for running a good race."

Iris cringed. She realized she hadn't told her mother she hadn't gotten the position. Her mother would be glad she was out of the political spotlight, and that would make her loss feel even worse.

Davis seemed to notice her expression. "I know the loss stings, but it's not too soon to start planning another campaign. You plan to run again, right?"

"I– guess? I don't know. Based on the recent election results, it doesn't seem like my platform is very popular."

"People are just afraid to speak up, for now. But I can tell you the sentiment *is* there and growing."

Iris raised her eyebrows. "Are you telling me that *you*– Chairperson Dawan's trusty right-hand man– are pro-integration too?

"I told you I voted for you, didn't I?"

"I thought you were just being nice."

Davis chuckled. "You're selling yourself short. You ran a good campaign. Even if you didn't win, it was close. You've started the momentum. Now it's time to keep it going."

"Maybe," Iris said with a sigh. "It's just that... when we first met, you told me that I was special with my two secondary powers."

"You are."

"Then why is it taking me so long to advance in politics?" Iris tried to stay calm, but a hint of anger wavered her voice. She couldn't help it. Davis had raised her hopes and put her on this path in politics.

Davis spread his hands. "Time is very relative here. You may still be gauging your progress based on a Static's lifespan. In terms of a Shifter's life, you're definitely on the fast track. You *are* special. Don't give up. You're just getting started."

She didn't want to admit it, but his words comforted her, and she let some of her hopes pour out.

"It has been my dream to change the Shifter system. At first, it was just to help my parents, but now it has spread to a desire to help all Statics. They shouldn't have to settle for less. They shouldn't have to grow old and die before their time if we can help them. Shifters need to unite in our special abilities. Show we're not afraid. Be visible and strong. Not to mention the financial opportunities there could be for Shifter powers."

Davis clapped. "I couldn't have said it better myself. I know that I speak for many others when I say that I'm tired of living half a life; of hiding in plain sight; of being told where I can go and who I can socialize with."

The corner of Iris's mouth quirked up. "Are you available for campaign speeches?"

Davis returned Iris's amused smile before assuming a businesslike mode. "It's important to start your campaign early. I could help you." At this last phrase, his voice softened before resuming his business talk. "That is if you want me to. The way you present yourself is important. We could go by your first name if you prefer. It may be more personable. That's what I do."

Iris took the flask and almost choked on the whiskey again. "Davis is your first name?"

"Why yes," he said with a chuckle. "Davis would be an unusual Chinese last name, don't you think?"

"Yes, well— I didn't want to make any assumptions. You could have a different ancestor somewhere in the mix or have been adopted."

"Very true. I stand corrected."

"So, what is your actual last name?"

"Sun."

Iris lit up. "Oh! Like Anna Sun!"

Davis laughed. "No relation. It's a very common name. That's why I always went by Davis." He sipped from the flask and passed it back to Iris. She took another swig, managing not to cough this time. "Just think of it as Davis. It's easier that way."

"You want me to think of you as Davis Davis?" Despite her sadness, Iris laughed. Davis joined in. She didn't know if it was the whiskey, but it felt nice to laugh, to leave her troubles behind for a moment. They looked at each other, their gazes lingering, then Iris flushed and looked away. "Well, I'm going to get going on my walk. Thanks for the drink."

Davis stepped forward. "Mind if I join? It's a beautiful night. Just look at that bright full moon."

Iris tensed up. He wanted to walk with her? She couldn't believe that he would be interested in her. This must be for professional reasons or because he felt bad for her. She didn't want his company out of pity. At the same time, he was her superior. She needed to keep him on her side if she ever wanted to advance in the Council, and he had already offered to help on her next campaign. Plus, she could use a little more whiskey.

"Sure, but I don't really know this place that well."

"You could *find* us a nice place to go? Maybe by the ocean?"

She realized Davis was suggesting she use her power of

locating. "It doesn't work that way. It has to be something more specific. For instance, if you had a photo of the spot you wanted to go to. Or had left an object in that location. If I had already been there and didn't remember the way, then I could use my abilities to think of the place and lead us there."

"I see."

Iris thought for a moment. "There's a trail along the cliffs, not far from here. I walked there with my mom yesterday."

Davis extended a hand to the side. "Lead the way."

They walked down the sidewalk and onto the forested dirt trail beyond, sipping whiskey all the way. By the time they reached the cliffs, Iris was feeling downright jovial. The sea breeze was crisp and invigorating. For the time being, Iris let it blow away her worries. She spread her arms out to either side, feeling as if she could float away. Then she came to a halt. A sign blocked their way.

Private Property No Trespassing.

"I guess we can't go any farther," Iris said. "That's private land."

"I won't tell if you won't," Davis said with a wink. He took her hand and pulled her past the sign.

Iris let herself be led, feeling a thrill at the touch of his hand and at their misbehavior. They found a large rock to sit on, close to the cliff's edge with a view of the waves lapping at a narrow strand of beach forty feet below. Her inhibitions were lifting. Boundaries blurred. For the first time, she allowed herself to truly feel her connection to Davis.

This is silly, she thought. *I don't really know him.* At the same time, she didn't care. She was enjoying his company.

Through the happy haze of the whiskey, Iris stared into Davis's eyes. Being this close to him, the blackness of his pupils seemed to almost encompass his whole iris. They gave him a wild look. This time, she held his gaze. He was very handsome. He always had been. Plenty of people would love to be in her position right now. Mindy Le, for one… But, so what? He was here with her, not Mindy. Why should she deny herself a little fun? Why had she been so resistant all this time? How else was she supposed to get to know Davis without letting loose a little? He leaned forward, and she held her breath, expecting to soon feel his lips press on her own.

"Iris?" he murmured.

"Hm?"

"I want to let you know I'm here for you."

Iris breathed out. "Oh?" She inched her face closer to his.

He turned away and sighed. "I also know what it's like to lose a parent. My father died last year."

"Oh." Iris tried to hide her disappointment. "I'm so sorry. I didn't know." She put a hand on his hand. He closed his fingers over hers, and she felt another thrill up her spine.

Davis looked up at the moon. "It's strange. Even though he's gone, I still have this desire to make him proud. I guess it never goes away."

"Parents," Iris sighed. "What about your mother?"

"My mother died when I was a teenager."

Iris felt a pang of sympathy for Davis. He was all alone in the world now. At least she still had her mother. After this walk, she would go home and try to be more appreciative of her.

"Before she died, she gave me this." Davis let go of her hand, pulled something out from his pocket, and handed it to her.

Iris examined the object. It was a round, dark stone, smooth like glass.

"What is it?"

"A good luck charm." He smiled. "It changed my life."

Iris rolled the stone between her fingers, thinking about loss and family. Was there something magical about this stone? Something that could help her in her grief? It seemed like a plain old stone. A polished and shiny stone, but plain all the same. She waited for him to elaborate on how his life had changed. When he didn't continue, she didn't probe him, understanding the delicate nature of emotions surrounding loss. She tried to hand it back to him, but he shook his head.

"My mother told me she got the stone around this area," he said. "I was wondering, do you think you can find more?"

"You want me to find you more stones?"

"Not just any stones. Stones exactly like this one." He smiled sheepishly. "I know it's silly, but this one has been so good to me. I would be honoring my mother's memory if I could add to my collection. And maybe it could help you like it's helped me."

"That's really sweet." A lump formed in her throat as she touched her bracelet. "Let me try."

She closed her eyes and focused on the stone in her hand. The familiar tug developed in her mind, pulling her down, down. She opened her eyes and drew in a breath.

"There are some close by!" she exclaimed.

"Really?" Davis jumped to his feet and looked around. "Where?"

She stood up and peered over the edge of the cliff; A jagged, slate facade, slick with ocean spray. The tug in her mind grew stronger, and she teetered with the effects of the whisky. Worried she might tumble over, she plopped down onto the ground. She stretched out a finger and pointed.

"There. There are more stones. A lot more."

CHAPTER THIRTY-EIGHT

Nivi

Summer 2000

Rays of light scintillated through Main Street's maple trees, casting shadows that danced around their feet. In a couple months, the foliage would be ablaze in yellows, oranges, and crimsons, and Yuras's population would double with the tourism the display would attract.

"How are you feeling?" Ling Guang asked.

"Better," Nivi said. She kept her attention on the ground, dreading what her grandmother might say.

Nivi had apologized for her behavior the other night and everything seemed back to normal for a day. Then, out of the blue, her grandmother suggested they go for a morning walk downtown. She had something she wanted to discuss.

"I found a new book about Algonquian languages at the library. Well, new to me. It's actually very old. You should try learning some languages with me now that you'll have some more free time."

Was this what her grandmother wanted to talk to her about? She didn't see why they needed to go on a special walk to discuss this. Maybe this would be a good time to tell her grandmother she didn't plan on continuing violin, even after she healed. She opened her mouth but couldn't bring herself to say anything. Doing so would make things so final. Her arms, covered by a long-sleeve shirt, hung heavy by her sides.

"Did I tell you it was an old friend who got me into the local language? I'll have to tell you more about her one day. She has a really interesting story."

Nivi nodded politely but remained silent. They continued down the street in silence. Ling kept giving her strange looks as if she were about to say something but kept changing her mind. It seemed they were both having trouble speaking. As awkward as this was, Nivi wasn't going to be the first to break their silence. Her grandmother was the one who wanted to have this talk anyway. Instead, Nivi focused on the scenery around her.

Something was off. She shivered despite the warm summer day, and the sky seemed to darken in response. The light gray trunks of the maple trees blurred together, and a little house came into focus. It was a white, one-story house with a dark gray pitched roof and powder blue shutters. For some reason, seeing this house made her stomach jump. It was familiar, yet Nivi had no memory of it. It was as if she were seeing it for the first time and the thousandth time. In a flash, the house charred into rubble, and the leaves of the surrounding trees erupted into brilliant red flames. Nivi gasped. She stumbled, disoriented and dizzy, and the scene faded away. The bright sunny day and majestic trees returned unscathed and unchanged. There was no house in sight.

"There's something I need to tell you," Ling said, turning to Nivi.

Nivi wasn't listening. She swayed back and forth before collapsing into her grandmother's arms.

⌁

Nivi lay in the middle of her beige bed, staring absently about her room. A couple of violin posters decorated the walls, and a shelf filled with sheet music and music books stood in a corner beside her desk. On the desk was the framed photo of her parents, which she had moved from the altar. The last piece of sheet music she had practiced before the fire lay open on the music stand. Nivi looked at her scarred arms. The lightness she had felt after being liberated from her violin obligations was fading, and a new dread she couldn't explain was setting in.

Her head had been pounding since the walk, and now, with the night advancing, it didn't seem she would have a reprieve any time soon. *It's just part of the healing process,* Nivi told herself as more images flashed through her mind. She kept seeing the white house with blue shutters burst into flames. Each time the scene replayed in her head, more details came into focus. In the scene, she realized she was four years old and it was raining– no, storming. Thunder and lightning shattered the dark sky, and water streamed down the car windows. *That's strange. A fire in a rainstorm.* She didn't understand why this house was having such an impact on her. She had only ever lived in one home, the one she was in now, beige inside and out. She had lived here with her parents and her grandmother, and then, at age four, her parents had died in a car crash. Then, it was just her and her grandmother.

"Where are Ma Ma and Ba Ba?" Nivi remembered asking. Her parents were both engineers who worked a lot, but they were never out this late.

Po Po responded in her usual stoic manner. "You won't understand this yet, but they're gone."

Nivi had stood there in the room, watching the water drip from her hair and clothes, forming a small pool around her feet. "When will they be back?"

"They won't."

Wait. Why was she dripping wet if she was waiting at home indoors for her parents that night? There must be some connection to the burning house. It was raining the night that house was on fire. Nivi was dripping wet the night her parents died. What was the connection? She racked her brain until it throbbed as if to the beat of a metronome. All the images blended into a shapeless and meaningless clump. Thoughts scattered as she drifted into a fitful sleep. She tossed and turned in her bed, feeling the sweats come on again. She got up to open the window, then returned to bed, eventually kicking her covers off to cool herself. A bead of sweat dripped from her furrowed forehead.

Nivi wiped her brow and opened her eyes. The beige walls of her room faded from view. In their place was a wall covered in colorful child drawings. She blinked several times, confused by what was happening. Where did her room go? She tried to get up, but her body didn't move. She tried to speak, but nothing came out. Only her eyes responded. Trying not to panic, she looked around, taking in the scenery.

Wooden dolls painted in Chinese garb lined the shelves, and red paper lanterns glowed from the ceiling, acting as a nightlight. Under the lanterns lay a heap of pillows in bright blues, reds, and golds, and on top of it sat a little girl holding a stack of paper and a box of crayons. Her curly, brown hair was cut short with bangs that fell into her eyes as she drew. Beside her sat a woman watching the little girl draw. The woman had a similar tan complexion as the girl and black hair with a gray streak over her forehead. Nivi sucked in a breath. The hair was just like her mother's. Could this be a memory? If only she could remember her mother's face more. She tried to look at the photo on her nightstand, but that was gone, too.

While the little girl was in the middle of drawing a picture, a gust of wind from the window blew the paper out of her hands and across the room. The little girl looked dismayed, but the woman spoke with an air of mystery and excitement.

"Ooo, May, do you know who that was?"

The little girl, May, looked up with wide eyes. "Who Ma Ma? I didn't see anyone."

Both their voices sounded far away as if they were on the other side of a glass barrier.

"That was the wind god, Fei Lian," her mother said. "He must be trying to tell you a secret."

"A secret?" May cupped her ear and scrunched her face.

Her mother laughed. "He doesn't always speak in words. Sometimes, he shows you things by using the wind."

The little girl looked confused, but that only lasted a moment before her face lit up. "What does Fei Lian look like? I want to draw him." She ran across the room to gather her papers, then plopped down on her heap of pillows.

"Well," her mother said when May had settled herself, "he has two forms. A human form and an animal form."

"I want to draw the animal form."

"Ooo, good choice. Fei Lian's animal form is very interesting. He has the head of a bird, and on that head, he has two horns like a bull."

"Wait, Ma Ma. You're going too fast." May scrunched up her face and put down her crayons. "It's too hard."

Her mother picked up the crayons and handed them back

to May. "You can do it. Just take a deep breath. Now, let it out. There you go." Her mother spoke more slowly this time as May scribbled to keep up. "And then he has the body and legs of a deer and a really long tail like a snake. His body is covered in spotted fur, like a leopard."

May worked on her drawing for several minutes before presenting it to her mother, who oohed and awed over it.

May looked out the window as another gust blew in. "How does Fei Lian control the wind?"

"He keeps the wind in a big yellow bag. Some say it is also a bag of secrets, memories, and answers, and if you listen to the wind or watch the movements caused by the wind, you might learn something useful."

May looked as if she didn't fully understand. "Is Fei Lian real?"

"The ancient Chinese believed he was."

That seemed a good enough answer for May, and she continued drawing. Meanwhile, the wind picked up from the window, lifting their hair into artful spins and twirls.

Nivi felt the wind hit her face, too. She shielded her face from the gust, relieved she could move again. When she lowered her arms, her room had returned to the plain beige walls and violin posters. May, her mother, and all the colorful drawings and decor were gone.

The sun was still up, and the wind gusted outside. The house moaned under its force. Nivi found that she was breathing hard. She slowed her breathing and tilted her head to listen to the wind. Maybe Fei Lian would know what was going on with her or what really happened to her parents. She glanced at the photo of her parents on her nightstand, but the memory of the woman in her dream had already faded, and she couldn't be sure if it was her mother or not. Even if it was, it didn't matter.

It was just a dream conjured up by her subconscious because she was frustrated by her lack of answers and her inability to do anything about it. So what if going to the morgue had jogged her memory? It still brought her nowhere nearer to understanding why the man followed her and attacked her, let alone why her grandmother had been acting strange.

She got up from the bed and went to the window to close it. Behind her, a rattling sound came from the other side of the room. Nivi left the window and walked over to investigate. A piece of paper had blown up against the opposite wall and was shuffling from side to side. Nivi approached it, thinking of the child's drawings from her dream. *No, it can't be.* She stooped over to pick it up. Flipping it over, she scanned the images with a laugh, although she couldn't help feeling disappointed as well.

It was a photocopy of a section of a newspaper. At first, she thought it might have been from a class assignment, but she didn't recognize it. It must have been some random trash that blew in with the wind. If only it could've been Fei Lian. Nivi carried it to the trash can, crumpling it in her hand. Before throwing it away, she glanced down at it once more, feeling stupid for her false hope. On the bottom right was a photo of the remnants of a white, one-story house with a dark pitched roof and light shutters. A chill went through her body. Even though the house was mostly destroyed, she recognized it immediately. It was the home from her vision. The one that had been on fire.

CHAPTER THIRTY-NINE

Iris

Summer 1990

DAVIS PACED BACK and forth along the cliff ledge looking for a way down. He seemed anxious and excited after Iris told him more stones were nearby. Iris had moved back from the cliff and was sitting on the large rock, clutching the flask of whiskey. She watched him through an alcoholic haze, not understanding why he was so worked up over a simple stone. Then she thought about her father. Her heart ached, and she understood how something so simple could mean so much once the person was gone.

Davis walked back toward Iris, rubbing his hands together with a decisive look.

"Iris." He took the flask from her, finished the last sip, and put it in his jacket. Then he took her by the hands. "This is such a fortunate development. You can't know how happy you've made me tonight. I thought this would be much harder and take much longer, but you've made my job so much easier."

"You're welcome," Iris said, almost like a question. That was a strange way of phrasing his search for the stones: a job.

"Once I have the new stones, I want to do something nice for you to thank you. How would you like to live closer to your mother?"

Iris was caught off guard. "Uh. That could be nice, but that's not possible. I need to stay close to the office in San Francisco if I ever want to be the Northern California representative."

Davis's voice escalated in pitch and speed. "Who says it has to be in San Francisco? What if we moved the office around here? What's the closest bigger city?"

Iris blinked, trying to absorb the deluge of questions and manic energy. "I think Crescent City is about an hour away."

Davis clapped his hands together loudly, causing Iris to jump. "Crescent City it is!"

Iris laughed. His enthusiasm was rubbing off on her, but then she remembered her conversation with the chairperson earlier in the week. "Chairperson Dawan would never go for it. He's very old-fashioned. He likes to follow the rules."

"Rules, rules, rules. That's all I've ever heard my whole life. Davis, you're not good enough. Davis, you're a disappointment to our family. All because of the stupid rules!"

Iris furrowed her brow. She wasn't sure what to make of what he was saying. They'd both probably had too much to drink.

"But guess what," he continued, pointing a finger at no one in particular, "I've made something of myself because I've made my own rules. All thanks to this." He tossed the dark gray stone to Iris.

She fumbled to catch it. "OK. Now you *have* to tell me. What is so special about this stone?"

"All in good time. All in good time." He put an arm around

her shoulder as they walked along the cliffside. "When I'm chairperson, I'll promote you to NorCal rep, and we'll make new rules together."

Iris snorted and put the stone in her jeans pocket. "Be prepared for a long wait. I don't think Chairperson Dawan is going anywhere anytime soon. And besides you, his current senators and reps are not about to vote him out."

"We'll see about that," Davis said, almost to himself. Then, louder, "First, we need to figure out how to get down there."

"Too bad we couldn't just use our powers."

"Of course! We can use our powers! Why didn't I think of that?"

Iris stopped walking abruptly and turned to Davis. His arm was still around her shoulder, and with her sudden change in position, she collided with his chest. Heat rose to her cheeks, but she didn't back away. Instead, she looked up into his face and spoke with an authority fueled by whiskey.

"Because one, it's against the rules. And two, I don't want to lose my powers permanently as punishment for a reckless, drunken decision. Although getting a mark would make my mother's day." Iris laughed.

Davis put both arms around Iris. He looked down into her eyes and spoke in a soft, teasing manner.

"There you go with the rules again. Look around. There's no one here to see us."

The heat in Iris's cheeks spread through her whole body. Her skin tingled. Their closeness magnetized the attraction she had always felt toward him. Her thoughts were a blur. All she could do was stare at his lips. She tried to protest faintly.

"We can't. It's…"

Davis leaned down and pressed his lips to hers. Iris inhaled sharply, and then she was kissing him back. He ran his hands through her hair and down her back. Any resistance Iris had to Davis's proposition faded with his touch. Iris was completely drawn in, intoxicated in his embrace.

Drawing Iris even closer, Davis moved his mouth toward her right ear and whispered.

"Please."

Iris's legs wobbled. She clung to Davis. What were they talking about? She wanted to keep kissing him, but Davis kept his head by her ear and whispered again.

"Please. For me. For us."

Iris squeezed her eyes shut, trying to clear her mind. Davis drew back his head and looked at Iris with a pleading expression. This slight, physical separation was enough to allow her conviction to reform. As much as she wanted to stay in Davis's arms, she felt strongly about this. She pushed herself gently away and shook her head.

"We can't. It's not like when I use my finding skill. Shifting is so much more visible. Someone could see us. We could both get in serious trouble." She lowered her voice to a whisper as if someone could overhear. "What if the chairperson saw us?"

Davis laughed. "You think that old bore would be up at this time of night?" He looked at his watch.

He was probably right. Chairperson Dawan stuck to a rigid schedule. Could she risk it? She wanted to help him, but there had to be another way.

Iris turned away from Davis and looked over the cliff. She scanned the cliffside. It was too steep to climb down in their current forms. As a snake, she would be able to navigate the sheer face. Her belly could wedge into and grip the uneven surface, and she could even coil her tail around a tree before descending if needed. She pushed the thought from her mind. This was ridiculous. She had worked so hard to form relationships with Chairperson Dawan, Senator Springston, and others. This could ruin everything. How could a stone be worth that much?

"Aren't you afraid of the consequences?" Iris said.

"I'm more afraid of the restrictions. Don't you feel how unnatural it is to keep your true self caged up? Locked inside. You can feel it, right? The urge to break free."

Iris furrowed her brows. "I– don't see what this has to do with anything. It's just a stone."

Davis took her hand. Each time he touched her, her attraction to him grew. She could feel her resistance fading again. Was it just the alcohol? Her grief? It felt so much stronger and deeper. Like she was losing control. Like all that mattered was to be near him and make him happy. He drew her to him, and she didn't resist. He kissed her again, and with that, all her willpower melted. What had following the rules gotten her anyway? A dead father. She was sick of always being so good and proper.

"It's more than that," he said. "I will show you. It will change everything."

She stared into his face, mesmerized by the dark, depthless pools of his eyes, the strong angle of his jaw, the way his lips parted, and the sweet, spicy whiskey on his breath. Slowly, she nodded. "OK."

"Really?" He embraced her and then turned to squat next to the cliff. "If you can get me to the location, I can carve out a tunnel for us to stand in. Then you can transform back and let me know where to dig."

"You can carve rock, too? I thought you told me I was an outlier with my two secondary powers."

"Shh. Don't tell anyone," he said with a wink.

"Then couldn't you carve a path down for us now?"

"I'd prefer to make one later, from further below. I don't want to create a ramp that anyone could use." Iris lifted her eyebrows, and Davis put up his hands. "I'm not saying anyone will come now. I just don't know if I'll be able to reform the rock to its original position after carving it, so whatever I carve might be permanent. If I make the ramp from up here, it will be really visible to anyone who happens by in the future. I mean, we *are* trespassing." He grinned.

"Thanks for reminding me. But couldn't you put a camouflage stone by the ramp?"

"I'd have to request that officially, and this is *unofficial* business."

Iris was a little reluctant, but she was also excited. This felt like an adventure. What harm could finding a stone do? She took the stone out of her pocket. She shook out her shoulders, trying to focus. Concentrating on the stone in her hand, she felt for the location of the other stones and committed it to memory. She handed the stone back to Davis, then looked behind her shoulder to make sure no one was around. The dark forest looked back, unstirring, crowned in moonlight. Satisfied, she closed her eyes.

Heat moved through her veins and coursed through her body. Her eyes began to burn. When she opened them, the world was cast over in a crimson hue. Her arms fused to the side of her body, and her legs merged into one. The ground shrunk away as her body elongated. Her skin became taut and restrictive, a temporary discomfort. Scales of pliable, white armor broke through her skin and replaced her clothing. Davis was right. It had been so long since she could change forms. She was free. It was exhilarating.

Davis gave a low whistle. "Call me impressed. I'm glad you're not my enemy."

Hissing, Iris lowered her head to the ground. Davis climbed on, grabbing a hold of one of her ivory horns. She slithered over the side of the cliff, her belly tensing as it gripped and released the rocky projections. The water lapped at the base of the cliffside. Ocean spray stung her eyes as she descended to just above sea level. She stopped and nodded to indicate this was the spot, then turned her head to the side to bring Davis close to the wall. He stepped forward, holding one hand to the slick stone while keeping the other firmly grasped to one of her horns. A coppery light emitted from his outstretched palm. The rock rumbled and small fissures formed. As Davis moved his hand, the rock slid aside as if it were putty. From time to time, a piece of unsupported rock cracked off and splashed into the retreating tide below.

Davis made quick work of carving into the rock, and in a matter of minutes, he had created a ledge and the beginning of a tunnel big enough for the two of them to stand in. Once he was in the tunnel, he used both hands to work even faster. Iris placed her head into the tunnel entrance and contracted her body, shrinking until she was back to human form. She reached up and touched the bands of stones that formed the arch over them.

"Nice work," she said, breathless from the adrenaline rush.

"Couldn't have done it without you. Wait here. I'm going to create that ramp now. That way, you don't have to risk transforming in public again, and we can come back any time we want to. I'll keep it far enough below the top of the cliff so it's not visible from above. "

He handed her the stone, then extended his arms outside the entrance. The rocks seemed to melt under his touch, collapsing away into dust. He stepped onto the newly formed ramp and continued to shape the rock before him, walking up the incline as he went. When his head was a foot shy of the top, he leveled the ramp off and returned to the tunnel entrance.

"We can easily climb the rest of the way out."

"I hope so."

She turned her attention to the stone in her hand and directed him where to carve. They moved into the cliffside, led by Davis's hands and their rock-carving glow that illuminated their way. Deeper and deeper they went. The sounds of lapping waves faded behind them. Cold stone and stagnant air encased them like a tomb. Davis's breath was beginning to sound ragged.

"Are you OK?" Iris said.

"I'm fine. How much farther?"

"We're getting really close. Wait. Stop. Just under here. Go very slowly."

Davis switched to one finger and touched the rock surface as if trying to remove a smudge. From beneath the glow of his finger, the rounded, glassy surface of a stone emerged.

"It really is here!" he exclaimed. "Can you create more light to help me see?"

Iris put the stone in her pocket and lifted her hand, summoning a flame that she cupped in her palm. Wavering, orange light flooded their immediate surroundings. Davis tried to continue to remove the stone, but he was trembling. Sweat beaded his brow. With a gasp and a cough, he slid down to the floor.

"What's wrong?" Iris said, dropping down next to him. She lifted the flame on her palm to look into his face. The color had drained from his complexion, and his eyes were glazed over. He tried to wave her off.

"I'm fine. I just need a minute," he wheezed.

Iris didn't understand. His powers shouldn't have taken this much out of him. Not from someone of his age and experience. Did he breathe in something toxic? Something released while excavating the rock? But then she should be feeling it, too. Maybe he was sick?

Davis pushed himself back onto his feet and leaned his forehead against the rock.

"Just a little more. I can do this."

Iris laid a tentative hand on his back. "Are you sure—?"

"I'm fine!" he snapped.

She shrunk back but stayed near in case he became unsteady again, holding up her palm like a torch. Davis continued his painstaking work, scratching around the stone with the tip of his finger. Finally, the stone fell into his hands. Cupping it like a baby bird, he sank to the floor and laughed. It was an exhausted and crazed sound that made Iris cringe. But then he looked at her and smiled his disarming smile, and she melted back into an arduous infatuation.

"We did it. We did it," Davis said over and over. He beckoned to her. "Come. Sit with me."

Iris sat beside him, cradling her flaming hand in her lap. "Now what?"

He held the stone up before her. "This is going to change the rules. *We* are going to change the rules." He looked around. "But we're going to need help. I don't think I can access any more on my own. You said there were lots more down here, right?"

"Yes. But why do you need more? I thought you just wanted one as a keepsake. And why can't you access them on your own?" Her eyes focused on the newly unearthed stone, and she realized it looked different from the original. They both had glossy surfaces, but the original was a dark, flat gray. The new one was light gray, and there was something else about it. "Wait. Is it moving inside?"

Davis withdrew his hand and closed it. He hesitated. "It is."

Iris suddenly felt very sober. "Davis. Tell me what's really going on. What is this stone? Why are you so exhausted? Was the story about your mother true?"

"Yes. Everything I've told you is true. Right before she died, my mother gave me one of these stones."

"One of those? You have more? What else are you not telling me?"

"I can't tell you. Not yet." He got up. "I need to talk to Chairperson Dawan first."

"Now?"

"Yes." He began to walk toward the tunnel entrance.

Iris followed, extinguishing the flame in her hand as they approached the moonlit entrance. When Davis didn't slow down, panic crept up her chest.

"You can't go now. You'll wake him up. He'll figure out what we've been up to and be really mad. What if you lose your position? What if you get a mark? What if we both get a mark? Then, I'll never be promoted. Please stop. Wait and think before you go."

"There isn't time. I have to talk to him again before the vote tomorrow."

"Again? The vote?" The pieces clicked together. Her heart sank. "You *were* here on business. Not to check on me."

Davis stopped. He swung around to face her. The stern expression he wore caused her to back up against the wall. When he spoke, his voice came out cold and hard. Nothing like the charm she'd known up to that point.

"If you must know, yes. I was here on business. I met with Chairperson Dawan just before I came to your place." He took a few steps toward her until he was right in front of her. Her body tensed. A red glow illuminated the space between them as her eyes ignited from within. His expression and tone softened. "But I was worried about you as well. It just so happens that we can help each other. Chairperson Dawan gave me the idea. Not intentionally, I'm sure." He seemed to sink into thought for a moment. "Anyway, you have already helped me immensely tonight, and I plan to repay the favor if you'll let me. There are things going on right now that you don't know about. If you want to change the system and be a representative one day, then come with me. If not, then go home and forget about what happened tonight."

He strode away and started up the ramp. Iris stayed glued to the wall, heart thumping and mind racing. None of this made sense. But Davis seemed so convinced that this stone would make a difference in the vote. A vote to relax the restrictive measures barring most Shifter and Static interactions, especially Shifter interventions in Static affairs. If it passed and her father were still alive, it could've saved his life.

Iris winced at the thought. How could her parents willingly choose a shorter life? Maybe her parents had been through dangerous times, but things were different now. They shouldn't have had to hide. They shouldn't have had to give up their powers. Tears brimmed her eyes. How could Shifter law let her father die? Iris gritted her teeth and ran up the ramp after Davis.

The tide was rising toward the cave entrance. When she caught up to Davis, he smiled and took her hand. A look of determination crossed his face.

"Let's do this. Together," he said.

Iris looked back toward the tunnel. "The tide is coming in."

"Don't worry. I took care of it."

"Oh, right." She had forgotten about his water skills after all the rock carving tonight.

Together, they walked in silence through the woods toward Chairperson Dawan's house.

CHAPTER FORTY

Ling
Summer 2000

Ling sat on the porch looking through The Classic of Mountains and Seas. Nivi was in her room resting after her episode during their morning walk. Ling had wanted to tell Nivi everything then and there, but Nivi looked so shaken and pale that she couldn't bring herself to put more on her shoulders. She would let her rest for a while, then go in and speak to her. She heard footsteps on the sidewalk and looked up to see Meng walking up to the house. Her heart jumped.

"Do you have a moment? I need to show you something."

Ling nodded, closing the book. "Let's go to the backyard. Nivi is inside resting."

They sat at a table under a wooden pergola. Around them, birds chirped in the lush backyard and played in the trickling fountains. A small Japanese maple tree wavered in the breeze, its bright green leaves tinged with red.

Meng leaned forward. "You didn't tell her yet?"

Ling avoided Meng's gaze. "I was about to, but she's not feeling well."

"Of course she's not. She will feel better knowing why she is feeling this way."

"Please, let her rest a little longer."

"She needs to know everything. That her parents didn't really die in a car crash. That they died in a fire in their house. What we had to do to protect her. What you gave up. What we both gave up."

"I promise I will. Is this why you're here?"

Meng shook her head. She put her hand in her coat pocket and brought out the gray stone. Pale blue swirled inside, pulsing from time to time like a cloud illuminated by lightning.

Ling perked up. "Is that–?"

"A transfer stone. It took me a while to remember what it was."

Ling took the stone and marveled at it. "It has been a century since I last saw one. I thought they were banned."

"They were."

"You activated it?"

"Not on purpose. A Static was wearing it around his neck, and I asked to see it."

"You were fortunate he was unaware of its powers and didn't intentionally try to use it on you." Ling tried to hand the stone back.

Meng put up a hand. "Keep it here for now, in a safe place. I need to use it for evidence, so I don't want to take back my powers yet and deactivate it. There is only a small amount of my power in there, but we don't want it to get into the wrong hands."

Where did the Static get it?"

"By the Cliff Trail."

"Will you let the Council know?"

"Not yet. I think there might be a transfer stone mine nearby."

Ling put a hand to her mouth. "A whole mine?"

Meng nodded. "I'm going to go investigate this afternoon. And, there's something else…"

Ling listened intently.

"I was in the forest by the Cliff Trail, and I believe I saw– a horned fox."

Ling's eyes widened. She sucked in a deep breath. "Here? In Yuras?" Hope flooded through her body.

"Do you think it's possible?"

Meng reached forward and took Ling's hand in her own. She looked at Ling with a softness in her eyes that Ling hadn't seen in a long time.

Ling looked back, her eyes moistening. "But where could she have been this whole time? Where is she now?"

Meng shook her head. They were still holding hands, looking deep into each other's eyes when the front door slammed. They jumped up and Ling rushed inside.

"Nivi?" she called as she walked through the house. She came back to the backyard. "Nivi's gone. Do you think she overheard us?"

"I need to check on the transfer stone mine. You go look for Nivi. I'm sure she is OK but she needs to hear everything now. I'll meet you back here tonight."

CHAPTER FORTY-ONE

Davis

Summer 1990

MOONLIT MIST SHROUDED the white, one-story house with the dark gray pitched roof and powder-blue shutters. A faint light glowed from a window to the left of the front door, diffusing through the moist air. Otherwise, the house was dark.

Dry pine needles crunched beneath their feet as Davis and Iris made their way up the front walk. They passed a lone redwood to their right that towered in front of the house, then walked up four steps to the front door. Davis raised a hand to knock, paused, and turned to Iris.

"Why don't you wait out here? I'll talk to him first and come get you in a little bit."

Iris retreated behind the redwood tree. Davis knocked at the door and waited with his hands in his pockets, cradling the stone in his left hand. Light sprinkles of rain began to fall. He waited and then knocked again. A light came on in the house. Footsteps approached. After a moment, Jackson Dawan opened the door. He looked sleepy, and his tone didn't hide his irritation.

"Vice Chairperson, do you know what time it is?"

Davis looked up at the sky as if it were a clock. "I believe it's past nine."

"Very much past nine."

From somewhere in the house, the sound of a violin drifted haltingly to the door. Davis leaned his head into the doorway. "It sounds like someone's still up."

Jackson Dawan sighed. "Yes, well, I don't want to restrict our enthusiastic and budding musician. You might as well come in. What is this about? I thought we had finished our discussion earlier."

"I was hoping to appeal to you one last time."

As Davis followed Jackson into the house, an unrealistic series of thoughts popped into his mind. If Davis could get Jackson to change his mind about the vote, maybe he wouldn't have to use the transfer stone. If Shifters and Statics could mingle again, maybe he could keep his position in the Council even if he didn't have powers because maybe, just maybe, he could reveal what he really was.

Jackson stopped in the living room, his back to Davis, and placed a hand on the mantle over the brick fireplace. "I've already made up my mind. Your showing up here in the middle of the night is not doing you any favors."

"Chairperson, if you would please reconsider—"

Jackson swung around with a penetrating look that gave Davis a chill. "I've given you the benefit of the doubt because you have served me and our community well. But it's time for you to tell me the truth. What is going on with you? What is this really about?"

Davis didn't respond. His heart raced. His hand pulsed around the stone. Jackson didn't know his secret. He couldn't know. Davis would've never made it this far in politics if Jackson had known this whole time.

"You know I can tell, right?" Jackson said. "I'm not sure others can, at least not yet. I don't understand it. I've never seen anything like it. Your aura... I only noticed a few months ago, and it's getting worse. Tell me what's going on. Maybe there's something I can do to help."

Davis hung his head, his hands still in his pockets. His aura and his powers were fading. He had to act now. How silly to think he could change Jackson's mind. There was no getting through to him. Davis would never be accepted by the Shifter community, not in his true form. And he couldn't forget Jackson was the enemy. Jackson killed his mother. He would finally get his revenge. This is what he had been waiting his whole life to do. But something held him back. All his time around Jackson over the past years had sowed a seed of doubt. The Jackson he knew wouldn't kill someone. There was only one way to find out.

"Actually," Davis said, lifting his head, "there is something you can do to help. Tell me why you killed my mother."

A look of surprise replaced Jackson's sleepy and annoyed expression. "Your mother...?" Then, realization crossed his face. "Chairperson Sun. I thought you said there was no relation."

"I lied."

Chairperson Dawan's voice was steady. "I didn't kill her."

"Now you're lying." But something didn't sit right with Davis. The seed of doubt sprouted. He soldiered on. "Because of you, my father blamed me for her death. I know you and my father were enemies. You wanted to stop my mother's integration policies, and with her out of the way, you could as chairperson."

"Enemies? No, if anything, your father and I worked together." Jackson hesitated. "I'm sure you're aware of the type of company he kept. I'm not proud of my past. I've directed people to do some unsavory things to get to where I am. But I've matured. I've changed. And I've never had anyone killed."

Tears stun Davis's eyes. He blinked them back. Despite everything, he believed Jackson. Davis let the stone slip from his fingers back into his pocket.

Jackson's eyes stared off into space, and he spoke as if he were thinking aloud. "When Randall Sun disappeared from Shifter society, it was the best thing to happen to me because it allowed me to escape that life. I became an honest man and have done my best to support and protect my people. How is your father these days?"

"He's dead."

Jackson's gaze turned to Davis. He seemed to be evaluating Davis, inside and out. "When the transfer stone mine was created, I was tasked with eliminating the memory of all those involved. I was supposed to direct one of those people to erase my memory as well. After using most of the oblivion tincture, there was only one other man, other than me, who knew where the transfer stone mine was, but he was so drunk all the time I didn't think he'd remember. At that time, I was still immature and selfish. I figured the mine could benefit me in the future. So I lied and said that that man and I had finished using the tincture on each other. Who would've thought he'd go and tell his *Static* son?" Jackson's voice took on a tone of disdain.

Davis tensed. His fingers curled back around the stone in his pocket.

Jackson continued speaking. "I grew up. I matured. I realized that mine was dangerous and no one should use its contents. So I moved to this area to keep an eye on the mine. Over time,

I grew lax, and I assume full responsibility. I should've erased both Randall and my memories that day." His gaze turned into a glare. "You may take our powers, but you'll never be one of us." He spat on the ground.

A jolt of self-loathing ripped through Davis's heart. How could he be so stupid to think that Jackson thought of him as an equal? Jackson may not have killed his mother, but he was still the enemy. Davis would show him. He would be more powerful than any Shifter ever was. Without a second thought, he touched Jackson with the stone.

White light shot out where Davis touched Jackson. Heat surged up Davis's arm and through his body. His skin tingled. His blood pulsed. His muscles swelled. He felt invigorated. This was what he needed. Power.

Jackson fell into a crouch, shaking his head. Suddenly, he lunged up at Davis and tackled him to the ground. Davis, caught off guard, struggled under Jackson's grip. Even without his Shifter powers, Jackson was surprisingly strong. Davis jumped up from the ground, and Jackson followed him. He lunged at Davis again. Before Jackson could get ahold of him, Davis released a fireball from his mouth into Jackson's chest. Jackson flew across the room into a wall and burst into flames. He lay slumped against the wall, a gaping hole seared in his chest, as the flames licked up the wall and spread. Before long, the whole room was on fire. Davis covered his mouth, a moment of panic before he composed himself. That foolish Static. What was he thinking, attacking someone more powerful than him?

Davis turned toward the door. A figure appeared in the hallway that led to the rest of the house. A woman. Mrs. Dawan. Davis froze, but then he realized he now had Jackson's powers. Mesmerism. He strode toward Mrs. Dawan and touched her forehead. Her eyes glazed over, and she swayed from side to side. Davis could feel the control he had over her. All he had to do was give her a command, and she would obey. But he also felt the strain. He wondered how many people he could control at once before he lost the secondary power. Mrs. Dawan would prove useful to help him mine the transfer stones. If he needed more help, maybe Statics would be easier to control than Shifters.

Iris would be useful as well. He needed her as an intermediary so that he wasn't seen too often near the mine. Once he had a few more stones, he could take Iris's power for himself, and he wouldn't need her anymore for her finding abilities. Although that ability in him would only last a few decades at most. What if he lost the ability and couldn't find any more transfer stones? He couldn't risk that outcome. For now, he would also have to mesmerize Iris.

As Davis left the burning home, he glanced down the hallway toward where the violin music had been coming from. The fire would take care of the child as well. It was better this way. Davis knew better than anyone what it was like to grow up without parents. He was doing the child a favor.

CHAPTER FORTY-TWO

Iris

Summer 1990

Iris was already having second thoughts about their late-night visit to the chairperson's house. She thought about turning back, but she stayed where she was. Every time a doubt popped up, she only needed to look at Davis and her mind would be put at ease.

She waited behind the redwood tree, feeling like a silly child playing hide-and-seek. A subtle fragrance emanated from the tree. Spice, earth, and a tinge of sweetness. She leaned against the rough bark, closed her eyes, and steadied her breathing.

There was a knock on the door. Iris tilted her head to listen. Nothing. An owl hooted in the distance. Mist coalesced at her feet; ghostly tendrils rising up to grasp at her jeans. A breeze picked up, and the top of the redwood rustled and swayed. Darkness glided over the land, blotting out the moon. Swollen clouds drifted overhead, and sprinkles blew onto her forehead and cheeks. *Great,* she thought, pulling her cardigan around her.

Another knock. A moment later, the door opened. Iris craned her neck as far as she dared. Chairperson Dawan's deep voice greeted Davis. He sounded surprised and tired. Maybe a hint of irritation. Iris bit her lip. Footsteps moved into the house, and the door swung on its hinges. Heavy rain droplets began to fall, rehydrating the dirt and pine needles into a fragrant mud. Drumming her fingers on her thigh, she decided to creep over to the door. At least she could get shelter from the rain under the awning.

Holding her hands over her head, she trotted over. She leaned on the door frame and peered through the glass in the door. Davis's back was toward her. Glimpses of Chairperson Dawan's broad shoulders and chest came in and out of view from beyond. He was pacing. Even though Chairperson Dawan was at least five inches shorter than Davis, he had a daunting presence. Iris put her ear to the door.

"Your aura," Chairperson Dawan was saying, "I only noticed a few months ago, and it's getting worse. Tell me what's going on. Maybe there's something I can do to help."

His aura? Iris looked back through the window. She focused on Davis, feeling his internal energy, the glow that identified all Shifters to each other. It was there. What was wrong with it? She adjusted her positioning and view and compared the two men's auras to each other. Chairperson Dawan's was brighter, but that wasn't unusual in itself. What was it then?

Something caught the corner of her awareness. A flicker, ever so slight, almost imperceptible. Was it really there? It happened again as if Davis's aura was vacillating in intensity. No, it wasn't the intensity. It had completely blinked out, only for an instant. How could that be? The existence of the aura was directly related to whether or not someone was a Shifter. How could he suddenly not be a Shifter, even for a fraction of a second?

She put her ear back on the door, but rain battered the roof and ground and blotted out the voices from inside the house. Iris returned to the door window. A blinding white light flashed through the glass. She pulled back, blinking rapidly to clear the spots from her vision. What was that?

Yells arose from within the house. Iris stepped back from the door. Her pulse quickened. What was happening? Should she intervene? Whatever trouble Davis was getting into could bring her down as well. What if the chairperson brought them both before the Council for marks? She hesitated, wringing her hands, no longer noticing the chill of the wind and rain.

The door opened and Davis ran out, almost crashing into her. Behind him, a fire engulfed the living room, and Chairperson Dawan lay on the floor. Iris gasped. Before she could say anything, Davis reached out a hand and touched her forehead. The world clouded over. The events of the night bled together. Her memories became a muddled mush.

She blinked and saw Davis next to her. Handsome, strong, caring Davis. She smiled. He took her hand, and her heart swelled. She blinked again. They were standing in front of a white house with powder blue shutters. Where were they? That's right. This was Chairperson Dawan's house. But why were they here?

Anger flared in her chest. A raw, unrestricted, primal rage. She was furious with the chairperson and his wife. How could they have let her father die? It was all their fault. They could've helped, and they chose not to. Smoke fumed from the back of her throat, coalescing into flames that licked at her lips. They erupted. Igniting the wood floors. Blazing up the curtains and walls. Pooling against the ceiling. Consuming all in their path. The whole world was red. And then it faded to black.

Iris opened her eyes. She was on the ground under a large redwood tree, cold and drenched. Her forehead ached. She sat up. Heat and light met her face. She squinted. There was the little white house with powder blue shutters engulfed in flames. *Oh my God,* she thought as jumbled memories flooded her mind. *What did I do?* She tried to remember what happened, but her mind was confused; stifled; stagnant. Rain poured down, but it did nothing to stop the flames.

Someone grabbed her from behind and lifted her up.

"We have to go. Now!" came Davis's voice.

"But… fire," Iris said. "We have to help." She pulled away from his grasp and tried to move toward the house.

He caught her arm and brought her back toward him. "There's nothing we can do. We have to go! Don't you understand? *You* did this! If anyone catches you here, that's it. You're done for."

"I? What?" Iris began to tremble. Her heart raced. Rain streamed down her face and across her vision. This couldn't be happening. "There must be something we can do."

"It's a magic fire. We need someone with water powers to stop it, and by the time we get someone here, it would be too late anyway."

Water powers? Somewhere in the distant recesses of her mind, she thought this sounded familiar. Did she know someone with water powers? She grasped at the thought. Tried to bring it closer. The slip of memory flickered at the edge of her consciousness and then fluttered away.

Iris grabbed her pounding head. Suddenly, she realized they weren't alone. A woman stood next to her, also drenched.

"Mrs. Dawan!" Iris exclaimed, letting out a sigh of relief. The chairperson's wife was alright. Maybe that meant Chairperson Dawan and their daughter were already out of the house.

Mrs. Dawan didn't say anything. She swayed in the rain, eyes glazed.

"Mrs. Dawan?" Iris said again, waving a hand in front of her face. "What's wrong?"

"I had to," Davis said. "She saw what you did. I did it to protect you."

"You did… what?"

"Mesmerism. I mesmerized her. It was the only way."

"You can mesmerize people? Since when?"

"There's a lot about me you don't know."

"Where is the chairperson and their daughter?"

Davis looked at her. He didn't need to say anything. Iris's knees went weak. Tears burned her eyes. She was an arsonist. A murderer.

"Now, let's go." He took her and Mrs. Dawan by the arm and led them deeper into the forest. A siren sounded in the distance.

"But what about…?" She looked at Mrs. Dawan.

"Don't worry. I have an idea."

A strange sense of gratitude spread through her. She had done something terrible, unthinkable. Yet here was Davis, staying with her, helping her.

The pounding in her head continued as they rushed through the forest, away from the fire. If only they could find someone with water powers, the fire could be extinguished, and maybe they could explain that it was all a mistake. Her fire power got them into this mess, and her location skills only worked on the inanimate. Davis could carve rock and… mesmerize? Were those his two powers? She remembered being surprised that he also had more than one secondary power like she did, but was that all? She couldn't shake the feeling she was forgetting something.

Fire and location. Rock carving and mesmerism. The powers repeated in her head until the throbbing became so intense that she had trouble even remembering those. A sense of alarm shook her body as her memories became more and more obscure. What was happening?

Sloshing footsteps brought her back to the moment. Rain pelted down between the trees, bringing down pine needles that caught in her hair. Mrs. Dawan followed from behind in a stupor, like she was sleepwalking. Iris looked at Davis leading the way. Strong, handsome, determined. Somehow, his presence calmed her. She could trust him.

He turned to her. "By the way, as I promised, you have been promoted. Congratulations, Representative Bai."

CHAPTER FORTY-THREE

Ling

Summer 1990

Smoke filled Ling's lungs, and she inhaled deeply. Smoke. Heat. Flames. This was the environment she was born for. It invigorated her, and this was a time that needed her complete focus and presence. She flapped through the house, gently grasping the unconscious four-year-old child in her talons. Her vermilion bird form, immune to fire, shielded them both from harm.

At the edge of the driveway, Meng waited for her. Ling glided out of the burning house, fluffing her feathers at the touch of the night chill. She placed the child on the ground and returned to her human form.

"Any other survivors?" Meng said.

Ling shook her head. Her nails dug into her palms. "Who would do this?"

Meng lowered her voice as if sharing a secret. "If I had to

guess, I'd say Vice Chairperson Davis. He'd benefit the most from the chairperson's death."

Ling gritted her teeth. "And he's callous enough to kill the chairperson's wife and child in the process."

"Luckily, we spotted the fire in time to save the child. Now, we must keep her safe until I can get proof."

"Can't we just wait until the authorities arrive?"

"We have no way of knowing if any of them are involved. But, I have a plan. We must act quickly." Meng reached into her blazer pocket and produced a red dot about the size of a quarter.

Ling's breath caught. "Is that what I think it is?"

Meng nodded solemnly.

"No," Ling said. "You can't give up your powers."

"It's not for me." Meng extended her hand.

Realization dawned on Ling. She shivered.

"I know it's a lot to ask," Meng continued. "But this will allow you to hide from the Shifters with the child. And with my position as the representative leader, I can monitor things from the inside until I can get proof."

Ling lowered her eyes and stared at the child on the ground. The red mark would be practically permanent, only reversible by combining specific Shifter powers. It would strip her of her longevity, strength, and ability to transform. She would be ostracized from the Shifter world. Her aura, the internal glow all Shifters had and could see within each other, would be gone. All that, of course, was how she would hide from the Shifters. It was a fate almost worse than death.

Meng took Ling's hand in her empty hand. "I know you didn't have the best relationship with the child's mother. I wouldn't ask this if it wasn't important. I believe this is just the beginning of Vice Chairperson Davis's plans, and we have to stop him before he hurts more people."

Ling winced, thinking of her estranged daughter. It was her own fault they didn't speak. If there was one thing she could do to make it right, this was it. She set her jaw. "I'll do it."

"You are sure? We can talk about this more."

Ling looked into Meng's slender, icy blue eyes. So unusual for a Chinese woman, and so striking against her pale skin and jet black hair. She absorbed this final moment with her. The sound of cars in the distance disrupted her thoughts.

Ling grabbed the mark from Meng's hand. "They're coming. We don't have time." She squeezed her eyes shut and slapped the red dot onto her left shoulder.

Instantly, a strange sensation arose in her chest. Tingling spread outward to her limbs like a million ants racing across her body. Then, it was gone, leaving her lightheaded and wobbly. She bent over and put her hands on her knees. What had she done?

Meng watched her with a look of pain. She touched Ling's shoulder once, then turned to the child on the ground. The child's breathing had become more even now that she was out of the smoke, and she looked almost peaceful. Except for her brown hair and a dusting of freckles, she looked just like her mother. Her small form, brown skin, and round nose weren't too dissimilar to Ling either.

Meng withdrew a vial of liquid from her blazer and sprinkled a few drops on the child's head. She turned to Ling. "An oblivion tincture. When she wakes, whatever you tell her will become her new reality."

Tears filled Meng's eyes. Ling, never one for much emotional display, held Meng's gaze for a few seconds, then lifted the child from the ground. The weight of the child took Ling by surprise. What should've felt like nothing with her previous Shifter powers suddenly took some effort. With one more glance at Meng, Ling ran past the burning house and into the forest.

Back by the house, cars screeched. Doors opened and slammed. They were here. Too soon. They would see her running away.

She tried to run faster, but her previous inhuman strength was already gone, nullified by the mark on her left shoulder. The only advantage was that her magical aura was also gone. It was no longer a visible tracker. She would blend in with the normal people of the world, the Statics, except there were no other people around right now.

Behind her, two-legged steps transformed into the galloping of a large creature. Ling glanced back. The creature's sleek, black body was almost invisible in the darkness. It lifted its head and sniffed as it ran, its breath fogging into the air. Ling recognized the panther, the Shifter's head of police. He always caught his target.

As Ling went deeper into the forest, the darkness encompassed her. Even though her vision was poor, she couldn't slow down.

Her left foot caught a tree root. She fell to her knees, barely managing to hold onto the sleeping child in her arms. Pain shot through her ankle. Her breath caught, and she held in a yelp. She tried to get to her feet, but her ankle crumpled under her weight. Panting on the forest floor, Ling glanced wildly about. She wouldn't be able to escape with the child, not with a twisted ankle. She would have to hide the child and lure away the panther and the rest of his search team. It was the only way to keep the child safe. In a house fire of that magnitude, it would be assumed that the child had perished with her parents, which is what she hoped the arsonist believed as well.

Ling felt around on the ground until she encountered a

shrub. She spread the branches and placed the child inside. Struggling to her feet, Ling hobbled along. When she had put a little distance between herself and the girl, she let out the yell she had held back when twisting her ankle. Twigs snapped as the panther skidded and altered course to trail her. Ling hung at the edge of the forest, following it until she came to a cliff. Without time to think, she scrambled over the edge.

She gripped the craggy cliff face, her fingers trembling under the strain. Sweat dripped from her brow, and her clammy hands threatened to lose their hold. Below, waves crashed against jagged rocks that pointed toward her like pikes.

The air whooshed overhead. A blue-green, serpentine dragon undulated over the cliff edge, its wingless body gliding effortlessly through the air, leaving crackles of electricity in its wake. It was Meng in her Shifter form.

Only moments ago, Ling could've transformed as well and flown away with Meng from this mess, fire flickering from her red feathers. What had she been thinking to relinquish her powers and leave the life she had known as well as the love of her life? To protect a child she barely knew? Maybe Meng had been worried about nothing, and the child would've been safe in Shifter hands.

The dragon circled in the sky, its four taloned feet clawing the air, then glided down to Ling's level. Two horns protruded from its silvery mane. Whiskers floated around its toothy snout. Iridescent scales glimmered like sunlight sparkling off the ocean water. A sudden dread pitted Ling's stomach. What if Meng had changed her mind? Or worse, what if Meng was the arsonist or an accomplice? They had assumed the arsonist was someone high up in the Shifter Council. Someone who would benefit politically from the chairperson's death. Davis wasn't the only one who fit that profile. Meng did as well.

Gravel sprinkled down onto Ling's head. She couldn't see it but could hear the panther's heavy padded steps above. All Meng had to do was indicate to the panther that she was down here. Another horrible thought entered her mind. With just a flick of Meng's tail, Ling would go tumbling down to her death. Maybe this had been Meng's plan all along. Fabricating a plan to strip Ling of her powers with the pretense of hiding her with the Statics.

Meng's breath puffed against Ling's face. Then she turned and flew back up. Voices came from above. Meng must've transformed back to her human form.

"There's no one out here," Meng said. "It must've been a neighborhood child that came to gawk at the fire."

Ling let out a held breath and almost smiled. Her small stature could very well pass for a child. She had been silly to think Meng would turn against her after all their years together. She was weaker than she thought, letting her emotions get to her in the heat of the moment.

"You may be right," the police chief said. "Let's do one more sweep back toward the house to make sure."

Ling heard them depart. She waited as long as her remaining strength would allow, then pulled herself onto the cliff edge. Dawn was breaking over the horizon, spreading a rosy glow over the ocean. She lay on the ground for several minutes, resting her aching arms and listening for any indication that the search party was coming toward her. When she didn't hear anything, she limped back to the shrub where she had left the child. She sighed, running through various versions of what she would tell this child. It had been so long since she had had a child of her own, and then that child ended up not speaking to her. Even if it was her duty, how was she qualified to raise this child? Maybe the child would be better on her own. She could take the child to town and find her a nice family, then return to Meng and live just as they had before. With this thought, she parted the shrub branches.

The child was gone.

Panic seized her. This had to be the right bush. She started ruffling through every bush in the area. It was no use. The child had vanished. Had the Shifters found her? If so, this was all for nothing.

An unexpected pain hit her heart. She hadn't expected to feel such a loss. The child was not just any child. She was family. Her granddaughter. Even though Ling's daughter had been estranged, the child had not had any agency in the matter. Ling had grown used to not speaking with her daughter, but her daughter had always been there. In the back of her mind, she knew there was always a chance they could reconcile in the future. Now that chance was gone. Ling hadn't allowed herself to mourn, but now that the child was missing, she had lost the last remaining part of her family.

Ling put her head in her hands. A sob threatened to shake free. She wandered in a circle, not sure where to go. As she began to leave the forest, a movement caught her eye on the road. There was a small figure walking just ahead. Ling broke into an uneven run and stopped when she reached the back of the figure.

The child turned and looked at her with an innocent expression. "Hello."

Elation filled Ling's heart. She had a second chance at repairing her family. She knew then what she would tell her. Her new reality would start with the truth.

"Hello, my granddaughter."

CHAPTER FORTY-FOUR

Davis
Winter 1998

Davis left the tunnel, taking with him a small bag of transfer stones. These would have to do for now to replenish his powers. Especially his water abilities, which were critical to keeping this mine dry when the tide came in. Where should he go this time to find his victims? Africa? China? They had plenty of tiny villages where he had found a lone Shifter living among Statics that he could easily target without causing much of a fuss. Oftentimes, the Shifter didn't really understand where the powers came from, so didn't know the full extent of what losing them meant. Other times, he was able to find someone young and newly coming into their powers and snatch them away before much realization developed.

Mining had taken more time than he realized. He needed more stones. As many as he could get his hands on. At first, he thought taking care of Jackson Dawan would finally fulfill his promise to his father. Make him worthy of his father. But it wasn't enough. Davis was still a weak Static masquerading as a Shifter.

After making sure his water barrier spell was intact, Davis walked up the trail along the cliff face. When he reached the top, he hefted the sack onto the cliff, then started climbing up himself. Even in the middle of the day, he wasn't worried about anyone seeing him since he had on his camouflage pendant. Any Static passerby would continue on without noticing him.

There was the crunch of footsteps in front of him. Davis didn't pay much attention and even chuckled, thinking about how he could frighten a passing Static. But then he felt it. The glow and warmth of a Shifter's aura. His first inclination was that it was Representative Bai. But she shouldn't be here, not without his direction. A slight concern came over him. Had he been discovered? Well, he was prepared to fight with what he had. He pulled himself the rest of the way up and took a couple of transfer stones out of the bag to have ready.

A woman stood before him. She had long, dark brown hair that cascaded in curls down her back. Wide-set, dark brown eyes. She stood frozen, a look of shock on her face, before she slowly started backing up.

This was a surprise. In all his years of frequenting this area, Davis hadn't come across any Shifter residents, not since the Dawan family had been *taken care of.* The way she was acting, it didn't seem like she was part of the authorities come to investigate his operations.

"Hello," he said, taking a step forward. "Who are you?"

"Please," she said. "I don't want any trouble."

"There's no trouble at all. I'm just passing through."

"I know who you are. You're going to turn me in."

"Turn you in?"

"I just want to be left alone with my family."

"I wasn't aware of any Shifter families in this area."

The woman's face grew pale as if she knew she had said something she shouldn't have. Her gaze went to Davis's hand. Davis realized in his attempt to appear unthreatening, he had opened his hand and put the transfer stones on display. The woman glanced from his hand to his face several times, her expression now fearful.

"My family and I, we don't intermingle with other Shifters at all."

"If you don't want to intermingle with Shifters, why not take the mark?"

The woman winced. "I've heard it can be hard to give up a part of yourself, and that loss can be unbearable. I thought I could remain hidden here."

"And the rest of your family felt the same?"

The woman looked off to the side and didn't answer.

Davis suddenly realized why the woman was afraid of being turned in. She was a Shifter. Her family was not. Could he trust her to keep his secret? But now she knew where the transfer stone mine was. Even if she didn't know what the stones were, he couldn't risk it. He put on his most innocuous smile and turned on his allure power.

"You have nothing to worry about. If you know who I am, you know I am *for* integration. Change is always slow, but I've been doing everything possible to start the process."

The woman looked hopeful. "But I'm breaking the current laws."

Davis took a couple of steps forward. "Your secret is safe with me."

The woman's body relaxed. "Thank you."

Davis took another step forward. "Of course." He was almost close enough to touch her.

He made his move. A flash of light, and she fell to her hands and knees with a cry. Now that she was a Static, she would be much easier for him to mesmerize. He grabbed her shoulder to turn her toward him so he could touch her forehead, but she bolted, scrambling to her feet and running in an uncoordinated zigzag.

She wasn't fast, and she was disoriented. It would be easy to catch her. Davis ran after the woman, but she suddenly veered toward the cliff's edge and tripped. Leaping forward, Davis threw his hands out to stop her fall. His hands transformed into lion claws to better grip the falling woman. The sharp nails dug into her clothes and across the woman's chest, but she continued to fall. Screaming, she plummeted over the edge.

"No!" Davis yelled.

He fell to his knees by the cliff edge and desperately grasped at the air. The woman thudded against the rocks below. Davis's breath came in such rapid succession that he began to gag. What had he done? It was one thing to kill Jackson Dawan. That was vengeance. But this was an innocent bystander.

Stop it, he told himself as he slapped his own face. *She was a necessary casualty. She would've turned you in. And you would've stretched yourself thin if you needed to mesmerize another person. Stop being such a weakling. This is what great leaders have to do. Make sacrifices.*

His breath slowed. He wiped his face and stood up. Dusting himself off, he took one last look over the side of the cliff. Waves lapped at the woman's unmoving body as seagulls cried overhead. Davis turned and walked away.

CHAPTER FORTY-FIVE

Nivi

Summer 2000

NIVI RAN DOWN the street, unable to breath. She didn't know where she was going, so she just ran and ran. *Her parents didn't die in a car crash. They died in a house fire.* The words spun through her head. It all made sense now. Her grandmother had been lying to her all these years. Ten years of secrecy and avoidance every time Nivi asked about her parents. She had assumed her grandmother was from a generation that didn't dwell in the past or express feelings. Maybe it had even been too painful for her grandmother to speak about. But now, the only thing Nivi could think of was that her grandmother had something to do with her parents' death. Why else would she hide the truth from her? It wasn't pain that had kept her grandmother from talking. It was guilt. And that guy who had attacked her. Maybe he was involved too. He had come back to finish the job, so she couldn't turn him in. She couldn't go back home. She couldn't trust her grandmother.

When she finally slowed down, she was deep in the forest. She keeled over and put her hands on her knees, gasping and choking as she fought back tears. A large, round rock lay a few feet ahead, so she climbed onto it and sat down. She wiped her face and stared straight ahead with blurred vision, trying to process her thoughts. Who had her parents been? Was their death intentional or an accident? Did the fire at the school have anything to do with the fire that had killed them? And who had killed the man who attacked her?

Nivi took a deep breath. Dust particles danced in streaks of light from above, and a light breeze tickled her bare shoulders, mingling ocean and pine scents. She brought her knees to her chest and laid her arms and head on them. Tears streamed down her nose and onto her jeans.

A hand touched her arm.

Nivi shrieked and jumped off the rock. She was past the point of composure. Heat flashed through her body, and her arms burned. A familiar woman stood on the rock where Nivi had been sitting. Blue scrubs. Tall, lean, and muscular. Short black hair with a gray streak in the front.

"You're– from the morgue!" Nivi exclaimed. She was glad to notice the woman was cleaner than their first meeting. "What was your name again? Ji?"

"Yes. I'm sorry to startle you." Her eyes moved to Nivi's arms. "You're... a Shifter. Of course, I see your aura now. It's faint, but that's because it's new."

Nivi looked down. The veins on her arms were undulating and glowing like pulsing lava creeping up her arms. As they advanced, her skin transformed into blue-green iridescent scales that scintillated gold and purple. Fire ignited from her hands. It ran up the sides of her arms along her twisted veins. She gasped and swatted at the flames, attempting to put them out. Stepping back, she tripped and fell to the ground. She wanted to scream, but her panicked, short breaths smothered her voice.

Ji jumped down from the rock. Crouching down in front of Nivi, she spoke in soft tones. "It's OK. Just breathe with me. You can do it. Deep breath in. Now, let it out. Keep going, in and out. There you go. Good."

Nivi followed Ji's prompts. Eventually, she felt her pulse returning to normal. As she relaxed, the fire and scales faded from her body, and her veins returned to a faint blue behind the raised scars. Miraculously, the fire didn't seem to cause any harm. Her mouth was dry, and she coughed several times before she was able to speak.

"What's happening to me?"

"You're a Shifter. My memory's still a little fuzzy, but it seems you're going through your first changes. Is this the first time you've seen this happen?"

"Um, kind of." The night Nivi returned from the hospital, she thought she had seen her veins glowing. She had told herself it was just in her head. Maybe this was still in her head. She had fallen asleep on the rock, and she was dreaming.

"Kind of?"

Nivi started out of her train of thought. She was definitely awake. But how could this be real? The scales on her arms weren't like any animal she'd ever seen. And how could she produce fire, let alone be immune to being burned? A sinking feeling filled her stomach. Maybe Amber was right, and she *had* caused the fire at the school. She didn't know how much she should tell Ji.

"It's a long story." That much was true.

"I don't know if I should be the first one telling you this. You should speak to your parents." Ji got up.

"They're dead. You can't just spring this on me and leave me here."

Ji sighed and helped Nivi to her feet.

"Maybe we should find a comfortable spot where we can talk for a while."

They hiked through the forest until they came to a bench on the cliff overlooking the ocean. A cool ocean breeze mitigated the hot sun. Ji's strip of gray hair looked silvery in the light. They sat down on the bench, and Ji spoke.

"A Shifter can transform into another creature."

"OK…I wouldn't have believed you if I hadn't seen what was happening to me. How do you know this anyway?"

"Because I'm also a Shifter."

Nivi's eyes widened, and she murmured to herself. "Monster people have been real this whole time?" She shook her head. If she wasn't dreaming, maybe she was going crazy.

"Well, I wouldn't call us that," Ji said with a hint of mirth in her voice. "Look at me. Can you detect my aura?"

Nivi looked at Ji. She didn't know what she was looking for, but then there it was. A glowing from Ji's chest.

"I see it! And feel it?" There was a warm feeling inside Nivi's chest as well.

"Yes. That's it. That's how you will be able to recognize other Shifters. How did you not know you were a Shifter?"

Nivi slouched back. Her thoughts were going in circles, but then she chuckled to herself. If she was going crazy, there was nothing she could do. So there wouldn't be any harm in finding out more information. "I don't know. My Po Po has a lot to explain if she even knows what I am. What can I turn into anyway? Some kind of fire lizard?"

"We'll have to wait until you fully transform to see." Ji gave her a small smile and gazed out toward the ocean.

Nivi eyed her from the side. "What can *you* turn into?"

"I'm not sure, exactly. A kind of fox."

"You don't remember? You can't be *that* old. Like forties, right?" Maybe age-related memory loss started earlier than Nivi realized.

Ji chuckled. "You'd be surprised. And it's not that. I have a spell on me that's affecting my memory."

"Oh great! There are spells, too?"

Ji nodded. "Some good. Some bad."

An idea popped into Nivi's head. Would it be rude for her to ask? But how else was she supposed to believe all this? She took a deep breath. *Here goes nothing.* "Can you transform now?"

Ji looked momentarily surprised, then seemed to understand Nivi's intent. "Sure."

Ji glanced around. When she seemed satisfied there were no onlookers, she stood up from the bench and immediately fell forward. Nivi jumped forward to prevent Ji from hitting the ground, but in midair, Ji transformed. White fur replaced her clothing and skin. Her ears grew long and pointy, tipped in black, and her face elongated into a toothy snout. A curved horn sprouted from her forehead, its silvery surface gleaming in the sun. She landed softly on padded feet. A bushy tail, also tipped in black, swished silently behind her.

The change had occurred so quickly, Nivi still had her hands out as if to catch Ji. Yup, she was definitely going crazy. There was no hope for her now, so she might as well go with it. This realization calmed her anxiety, and she reached forward and touched Ji's back without thinking. Although the fur looked fluffy, it was surprisingly thick and coarse. Nivi smiled, then realized she was basically petting someone even though she wasn't in human form. She jerked her hand back.

"Oh god, I'm so sorry. That was so creepy of me."

Ji transformed back into a human, laughing. "I'm glad you

realized. You'll get used to the etiquette." Nivi sat back down on the bench, feeling mortified. Ji joined Nivi on the bench. "It's OK, really. I don't hold it against you at all."

Nivi rubbed her palms on her jeans. What was wrong with her? This was why she didn't interact with people: because she did stupid things like this. She looked out toward the sea, her tone cold. "How did you find me anyway?"

"I followed you."

Nivi scooted away from Ji on the bench. "That's more creepy than me petting you." She tried to sound condemning, but then she giggled, and then they were both laughing.

"I'm sorry. After you came and asked about Allen, I needed to know if you knew more."

"Allen?"

"The man that died in the fire."

That sobered them both up. Nivi fiddled with her fingers, looking at her scarred veins that had just been alight with fire. She couldn't be responsible for the school fire or his death. Even if she *had* done something, it was in self-defense, right? That thought didn't relieve her of the suffocating guilt of potentially killing someone. Oh my god, what if she *had* killed him? The more she thought about it, the more it made sense. How else could she have emerged mostly unhurt from the fire? The fire that came out of her didn't harm her.

Another terrible thought manifested in her mind. She tried to reject it as nonsense, but it pushed its way to the front until it was all she could think about. Her abilities could also explain her parents' death. Maybe that's why her grandmother had lied to her and hid the truth about her abilities. Because Nivi had started the fire that killed her parents. How could she ever go home and face her grandmother?

"I don't know anything," Nivi snapped. She turned her face

away from Ji to hide her anguish. She wasn't going to tell this stranger anything. "I'm also having memory problems."

Ji's voice was soft. "It's… the shifting. Your first shifts can be physically and emotionally traumatic. They can cause temporary memory loss."

"Lucky me."

Ji didn't seem to be bothered by Nivi's sudden attitude. "The good news is that it'll eventually pass, and all your memories will come back."

Nivi jumped up. That was not what she wanted to hear. "I'm leaving."

She didn't know where she would go, but she couldn't stay here and listen to more of this nonsense. She didn't want her memories back. She wished she could forget everything she just learned and go back to how things were before. She'd even go back to playing violin if she could resume her life before all this craziness. A pit developed in her stomach, making her wince. Why did the violin affect her so much?

Ji stood up. "Wait. I'm sorry. I know this is a lot for you. I don't actually work at the morgue. I didn't mean to trick you. I was there looking for Allen, too. And then you came in and– I didn't know what to do, so I just pretended to be an employee."

Nivi tensed. More lies. "Don't follow me again." She began to walk back toward town.

Ji called after her, speaking quickly. "Allen was a friend. We were together in that cave."

That made Nivi pause. Suddenly her memory cleared more. She remembered the noises that Allen had made before he attacked her and how she had heard the same noises in the cave – from multiple people. Allen hadn't been alone. Fear tensed all of Nivi's muscles, preparing her to run. Was Ji going to finish off the job that Allen failed to do?

Ji continued talking, her voice taking on a pleading tone. "Allen and I were under a spell that kept us in that cave, and maybe another that kept us alive. We didn't eat. We didn't sleep. We were either working or not working. And when we weren't working, we were kind of idle in one part of the cave, on standby. When you entered the cave, something activated in us and we approached you, like we were instructed to defend against intruders. After I touched you, something happened, and it was like the whole spell had been lifted. We left the cave and were hungry and thirsty and tired for the first time in ten years."

"Ten years?" Nivi was still on high alert, but Ji's story was sucking her in. Ji seemed so sincere, it was hard for Nivi to imagine why she would make something like this up. "Then what happened?"

Ji hesitated. "We were walking by a high school…"

Nivi tensed again. This was it. She would see if Ji told her why Allen attacked her.

Ji continued. "Suddenly, Allen was overcome by the spell again. He took off into the school. I ran after him but saw the master walking in after him, and I hid."

"The master?"

"He's the one that put the spell on us and made us work in his mine. I don't know his name, and I can't even remember what he looks like. But I'm sure I'd know him if I saw him. He would come periodically to pick up stones." Ji sighed. "I can't help but think if I had gone in after Allen, maybe I could've helped him, and he wouldn't have died."

And maybe I'd be dead, Nivi thought. She tried to hide her skepticism. Was this all an act to get her to trust Ji? But why would Ji need Nivi to trust her? If Ji wanted to kill Nivi, she could've done it already. And did Ji really not know that Allen had attacked her? Nivi hadn't seen anyone else in the school hallway except for Allen, although her memory was still fragmented from that day, so she couldn't really say if this *master* was real or not. She decided to tell Ji what happened to see how she'd react. "Allen– attacked me."

Ji put her hands to her mouth. "It must have been the spell the master cast on us. Allen had no control over what he was doing. But why would the master want to hurt you?"

Nivi looked down and shook her head. She didn't know what to believe, but it seemed less and less likely that Ji was here to hurt her. What if this master had known what Nivi was capable of and had come after her to prevent her from hurting other people? She turned her palms up and down, looking at the scarred veins, remembering the fire that had leaped from her skin just moments ago. Her hands trembled. Amber had been right. Nivi must have started the high school fire. She didn't mean to, but she was still an arsonist and a murderer. Her breathing grew more rapid. Her head pounded. She clenched and unclenched her hands, sucking in short breaths. Before she could stop herself, her insecurities poured out of her mouth. "What if *I* killed him? What if I burned a hole through his chest?" She almost said *what if I also killed my parents?*

Ji furrowed her brow. "I don't think that's the case. When powers first come out, they are nowhere near their full strength yet. You wouldn't have been able to do that if you had tried."

"Are you sure?"

"I'm positive."

"And I wouldn't have had any powers as a child?" She wasn't going to cry. She wouldn't let herself.

"No."

That little word was such a relief. Nivi's legs wobbled, and she made her way back to the bench and sat down before she got too lightheaded. Ji came to the bench and touched Nivi's shoulder but quickly withdrew and remained standing. Nevertheless, Nivi felt comforted. For some reason, she trusted Ji. Ji said she couldn't have killed Allen. Ji said she couldn't have had her powers as a child. Nivi wasn't responsible for anyone's death. She took a deep breath and let the ocean air wash over her face. The relief was brief as she began to think about her parents' death again and the fact that her grandmother had lied about it. What was she going to do? She shifted on the bench and heard a crinkle from her back pocket. Standing up, she pulled out the photocopy of the old familiar house.

"What's that?" Ji said.

Nivi decided to take a chance and tell her about the house and her parents. "I've been having visions of a house on fire. Then I found this copy of an article about a house fire, and it's the house from my vision. And then, I learned that my parents died in a fire. It seems like too much of a coincidence, except the article says the house was abandoned."

Ji looked at the paper and sucked in a breath. "I know that house." She ran her fingers over the photo of the burnt house. "I know where it is."

"How?" Nivi's heart thumped. After all these years, would she finally know the full truth about her parents' death?

"I don't know. I just know where it is. Follow me."

CHAPTER FORTY-SIX

Meng
Summer 2000

ENG CREPT THROUGH the forest to the Cliff Trail. Her heeled boots crunched over fallen leaves and pine needles. Mosquitos flitted about her sleeveless dress. She should've worn something more practical, but she didn't bring anything besides business suits and dresses. At least this time, she wore her camouflage pendant. She wasn't going to have a repeat of the other night. Too bad the pendant didn't protect against mosquitos. She swatted at her shoulders and arms.

She sat down on a stump and waited. Not long after, she heard footsteps approaching. Standing up, she watched Amber and a boy come into view. They walked along the cliff and passed her, chatting loudly as if they didn't expect anyone to hear them in this area. Continuing on, they veered off the main path to follow the cliff, passing a *Private Property No Trespassing* sign.

Cheeky teenagers, Meng thought. She lingered where she was until the teenagers were just out of view, then trailed them, keeping within the tree line. With the camouflage pendant on, she didn't necessarily need to be this careful, but why take any chances? There might be Shifters involved with this cave.

When she passed the *No Trespassing* sign, she no longer saw them. Where could they have gone? She could see all the way down the coastline, and there wasn't anyone along the whole cliff. She decided to make herself comfortable against a tree and wait for them to come back from wherever they went. After a while, the sound of voices snapped her to attention. She sat up and saw the kids climbing up over the cliff edge. Both Amber and the boy looked spooked.

"I don't understand," Amber said.

The boy ran a hand through his hair. "I don't think it's as abandoned as we thought. Let's get out of here."

They took off in a jog back the way they had come. Once they were gone, Meng looked over the edge. There was a ledge and a ramp leading down to the ocean. This had to be it. She climbed down onto the ramp and walked to its base where a tunnel led into the cliff. She stepped into the dark, cavernous entrance. Holding out a hand, she opened and closed her fist until an electric current built along her tissues. Blue electricity sparked along her palm and between her fingertips. Sparks crept up her skin until her whole body glowed with electricity. The emitted light illuminated her vicinity.

She walked through the tunnel, following the largest branch until she entered the open room at the end. There was evidence of mining. Picks and buckets full of black rock lay about, but there were no transfer stones that she could see. She let out a sigh. Maybe she had been wrong. Maybe the stone she got from the man in the flannel was alone and unique. She stepped back, scanning the room and floor. Something crunched under her foot. Leaning over, she sorted through broken bits of cave stone. Nothing.

Whispers echoed from the tunnel. Meng stood and turned around. The whispers continued, emanating from a small tunnel offshoot. Muscles tensed, Meng walked toward the sound. She stepped methodically into the offshoot, trying not to make too much noise. Blue light glowed off the rocks around her. A soft, electric buzz emanated from her skin. She came to the end of the offshoot and gasped.

"What the…"

Four people stood with their hunched backs against the wall. Their sallow skin shone green in Meng's light. Flesh drooped on their faces and arms. They muttered and swayed side to side as if in a trance, their eyes glazed over. Meng felt no internal warmth or glow from them, so if they were once Shifters, they weren't in their current state. She waved a hand in their faces.

"Hello? Hello there?"

There was no response. What was this? She inched forward and touched one of their hands. It was rough and calloused. She thought back to the tools she saw in the other room. They were miners. But they didn't seem to have any personal initiative. Was this some kind of magic slavery? Were they mining transfer stones? The vein by Meng's temple throbbed. This was too big to keep to herself. She would have to alert the Council, or at least Representative Bai since this was her jurisdiction. She could still keep Nivi out of the radar since this didn't seem related to the school fire. She still didn't know who was responsible for killing Nivi's parents and couldn't take the chance that whoever did it would come back to finish the job.

With one more glance at the four figures, she turned and ran toward the cave entrance. The sound of her footsteps bounced off the walls as she gained speed. Her camouflage pendant snagged on a sharp protrusion in the tunnel, and the necklace fell to the ground. She didn't have time to look for it in the dark, and it wouldn't do her much use once she transformed anyway. Electricity crackled around her body. Ocean air whooshed past her ears. She ran faster and faster. When she reached the entrance, she dove head first into the open. As her head and body cleared the tunnel, she transformed.

Whiskers and horns grew from her face and head. Her body elongated, becoming long and sinuous. Blue scales erupted across her skin and replaced her clothes and shoes. They settled into place with a tinny clang. Pointed claws grasped at the air as she took flight. She was taking a risk shifting in broad daylight, but this was an emergency. The fastest way to get to Representative Bai and bring her back here was by flying. She wanted to get back with reinforcements before whoever was doing this got rid of all the evidence.

She flew out to sea, staying far from shore and close to the water's surface in hopes that her colors would keep her camouflaged. The setting sun dazzled off the surface of the ocean. Salt spray stung her eyes. She blinked away the sting and watched the coastline. Half an hour later, the Crescent City government building came into view. From Meng's viewpoint, the reflection of the ocean in the floor-to-ceiling windows made the boxy, redwood structure seem like it contained its own water. She veered toward land. Waves crashed at the base of the cliff under the building overhang.

Meng flew up onto the cliff ledge and transformed into human form. She wiped the salt from her eyes and walked into the building, straight into Representative Bai's office without knocking. Iris looked up as she came in. Her expression was hard to read. Meng didn't wait for her to say anything.

"We have a problem."

Iris kept her eyes on Meng. She didn't respond.

"There's a lot to explain and not a lot of time. There's a mine in the cliffs of Yuras. I can't be sure, but I suspect it's a transfer stone mine. I don't know if you've even heard of these stones. The short of it is that they're illegal. And there are enchanted prisoners in there. I need your help to secure the mine while we contact the Council."

Iris blinked. A smile came to her lips. "Of course. You came at a perfect time. Her eyes flicked behind Meng.

Meng felt a presence at her back. She turned around to find Chairperson Davis. He was dressed in his usual suit and tie. He stood with hands in his trouser pockets, a crooked smile on his face.

"Chairperson?" Meng said, surprised. "You're here? That *is* perfect timing. Did you hear what I told Representative Bai?"

"I did," Davis said with a nod. His dark eyes were intense and shining. He took a hand from his pocket and placed it on Meng's bare shoulder. "Thank you for telling us."

Davis gripped Meng's shoulder and squeezed. Confused, Meng looked down at her shoulder and back up at Davis. A searing pain shot through her skin, like a screw being driven in. She tried to jerk her arm away, but her arm felt numb. In fact, her whole body felt numb. Something was different, wrong. She wobbled. Her legs went limp. Davis caught her under the arms and lowered her to the floor.

Her head lolled to her left. She looked down at her shoulder and gasped. There, seared into her skin, was the bright red, power-stripping mark. Her chest constricted with panic. Rapid breaths came in quick succession. Her vision blurred.

"What– did you do?"

"Don't worry," Davis said. "The weakness goes away pretty quickly. I'm sorry I had to do that, but I can't have you sounding the alarm before I'm ready." He walked behind the desk and put a hand on Iris's shoulder. She sat there, not moving, but the expression on her face seemed strained. "Or I should say until *we're* ready. I've found that mesmerizing Shifters can prove unreliable. Now that you're technically a Static, I should have better luck with you."

He walked back toward Meng, his hand outstretched. Meng struggled to move, to dodge his approaching hand. She was too physically weak. All she could do was tilt her head so that it nodded forward. She watched his hand approach, wincing as his cold fingers touched her in the middle of her forehead. Her mind went blank.

CHAPTER FORTY-SEVEN

Nivi

Summer 2000

JI LED THE way through the forest in a direction parallel to town. At one point, Nivi wondered if she was making a big mistake, following Ji through the forest. But Ji trudged ahead, seemingly without any malicious intent, and eventually, Nivi relaxed. Her desire to see the house outweighed any reservations she had. They came upon an indistinct dirt road overgrown with vegetation. It looked like it hadn't been used in years.

Ji turned left onto the road, away from town, and followed it as it meandered through clusters of pines and redwoods. Nivi pulled out the newspaper article and skimmed the information again. This must be Redwood Road. She had never heard of this road before reading it in the news article. Was it as unfamiliar to everyone in town as it was to her?

They passed a house on the right that was in disrepair and then another on the left. Paint was peeling off, roof shingles were falling down, the yards were overgrown, and windows were broken.

"Are all the homes on this road abandoned?" Nivi said.

"It looks like it," Ji said. "Very strange."

At the end of Redwood Road, one more house stood off to the left. Nervous excitement filled Nivi as they approached. They walked onto the neglected driveway obscured by dirt and pine needles. A large redwood stood to the right of the driveway. At the end of the driveway were the charred remains of a house. The roof had caved in. Fallen beams lay at odd angles. Plants grew through open walls.

Nivi stood frozen next to Ji. This was it. She couldn't believe it. None of the colors of the original house survived, but the sense of knowing this place was stronger than ever. She rubbed her face and searched her memories to no avail.

"I can't remember how I know this place," Nivi said in frustration.

"Me neither," Ji said. "But I know it was important to me."

"Me too. But it doesn't make any sense. Why should an abandoned house be important to us? And why should the two of us strangers know it?"

"Maybe it used to be an important part of the community?" Ji offered. "If we ask around, maybe more people will know this place and be able to tell us why it was important."

They walked the perimeter of the house and peeked in through the wreckage, scanning for anything that could tell them more. The daylight began to fade. There was nothing.

As they prepared to leave, Ji seemed to realize something. "Look at the surrounding trees. Not a single one is burnt. Not even a little bit."

Nivi flashed back to herself standing in her grandmother's living room, dripping wet.

"I think it was raining."

"It's more than that," Ji said, walking toward a tree and

examining its trunk. "A very targeted, contained fire... This was Shifter magic."

Nivi felt a chill and looked at her hands. The raised scars seemed to pulse a little brighter. What if Ji was wrong, and Nivi had been the one to cause the fire? A scenario began to emerge in Nivi's mind. She had been exploring the forest with her family and had found this abandoned house. She ran inside to play, and her parents followed her. Something scared her, which caused a spark from her hands to set the house on fire. She escaped with her grandmother, but her parents didn't make it. Before the thoughts got out of control, Ji spoke.

"A targeted fire killed Allen. The master... he might have set this fire too!" Ji turned to Nivi. "Are you sure your parents died here?"

Nivi wasn't sure. All she had were overheard words, a vision, and a photocopy of an old newspaper article. But the newspaper article was from the week her parents died, so it couldn't be just a coincidence. "I'm pretty sure, but one thing doesn't make sense. The newspaper article didn't mention any deaths."

"They wouldn't mention it because your parents were Shifters. The Shifters keep their society and lives separate from the Statics – the non magic people."

Nivi hadn't thought of that possibility, but it made sense. "How would they do that?"

"There's a Shifter Council that oversees different aspects of Shifter life. They probably sent someone out here to *take care* of things."

"That sounds ominous."

"Nothing too awful. Probably just oblivion tincture. Something that erases memories."

Nivi looked back down Redwood Road toward the other abandoned houses. "Maybe those other houses were owned by

Shifters, too. Maybe this was a whole Shifter community, and that's why I had never heard of this road before either."

"That very well may be," Ji said. "Again, strange. A whole abandoned area of Shifter homes. I feel like my memories will come sooner or later. We should get going before it gets too dark to find our way back."

Nivi looked up toward the fading light beyond the trees. She hadn't realized how dark it was getting. "Where will you go?"

"I'll find a comfortable and safe place in the woods."

"You can't do that!" The thought of a night alone in the woods made Nivi shudder. But the only other place they could go was back to her home where she would have to confront her grandmother. She had never had an open conversation with her grandmother, but maybe with Ji beside her, her grandmother would be forced to answer her questions. "Come to my grandmother's house... my house."

"Are you sure she'll be OK with a stranger?"

"You're not a stranger anymore." Nivi smiled.

As they walked past the burnt home, Nivi glanced through the fallen beams one more time. The shadows were growing darker, and the last of the light came in unsteady bursts between the swaying branches. In the corner of what might have once been a bedroom, something lay on the floor. Nivi stared as another ray of light illuminated it for a moment. The item was badly burnt, but the side had a characteristic hourglass curve that Nivi recognized immediately. Then the light was gone, and the item looked like just another pile of rubble. She had probably just imagined it. And even if it was what she thought it was, it could just be another coincidence. Another coincidence. Her mind was probably reaching for connections where there weren't any. A burnt home where her parents probably died, and in one of the rooms, a child-sized violin.

CHAPTER FORTY-EIGHT

Ling
Summer 2000

LING SAT OUTSIDE in her garden as the setting sun cast shadows and a cool air settled around her. Where was Meng? She should've been back by now. She went inside to grab a shawl, then returned outside with it draped over her shoulders and a book under her arm. Even though the light was fading, she liked to absorb the last of the daytime hours. She read a page, but her mind kept wandering. She decided she was too antsy to read and she'd walk a lap through town. If Meng was on her way back, she would see her on the streets. She set the stone down in the kitchen and left a note on the dining table, just in case Nivi or Ming returned before her, saying she was walking in town and would be right back.

The wind picked up as she walked through town. She scanned the streets, which were mostly empty since it was dinner time. A person scurried home here. Another there. She passed a neighborhood cul-de-sac and another as she made her way through downtown. Then, on the last cul-de-sac, she saw a figure moving strangely toward the end of the street that led through the woods to the Cliff Trail. A woman. *Is that Meng?* It looked like Meng, but her hair was disheveled, and her walk was different. A sort of unsteady swaying. *Something's wrong.*

She hung back until Meng entered the forest. Then she walked quickly to the dirt trail to follow, trying to keep her feet as light as possible. The rustling of the wind on the treetops hid the crunch of her steps as she followed from a distance, keeping trees between their line of vision whenever possible. When they emerged from the trees, the wind was gusting, blowing debris into her eyes and making it impossible to hear. Once she blinked out the dust in her eyes, she saw Meng continuing toward the cliff edge. As Meng teetered closer to the edge, Ling dashed forward, ready to stop Meng from falling over. But a man emerged from the trail and ran after Meng. Ling stopped and hung back in the trees, watching. Before the man could reach Meng, he suddenly twirled in the air and fell to the ground. Two more people came running from the woods and knelt over the fallen man. Meanwhile, Meng stopped at the cliff edge and hopped over.

Ling panicked. The fallen man had two other people with him, and one of them ran back toward town, probably to get help. No one was helping Meng. She crept out from the forest and ran behind the fallen man and the other man huddled over him. She reached the cliff's edge and got on her belly to look over. Thank goodness. There was a ramp, and Meng was walking down it. At the base of the ramp, Meng disappeared into an opening in the side of the cliff wall.

Ling lowered herself down the cliff, her joints creaking and her foot getting a shock of pins and needles when she landed on the ramp. A feeling of vertigo rushed through her head, and she crouched with her head between her knees for a minute until it passed. Keeping one hand on the rock wall, she hiked down the ramp to the tunnel. Belatedly, she realized how dark it was. It was too late to go back for a flashlight. If Meng was in trouble, she needed to go in now. She stepped into the tunnel, feeling along the walls. Following the sound of footsteps ahead of her, she walked into the darkness.

CHAPTER FORTY-NINE

Amber

Summer 2000

AMBER WAITED ALL day for a phone call from Nivi. Nivi must've seen the copy of the newspaper article by now. Did she not realize it was from Amber? Or worse, did she know and still didn't want to speak to her?

As the sun began to set, the phone finally rang. Amber jumped up from her bed and picked up her room phone before her parents could answer from another room. It was Arav.

"Try not to sound too disappointed," he said.

"Sorry," Amber said. "I was expecting a call from Nivi."

"Well, this should perk you up. Kabir thinks he saw that woman, the one with the blue eyes. He's gone downtown to try to question her."

He wasn't wrong about her perking up. "Really? We need to go there too!"

"It's better to let him do the police work. We can find out what he knows later."

Amber was already picking up clothes from the floor and getting dressed. "Meet me at the corner of Peninsula Street in ten minutes."

Arav sighed. "We really should wait…"

"See you soon!" She hung up before Arav could protest more.

A few minutes later, she was out the door and headed to Peninsula Street. She figured if they started at the northernmost end of downtown, they could peek into buildings as they went south and eventually cross paths with Kabir and that woman.

Arav jogged up behind Amber as she reached Peninsula Street.

"Did you see them on your way here?" she asked.

"No, you?"

Amber shook her head.

They walked back down Main Street, looking into stores as they went. Each time Amber poked her head into a building, she could barely contain her anticipation. Only when they were halfway through Main Street did she realize she didn't know what they would do if they actually saw the woman. If Kabir was already there, they could eavesdrop and see what he learned. But if he wasn't, then what? Amber pushed the thought from her mind. She'd worry about it when it happened. The important thing was to finally get some answers.

They approached Cedar Lane, and Amber even volunteered to check inside the library. She roamed the bookshelves and went into the basement, feeling like a seasoned bookworm, but with each dead end, her hopes deflated. Where could they be? Maybe Kabir had been wrong. Maybe he hadn't found the woman and had already gone home while they were still at the north end of Main Street. Amber emerged from the library and joined Arav on the sidewalk.

He shrugged. "I guess that's it, huh? We could go back to my place and see if Kabir beat us back there."

Amber nodded, but she didn't expect much. She'd never get any answers. Nivi would never be her friend again. They'd finish high school, and Nivi would go off to some fancy university while Amber was stuck in Yuras playing violin in the local community center. Would that be so bad? She had plenty of friends who would also stay in Yuras. Plenty. They could spend summers on the beach between rehearsals and performances, just like she did now. It would be fine. Like nothing had changed.

Amber chewed her lip as she and Arav crossed Main Street and walked south one more block to Forest Lane. As they neared Arav's house, he suddenly stopped and squinted at the forest.

"There he is," Arav said, pointing.

At the start of the Cliff Trail, there was a scurry of motion.

They jogged into the forest and slowed down when they neared Kabir, who had his back to them. Arav motioned for Amber to join him behind a tree.

"He's following a few people," Arav whispered. "It looks like they have that woman restrained or something."

Amber peeked out from behind the tree. She saw Kabir inching along, and in front of him, she saw the woman. This was it! Kabir was going to get some answers for them! But something felt off. The woman was by herself, bent over and moving strangely as if trying to resist moving forward even as she continued to walk.

"She's by herself," Amber said. "Why is Kabir holding back?"

Arav peered around the tree. "No, she's not. Two people are pushing her along the road."

Amber tried to look again, but they must have advanced further through the forest because she couldn't see anything.

Arav and Amber moved out from behind the tree and walked quietly to keep up with Kabir without being detected. When they reached the forest's edge, they hung back in the trees. Suddenly, Kabir twisted around in a strange, inhuman way. Then he dropped onto the ground.

Arav ran out into the open. "Kabir!"

Confused, Amber ran after Arav. Kabir lay on the ground near the edge of the cliff. How had he moved like that? Did he trip and fall? But that wouldn't explain how he twisted around, almost like he was floating in the air.

Arav ran up to Kabir and dropped to his side. "Kabir! Kabir!" He shook Kabir, but he didn't move.

Amber followed and watched from over Arav's shoulder. Arav pressed his hands firmly into Kabir's stomach. Something bubbled up between Arav's fingers and spread across Kabir's shirt, creating an expanding dark spot on the police uniform. It was blood. Lots of it. Amber covered her mouth, her mind spinning.

"I– I'll go get help."

She ran back through the forest and up to Arav's house. To her surprise, the door was locked. She banged on the door and peeked in the windows but didn't see anyone. For all she knew, Frank Markson probably locked the doors due to his paranoia and was passed out somewhere inside. She ran around the house in a panic, yelling and banging on the windows.

The old man who lived next door came out onto his porch.

"We need help!" Amber called to him. "There's been an accident! Kabir. Arav. On the cliff."

CHAPTER FIFTY

Nivi

Summer 2000

NIVI ARRIVED BACK home with Ji. She pushed the front door open while calling out.

"Po Po? Are you home?"

She turned on the lights around the house while she searched. The house was empty. She checked the backyard where she had last seen her grandmother. Her grandmother's book was still lying on the table on the outdoor patio. Where could she have gone? Her grandmother was usually preparing dinner at this time. Deep down, Nivi felt partially relieved that she didn't have to confront her grandmother about all the lies just yet. She went back inside, where Ji was leaning over the dining table.

"Is this from her?" Ji said, picking up a piece of paper. "It says she went for a walk and will be right back."

Nivi looked at it. "That's her writing, but she wouldn't still be out this late." She paced around the table. "What if something is wrong?"

"Why would something be wrong?"

"Oh, I don't know. First, I'm attacked at school, and there's a crazy fire. Then my grandma's mysterious old friend shows up. Then I find out my whole past is a lie and that there's a whole secret society of magic shapeshifters."

"OK. I get it."

Nivi picked up the note and flipped it over, searching for any other note her grandmother may have left. Then she went outside and picked up the book on the table. She flipped through it and shook it. There was nothing. She let out a sigh of frustration and went into the kitchen. Something glinted from the counter as she turned on the kitchen light. It was a stone from the cave. She must've made a sound because Ji called out from the dining room.

"What is it?"

Nivi took the stone back to the dining room. "It's one of those stones my friend Amber and I found in the cave."

Ji's eyes widened, and she suddenly contracted forward and brought a hand to her head.

"Are you OK?" Nivi asked.

"These are the stones that I was forced to mine."

"Why would my grandma have this? Unless… I think she might be there." Nivi turned toward the front door.

Ji put a hand on Nivi's shoulder. "It's dangerous. What if whoever did this to me does the same to you?"

Her apprehensions about a confrontation with her grandmother or going into strange caves at night vanished with the thought of her grandmother in danger. "If that's true, then I need to help my grandma. I understand if you don't want to come."

Ji clenched her jaw and set the stone on the dining table. "No. I'm coming with you."

CHAPTER FIFTY-ONE

Amber
Summer 2000

There had been so much blood. Amber couldn't get it out of her mind. She sat on her bed, wanting to call Arav. Wanting to go to his home and comfort him. But he had asked to have some time to himself. That was understandable. Of course it was. Arav's brother had almost died today, so she could definitely understand why he wanted time to process.

All night, she tossed and turned, thoughts of blood-soaked clothes and blood-stained hands preventing her from sleeping. She couldn't understand what had happened. Arav said that there were other people there, and one of them attacked Kabir. But Amber had been watching the whole time and never saw anyone else. She only saw Kabir fall. Could a simple fall cause gashes like that?

When the sun rose and shone into her room, Amber sat up in bed. There was no point trying to sleep. She stared down at her hands. They were trembling. She grabbed them to make them stop. They kept trembling. She just needed something to do. Something to distract her. She got up and started picking up clothes from her floor and putting them in her laundry basket.

Before long, she had gathered all her dirty clothes and took them to the washer in the hall. Her father saw her walking by from where he was sitting in the kitchen.

"What are you doing, Amber?" he called from behind his newspaper.

"Laundry."

That made him drop the newspaper on the counter. "Do you *know* how to do laundry?"

Amber didn't respond. Her eyes burned, and she blinked back tears. She placed the laundry basket on the floor and pretended to turn the dials on the machine. A moment later, her father joined her. Without saying anything, he leaned over and began to load the washing machine in a way that seemed like he was just helping Amber instead of teaching her.

With the laundry started, Amber returned to her room and sat on her bed. Her floor was clean. She had put her clothes in the washing machine for the first time. Now what? She could barely do her own laundry. She had nothing. Nothing to do. No future. She was doomed to stay in Yuras forever as a second-rate community center violinist. Not like Nivi, who could go to any college she wanted and be whatever she wanted to be, first chair violin in a famous symphony or anything else she decided on. Amber wished she could be that smart. What she wouldn't do for a chance to live in a big city and work for some big fancy company. Her eyes fell on the school books stacked in the corner of her room. She *could* go to the library and start studying now for the school year. The thought made her chuckle. She'd be such a loser. But then her mind drifted again to thoughts of big city living, and before she knew it, she was wandering over to the books and sorting through them.

English. Algebra. Biology. History. It was too much. She would never be able to learn all this, especially not on her own. Sighing, she looked out the window at the lightening sky. When she looked back at her books, the brightness of the outdoors caused everything to look dark and unfocused. All the books blended together except for one red book. Amber pulled it out of the pile. It was a math book from when she was in middle school. She flipped through it, doubting if she would even understand anything from the book.

A paper fell out of the book, and Amber held it up. It was a math test with a score of 100% at the top. And it had her name on it! She couldn't believe it. She had no memory of ever scoring so highly in math. Her recent memory only contained a string of fails and barely passing grades. She flipped through the pages and found another test, also with 100%. Again, her name was on top. This was incredible. Maybe she was able to do this. At least she could start with this book and work her way up from there. She dressed, placed the book, a notebook, and pencils into a bag, and headed to the library.

She spent a few hours at the library, starting at the beginning of the book and working her way through. Each time she remembered how to solve particular equations, she got more and more excited. On top of that, the library was not that bad, especially sitting in the upstairs area where the light cast a soft rainbow through the stained glass windows. It was peaceful and kept Amber's mind off the previous day's events. If she was truly honest with herself, she liked it. As she left the library for the day, she already knew she'd be back the next day.

As she walked home, she paused before turning onto her street. If anyone could appreciate Amber's excitement about the library, it would be Nivi. It wouldn't hurt to just walk by Nivi's house and see if she was around. Amber continued down Main Street, past her street of Maple Lane and turned onto Pine Lane. As she approached Nivi's house, she saw the door was open. That meant that Nivi or Grandma Ling was probably going in and out of the house, so she'd see one of them any moment. How would Nivi respond to her visit? She paused in front of the beige house and loitered on the sidewalk. After a few minutes, she walked up to the open door and listened for activity inside. All was quiet.

Amber stuck her head inside the door and called out.

"Hello? Nivi? Grandma Ling?"

She crept into the house, still calling out as she checked the rooms, and ended in the kitchen. No one was home. They must've gone out and not fully closed the door, or maybe a breeze blew it open. An unexpected pang hit her. Before, Nivi would've invited her to wherever she was now. Amber sighed. As she turned to leave, something glinted from the kitchen table. She ignored it at first, but it happened again. A sudden, bright light like a spark of electricity. It was coming from a smooth, gray stone. It was one of the stones from the cave! She had never brought one out of the cave. Is this what they all looked like in the sunlight? She picked it up and studied it. There was definitely a bluish spark inside that looked like electricity. She debated taking it with her. This might lift Arav's spirits a little. She could just borrow it to show him, and she'd bring it back later, slip it back onto the kitchen table when no one was looking. With that thought, she picked up the stone.

A strange sensation met her fingers, almost like the stone caused her skin to tingle. In the back of her mind, there was an urge for Amber to accept something. A gift. What a silly, random thought. But with the stress of recent events, she couldn't blame her mind for trying to bring joy back into her life. A gift was better than a curse, so why not? As she put the stone in her pocket, she allowed her mind and body to accept any gifts the universe would send her way.

A sudden electric shock zapped her fingers, and her whole body became warm. Amber shook her head and rubbed her hands together. The stone had given her an intense static shock. Some gift. She left the house, making sure to close the door behind her.

At home, her parents told her Arav had called. She ran to her room and called him back right away. He sounded down, but he invited her over to talk about how Kabir was doing. Amber fingered the stone in her pocket and said she'd head right over.

When Arav opened the door for Amber, she held back, not sure how to greet him if he still wanted some space. Something seemed different, almost as if he was glowing. He gave her a little smile and hugged her. She let out a breath. He was OK. They were OK.

Almost as if he were reading her mind, he looked at her as if he were evaluating her. "You seem to be doing well. You're glowing."

"I was actually thinking the same about you, all things considered." Amber followed Arav to his room. "How's Kabir?"

Arav ran his hands through his hair and took a deep breath. "He's doing alright. He was awake and eating this morning at the hospital. They might discharge him in a few more days."

"That's great."

Arav suddenly laughed and shook his head. "I can't believe it. He was right."

"Who was right?"

"My dad. About the monster people."

Amber furrowed her brow. "I don't understand."

Arav took Amber's hands. "This whole time, I thought my dad was crazy. Drowning his sorrows in alcohol and made-up villains. But they're real. The monster people are real. They're a danger to our community. First, my mom. Now Kabir. We have to protect ourselves. We have to defend ourselves."

This was not what Amber expected Arav to say when he said he wanted to talk about Kabir. She hadn't seen anyone else on the cliff other than Kabir that day and was worried that Arav had imagined something that didn't happen, but she didn't want to contradict him now. Not when his brother was still recovering from surgery. Afterall, hadn't she also *seen* some things that probably hadn't occurred during the school fire? Her parents were probably right all along. It was normal to see strange things in the heat of the moment. But remembering how she had felt when no one believed her, she resolved to be as supportive as possible.

"How will we do that?" she said.

"There's this group. They have a meeting coming up. Will you come?"

Amber wrung her hands. Would this be like some sort of cult? But one meeting couldn't hurt, and if needed, she could be a voice of reason to Arav. She put on her most supportive expression and nodded. His smile confirmed that Amber was doing the right thing. He seemed more relaxed now. More like himself.

"Oh!" she said, remembering the stone in her pocket. "I wanted to show you something." She handed it to Arav. "It's one of those stones from the cave!"

Arav looked at it and smiled. "It is."

Why wasn't he as amazed by it as she was? "Look inside it!"

Arav looked at it again. "What am I looking for?"

Amber reached out and took the stone back. "It's…" The stone was an opaque, dark gray. The blue electricity was gone. "I… it looked different before."

"Maybe it was the lighting. Did you go back there recently?"

"No, I found it at Nivi's. Must've been from when I showed her last."

Arav was probably right. There was probably some blue appliance light in Nivi's kitchen that had reflected off the stone. She was just having strange hopes and thoughts about gifts and the stone being special. She put the stone back in her pocket and planned to return it on her way home.

CHAPTER FIFTY-TWO

Nivi

Summer 2000

Nivi raced down the ramp from the cliff edge. She turned around and saw Ji holding back.

"Come on," Nivi said. "We're almost there."

"Something doesn't feel right," Ji said.

Nivi stopped walking. Of course Ji wouldn't feel comfortable. This was the place where she had been imprisoned for ten years.

"Maybe you should stay here."

Ji shook her head. "I'll be OK. I won't let you go alone."

Nivi tried to protest, but Ji moved forward, taking Nivi with her. They continued together down the ramp and into the tunnel. The way was dark except for the small point of light from Nivi's flashlight. As they went deeper and deeper, voices echoed from the depths of the tunnel, bouncing off the cold, stone walls as if a howling wind were passing through. Nivi took a deep breath. Fear pounded at her chest, but concern about her grandmother's welfare drove her on.

As she approached the large cavern of stones, she turned off the flashlight and slowed her pace. A glow emanated from the cavern ahead. Nivi kept one hand against the tunnel wall to guide her steps. She peeked around the corner and held her breath, squinting to make sense of the dim shapes in the room.

A couple of electric lanterns sat on the ground. Her grandmother and Meng stood facing the doorway. Nivi waved and beckoned to them before realizing something was wrong. They were swaying slightly from side to side as if they were mindless pieces of kelp, waiting for instruction from the ocean current. Four other figures stood around Ling and Meng, also limp and swaying. In front of them, two people stood with their backs to Nivi. She couldn't tell who they were. Then the two people turned to speak to each other, and she could make out from their profiles that it was a man and a woman.

Was her grandmother a member of some strange cult? That couldn't be. Nivi would've noticed something sooner. Guilt filled her gut. Would she have noticed? All these years, she had barely spoken to her grandmother. She realized, with a pang of regret, they didn't know each other at all.

Suddenly, Ji bumped into Nivi from behind, knocking her forward into the cavern. Nivi, thinking that it was an accident, panicked and turned to look at Ji so they might run from the cave and get help, but Ji had assumed the same glazed look as her grandmother, Meng, and the four others beside them.

"Ji, what's wrong?" Nivi whispered, waving a hand in front of Ji's face and trying to push toward the tunnel.

"Why hello," the man said. "So nice of you to join us. And who do you have here?"

Nivi turned to face the man. That thick, black hair. Those

intense, dark eyes. The familiarity of them prickled her skin as if tiny worms wriggled beneath. Her heart began to race, and she felt woozy and faint. Her mind became a wavy blur, and when it cleared, she saw her home. Not her grandmother's house. The one from *before*.

Nivi was practicing violin. Several loud thumps came from the living room. She rushed out and saw a man struggling with her father in front of the fireplace. The fighting startled her, so she ran back to bed and pulled the covers over her head. The vision faded, leaving her staring into the face of the same man who had fought with her father.

The man watched her with furrowed brows. "You look so familiar. How do I know you?"

The panic was growing more intense, and a wave of nausea washed up Nivi's throat. This was such a mistake. She should've stuck to her instincts and stayed home, especially at night. She tried again to turn and leave the cavern, but Ji grabbed her arms and blocked her way.

"Ji! Let me go!" Nivi twisted and pushed to no use.

The man's eyes went back and forth between Ji and Nivi. His furrowed brow relaxed, and he smiled.

"Ah. I see," he said. "How precious is this? Reunited. All of us."

Nivi's pulse grew so rapid it threatened to strangle her voice. No, she wasn't going to have a panic attack now. She wasn't going to give this man the pleasure of seeing her crumple in fear. She took a couple of slow breaths.

"Who are you?" she managed to squeak. "What do you want?" It was then she noticed the woman standing beside the man also had a somewhat glazed look.

The man put a hand on his chest. "You don't remember me?

I'm hurt. Well, to be fair, I'm not sure we've ever formally met. My name is Davis."

This must be the master, Nivi thought. Of course. This wasn't a cult, although she now wondered which would be worse. "What did you do to everyone?"

"Why don't you come a little closer, and I'll show you?" Davis said.

Ji began to push Nivi toward Davis. Nivi struggled against Ji. Sweat pricked her brow as heat rushed through her body. The branched scars on her arms bulged and pulsed. Davis crossed his arms and tapped his foot. He looked at his watch. Ji pushed Nivi closer and closer. As Nivi passed by her grandmother, she reached for her arm, just grazing her skin with her fingertips.

"Po Po!" she yelled.

Her grandmother's head twitched.

Davis moved toward Nivi's forehead with an outstretched hand. Nivi braced herself. She was going to become one of these mindless workers. Why did she ever decide to go with Amber to this cave? None of this would have happened if she had just stayed put in her room and stuck to violin and studying. It was so tempting to blame it all on Amber, but the more Nivi thought about it, the more she realized that wasn't true. If she hadn't come to the cave, her powers would have still developed and brought attention to her. At least she was able to set Ji free for a little while. But then maybe Allen would have survived if he hadn't gotten out of the cave. It was all a mess. She didn't know what to think or what would've been better. None of it mattered now. They would all be doomed to live out their lives in this cave.

All of a sudden, Ling ran at Davis. She grabbed his hands and pushed them away from Nivi. Davis seemed surprised but quickly regained his composure. He sneered and pushed Ling with such inhuman strength that she flew across the room. She hit the wall with a crack and fell to the ground.

Nivi gasped. For a moment, she stood frozen in shock. Did Davis just kill her grandmother? Then Ling moved, and Nivi let out a breath.

Moaning, Ling pushed herself to her hands and knees and stared at Davis with a look of contempt. "I can feel your weakness, Davis. You won't be able to control your powers forever."

Davis laughed. "You are one to talk."

But sweat beaded his brow, and his limbs trembled ever so slightly. He clenched his jaw, and the veins in his forehead protruded. He turned back toward Nivi, again trying to touch her forehead. Nivi struggled against Ji who was pinning her arms behind her back. Ling rose to her feet and ran toward Davis. He saw her approach. His face stretched, taking on a feline look with wide-set eyes, a broad nose, and teeth that elongated into fangs. His skin mottled with stripes of orange and brown. Before Ling got to him, Davis opened his mouth and released a ball of fire with a roar. The fire sizzled through the damp cave air and hit Ling. It threw her back into the wall and burst. Ling crumpled to the ground in a blaze. Her form collapsed into a pile of ash and embers.

"No!" Nivi screamed. This wasn't possible. It wasn't real. Her grandmother would be OK. She had to be OK. Nivi struggled even harder against her captor, choking on her sobs.

Davis's face returned to human form. He looked pale and seemed to struggle to stand up straight. He wiped his brow. A sneer curled his lips.

"As much as I'd love to stay for the finale, I don't have time for this. Iris, finish them off. All of them. I'll take away the water shield on my way out so the tide will come in and wash away the evidence."

Davis picked up a box of stones from the ground. It seemed most of the stones had been mined from the cave. Only a few remained in the walls. He strode past Nivi, and she spat at him. A little of her spittle landed on the sleeve of his suit jacket. The smoldering pile of ash that was her grandmother immediately eclipsed what small satisfaction that may have given her. She felt like she had been punched in the gut, and the punching continued, driving her stomach deeper and deeper into herself. She couldn't breathe or think. She was numb and empty.

Iris stood in the center of the room, her eyes glowing a fiery red. Her skin glistened, her neck elongated, and her whole body stretched until she filled the cavern. Nivi was face-to-face with a giant, toothy snake. Smoke curled from the snake's nostrils.

Nivi's despair dulled her fear. Instead of breaking down into a panic attack, she was able to think. She couldn't just stand there and let them all die. She had to do something.

"Please don't do this," Nivi yelled. "You're under his spell. Try to fight it."

The snake seemed to pause. Hope soared in Nivi but quickly sank when the snake arched back and opened its mouth. From deep in its throat, a rumble emerged. A stream of fire spewed forth as thick as lava.

Nivi watched the fire approach. Unable to break free of Ji, she screamed. Dozens of thoughts flooded her mind in a fraction of a second. Her grandmother had lied to her, and now she'd never know why. Soon, she'd be dead as well. All the time she spent stressed about school and violin and rarely socializing was for nothing. No one would miss her. Not even Amber. Nivi couldn't blame her. It was her own fault. If she hadn't kept everything inside this whole time and had talked more openly to Amber and her grandmother, maybe things would have been different.

Regret twisted her heart. It was all so unfair. First, she lost her parents. Then Amber. Now, her grandmother. She was just starting out with her life. This couldn't be it. If she ever got out of here, she would make sure that awful man suffered the way they were now. She wanted him to feel hopeless and afraid. She almost laughed. What good were these thoughts now? She should've done more sooner.

Her scream morphed into an indignant roar. Heat erupted through her body. She closed her eyes and braced herself for the impending impact, the burn that would melt away her flesh like wax.

The impact didn't come. Nivi opened her eyes. The stream of fire had stopped as if it were encountering an invisible force-field. A sphere surrounded her, as thin as a bubble. The surface of the sphere wavered like a mirage. Flames licked up her legs, sending heat through the air. At first, Nivi thought the snake's fire had hit her. Then she realized the flames were coming from herself. The veins on her arms were pulsing bright red. Sparkling embers floated off her skin, forming the shield around her. Her anger blocked any sense of shock or wonder. For the first time, she didn't fight her transformation. She allowed the energy to flow through her. Ji released her. She was sure Ji's iron grip would return at any moment, but Ji stood off to her side, shaking her head as if coming out of a daze.

Nivi's body grew. Her wrists sprouted golden fur, and her fingers fused into hard, gold hooves. Iridescent scales coated her body and replaced her clothes, at one time appearing green, at another all the colors of the rainbow. Her joints popped, and her bones cracked, but there was no pain. She fell forward onto all fours, feeling as natural in this form as if she had always been a creature of four legs. Fire continued rising up the sides of her legs and body, as much a part of her as the fur and scales.

The shield throbbed around her, filling with a palpable energy. Pressure built up within her and around her until it could no longer be contained. The shield burst with a blinding white light that illuminated the whole cave. Then it was gone, and all went dark.

⌁

Nivi opened her eyes. For a moment, she forgot where she was. She saw herself in her previous home as a little girl with her father and… Ji. Why was Ji there? Then she was back in the cave, in human form, lying on her side on the floor. Salty liquid wetted the corner of her mouth. It trickled through her hair and against her body, seeping through her clothes. The tide. It was coming in, just like Davis said.

She tried to sit up but quickly lay back down. Her body ached, and she was dizzy and thirsty. From the ground, she looked around the dimly lit cave. The two electric lanterns were still sitting on the ground. Iris lay across from her, also pushing herself up. Worried that Iris would attack again, Nivi pushed herself to her feet, ignoring her dizziness and protesting muscles.

"It's OK,' Iris said, putting her hands up in surrender. "You did it. You broke the spell." Tears streamed down from her eyes. "I'm so sorry. I didn't– I couldn't control–" She put her hands over her face.

The tension left Nivi's body. With the imminent threat of death gone, reality and shock overcame her. Her breath came rapidly, and she clutched her hands over her chest until she was able to speak. Only one word came out.

"How?"

Next to Iris, Meng stirred as well. Her light blue eyes glowed in the lamplight. "You're a qilin." Her voice was ragged, but her tone was deferential. "You are a protector. You can defend against magic and nullify spells."

A qilin. "But that's just a legend…" She trailed off as she thought about the events that led to this point. Was being a qilin really impossible after everything that had happened? Still, she shook her head, unable to take it all in. "What about the fire on my body?"

Meng stood up and brushed herself off. A tremble in her voice marred her usual composure. "It's a protective fire. It forms a shield against magic that would harm you or those in your vicinity." Suddenly, her eyes went wide as she looked to Nivi's side. "Ji? You're… alive?"

To Nivi's side, someone spoke with a shaky voice. "May?"

The name and voice sent a chill of recognition up Nivi's spine. Somehow, she knew that the name was being addressed to her. And the voice, it was that of her mother. How could that be? Her mother was dead. She slowly turned and saw Ji sitting beside her. Only now, she recognized Ji for who she really was. Her mother.

Tears flowed from her eyes. She opened her mouth to speak, but nothing came out.

Ji scooted over, and they embraced. She smoothed Nivi's bangs across her forehead and wiped her tears.

"You broke the spell on yourself as well," Meng explained. "Ling and I put an oblivion spell on you when you were a child to make you forget your past. To protect you. We didn't know Ji— your mother— was alive until now."

Nivi blinked through her tears. The memories and visions flooded back. The child in the bedroom drawing animals with her mother. That was her. The white house with the blue shutters. That was her home. The realization overwhelmed her. She was May. She always had been. But she had spent so much time as Nivi as well. It didn't feel quite right to identify with one name or the other. She couldn't help but feel anger toward Meng and her grandmother, even if they were protecting her. How could they have taken away her memories?

Her grandmother! In the deluge of events, she had briefly forgotten what had happened to her.

"Po Po!" Nivi jumped up and ran to the wall where the pile of cloth and ashes lay, smoldering and hissing in the seeping ocean water. "Oh no! No!" She glanced wildly at Ji and Meng and Iris as if one of them could undo this reality.

Ji and Meng walked up next to her.

Ji knelt and placed a hand on the pile. "Ma Ma…" Her voice caught.

Iris hung back, wringing her hands and furrowing her brow.

Meng crouched beside Ji and put a hand on the rags. "Please say she got to you in time." She turned to Nivi. "Did you touch her before she was hit?" Nivi nodded. "Then we may still have a chance. Ling received a mark." She pointed to her left shoulder, and Nivi knew she was talking about the raised red scar on her grandmother's shoulder. "It was something that took her magic away so she could blend in and keep you safe from the people who set fire to your house. We figured it was a politically motivated attack, and they wouldn't want any survivors. But if you broke the spell of the mark before she was hit…"

Nivi wished with all her might that what Meng said could be true. If her grandmother could come back, they could start again. Develop a real relationship. For the past ten years, Ling was the only family Nivi had. So Nivi wished and wished in the same way she had when she found out her parents had died, with the same childish thought. If she just wished hard enough, it would come true.

The pile of clothes crumpled and collapsed down further into ash. Meng bowed her head. Nivi bit her lip as more tears flooded her eyes. Ji stood and pulled Nivi close.

Guilt constricted Nivi's throat. Her grandmother did this all for her. To protect her from the people who killed her father. More flashes of memories appeared in her mind. She again saw Davis and her father struggling in the living room. In fear, she ran to her bedroom. She looked out her bedroom window and saw…Iris.

Nivi turned on Iris, pointing a shaky finger at her. "You were there that night of the fire. With Davis when he fought with my father. You're just as responsible as him. You helped kill my father and my grandmother!"

Meng and Ji turned to look at Iris.

Iris took a step back. "I– I don't remember much from that night. At least not until now."

Meng spoke with a diplomatic tone. "We cannot rule out that she was under Davis's spell then, too. We will get to the bottom of this, I promise."

Nivi seethed. She wanted Iris to be guilty. She needed Iris to be guilty. Who else could she direct all this anger at? Davis was long gone. And her father and grandmother were dead. How could Meng be so calm about things?

She looked back toward the pile that was her grandmother. Some of the ash floated into the air. It danced in the lamplight, then disappeared into the darkness of the cave. Nivi sniffed and wiped her sleeve across her eyes. Water sloshed around her feet.

"We'll have to get going soon," Ji said softly.

Nivi looked up at her mother and saw that Ji's jaw was tense, and her eyes were red. Ji must be as angry as she was. Nodding, Nivi turned away from her grandmother's remains. As she took a step, something flew in front of her face. More ash. She glanced back. Even more ash flew into the air. There was no breeze, but Nivi figured it was due to the tide disturbing the cavern air. Still, it was strange. The ash continued to rise, plumes of it. All of a sudden, the gray cloud ignited like sparks flying off a fire. Soon, all the ash was alight in specks of bright red and orange.

Alarm shot through Nivi's veins, and her arms heated up. "What's happening?" Had Davis left yet another spell to finish them off?

A smile brightened Meng's face, and her shoulders relaxed. "You did it."

Ji hugged Nivi tight. "She's going to be OK."

Confused, Nivi looked back and forth from Meng to Ji, seeing the dots of red sparkles in their eyes.

"Give her some room," Meng said, putting out her arms.

They all backed up. A mass of sparks filled the air above Ling's pile of clothes like a suspended firework. The remains lit up and trembled, coalescing into a luminescent, red ball. Cracks formed along the top of the ball, and white light streamed out. Nivi shielded her eyes. Through the light, she saw a creature emerge. Expansive wings spread. The light died down and revealed an enormous, fantastic bird. Vivid red and gold feathers crested the bird's head. Large, long plumes extended from its tail like a waterfall of fire.

"Is that… Is she a phoenix?" Nivi said.

"A Zhu Que or vermillion bird," Meng said. "Similar to the western phoenix with her ability to be reborn."

The bird arched its back and neck and shook out its feathers that undulated around its body like a cloak of flames. It folded its wings on its back, then shrank in size and dimmed in color and brightness until a human form took shape.

"Po Po!" Nivi cried and ran to hug her grandmother.

Ling was in a pale dress with her long black hair hanging to her waist. She stood straighter and looked younger.

"May," Ling said, returning the hug and patting Nivi's back. "I'm so sorry for everything. We were supposed to protect you from all this."

"It's OK, Po Po. I'm just happy you're alive."

Ling released her and turned to Meng. They looked at each other for a while with bright eyes, and Nivi thought they seemed full of hurt. It was then that Nivi realized how worried Meng had been and how much she had been holding inside. Ling held out a hand, and Meng took it, intertwining her fingers. They embraced, and Meng ran her fingers through Ling's hair while speaking softly into her ear. Nivi couldn't hear what they were saying, but it was obvious that they had forgiven each other. Her grandmother had given up her powers and Meng to care for her.

Ling separated from Meng and looked at Ji. "You're alive."

Ji stayed where she was and nodded. There was an awkward tension between the two of them. "As are you."

Then Ling smiled, tears in her eyes, and embraced Ji. Ji smiled back and the group quickly turned to laughing and reminiscing.

"Thank goodness," Iris said.

Nivi had forgotten she was there and whirled around.

"Detain her," Ling said, stepping away from the reunion.

"Wait." Nivi gritted her teeth at what she was about to say. She still didn't trust Iris, but the joy of seeing her grandmother alive made her feel she should at least try to be as diplomatic as Meng. "She didn't know what she was doing. She was under the same spell."

Meng nodded. "Mesmerism."

Ji gasped.

"What?" Nivi said.

"That was your father's power."

"Yes," Iris said. "He used a transfer stone to steal Chairperson Dawan's power and mesmerize me and Ji. Although, for some reason, it only had a partial hold over me over the years."

"He can't control all that power," Ling said. "He's taking on more than he can handle."

"All these years," Iris said, "I thought I was responsible for the fire that killed Chairperson Dawan." She looked at Nivi. "Now that you've broken the spell, I know that it was all Davis. He used me. But it's still my fault that I led him to the stones."

"You didn't know," Meng said.

"I'm afraid he's going to do something worse. He's been waiting to get enough stones, and now he has them. He has a meeting with all the Senators and Representatives tomorrow morning."

Nivi took a step and her foot made a splash. "Do you think we can stop him? Whatever he has planned?"

"First, we need to get out of this cave," Ji said.

She picked up one of the lanterns from the floor and held it out in front of her. Four figures stirred from the wet ground. The other mesmerized people.

"Statics," Ji said. "Like Allen. We can't just leave them here. They were victims like us."

"Allen?" Ling said.

"The one who attacked me at school," Nivi said.

"Bring them with," Meng said. "We'll drop them off somewhere safe until we know what to do and what we're up against. Most likely, we'll be using an oblivion tincture on them."

Nivi gaped at Meng. After having lost her memories for all these years, she didn't like the idea of doing it to someone else. What was the point of life if their memories could be erased at any moment.

"It's not up to me," Meng said. "The Council will have to decide. Either way, we'll ensure they're safe."

"Speaking of oblivion tincture…" Iris reached into her pocket and brought out a small glass vial with black liquid inside. "I was holding onto this in case I got a chance to use it on Davis."

Meng narrowed her eyes and swiped the vial from Iris. "It might still come in handy."

They quickly explained the circumstances to the very confused Statics. Then Ji led the way through the tunnel. Everyone followed quietly, the only noise the sloshing of their steps. They reached the cave entrance and walked up the ramp to get out of the water.

"How was the tide prevented from going in the cave before?" Nivi asked.

"Davis has water magic as well," Iris said. "He created a barrier to the cave, which he removed when he left tonight."

Nivi looked out at the horizon where the rosy glow of dawn extended its fingers, and her heart sank. It was already morning. Davis would be meeting with the Council soon. "If Davis is planning something this morning, we'll never make it in time."

Ling looked at Meng. "I know a way, but it risks exposing us to the Statics." She glanced back at the four Statics. "That is if we're not exposed already. Are you willing to risk it?"

"It's not more exposure than I've already risked," Meng said. "And we don't have another choice." She walked to the edge of the cliff. "I'm going to have to carry you."

Before Nivi could ask how, Meng dove from the cliff. A yelp rose in Nivi's throat, only Meng didn't fall. She hovered in the air. Blue scales covered her lengthening, snake-like body. Whiskers sprouted from a toothy snout. Plates and spikes poked through a mane that ran down her spine. Great claws gripped the air as if it were as substantive as the ground. Electricity crackled around Meng, making Nivi's hair rise. The Statics gasped.

"Come on, let's go," Ling said, climbing onto the dragon's back.

After a brief hesitation, Nivi and the others followed, and they flew out over the ocean.

CHAPTER FIFTY-THREE

Iris

Summer 2000

As they flew along the coast toward the Council headquarters, Iris huddled into the dragon's mane to shield against the brisk morning air. Since the mesmerism spell was broken, guilt and confusion riddled her thoughts. She should be relieved, and she was to a degree. All this time, she thought she was responsible for the fire that killed Chairperson Dawan and his family, but it had been Davis all along. And Ji and Nivi were alive. That was great.

A dense layer of fog sat over the Bay. Iris glanced down at her tightly clenched right fist. Inside was a transfer stone. All these years under Davis's spell, she had never been able to pick one up until now, thanks to Nivi. She should be furious at Davis. He had manipulated her. Yet, she was conflicted. Davis had given her the option to turn back that night many years ago. She had chosen to go with him because he promised to help her advance in politics, and he had kept that promise. Now she was a representative, in a position to actually make a change in her community. What would happen if they stopped Davis? Would the Council strip her of her title?

Meng's sudden descent indicated they were approaching their destination. Iris glanced back at Nivi, Ling, Ji, and the others, all clinging in an undulating line along Meng's back. The flight was smoother than she expected. Instead of an up-and-down motion as with the pumping of wings, it was more of a gliding and curving through the air since Meng was a wingless dragon.

They descended into the marine layer. The air became thick and damp. Iris could barely see the people behind her. Cold bit her skin with icy teeth as she hunched into the dragon and fin-gered the stone in her palm. Maybe she could use this stone to take Davis's power and disarm him. The Council would reward her and maybe even promote her. She didn't know if the transfer stone would be able to take so much power from one person, but it was worth a try.

Meng flew to the floating dock next to the large white building where the Council board room was located. Everyone dismounted, and Meng returned to human form on the dock beside them. She pulled up a pendant from around her neck and held it to the wall. The door outline appeared, and the door slid in and back to let them pass. A crowd of people waited in the main reception area. All the country's senators and repre-sentatives were present.

There was a commotion as they walked into the room. Murmurs of recognition and disbelief.

"Is that Mrs. Dawan?" "Ling Guang?" "I thought she was dead." "Shh, don't say that." "But it's true." "There was that fire." "Are those Statics?"

Senator Kris Springston walked up, surprise on her face.

"Vice Chairperson Meng, I thought you weren't going to be able to make it today."

"What's going on?" Meng said.

"We're having individual meetings with Chairperson Davis before he announces the new direction the Council is taking. I thought you would know."

"How many people have already met with him?"

"Maybe half of us."

Iris jumped forward. "We need to get down there now."

"You all go," Ji said. "I'll stay here and keep others from going down. Or should we tell them what's going on? We might need their help."

"It's too dangerous," Meng said. "We can't risk losing more of our leaders. We'll need to bring in our military." She turned to Kris. "Senator, we don't have time to explain everything. The short of it is that Chairperson Davis is stealing powers with transfer stones. Can you find a safe place for these Statics until we have a chance to evaluate the situation?"

"I can do that," Kris said. "I've always trusted you, Vice Chairperson Meng, so you can fill me in on the details later. I'll make some calls and have the military meet us here." She motioned to the Statics. "Follow me."

"I'll tell the remaining council members that the meeting has been canceled," Ji said. "I'll try to clear the building as quickly as possible."

"I'll help," Ling said. "It'll go faster that way. Then we can come down and help you when everyone is safe and gone. You should be able to handle him in the meantime. He won't be able to control that much power much longer. He was already showing signs of breaking down in the cave."

Meng nodded. They walked toward the elevator. Northern California Representative Ariana Peters waited in front of the elevator doors. Maybe they should take their time and allow Ariana to go down the elevators. After all, if Ariana were no longer a Shifter, Iris could take over her position as the runner up. But Meng waved Ariana over and explained the situation, and she left the building.

They continued on toward the elevators. Marcus stood up from behind his gold desk. He spoke with a monotonous tone.

"You can't go down. Chairperson Davis requested private meetings with each councilmember."

"This is an emergency," Meng said. "I'm the Vice Chairperson."

Marcus didn't budge. He continued to stare at them with unfocused eyes. "Chairperson Davis explicitly told me that this was a private session for he alone and each council member. He told me not to let anyone pass whose turn it wasn't."

"Davis mesmerized him," Ji said. "I'd know that look anywhere."

Nivi placed her hand on Marcus's arm. The veins on her skin raised and lit up. A glow spread through her hand toward Marcus. Marcus's eyes cleared, and he shook his head.

"What happened?"

"We will explain later," Meng said. "First, we need you to open the elevators."

Marcus put his finger on a scanning button, and the elevator doors opened. Ling turned to Meng and touched her face.

"Be careful."

Meng took Ling's hand and nodded. She stepped into the elevator where Iris was waiting.

Nivi hugged Ji.

"You have what it takes to keep his powers from being used on you," Ji said. "Just help Meng get close to him."

Nivi set her jaw and joined Meng and Iris in the elevator.

The doors closed. A gentle rumble resonated in the walls as the elevator descended. Iris still clutched the stone in her fist. Her thumping heart pulsed in her palm.

The doors opened. A blinding light flashed, and they shielded their eyes. When it faded, Davis stood at the front of the room next to a wooden box. He held Representative Mindy Le's hand as if they had been shaking hands. Mindy fell to her knees. White light flowed up Davis's arm and diffused through his body. He seemed to grow a little in size. He let go of Mindy's hand and stretched, cracking his neck from side to side. Part of Iris smiled inside. Mindy Le, who had always been so condescending and infatuated with Davis, was literally falling at his feet. She would no longer be a threat to Iris.

Meng stepped forward. "No one else is coming down. You won't be hurting anyone else."

Davis snapped his head toward them, eyes widened. Then he sneered.

"You're too late. I'm already more powerful than all of you. You can't stop me."

He dragged the limp representative as easily as if she were a sack of potatoes to the side of the room. Iris, Meng, and Nivi followed at a distance.

Around the corner, dozens of council members lay on the floor in a cage made of ice. Several were not moving. Others were trying to move but shaking and collapsing. Davis approached the cage, dragging Mindy behind him. He melted a bar of ice, threw her inside, and reformed the bar.

Davis turned toward them, glowing brighter and brighter. Magical power pulsed within him. Warm yellow undulated into brilliant greens, blues, and reds. Light reflected off the glass-encapsulated room like the inside of a cut gemstone.

"Now you see," Davis said. His voice was inhuman as if

multiple voices resonated in his torso at the same time. "I am too powerful. I am *all* powerful. Soon, I will have all your power."

As Davis spoke, he grew in size. His body bulged and contorted. Lumps boiled across his flesh. Appendages of all shapes and sizes– wings, claws, flippers and skin, fur and scales– alternately erupted and reabsorbed into his skin. Multicolored light flashed across his body like a psychedelic disco ball.

Iris's heart raced. She stood transfixed, watching Davis's horrible transformation. How could she stop that? Ling was wrong. He wasn't breaking down. He was getting stronger and stronger. The only chance she had was to get Davis on her side. He slapped a taloned hand onto the ground toward Nivi. Iris jumped. Nivi's body went taut, and a burst of energy emitted from her limbs. The energy formed a shield that surrounded her, Iris, and Meng. Iris breathed a sigh of relief. At least they had Nivi's magic nullifying shield.

Meng grabbed Nivi by the shoulders. "Go help the council members. I'll try to keep his attention on me and get close enough to use this on him." She held up the bottle of oblivion tincture.

Nivi nodded, and her shield dissipated. Iris was again exposed to Davis. She squeezed the stone in her hand. Could one little stone transfer all that magic? And what would that amount of magic do to her? Davis took another step forward. The impact of his foot shook the room. Iris's breath quickened, but she couldn't get enough air. The room became fuzzy. Her mind went blank. She took several steps back, turned, and ran.

CHAPTER FIFTY-FOUR

Nivi

Summer 2000

A FLURRY OF MOTION at the back of the room caught Nivi's attention. Iris was running up the stairwell. She pointed, mouth agape.

"Never mind her," Meng yelled. "Help the council members!"

Meng ran toward Davis and transformed into her dragon form, baring her teeth and curling her tail around Davis to keep him from moving. Her azure scales shone brightly, and electricity crackled in the air around her body.

Nivi froze. There were only two of them against Davis. Her hope began to fade, replaced by the familiarity of panic. She stared at Meng and Davis's clashing figures and was once again transported back to the night Davis attacked her father. As her father and Davis tumbled in the living room, Nivi ran to her bedroom and looked out the window. There was Iris, watching the house. Something didn't make sense. Iris said she was mesmerized by Davis. That's why she helped him. But mesmerism was Nivi's father's secondary power, and he still had his power that night until Davis took it. That meant that up to that point, Iris had been voluntarily helping Davis.

Nivi shook herself out of her daze. She had to help Meng defeat Davis as quickly as possible. What if Iris was upstairs planning something to help Davis? Nivi needed to get up there to make sure her mother and grandmother were alright.

She crept over to the ice cage. The bars were cold in her hands. She closed her eyes and focused, feeling the warmth travel from her core and out to her arms. The veins on her hands throbbed, glowing faintly. A loud rumble from behind snapped away her concentration. She looked back. Davis had grown. Even bent down onto all fours, his head touched the ceiling. He opened his elongated mouth and roared. Spittle flew past rows of knife-like fangs. Shaking, Nivi turned back to the cage and forced herself to focus. Her veins shone fiery red, and the icy bars melted in her grip. She rushed inside the cage and helped the groaning council members to their feet.

"Can you walk?" she asked them.

They were unsteady, but one by one they followed her slowly from the cage. Nivi guided them to the back of the room and hailed the elevator.

"Go somewhere safe until this is over," she said to the first group as the doors closed.

Some of the council members were able to make it up the staircase. The rest waited for the elevator to return, weak and nervously glancing at the fight between Davis and Meng.

At the front of the room, Davis broke free from Meng's coils. He lunged at her, and she released an electric bolt to fend him off. The bolt cracked into Davis's chest and propelled him backward. He rolled quickly onto his feet and charged Meng again.

Nivi waited until the last council members were safe in the

elevator, then ran to Meng's side. She transformed into a qilin, emitting her shield of flame just as Davis struck out with newly sprouted tentacles. The tentacles flew straight through Nivi's shield and knocked her and Meng to the ground. The shock knocked the air out of Nivi and caused her to revert to human form. Davis's tentacles resorbed into his body. He looked down at himself, seemingly confused, but immediately sprouted new tentacles. Nivi realized Davis's magic was indeed stronger than her own. His tentacles were able to penetrate her shield before her nullifying magic was able to break their spell.

Gasping for air, Nivi struggled to her feet. As soon as she stood, another blow knocked her on her back. Without her qilin scales, her soft flesh was more vulnerable. She gasped for breath and tried to move. Pain shot through her limbs, and she curled into a ball, expecting to be hit again and again, but Davis turned his focus to Meng, driving her back despite the dragon's bites and bolts of lightning. Dread filled Nivi's spinning head. They were no match for Davis. She squeezed her eyes shut, holding back tears. At least they had gotten everyone else to safety. Still, she couldn't give up. She opened her eyes and pushed herself onto her feet. If her magic nullification was not strong enough to stop Davis's attacks, she would defend herself physically.

Falling forward onto all fours, Nivi transformed. Her golden hooves clanged on the floor as she galloped toward Davis, whose back was toward her. He was striking Meng over and over with his dozens of tentacles. Splatters of red marred Meng's beautiful blue scales. Blood trickled from her mouth. Nivi leaped and grabbed several of Davis's tentacles between her sharp, dragon teeth. The rubbery flesh separated with a soft crunch. Blood flooded her mouth. Davis roared. He retreated to the front of the room where the wooden box sat.

Nivi spat and trotted over to Meng. Meng had some cuts and bruises but otherwise seemed alright. Had it been that easy to beat Davis? Davis seemed to cower at the front of the room. His massive, grotesque form hunched over the box, his tentacles groping inside, blood oozing from his injuries. A moment later, he sprang back toward them. He came so fast that Nivi barely had time to jump out of the way. Davis pinned Meng's sinuous body against the floor with his tentacles. Meng writhed but couldn't extradite herself. Davis brought a free tentacle toward Meng's body. A gleam of something round and gray was in one of his suckers. A transfer stone.

"No!" Nivi screamed.

Meng twisted, hissing and snapping her mouth at Davis. The tentacle with the stone came down on her side. There was a flash, and Meng shrunk back to human form. Davis's body became more sinuous and lightning flashed off his sides. Nivi felt sick, seeing Meng's powers now in Davis.

Meng began to crawl away, pulling herself toward the side of the room. Nivi saw what she was going for. The bottle had fallen from her hands with Davis's blow. Davis leaped over Meng and slammed a large tentacle down, smashing the bottle to pieces, and with it, the last of Nivi's hopes to defeat Davis. Nivi reverted to human form and ran to Meng. She pulled Meng up and put an arm under her shoulder.

"Run!"

They scrambled toward the staircase, bodies awkwardly colliding with each other. Before they could reach the stairwell, Davis was on them. Suckers latched onto their legs and pulled them off their feet. Nivi clawed at the ground but couldn't break free. Davis dragged them toward his gaping, drooling maw. He lifted them into the air before him. Nivi choked on his hot, putrid breath.

A flutter of fiery feathers exploded out of the stairwell. Nivi stared at the creature. It was her grandmother in her vermillion bird form. Ling landed on Davis's face, squawking and clawing at his eyes. Davis dropped Meng and Nivi as he flailed. Blood dripped down his face. He thrashed and roared, changing forms between birds and canines and felines before settling back on tentacles.

Nivi helped Meng to her feet, and they moved toward the stairwell. She hesitated, not wanting to leave her grandmother alone with Davis.

"Don't worry," Meng said. "Once we're up the stairs, she'll be right behind us."

Nivi wanted to ask how Meng could be so sure, but she started up the stairs without a word. Meng managed to keep up despite being hunched over and shaking. Nivi made it to the top of the stairs first and held the door open into the lounge just long enough for Meng to stagger through. Then she ran back down the stairs, yelling.

"Po Po! We're safe!"

Ling took flight, leaving Davis to rub his bloody face with his tentacles. Nivi waited for her grandmother to reach the stairwell before she started up the stairs, but Ling stopped mid-flight, as if she were suspended in the air. Nivi turned around. A tentacle had wrapped around the great bird's body. Another tentacle reached forward and touched Ling, and there was a terrible, bright white flash.

"No!" Nivi screamed.

Ling transformed to human form, still suspended in the tentacles. Nivi ran at them and jumped, changing into a qilin mid-leap. She extended her jaws and clamped down on the tentacle holding her grandmother. There was a squeal, and Davis dropped Ling. Nivi landed beside Ling, back in human form.

"I'm so sorry, Po Po."

She put her grandmother's arm around her shoulder and pulled her up the stairwell. Davis tried to follow, but he crashed into the opening. He couldn't see well, Nivi realized, thanks to her grandmother. They reached the top of the stairs and went through the door into the lounge. Nivi slammed the door behind them and sat her grandmother against the wall next to Meng. From below, thunderous footsteps shook the steps.

Ji hurried over. "What's going on?"

"Davis stole her power too," Nivi gasped, her voice cracking. "And he destroyed the bottle."

"No time," Meng said. "Push the desk here."

She pointed, and Nivi and Ji ran over to Marcus's desk and heaved it toward the stairwell door. Meng and Ling stood and hobbled away from the doorway. The desk was almost in place when Davis slammed against the door from the inside. The desk shot back a foot, and Ling fell to the ground next to the door opening. A tentacle pushed through and grabbed her ankle.

Nivi and Ji pushed hard against the desk into the door. The door slammed against the tentacle, causing it to withdraw and release Ling. Ling slumped over. Nivi and Ji pushed again, and the door closed. Meng stumbled over to the side of the desk where Ling lay. She sat on the floor with her back against the desk and cradled Ling's head in her lap. Ling looked up, pale with a sheen of sweat.

"I've been used to being a Static, anyway," Ling said with a wry smile. "I guess I'm in it for the long haul now."

The door pounded against the desk. Ling heaved herself up and put her back against the desk with the rest of them. They bent their knees and dug their feet into the floor.

"What do we do now?" Nivi said, choking down a sob.

"We need to get out of this building," Meng said. "Maybe we can lock him in until we can figure out what to do."

"The senators and staff have already evacuated," Ling said.

"Where's Iris?" Nivi said, suddenly remembering. "She can't be trusted!"

"She ran out of the building before the senators came up," Ji said.

Nivi would have to let it go for now, but she was still worried Iris was up to something.

"Ji, you help Ling," Meng said, "and Nivi you help me. When I say so, we run."

"We can run faster in our Shifter forms," Nivi said.

"I don't think we're strong enough to hold on," Ling said. "You'll have to use your arms to support us."

"I'll try to heal you as much as I can while we run," Ji said. She positioned herself next to Ling and pulled Ling's arm over her shoulder.

Nivi did the same with Meng. They waited for another strike to come against the door. As soon as it passed, Meng said, "Go!"

They ran through the lounge and past the rows of underwater windows. Ling and Meng loped alongside Ji and Nivi. Nivi glanced behind and saw the door crash open. The desk flew out and toppled over, and the bloated, contorted, monstrous shape of Davis lumbered into the lounge. He continued to morph, a jumble of teeth and limbs, scales and feathers. Light pulsed under his skin, looking like neon putrefaction, ready to burst.

"Go, go, go!" Meng yelled.

They ran through the hall and up the stairs. The floor shook, and the windows rattled with Davis's pursuit. They burst out onto the oceanside platform and turned to shut and lock the door. Davis plodded up the stairs. The tip of his snout was at the doorway. A tentacle shot forward, reaching for another victim. The door slid shut and locked.

"Won't he be able to get out with his own pendant?" Nivi asked between gulps of air.

"That's one thing I was able to get away from him," Meng said, holding up a pendant in her hand.

"Thank goodness!"

Nivi and Ji assisted Meng and Ling away from the door which was still pounding from within. They sat on a bench on the opposite side of the platform.

"What now?" Ji said.

"The senators are waiting for us back in the harbor," Ling said. "The Shifter military should be here soon."

"Is that so?" a voice came from beside the doorway.

Iris was standing at the door. Her pendant hung around her neck. The pounding stopped.

Nivi jumped up. "Iris! Don't!"

Iris put a hand on the door, and it slid open. Davis strode out in a humanoid form, stooping so his massive body would fit through the doorway.

He smiled, exposing sinews in his jaw. Teeth sprouted out in all directions, and his wounds appeared to have healed. "You cannot stop me."

His voice resonated like echoes in a cave. With each step he took toward them, he loomed larger and larger. Nivi looked frantically for a way for them to escape, but Iris and Davis blocked their way off the dock. They could try to swim, but Davis was sure to transform into something that could swim faster than any of them, and Meng and Ling were too weak to make it very far.

Iris put her hands on her hips in a triumphant pose and echoed Davis's words. "You cannot stop us."

Davis stopped mid-stride and turned toward Iris. "Us?"

Iris looked confused. "Of course. I helped you." Davis scoffed and began to turn away. "You need me. I've helped you all these years. And you will repay me by raising me in the Shifter Council ranks like you promised."

Davis turned back to Iris. "I never *needed* you. Even when my useless sister Anna failed to obtain your power for me, I didn't need you. I found my own way. I *made* my own way."

Iris looked confused. Gradually, her face took on the look of realization. "You told me there was no relation."

"I lied," Davis sneered. "How could you think I would ever need someone as dim as you? My father was the most powerful Shifter before *I* took his powers. And just to prove how dim you are, I will spell out the truth of your family's history. Your mother didn't lose her hand in Salem. She was an anti-integration gangster who used her powers to coerce people to do as she pleased until *my* father put her in her place by taking her hand."

Davis turned his attention to Nivi, Ji, Meng, and Ling. Spikes sprouted along his back and fists, and a twisted smile crept along his lips.

Tears came to Nivi's eyes. She turned to her companions. "I'm sorry."

Ji stood up next to Nivi. "Me too. But we won't stop without a fight."

Nivi wiped away a tear and nodded. She turned into a qilin and formed a shield around the four of them. Even though she knew it wouldn't hold Davis back much, it was the only thing she could do to slow Davis down before the Shifter military arrived. Ji transformed into a horned fox beside her.

Iris's face turned red. Her eyes blazed to match. She tensed her body, clenching her fists at her side and looking like she was about to transform, but then she relaxed, and the color faded from her face and eyes. Instead, she laughed.

"Is that what this has all been about? Poor little Davis. Did you ever get your father's approval?"

Davis paused his advance toward Nivi and Ji and growled. "Shut your mouth. You don't know anything about my father."

Iris took a step toward Davis. "I know he thought you were weak. He preferred Anna to you."

Davis puffed his chest and turned toward Iris. "He wouldn't call me weak now. I have more power than he ever did."

"I know he was just as unscrupulous as you. He did whatever he had to to get and maintain power. Just like you. Guess you're a chip off the old block." The back of Davis's head was turned to Nivi, so she couldn't see his reaction, but Iris's eyes widened in a look of mock surprise. "Oh, didn't you know? Your father setup the hit on your mother so he could change her policies."

"What?" Davis's stance wavered, and some spikes disappeared from his back and fists. His voice stopped resonating and sounded human again. "You're lying."

Iris shook her head with a very serious expression. "I was there when he told Anna what he did."

"He told me it was my fault. That I– killed her."

Iris closed the gap between her and Davis and put a hand on his shoulder with a sympathetic look. "It wasn't your fault."

Davis lowered his head and his body resumed its normal size. The remaining spikes resorbed into his body. At that moment, Nivi almost felt bad for him. He looked like a lost child.

Iris's body elongated. White scales covered her skin, and dorsal spines sprouted from her back. Her limbs shrunk until they were one with her body. She lunged at Davis, wrapping her giant snake body around him. Surprise barely registered on Davis's face before the force propelled them off the dock and into the water. They thrashed. A torrent of water erupted into the air. Screams and roars deafened their ears. Nivi dropped her shield and transformed back into her human form. As waves swelled beneath the dock, Nivi, Ji, Meng, and Ling crouched to maintain their balance.

Eventually, the spray and noise subsided. Nivi cautiously stood up. Her first impulse was to run away, but as the waters calmed to only a rippling at the surface, she inched to the edge of the dock. Davis and Iris had submerged. Multiple colors flashed through the tumultuous waters, growing dimmer and dimmer. Nivi clenched her fists, her muscles not ready to relax their defenses even as part of her began to mourn the loss of Iris and Davis. She should be happy to be rid of them after all the pain they caused. They separated her from her family and murdered her father. And yet… She kept replaying the expression on Davis's face, that of a sad, lost child. She knew what that was like.

A sudden explosion of light and energy burst to the surface. Water sprayed across the dock and knocked Nivi backward. She turned her head to shield her face and wiped the stinging salt from her eyes. Jumping to her feet, she made ready to defend herself again, but there was no more light or movement. Only bubbles remained in the water. No sign of Iris or Davis in the depths.

The tension slowly left Nivi's body. With the immediate danger gone, an awareness of pain surfaced. Bruised tissues, aching muscles and joints, and a debilitating fatigue. She hobbled over to her mother, who was also back in her human form, and embraced her. Meng and Ling joined them. The four of them put their arms around each others' shoulders and stared out at the water. Then they turned and headed back to shore.

EPILOGUE

Nivi stood in front of her home with her grandmother, Meng, and Ji. It wasn't her home anymore. She would be getting a new home with her mother.

"Does this mean I'm not allowed to associate with you anymore?" Nivi said.

"Maybe for now," Ling said. "But things are changing. The Shifter Council needs to rebuild. They need a new Chairperson and Vice Chairperson. And there are four Statics that have no family that they know of and may need to be integrated into Shifter society. After what happened, the old ideology will be reexamined."

Nivi ran forward and embraced Ling. There was still so much Nivi wanted to ask her grandmother. All these years together, she felt they were just starting to get to know each other. She now understood why her grandmother had been so silent and distant. Ling had had a large burden to bear. Neither of them had behaved well in their time together. There was still so much healing to do between them.

"They still need time to sort things out," Nivi said, "so it'll be several weeks before they bring me in for the pendant ceremony. And to replace my mom's pendant. They can't stop us from visiting you every day in the meantime."

Ling pulled back and cupped Nivi's cheek. "Of course not."

Nivi and Ji exchanged another round of hugs with Ling and Meng and made plans to get together for lunch the following day. As Nivi and Ji walked down the sidewalk, Nivi glanced back at the home she had known for the past ten years. Ling and Meng stood in front of the door where the qilin statue now stood, holding hands and waving. It was still a beige home, but it was no longer boring.

Nivi smiled to herself. She also had a lot of catching up to do with her mother. They were both starting life anew. "Where are we going?"

"First," Ji said, "We'll stop by the apartment and make sure there isn't anything else you need. Then we'll see about restoring one of those houses on Redwood Road."

"Really? But how can we afford that? You don't have a job yet."

"I have some interviews set up next week. And remember that inheritance you got from me and your dad? Since I'm alive, it goes back to me now. Sorry."

Nivi shrugged. "It was technically your money, to begin with. Plus, you made it so I couldn't touch it until I was thirty anyway, so it's not like I knew what it was like to spend it."

Ji laughed and put an arm around Nivi. "That's true."

They turned the corner. Ahead, Amber walked toward them, carrying some books. Nivi approached her awkwardly. She hadn't spoken to Amber since their fight, and it turned out that Amber was right all along. But she couldn't just tell her that, could she? Maybe she could, eventually. Amber was her best friend, after all.

Amber stopped in front of Nivi. "Hi."

"Hey," Nivi said. They stood unspeaking for several seconds.

"Hi," Ji said.

Nivi snapped to attention. "Oh my gosh. Sorry. Amber, this is my mom. Mom, this is my best friend, Amber."

"Your mom?" Amber's eyes widened.

"Nice to meet you, Amber," Ji said.

"It's a long story," Nivi said. "Maybe we can get together later this week to catch up? I have a lot to tell you. And… I'm sorry about everything. It's all my fault."

Amber's demeanor relaxed. "No, I'm sorry. Of course we can get together. I have so much to tell you, too. Like I've been studying at the library!"

"Really?" Nivi started laughing.

Amber joined in. "I know. It's hard to believe. I have a thing to go to right now, but maybe we can get together tomorrow or the day after?"

"Sure."

They smiled at each other.

"Nice to meet you, Mrs…." Amber began.

"Dawan. The same as Nivi," Ji said. "But you can call me Ji."

"OK, Mrs– uh– Ji."

They laughed. Amber waved and continued down the road. Nivi and Ji put their arms around each other and walked toward their apartment.

Meng and Ling went into their home. After ten years apart, it felt good to be back together, even as Statics. They sat at the kitchen table and Meng poured them some tea. Ling sipped hers and absentmindedly toyed with the stone on the table. After a moment, she picked up the stone.

"Didn't you transfer some of your magic into this?"

Meng put down her cup of tea and took the stone. "I completely forgot about that, but you're absolutely right. This stone looks deactivated now. How could that be?"

"Maybe Nivi deactivated it? It wasn't me."

"You're probably right." Meng took a sip of tea. "I just had a thought. Neither of us has a mark anymore, and we don't have any power. Would we be able to regain power using a transfer stone?"

Ling laughed. "Are you tired of being a Static already?" But then she sobered as she thought about it. "That actually might be a possibility. But that means we'd have to take the powers of someone else. We couldn't do that to another Shifter, even if we had more transfer stones to do it." She took Meng's hand in hers. "Besides, I don't need any powers as long as I have you."

Meng chuckled but seemed distracted. "I wonder... I was somehow able to transfer only a tiny bit of my powers into that stone. I barely even felt the loss of it. Maybe there's another stone in that cave that was missed. Maybe if we found another one, someone would give us a tiny bit of their power."

Ling stared wistfully out the window into the backyard. "Maybe."

Of course Ling wanted to feel whole again, but if she stayed away from the Shifter community, she wouldn't have to divulge the truth about Nivi's father. It wouldn't matter now anyway. Nivi's father had passed. Better to let sleeping dogs lie and not ruin Nivi's relationship with Ji. But the truth of it all was still mind-boggling. She had had everything wrong, thinking that Statics were inferior. It wasn't supposed to be possible to be part Static and still have powers. In the past, any Static contamination had prevented any powers from forming, at least that's what she had been taught. How many others were there out there like Nivi?

❧

Amber turned off Main Street onto Peninsula Street and entered a small boutique store. She moved through the displays of trinkets and clothes and exited the back of the store to an enclosed patio. Several other people were already there, organizing snacks, drinks, and paperwork. Amber stood by, fidgeting, not sure what to do.

Arav arrived soon after. He lit up when he saw her. With everything he had been through recently, Amber was relieved to see Arav in a lighter mood.

"Hey," he said. "So glad you could make it." He gave Amber a hug and a kiss on the cheek. "Ow." He pulled back. "You shocked me."

"I did?" Amber touched her cheek where he had kissed her. "I'm sorry."

"No worries. I'm just so glad you're here. It might just be everything that's going on, but I feel a literal warm fuzzy feeling with you right now. And you look so beautiful like you're glowing."

"Stop." Amber playfully pushed Arav, but she felt it, too. A warm connection with Arav. And like before, he also seemed like he was glowing. She couldn't explain it.

Did you sign in yet?" he said.

"No. Where do I do that?"

Arav led Amber to a side table with a sign-in sheet. Arav signed his name and handed the pen to Amber. Amber signed her name. She put the pen down at the top of the sheet, next to the club name and logo:

Monster Hunters United. Protect. Defend. Eradicate.

COMING SOON

The story continues…

June 2000

My Dear Nivi and Ji,

Destroy this once read.

I've heard Ariana Peters has become the new chairperson. Her strict anti-integration policies will include the liberal use of oblivion tincture. As one who used to administer this tincture, I can tell you that when they come, it will be unexpected. Say nothing of Nivi's ability to nullify magic. All they know at this time is that Nivi can block physical magic attacks with a shield of fire.

I fear this will be goodbye for now. Nivi, stay strong. It will be lonely being the only one with the truth. Take comfort knowing I have your grandmother as my companion. Cherish your mother's presence, even if her reality cannot be what you want it to be for now. I have hope that things will change. And when they do, you will reunite us.

Until then,

Meng

AUTHOR'S NOTES

Back in 2019, I went on a Wikipedia deep dive about Chinese mythology. Even though I grew up immersed in Chinese culture and language from my mom's side of the family, I wasn't deeply versed in some of the most popular mythologies and their historical significance. Eventually, I came across an article for *The Classic of Mountains and Seas*, or Shan Hai Jing, an ancient text written almost 2500 years ago. It depicts ancient geography, culture, and fauna, mostly fantastical, and serves as the basis for a lot of Chinese mythology. Some of the creatures I had heard of before: the dragon, qilin, and vermillion bird. Most I had not. If you have some time on your hands, I highly recommend an internet search to see some of these creatures for yourself. It's fascinating!

In addition to Shan Hai Jing, I read about the four deities that represent the directions, seasons, elements, and constellations. They are the azure dragon, vermillion bird, white tiger, and black tortoise. The azure dragon is named Meng Zhang, and the vermillion bird is Ling Guang. Another famous story is the legend of Bai Suzhen, a one thousand year old white snake spirit that is transformed into a woman.

Some of this may be starting to sound familiar. There were so many fascinating stories to read, I realized there was no way I would become an expert on Chinese mythology anytime soon. So, I decided to write a modern story, taking inspiration from and alluding to the mythology I'd learned with the idea that immigrants in the US would bring with them certain aspects of their culture. I hope you found this book as enjoyable as I found it to write. And I hope you will have as much fun reading the sequel.

ACKNOWLEDGEMENTS

I would not have started this journey without having signed up for UCLA Extension writing courses. Teachers Alyx Dellamonica and Jessica Barksdale Inclán inspired me as accomplished authors in their own right and taught me how to develop my writing skills and stay consistent in my practice. The wonderfully supportive online community at Other Worlds Writers' Workshop embraced the humble beginnings of my writing. Thank you to those members for all their critiques, especially Clark Sodersten, EJ Heijins and Doc Honour, for feedback on my very first draft of this novel. Special thanks to my writing partner, Karen Darger. In addition to keeping me on a schedule and giving me extremely insightful critiques, she and I shared lots of fun conversations, coffee, and croissants. Thank you to all my beta readers. I really appreciate Jan Solomon for catching my anachronistic errors.

For the beautiful cover and interior formatting, thanks goes to Damonza. For the developmental edit, thank you Wishing Shelf. Thank you, Melissa Nash, for the awesome map of Yuras. Thank you, Paige Lawson, for a wonderful line edit and the all-important proofread. And thank you to Muthahari Insani of Sweeneypen for the beautiful special edition art.

And finally, thank you to all my family and friends and anyone I unintentionally missed: my amazing husband Noah and sister Kim for listening to every idea and reading said ideas over and over again, my father Ken for being an early reader, and my mother Clara for advising me on Chinese matters, and my sister Jenny, Marcie, Sierra, and Krishna, for your support, suggestions, and enthusiasm. I love you all!

ABOUT THE AUTHOR

EMILY RENK HAWTHORNE

began her adult career as a dentist working with underserved populations. She loves reading fantasy books and always dreamed of writing her own. *Of Mountains and Seas* is her debut novel. Emily grew up in Southern California and now resides on the Central Coast with her husband and child.